He, She and It

He,

She

and

It

a novel by

Marge

Piercy

Alfred A. Knopf
New York
1991

to the memory of Primo Levi

His books were important to me.
I miss his presence in the world.

Contents

Contents

He, She and It

one

IN THE CORPORATE FORTRESS

Josh, Shira's ex-husband, sat immediately in front of her in the Hall of Domestic Justice as they faced the view screen, awaiting the verdict on the custody of Ari, their son. A bead of sweat slid down the furrow of his spine—he wore a backless business suit, white for the formality of the occasion, very like her own—and it was hard even now to keep from delicately brushing his back with her scarf to dry it. The Yakamura-Stichen dome in the Nebraska desert was conditioned, of course, or they would all be dead, but it was winter now and the temperature was allowed to rise naturally to thirty Celsius in the afternoon as the sun heated the immense dome enclosing the corporate enclave. Her hands were sweating too, but from nervousness. She had grown up in a natural place and retained the ability to endure more heat than most Y-S gruds. She kept telling herself she had nothing to fear, but her stomach was clenched hard and she caught herself licking her lips again and again. Everytime she called up time on her internal clock and read it in the corner of her cornea, it was at most a minute later than when last she had evoked it.

The room glittered in black and white marble, higher than wide and engineered to intimidate, Shira knew from her psychoengineering background. Her field was the interface between people and the large artificial intelligences that formed the Base of each corporation and every other information-producing and information-eating entity in the world, as well as the information utility called the Network, which connected everyone. But she had enough psychological background to recognize the intent of the chamber where with their assigned lawyers they sat upright and rigid as tuning forks for the blow that would set them quivering into sound. Perched around them were similar groups in waiting: breaches of marriage contract, custody cases, complaints of noncompliance and abuse, each group staring at the blank view screen. From time to time a face appeared, one of those ideal, surgically created Y-S faces—blond hair, blue eyes with epicanthic folds, painted brows like Hokusai brush strokes, aquiline nose, dark golden complexion. It would announce a verdict, and then a group would swirl around itself, rise and go, some beaming, some grim-faced, some weeping.

She should not be as frightened as she was. She was a techie like Josh, not a day laborer; she had rights. Her hands incubated damp patches on her thighs. She hoped their verdict would be announced soon. She had to pick up Ari at the midlevel-tech day care center in forty-five minutes, some twenty minutes' glide from the official sector. She did not want him waiting, frightened. He was only two years and five months, and she simply could not make him understand: Don't worry, Mommy may be a little late. It was her fault, insisting on the divorce in December, for ever since, Ari had been skittish; and Josh bitter, furious. Twice as alive. If he had loosed in their marriage the passion her leaving had provoked, they might have had a chance together. He fought her with full energy and intelligence, as she had wanted to be loved.

Everything was her fault. She should never have married Josh. She had been passionately in love only once in her life, too young, and never again; but if she had not married Josh, she would not have had Ari. Oh, she felt guilty all right as she looked at Josh's narrow back, the deep groove of his spine, vulnerable, bent slightly forward as if some chill wind blew only on him. She had promised to love him, she had tried to love him, but the relationship had felt thin and incomplete.

During their courtship, she had thought he was beginning to learn to talk to her, to respond more sensually and directly. In the born-again Shintoism of Y-S, they were both marranos, a term borrowed from the Spanish Jews under the Inquisition who had pretended to be Christian to survive. Y-S followed a form of revivalist Shinto, Shinto grafted with Christian practices such as baptism and confession. Marranos in contemporary usage were Jews who worked for multis and went to church or mosque, paid lip service and practiced Judaism secretly at home. All multis had their official religion as part of the corporate culture, and all gruds had to go through the motions. Like Shira, Josh had the habit of lighting candles privately on Friday night, of saying the prayers, of keeping the holidays. It had seemed rational for them to marry. He had been at Y-S for ten years. She had come straight from graduate school, at twenty-three. Y-S had outbid the other multis for her in Edinburgh—like most of the brightest students in Norika, the area that had been the U.S. and Canada, she had gone to school in the affluent quadrant of Europa—so she had had no choice but to come here. She had been lonely, unused to the strict and protocol-hedged hierarchy of Y-S. She had grown up in the free town of Tikva, accustomed to warm friendships with women, to men who were her pals. Here she was desperately lonely and constantly in minor trouble. Often she wondered if her troubles were caused by the particular corporate culture of Y-S, or if it would be the same in any multi enclave. There were twenty-three great multis that divided the world among them, enclaves on every continent and on space platforms. Among them they wielded power and enforced the corporate peace: raids, assassinations, skirmishes, but no wars since the Two Week War in 2017.

Josh had been born to an Israeli couple, survivors of the Two Week War a terrorist had launched with a nuclear device that had burned Jerusalem off the map, a conflagration of biological, chemical and nuclear weapons that had set the oilfields aflame and destroyed the entire region. He had been orphaned at ten, wandering without a country in the period Jews called the Troubles, when the whole world blamed them for the disasters that put an end to oil dependence in a maelstrom of economic chaos. Nothing had come easy to him in his life. The more he opened to her and told her, the more precious he seemed to her, in that fervid courtship, and the more she felt herself absolutely necessary to him. She was astonished that at first she had thought him cold. How he had suffered! He needed her like air itself.

He had seemed to be opening. Shortly after the marriage he had insisted upon, he began changing back. He acted happy. He seemed delighted with her; but from a distance. As for getting to know her better, as for sharing his inner life or taking an interest in hers, those pastimes seemed uninteresting to him, lacking in urgency. Ari was supposed to mend that breach. Since the birth of their son, all Josh's after-work energy focused on Ari. She often suspected that if they did not have Ari, they would have nothing to talk about. Their silence roared in her ears. Soon she was boiling with resentments. They fought forty skirmishes a day about nothing. As her grandmother Malkah had warned her when she married Josh, she had made a costly mistake. Living together combined for them the worst aspects of living alone and living with a stranger. Their major activity together was disagreeing. She had grown up in a benign household, for Malkah was feisty and opinionated but also loving and funny. People did not have to live unremitting desperate wars. Shira had summoned her energy and left him.

She called up the time on her cornea. Only four minutes had passed since she had last asked. Finally the long-skulled face appeared and spoke, in its uninflected way, their names: Joshua Rogovin and Shira Shipman, re the custody of child Ari Rogovin. Even in Y-S, with its male dominance, women did not change their names. Marriages were on the basis of five- or ten-year contracts, and name changing without purpose was inefficient. Still, Shira felt an odd chill as she heard Ari's surname given as his father's. That was not how she had registered him at birth, but Y-S had ignored her preference.

"In regard to this matter the judgment of the panel is to award custody to the father, Joshua Rogovin, status T12A, the mother, Shira Shipman, status T10B, to have visitation privileges twice weekly, Wednesdays and Sundays. This verdict rendered 28 January 2059, automatic review on 28 January 2061. Verdict recorded. Out."

Josh turned in his seat and glared at her. His lawyer was beaming and slapping his shoulder. "What did I tell you? In the bag."

"They can't do this!" Shira said. "They can't take Ari!"

Josh grimaced, almost a smile. "He's mine now. He's my son, he's a Rogovin." His light eyes, somewhere between gray and blue, seemed to read her pain and dismiss it.

"Your ex-husband has a higher tech rating than you do," her lawyer said. "I warned you they would take that into account. You've been stuck in the same grade for three years."

"I'll appeal. Ari needs me." And I need him, she thought.

"It's your choice, but you're throwing away your credits, in my opinion. Of course I'll represent you if you choose to retain me."

Josh and his lawyer had already swept out. Shira's lawyer stood over her, impatiently tapping his foot. "I have another client to see. You think about the appeal. I can start the process tomorrow if you choose."

Suddenly she rose and rushed out, realizing she was late to pick up Ari. "Start the appeal," she called over her shoulder. "I won't let him go."

She hopped the express lane on the moving sidewalk, nimbly jumping from track to track. It was considered poor form for gruds—Glop slang for professional and technical personnel of multis—to do that, although day laborers did it all the time, but she did not care. She was desperate to reach Ari. She sped past the gossamer structures of the official district. Since there was no weather under the dome, and since no structure could be taller than six stories, the prevailing style was long parabolic curves, fanciful spirals and labyrinthine grids of glittering translucent filigree. Almost everything was black, white or blue, like the backless business suits that came to mid-calf or lower, which all gruds wore. Almost every exec, male or female, had been under the knife to resemble the Y-S ideal, faces as much like the one on the view screen as each could afford.

The techies flashing past on the movers looked far more diverse, but they, too, dressed in suits of acceptable colors. People of the same rank greeted each other with ritual gestures, a bob of the head. Those farther down the hierarchy they usually ignored. Passing those above them, they awaited recognition and bowed deeply. How many times had she slipped into trouble by talking so intently she had inadvertently neglected to greet properly an equal or a superior? The day laborers wore overalls or uniforms in yellows, browns, greens: color coded for their jobs. If they were in the wrong place at the wrong time, it would be immediately evident. She leapt from track to track, never mind who saw her—who might report her—as undignified, lacking in proper Y-S decorum. She always felt too physical here, too loud, too female, too Jewish, too dark, too exuberant, too emotional.

The day care for the children of middle-level techies was just ahead now, behind a hedge of tall brightly colored crotons, the blue and white and black Y-S flag drooping over the entrance. She was not impossibly late, because she saw a few straggling mothers and one father as she ran the three blocks from the nearest mover. She realized she never saw an adult run on these streets. Everyone was too conscious of being observed, of being judged. This was the middle-tech compound of little houses, each in its yard. With Josh, she had lived in one of them. Four styles of house for this rank, with the same acceptable shrubs and manicured lawns, but a free choice of color. Nobody chose red or purple. The only vehicles that moved down the median strips were official: delivery trucks, repair and emergency vans, security apes, all battery-powered rigs that monotonously beeped.

The supervisor, Jane Forest, was noticeably cooler to her. "But, Shipman, a security assignee picked up Ari Rogovin eighteen minutes ago. We were informed this was proper. You are not authorized to pick up Ari Rogovin except on Wednesdays."

"An ape took him? But why?"

"Request information from security central, please."

Although Shira wanted to scream and argue, she was aware the supervisor would never alter orders given her; or Jane would no longer be a supervisor. Any protest Shira made would be ineffectual and recorded against her. She had to call her lawyer at once. Mostly she had a strong desire to call Malkah.

Even a month ago, she would have called her secretary, Rosario, for they had become close. But the low-level exec with whom Rosario had had a ten-year contract had not renewed their marriage. As was customary even for low-level talent, he had taken a new wife, twenty years younger. Rosario was forty-two, and Y-S let her go. Shira had protested that she needed Rosario, but she had no power. Women over forty who were not techies or supervisors or professionals or execs were let go if they were not the temporary property of a male grud. Female gruds were supposed to have the same privileges and, if they had enough position, often took young husbands.

Rosario had disappeared into the Glop. She might be tubed in and out of the enclave daily as a laborer, working in the laundry or cooking or doing any of the maintenance jobs not taken care of by robots, but Shira would never see her. Rosario had been pushed out of the safe fortress into the crowded violent festering warren of the half-starved Glop, where nine tenths of the people of Norika lived; if she was still alive, Shira would never know it. The Glop was slang for the Megalopolis that stretched south from what had been Boston to what had been Atlanta, and a term applied to other similar areas all over the continent and the world.

As soon as Shira reached the two-room apartment that was all she was entitled to by her own rating, one of the so-called bins for lower-level techies, she asked the apartment for messages. Every housing facility in the corporate enclave had a computer. Hers wasn't a sophisticated system like the one she had grown up with, programmed by Malkah, but it functioned as a message service. It told her that Malkah had called fifty minutes before. Shira called first her lawyer and then Malkah. She did not bother plugging in for conversations—nobody did. She just spoke her instructions. Malkah's round, slightly wizened face appeared, her hair, as black as Shira's braided around her head. "Shira, you look upset." Malkah had a deep resonant voice. Although she was Shira's grandmother, she had raised her. That was the way of her family, bat Shipman, until Shira had broken the pattern.

"Are you eating?" Shira asked politely. It was an hour later in the free town Tikva on the Atlantic, where Malkah lived, where Shira had grown up.

"What's wrong?" Malkah always came right to the point.

"Y-S awarded custody to Josh."

"Those pigsuckers," Malkah said. "Those poison belchers. I told you not to marry him. You're the first in our family to marry in four generations. It's a bad idea."

"All right, all right. I thought Josh needed the security."

"And could you give him security? Never mind. Come home."

"I can't just take off. Especially now. I'm lodging an appeal. I have to get Ari back. I have to."

"What does Y-S want?"

"From me? Nothing. They hardly know I exist."

"When you finished your graduate work at Edinburgh, six multis bid on you. And Y-S lets you sit and rot. It smells."

"I think my work's good, but nothing happens. Nobody here rates me as much."

Malkah snorted. "Come home. I can use you. I'm not working with Avram any longer. I'm designing full time."

"I thought that was an odd partnership."

"What he's doing is quite fascinating. But never mind. He's mad at me. He's a stubborn arrogant alter kaker, but he's a genius in his field, no doubt about that."

"Cybernetics has never drawn me. . . . Malkah, I can't stand to lose Ari. I miss him already." Tears began coursing down Shira's face.

"You should never have gone to work for those manipulators, Shira. You have a place here. You ran away. But Gadi's not living here. He's up in Veecee Beecee, making those elaborate worlds people play at living in instead of worrying about the one we're all stuck with."

"I made a lot of mistakes," Shira said. "But Ari wasn't one of them. He's precious, Malkah, he's life itself to me. I must have him back. He carries my heart in him."

"Daughter of my soul, I wish you strength. But a multi always has its reasons. It may take you a while to figure theirs, and when you do, that may not help you get your son back."

"So pray for me."

"You know I don't believe in personal petitions. All I can ever pray for is understanding."

Shira had forgotten to pick up a meal. She ate crackers and dates. Then she sat down at her terminal again and plugged in, inserting the male coupler from the terminal into the little silver socket at her temple, just under the loop of hair that always fell there. Rosario had had no plug; it was a class distinction here, but in Tikva, every child was raised to be able to access directly, taught to project into the worldwide Net, into the local Base. She moved quickly from her own private base into the Y-S Base.

Their logo greeted her, white and black double lightning against sky blue. The Y-S imagery of entering the Base was a road sign. She was standing on a crossroads branching in seven directions. Library access. She walked along the narrow white road. Of course she was sitting in her chair, but the projection felt real enough. A person could die in projection, attacked by raiders, information pirates who lifted from one base and peddled to another.

A building stood before her, white marble with a colonnade. The library. She climbed the shallow steps quickly. She was looking for the law section. She intended to master relevant Y-S law on custody. That was why she had not simply accessed in reading or aural output. In full projected access, when she was plugged into a base, learning was far faster than in real time. She was going to challenge them on their own terms. She would win her son back.

IN THE MORNING she was standing outside the day care center when Josh arrived, with Ari in tow. She darted to kneel before Ari. "I just want to tell you that I'm going to pick you up today. Tonight you'll be with me."

Ari had his thumb in his mouth, and he looked as if he had been crying. His Diddlee Bear tee shirt was on backward. His eyes looked sticky.

Josh said, in a voice that sang like a hornet, "I'm lodging a protest."

Indeed on her screen a security message appeared at thirteen hundred: "Shira Shipman is enjoined from interaction with the minor Ari Rogovin awarded to the custody of his father Joshua Rogovin except on the prescribed days and defined times of visitation. Any further breaches of this regulation will result in the cancellation of said privileges."

Shira locked herself in a waste disposal cell before she wept.

two

THE COLOR OF OLD BLOOD

Shira was up before Malcolm. It was the second night they had spent together, as she tried to put some distance between her ex-husband and herself. Every time she picked up Ari or brought him back, in the two months since the verdict, Josh and she clashed. Now Shira sat at her terminal going over the wording of her latest appeal, a little depressed about how long and leaden the evening had felt. As she was reworking an argument, the apartment computer told her she had a caller. It was a cheap model, not provided any personality, but she had given it a female voice that reminded her of the house of her grandmother Malkah. Most houses had female voices. "Put the incoming message on audio only."

"Shira?" It was Gadi's voice. "Put it on visual. I loathe talking to a blank wall. If you're not dressed, damn it, do you think I don't remember your body?"

As always when she heard his voice without warning, her heart collapsed like a crushed egg. "My body ten years ago?" She tried to sound flippant. She glanced at the mirror to assure herself she was presentable, wishing she could feel indifferent to how she appeared to him. She was still in her dressing gown, of translucent shimmering silk. Her hair was tousled, a scattering of gold grains from the night before still glinting against the black. She looked a little too girlish, too waif-like, as she always did without makeup, but she could not stand the idea of painting her face at nine on a Sunday morning. She spoke. "Visual on. Good morning. Where are you?"

"Back in Tikva, visiting Avram. Ah, our daily duels, our refreshing bouts of mutual insult. The new stimmie I was working on with Tomas Raffia is done, and I'm on vacation. Why don't you come home for a visit?" Gadi was dressed much as she was, in a translucent silk robe—from the mutated worms that were the rage. His was much more beautiful than hers, in colors that shifted as she watched. His face was gaunt but handsome as ever. He had dyed his hair a silver gray, not unlike his eyes. Only young people had gray hair nowadays. Most people looked dreadful that way, but it set off his face, dyed brown. He must look a little bizarre in Tikva, where everybody ran around in shorts or pants; but there he was an emissary of glamour from Vancouver, where the production of stimmies was centered. He was famous. People would expect him to look like a polished artifact. A designer of virons for stimmies was a star in his own right, able to move among the fans the way actors never could, their wired up and enhanced senses making them too vulnerable.

"How did the audience receive it?"

"Didn't you enter my stimmie?" His voice arched in pained disbelief. "It was absolutely raw!"

"Gadi, I've been getting ready for court, meeting my lawyer every other day for the last three months. Josh has taken Ari from me. Why don't you send me a crystal copy?" Then she would have to enter it. She hardly ever took the time to immerse herself in a stimmie, even now when she was living alone. She had lost the habit when Ari was born, for she could not cut herself off from him in that complete sensory overload, living out the exquisite sensations of some actress being pursued by cannibal dwarfs or balancing four lovers on Nuevas Vegas satellite, emotions pumped through her.

"Computer, note last request and fulfill. . . . How could he take your kid?"

"They have patriarchal laws here. The boy is regarded as property of the father's gene line—and, Gadi, you know I married him. Plus he has a higher tech rating than I do."

"Why did you do that foolish thing?" Gadi grimaced. "I told you not to marry that caterpillar. Single marriage is old-fashioned and dreary."

"You never tried to understand Josh. . . . Actually things are mean between us, vicious. I hurt him terribly, Gadi." It felt wonderful to talk. They always began with opening salvos and diplomatic couriers from their opposing forts, and then in five minutes they were exchanging confidences. They were still meshed in secret and subtle ways. Just last night she had thought of him as she was getting into bed with Malcolm, as she supposed she would for the rest of her life, and now this morning here they were chatting. "Gadi, in Y-S most people get married. There's pressure to."

"That man was born to be hurt—a moth who turned back into the worm he came from."

"Josh is someone who has endured more than either of us can understand. He has no one at all left, no one. He survived by accident. Imagine, his native land is the Black Zone." A large chunk of the Middle East was represented on maps as a uniform black, for it was uninhabitable and interdicted to all. A pestilent radioactive desert.

"You don't marry a man because he's bleeding on your foot."

Shira winced, the taste of salt in her mouth. "I thought I could make him happy."

Gadi snorted. "That's what women are always trying to do to me, and what does it get them? A sore ass from landing on it."

She decided to change the subject. "Your father has offered me a job, do you believe it?"

"Why you?" His forehead accordioned. "What does Avram want with you?"

"Gadi, I am very good at what I do, although Y-S doesn't appreciate me."

"Working for Avram is out of the question, but I'd love it if you were in Tikva. Then I'd see you when I skulk back here."

"Until my appeal is decided, I'm not going anyplace. I won't give up Ari. I was so stupid. I got married instead of giving my child to my mother. Now I wish I had. I broke our family line, and now I've lost him!"

"You sound as if you're feeling guilty, Shira. Why?"

"If I hadn't gone and married Josh, if I'd given my mother Riva my child, the way I'm supposed to, if I had only listened to Malkah, I'd have my child in my own family. It's my fault. I thought I was so smart, so in control."

"We all piss it out, Shira. Are you sure your mother wanted him? I've only met her twice in my life. I can barely remember what she looks like."

"She's a stranger to me. She works for Alharadek, that's all I know."

"It's hard for me to picture you with a kid anyhow, Shira. You're still a kid to me. I think you made up this imaginary Ari."

A tear rolled out of her eye, and she snorted in anger. "Don't be a complete turd, Gadi. He's more real to me than anyone in the world is—" She became suddenly aware Malcolm was standing just inside her bedroom, listening. Now he moved behind her so that his image would be transmitted.

Gadi looked amused. "You should have told me you had company. We can gossip any old time."

With Malcolm at her elbow, she could not say the truth: that she had forgotten him in the immediacy of her connection with Gadi. It was awkward all the way around as she signed off.

Breakfast was decidedly bumpy. "I didn't know you had another man in link." Malcolm scowled. He was as tall as Gadi but more solidly built, with thatchy brown hair and thick commanding brows, a habit of holding his chin jutted out as if commanding a charge.

"It's not that way. He's an old friend. We grew up together."

"You kept laughing when you were talking to him. It didn't sound like someone who's merely a friend."

"I never think of friends as merely anything. Friends are precious."

"The right word for him. Good-looking if you like the precioso type."

"He creates virons for Uni-Par."

"I never sink into those things," Malcolm said, which was the going line in Y-S unless it was an official program, but the corners of his mouth sagged. "I don't even own a helmet to go all the way in. I just use grungy old electrodes. . . . That wasn't Gadi Stein?"

Shira found herself irritated, which she politely attempted to cover by asking him about his sand sailing. It was a night sport but still dangerous. It would have been much pleasanter to go on gossiping with Gadi. She had not had time to ask about his father, Avram, about all their old friends, about the complicated relationships in Tikva, the newest political flap, the latest crazes. It was effortless to talk with Gadi and laborious to carry on the tedious, painstaking spadework of getting to know this man, who seemed less sympathetic by the moment. He was definitely sulking, whipping his coffee round and round, his spoon standing up in the cup like a pole, as if to punish it for his disappointment in her. She did not want to quarrel with him—she did not need yet another feud at work—so she would simply get through breakfast and ease him out. She herself was the problem.

"I thought you'd be . . . softer. You have this look sometimes like a little kid, so innocent," Malcolm said as if accusingly. His chin was thrust at her, his brows beetled.

She felt like telling him it was simply the neotonic effect: large dark eyes in a thin face provoked in mammals including humans the inborn reaction toward infants—the fawn, the kitten, the puppy, and the Shira. In college she had frowned a lot in order to compel those around her to take her seriously. She was not girlish, shy, innocent, blithe, and she often wished she did not present a facade that seemed to lure only men who wanted a child-woman. She was bleaker, thornier. And the truth was, she was too involved now in her efforts to get her son back to try hard with any man. She felt like apologizing to Malcolm for wasting his time. She was a mirage.

Today she would see Josh, one reason she had felt the need for pretending she had a real new relationship. She must simply go and confront Josh and try to reason with him. Then she would have Ari to herself for an entire twenty hours, from noon till eight a.m. tomorrow.

As soon as Malcolm left, she began preparing psychologically, in her dress and her manner, for the battle to come. Josh had been full of nasty games since she left him, but she knew they were just an expression of his pain. It was not that Josh had loved her passionately, although he would have insisted he did. Rather he had formed a conventional attachment, but one that was central to his personal economy of survival. He simply counted on her to be there.

No more postmortems. What she most wanted was to create a perfect day for Ari. She hoped he still liked fluffy omelets with the egg whites whipped separately. She had managed to buy three real eggs. She would ask him if he wanted to eat a cloud. Unfortunately the day was dark, the artificial light orangey. Probably a sandstorm was raging outside the dome. She had planned to take him to the park. She kept a few toys here, but spending all her credit on legal fees, she could not afford much.

She hurried through the neat, ever new and ever clean city of the enclave. Above the serrated rows of low-tech bins, the silver dome stretched. Three hundred thousand people lived here; as many tubed in and out daily from the Glop. Under the dome it was spring, and the climate was set for what it had probably been like here fifty years before, but the streetlights were on.

A crocodile of children in their Sunday blue uniforms marked with the Y-S logo marched past. She could tell they were children of management rather than of techies, because they had already been worked on surgically to resemble the Y-S ideal face and body. They were singing one of the corporate hymns, a security ape leading them and one bringing up the rear. The apes moved as heavily as robots, although robots were forbidden to be made in human form since the cyber-riots; apes were simply people altered chemically and surgically and by special implants for inhuman strength and speed. These were high-level children being escorted through the midlevel-tech shopping district to some special event. Normally they would not venture out of Paradise Park, the enclave within the enclave, built behind walls around a real lake of water. A tall elegant woman on a horsicle—a horse robot shining golden and lifting each cobalt hoof high into the air in a mincing gait—rode beside them. Teacher? More likely, from the horsicle—which cost a fortune—and her hair, braided with jewels, one of the mothers.

She thought of her own mother, Riva, as she had not in years. She had seldom met Riva. The last occasion had been when she was seventeen and about to go off to college. Her mother was a dowdy prematurely middle-aged woman, your typical bureaucrat or middle-level analyst—Shira had never quite grasped what her mother did, but obviously nothing important. The talent that made Malkah recognized worldwide as a genius and that had until recently secured Shira her choice of schools and projects seemed to have skipped Riva. Had Riva ever missed her as she was already missing Ari? She doubted it. Insofar as Shira could visualize her, she saw a fussy woman rubbing her hands together nervously. Riva had turned her over to Malkah with evident relief, Malkah had raised her, and everybody had been happy. No, Shira had not been able to take seriously the family tradition that she give her child to her mother. Her impression was that Riva would have been overburdened raising a gerbil.

Shira had grown up with cats and birds, but here only high-level techies and execs were permitted real animals. Everyone else made do with robots, but the good ones cost far too much for her. Ari's little koala was the best she and Josh could do. Ari was crazy about it, Wawa Bear, but Josh had forbidden her to take it along with Ari, saying it was too expensive to drag around.

Their street was like a hundred others, their house one of the four types for Josh's rating. Shira grimaced, standing outside the door, which no longer opened at her touch. The house computer had been reprogrammed to treat her like any other stranger. Recently when she picked up Ari, she waited outside for him. The last time she had been inside the house they shared, she had found the living room and kitchen ostentatiously unclean, food containers everywhere, unwashed crockery. The house had screamed neglect: look what you did to us! All Josh had to do was let the cleaning robot at its job. But he had chosen to say with the filth: this is what I have been reduced to. His anger was a stench in her nostrils. She had written a description of the incident in her latest appeal, citing the atmosphere in his household as unsuitable and unhealthy for a toddler. Two could fight with old food.

The house opened the door. "Come in. There is a message for you." The voice had been reprogrammed. Actually it sounded as if the house were on neutral, as if no one lived here. The voice was clearly a machine voice, no longer female, no longer familiar.

"Isn't Josh at home? Where's Ari?"

"Josh is not here. Ari is not here. Please receive the message left for Shira Shipman."

She walked through the foyer. Most of the furniture was in place, but personal things had disappeared, the photographs of Josh's family. He would never remove the pictures of his slaughtered parents and brothers while he occupied this house. They were officially listed as dead in a plague, but they had died fighting. The twisted and half-melted menorah recovered from the ruins was gone from its place. She ran quickly to the terminal. It was not the enhanced one they had always used. It was a minimal terminal, set to run the house, take messages, answer simple questions, control a cleaning robot. It was the caretaker type that lacked even a protect function. She felt as if her chest were filling with cold mud. She felt heavy, formless, chilled through. What was going on? She sank into the chair before the terminal and identified herself.

Josh's face appeared on the screen, his lips drawn thin. "I presume you have come here to argue with me. Any further appeals are useless. You left us, and now we have left earth. Yakamura-Stichen has transferred me to Pacifica Platform. I'm taking my assistant Barbra and Ari. I have the full permission of Y-S to take Ari with me. Unless you can get clearance to Pacifica, you'll have to wait till we return to earth at the end of our tour of duty. The standard two years. Josh Rogovin out."

She sat stunned. Then she ran upstairs to Ari's room. It was stripped. Y-S must have let Josh move Ari's little bed, his play desk, his toys, his koala robot. She ran through the house, calling hopelessly, futilely. Then she flung herself at the terminal and replayed Josh's message.

"You really took revenge on me. You really did," she said to his face frozen on the screen at message's end. She went on sitting there while the room darkened. Lights here would not turn on unless she requested it, and she made no request. How dingy and small the house felt around her, devoid of any traces of their marriage beyond wear and tear on the furniture, an occasional stain not yet cleared from the wall. Ari was gone. He was not even on earth.

It all came down to the simple fact that Josh's skills were more valuable to Y-S than hers. They had been trying to transfer plasma state physicists to Pacifica Platform, but according to the rights of Y-S citizens, no one could be relocated off-earth without consent. Everyone suspected that there was more hard radiation on Pacifica than the multi was letting on. Josh had never been interested in working in space. Life on a platform was claustrophobia fully realized. Josh had no right to take Ari to spend his childhood in such a place. He had done it to punish her. There was nothing, absolutely nothing she could do.

She hated Y-S. Her boss had not fought for her hard enough. She had been sacrificed to the need of the multi for scientists willing to spend two years in a large tin can. Two years. The tears slipped down her face. She did not want to cry in this abandoned house that had witnessed the last phase of her stupid misbegotten marriage. She blew her nose hard and went home.

For what it was worth, she logged a formal protest to Y-S. Then quite openly she sent a message to Avram. She did not speak to him but sent it through the Net, the public information and communication utility that served the entire world. She told him she would accept the position in his lab. As soon as she could clean up her affairs here, she would be with him and go to work at once. She had squandered her accumulated credit on legal battles.

She had no idea why Avram wanted her to work with him, but a temporary job in Tikva would give her time to think which way to jump, time to negotiate with multis, time to heal. It would be a pleasure to be home again, where Malkah would light the Sabbath candles and they would say the ancient blessings, where she would be free to be who she was. How grim to be returning torn from her child, whom she had so often imagined bringing to Tikva. She anticipated no trouble in resigning. Had Y-S wanted to keep her services, they would have ruled she might share custody of Ari. Had they wanted her as badly as they wanted a plasma physicist on Pacifica, she would have sole custody. Company justice. She was going home.

three

MALKAH TELLS YOD A BEDTIME STORY

Once upon a time is how stories begin. Half artist, half scientist, I know that much. A mother and a grandmother, I have been telling stories for fifty years. As the children grow, so do the tales, from line drawings in motion to the full range of colors and shadings, layered thickly as plaster or blood. Some moral tales belong to kindergarten, the age of being afraid of the dark, the age of venturing from the house alone for a short distance, admonitory fables in primary crayons. But other tales are always with us. We tell them to ourselves in midlife and in old age, different each time, accreting as stalactites press toward earth, heavier with each drop and its burden of secret dissolved rock and minerals, the many salts of the planet.

Thus, dear Yod, the story I am about to leave you in the Base is not the way I told it to my child Riva or to my child Shira or to Shira and Gadi when they would sit on their haunches like little frogs, all bug eyes and appetite. I am recording this story just for you in the nights of my ash-gray insomnia, when my life feels like an attic full of boxes I have put away, things once precious and now dusty and half forgotten but still a set of demands that I put it, all of it, in order and deal with it, as bequests, as trash, as museum to set open to the family or the world. This is a time of beginnings and endings, of large risks and dangers, of sudden death by mental assassination. It is also the time my sight is failing again, and this time it cannot be repaired. The darkness of night apes the darkness I dread, and sleep is the lover I fear perhaps more than I truly desire his soft warm weight on me.

This is the story, then, of the Golem: not you, my own little Golem

I call little although you are taller than me by the same measure as a tall man (like Razi, my second-to-last lover) and stronger than me by a factor too large to bother guessing. You can lift a block of marble over your head. No, little as an affectionate term, the way so many languages attach suffixes of endearment that diminish in size as they enlarge in affect. Avram has forbidden me to see you, but we can still communicate through the Base, and there I create my bubeh maisehs for you. I am not at all sure to what extent I am guilty of great folly and overweening ambition for my role in your programming, or to what degree I am instead that figure of Strength on the Tarot deck, the woman who tames the lion, who taught you to temper your violence with human connection. A task Avram interrupted.

I am telling this story for you as I lie alone in my own huge antique bed in the bedroom shaped to me like an old familiar garment, with the scent of narcissus from the courtyard, in this the house of my family with its oasis of green in the desert the world has become. I lie awake sensing the danger gathering around us in this fragile modern ghetto. This is a tale of my family from long ago when the world seemed to be breaking open. They called it rebirth. Renaissance. But nothing ever comes back the same. The world moves in epicycles on the human level, although at the time in which my story is wanting to be told, it was those very projected epicycles of the universe that were being discarded by a few brave astronomers in favor of a system that was simple, clear and utterly alien to the human or rather the man-centered universe held to be immutable and preeminently Christian by most of those living in Europe. But like the Ptolemaic universe, my story has a human center.

This is the story particularly of one Judah Loew, several men and women around him, and one un-man. But it is also the story of a city, and of a town within a city, a town as special and as isolated and as endangered as our own free town of Jews huddled here beside the rising poisoned sea. Prague is the city, beautiful Prague just taking on its gray and golden, mustard and terra-cotta, strawberry and pistachio stucco warmth, just beginning to be shaped into the city whose Baroque lineaments I walked through in the spring of my twenty-second year—2008—while I was studying philosophy with that brilliant man who was so great a teacher and so awkward a lover, and yet I thought the bargain of my flesh for his company and his conversation a worthy one, and I was right. I wandered those twisted ways and climbed the streets of stairs, dreaming of Kafka, whose stories I carried always with me, and dreaming, too, of Einstein, who had taught at that university while he was creating his theory of relativity. I was a bright, bright student, the best student of my professor and his momentary beloved besides while lilacs bloomed that spring.

Every day from the university buildings I looked back into what had been the ghetto; every day I crossed it, past the Altneushul, past the Jewish cemetery to my neighborhood of students and workers, a medieval warren of narrow streets, two- and three-story houses washed with mustard stucco over the ancient crumbling bricks on Rasnovka Street. In the Pinkas synagogue, built in the thirteenth century, a synagogue already old when Rabbi Judah Loew walked those narrow streets, on the stripped interior walls are written the 77,397 names of the Jews who perished into smoke from the death camps the year my mother was born in Cleveland, Ohio, forty-one years before my own birth. The lilacs were in bloom when I conceived my only daughter Riva, whom in my barely postadolescent silliness I carried away from Prague, a lump in my womb like a souvenir of delight, as other sojourners carried away artifacts of Czech crystal. Indeed Riva grew up about as malleable as crystal.

Inside 1600 Prague is Jewtown, the walled ghetto, the Glop of its time, with houses shoehorned into courtyards and families squatting in one room or several families jammed in a space hardly big enough for them to lie down side by side to sleep—the walls that seldom keep out the mobs that periodically rise to ravage and murder. It is not many years since a mob came raging through the streets and in a matter of hours slaughtered a quarter of the inhabitants, maimed and torn bodies flung down like bloody trash in the streets, fallen over cribs, impaled as they prayed, slashed open in the birthing bed. There was not one survivor who had not to bury a husband, a wife, a child, a mother, a beloved. In 1543 all the Jews of Prague were sent into exile, suddenly expelled from their homes with what they could carry and dumped into the hostile countryside to make their way elsewhere, anywhere else. Only yesterday the Jews of Prague heard talk from the burghers, from the crafts guilds too, that it is time they were exiled again. In Judah Loew's lifetime all Jewish books were seized, many burned and the remainder bought back by a huge ransom. Every year the Jews pay a "leibzoll"—a tax on their right to live.

They wear on their coats, men and women and children, a yellow symbol proclaiming they are Jews. It is not the six-pointed star, the Magen David, because that symbol is only a local emblem on the banner of the community of Prague and will seem most unusual when it is used, as it will be for one of the characters we will shortly meet, on his tombstone. No, the badge required is simply a cut-out shape of yellow that every Jew must wear so as to be identifiable instantly. It has not been so forever. In fact if things at this moment are briefly a little better for the Jews of Prague, it is only a respite. Life has gotten markedly worse within their memory, and fortunately for their ability to sleep at night, they do not yet have any idea how bad it is going to get in a few years, when the Thirty Years' War sweeps back and forth and back and forth like a mad scythe harvesting human heads.

For centuries we had occupied a small, dishonorable but necessary role, because we were the bankers, the pawnbrokers, the exchanges, the source of loans; it was the work permitted us. But once Christians became bankers, Jews began trying to do the same work as everybody else, even though most trades were officially forbidden us. We had to make a living, and we couldn't just take in each other's washing. Up to the time of the first Crusade, Jews lived mostly in their own neighborhoods as people do, near their relatives, their friends, but there might be three or four more and less Jewish neighborhoods in a city like Prague, and if a Jew wanted to live someplace else, who cared? But from the first Crusade, the Church was militant, expanding, determined to conquer or extirpate other beliefs. The Fourth Lateran Council decreed Jews should be locked up in ghettos or expelled.

In the ghetto at Prague there are a few quite rich Jews who still finance foreign trade and whose empire of interests is far-flung and daring, and many, many poor Jews. There are a handful, such as the Loews, in between the hell of the very poor and the heaven of the rich. But in Jewtown everybody, the rich Maisls, the middling Loews, the hungry searching through rubbish for a piece of kindling to burn, they are all crowded into a tiny place and they know each other by name and they all know each other's business. It is a hot tight place, noisy day and night, where the ragpicker may also be a great scholar and the drayman a cantor who can sing till the birds faint or a fiddler who can make your bones shiver. The rich Jews try every few years to buy a house or some land outside, but they are too hated. No one will sell to them. If anyone entertains an offer, something happens to that seller or else that house or land goes at once off the market. So the rich, too, are stuck in this large quarrelsome family, stuck with the resentments and suspicions of the poor whose shacks and tenements press to the very walls of the fancy houses and whose smells and cries enter through every window and crack, as do the rats that breed in the cellars. Rabbi Loew has quarreled with the wealthy, because he calls them to account, he scolds them, and he insists the poor have the right to the same education as the sons of the well-to-do.

Let's look at Judah Loew, about whom this story gathers itself like a cloud that rests on the shoulder of a mountain. He's called the Maharal. In those days big rabbis have nicknames like sports stars and stars of stimmies. In the embattled ghettos, they are culture heroes and entertainers besides. His given name: Judah Loew ben Bezalel, Judah the Lion. A lion among the Jews.

The Maharal is a bright fierce man, a hotheaded kabbalist, steeped in ancient tradition so that Torah haunts and informs and sculpts the world for him, but curious, open to the science and the speculation of his time. The Maharal is a crabby saint of towering intellect with a fondness for having at the opposition with every weapon in his arsenal, from reason to high rhetoric to sarcasm to ridicule. He is free with his invective, his insults. In any intellectual contest, the desire to win takes him over and he fights to kill his opponent. He is almost alone in his time in believing that any opinion has the right to be uttered—he believes anachronistically in free speech, not because he is a relativist. No, he believes in the truth of his religion. But he believes too strongly in the sacredness of the intellect to cripple it by forbidding any ideas whatsoever. He conducts running wars of words with most other famous rabbis of his time. But in December of 1599, he receives a summons to debate a priest in public, a dangerous agon, because as a Jew he is supposed to lose. If he doesn't, the opportunity of the Church for revenge will be multiple, swift or slow-moving as they wish, and never-ending—or ending the usual way. It is not a time when someone wishing the sight should lack for the spectacle of burning Jews. But how can the Maharal throw the debate? G-d would not accept less than victory. As a Jew, he is obligated to use his entire mind. The early Biblical critic dei Rossi, whose ideas the Maharal detests, said if you want to offer a sacrifice to G-d, offer it to truth, and perhaps that is the only thing Rossi ever uttered with which the Maharal is in agreement.

The Maharal prepares for a public debate with the priest, Thaddeus, a Dominican formerly in the office of the Inquisition in Spain. Thaddeus was recently posted to Prague, where it is felt a climate of some toleration has been flourishing under the emperor Rudolf, which cannot be permitted to continue or to expand. Judah finds in his heart fury and contempt for this opponent who causes such ruin, torture and death in other lives while enjoying the security of his own position, but he strives to overcome his rancor. He wonders if he should not plead ill health, but special pleading seldom works. His health is fine, although he is an old man, but he has been depressed this winter. He has not recovered from the death of his only son.

When he sees his son in his mind, he does not see the fifty-five-year-old with the gray streaks in his beard but rather the gifted but often too sensitive child with his weak eyes and quavering voice. He thinks he was a poor father to his only son and probably to his daughters as well, although he left them largely to Perl, his able balebusteh of a wife. He had huge expectations for the son for whom he had waited so long, the successor, the bearer of his name into the future. Now he has outlived him. This is a pathetic fate I particularly fear. I have raised an outlaw who operates far from me with a price on her head. Will I even hear of her death? While I walk through my busy comfortable days, often my mind drifts toward Riva. Like the Maharal, I have been a poor parent and a fine grandparent.

Although the Maharal is old—not as people call me old, and then I look with surprise in the mirror and say, Who is that bag with the crinkles and lines? Who loosened my teeth? Who slacked my tits? No, the Maharal was old enough to feel his age. My family tradition says he was eighty-one; the books report various birth dates and thus a medley of ages up to ninety-odd. I'll accept the family's memory. Nonetheless he is still active and still creative. His voice has lost none of its power, and his intellect is as honed as ever. He is perhaps a little wilder in his language, a little harder in debate than he had been in his middle age, for he feels himself with a short time left and much to do. His is a hard-driven and a passionate old age. He appears not shorter but taller than he had stood in his youth, with his eyes as bright and fierce as ever in a gaunter face. Instead of gentling his edges, age sharpened them. He is an eagle.

Judah moved to Prague forty years before, but always when it came time to choose a chief rabbi and he was the obvious man of eminence, he was passed over. Too deeply into the mystical kabbalah perhaps, too argumentative, too original a thinker. A troublemaker. Not that his light was exactly under a bushel. He ran a famous Talmud school. He was the friend of the wealthiest Jew in Prague, Mordecai Maisl. He was surrounded by disciples and colleagues. Just before he left Prague for the last period of exile, in 1592, the emperor Rudolf sent for him and saw him privately, unheard of treatment for a Jew.

For even a spry old man it was a long walk out through the gates of the ghetto, across the Karl Bridge over the wide Vltava with its white rapids, through the streets of the Malá Strana, where the nobility had been building themselves grand palaces among orchards and pastureland remaining within the walls. Above the steep winding streets, the castle bristling with towers and spires loomed over its cliffs. He leaned on the arms of his son-in-law Itzak Cohen and his current favorite disciple, Yakov Sassoon. Up the long stairway he struggled, his heart shuddering his slight frame, while they dodged against the wall to avoid the horses ridden or led by. Below them the voices of the city rose like bright flapping banners to hang over the red roofs.

Judah passed through the massive gateway and two courtyards and up a great ceremonial stairway and through room after room, each ornate, huge, empty of purpose but filled with idle courtiers dressed in brocade and silk and velvet, with their heads riding on ruffs as if on plates, till he was forced to leave Itzak and Yakov in an anteroom. He was led at last into a smaller room hung with velvet, where in cabinets were displayed a narwhal's horn, a two-headed embryo in a bottle, a mandrake in the form of a priapic man, all manner of minerals, lodestones. Judah had no time to stare before Prince Bertier greeted him, but Judah sensed another presence. As the interview proceeded jerkily, with long pauses and whispering, Judah deduced that the emperor was sitting behind a full-length velvet curtain, using Prince Bertier to put his questions. That didn't last. The emperor became impatient with whispering the questions to Bertier and started speaking from behind the curtain; finally he burst into the room and took a chair. The subject of this most unusual interview granted a Jew was a secret; the histories are silent. Even in his account for posterity Itzak did not commit the subject of the conversation to paper. But the family has its stories, doesn't it always?

Now the emperor held the Jews as his own—his own cow to milk, his own private tax vineyard out of which always more juice could be squeezed. With a great deal of fear and a hidden anger and his wits sharpened like throwing knives, the Maharal listened to the emperor. The subject that the emperor raised with him after much conversation about the universe and those strange new theories of Copernicus, which most people who had heard about them mocked openly and which the Church condemned, was astrology. All his advisers believed in astrology as a determinant of human character and fortune. His own fine astronomer, Tycho Brahe, cast horoscopes. What did the rabbi think?

The Maharal thought quickly. Astrology was a respectable business of the time, and as nowadays every rich macher has his chemistrician in residence to feed in exactly the right psychoactives and monitor trace elements and nutrients in the blood and allergenic and immune system reactions, so the rich and powerful then had their pet astrologer to tell them the right times to act and to refrain from acting, the auspicious time for marriages and ceremonies. Judah surmised the emperor had been given a prognosis that made him uneasy.

Rudolf had the reputation for being a weak and indecisive ruler. He actually didn't seem to like war much, considered a sign of a feeble character in his time. In truth, he encouraged science and the arts and practiced a mild religious tolerance, usually resisting the mad zeal of the Counter-Reformation, allowing both Protestants and Jews to worship as they pleased and giving the universities unusual freedom. Personally I'd rather live under him than under many a more famous and admired king of Prussia.

Why the Maharal? Now, only seven of the Maharal's books had been published at this time, but several had been circulated in manuscript. Judah could be pretty sure that the emperor knew he had written a long essay, thoroughly demolishing that pseudoscience. Obviously that was why the emperor had chosen him, and he was not about to recant. The emperor was seeking a rationale for ignoring some piece of astrologically based advice, Judah deduced, and he would provide it. So be it. That is, according to family legend, what happened between Rudolf and Judah.

Shortly after this audience, the Maharal was once again passed over for chief rabbi of Prague. He promptly accepted a post at Posen and shook the dust of Prague from his hat, departing with his family.

He didn't come back until they finally gave him what he wanted. Now, the legend that has attached to him belongs to this period when the Maharal has recently returned in triumph to Prague as chief rabbi. The Maharal is a learned man, not only in Torah and Talmud, not only in history, in the science and philosophy of his time, but also in the mysteries of the kabbalah. He makes an absolute distinction between the truths of science, which are based on observation and are always changing as the world is always changing (a radical concept because the world had been considered static and unmoving for centuries), and the truths of religion, which are of another order. In that sphere, thought is action and words are not signifiers of things or states but real and potent forces. This is of course the world of artificial intelligence and vast bases in which I work— the world in which the word is real, the word is power, energy is mental and physical at once and everything that appears as matter in space is actually immaterial. Perhaps that's why as I get older, I become more of a mystic. When I was young, sex and psychology obsessed me, fashion and flair; now that I come toward the end of my braided rope, I am fascinated by the holy and the powerful light that shines through history, the powers that enact their dramas through us, the good and the evil, the damage and the repair our wanderings and our choices commit.

Is it fair to tell this tale? It is a tale of kabbalah, of religious magic. Most scholars insist that it has no basis in the life of this exemplary religious thinker and educational reformer, this historian and polemicist. What has he to do with the creation of monsters? But as a woman who spends her working days creating fictions and monsters, how can I feel I am committing calumny against Judah? I believe in the truth of what is perhaps figurative, although Moshe Idel has found recipe after recipe, precise as the instructions for building a yurt or baking French bread, for making golems. I cannot always distinguish between myth and reality, because myth forms reality and we act out of what we think we are; we know on many levels truths that are irrational as well as reasoned or experimental. Our minds help create the world we think we inhabit. I am myself a magician who last fall seduced a machine, so I can project myself back into the Maharal and say that he, too, may have created the being that folk memory records as his. Do you not think, my friend, that you are something beyond the ordinarily human, a miracle?

Thus when the Maharal that winter begins to feel danger growing and a net of intrigue tightening around his people, where shall he turn but to mystical lore? The Prague Jews are penned in their ghetto, and there is nowhere to escape and nowhere to flee. The Jews of Spain who had lived a thousand years in peace and high culture were overnight exiled from the land they thought theirs, torn from their roots and their graves and their synagogues. The Jews of England were expelled to penury and wandering. The Jews of Portugal were ripped from their homes. How can he save the Jews of Prague?

Every year on the Day of Atonement, he recites from the pulpit the poem written by Avigdor Karo mourning the three thousand Jews slaughtered when the Prague ghetto was attacked by a mob armed with swords, maces, pikes and sickles. Afterward the royal chamberlain convicted the Jews of inciting to riot and fined them five tons of silver. If Rudolf is apt to spare them, he has other, more pressing concerns. The Jews are expendable. The rich local burghers hate them. As a visible separate people, they are always in danger. The Counter-Reformation is gathering intensity and momentum. The Church is militant and enraged at the stubbornness of the Jews, so like the stubborn refusal of the Protestants but easier to quash.

One new danger is the blood libel. At Pesach, we open the door at the Seder every year to let Elijah, the great prophet of hope and freedom, enter if he will come to us. I can remember explaining to Riva, I can remember explaining to Shira, and yes, Gadi too, for by then Sara was too ill to make a Seder and both Avram and Gadi came to us, how that custom originated in the terrible years of the blood libel. Then Christians believed that Jews put the blood of Christian children into the Pesach matzoh. It's a bastardization of the story of Exodus, the death of the firstborn and the Jewish children passed over by the Angel of Death, a confusion with the wine of the Seder altered in their Mass into blood. What have we to do with blood, who are forbidden to consume it? So we began opening the door, to show we have nothing to hide. Will Shira ever come home again for Pesach? Married to that arrogant and broken creature. Now divorced, but loitering in the closed corporate world.

Another increasing danger is the priest Thaddeus, who has come to Prague from Spain particularly to carry out the aims of the Inquisition. He simply cannot believe that Rudolf permits the Jews of Prague to have a publishing house that prints books in Hebrew, to march in processions, to engage however controversially in trades and sciences. He cannot believe that the emperor's own mathematician, the great astronomer Tycho Brahe, treats the Jew David Gans as a colleague and lets him work in his observatory, the most modern in all Europe, or that Johannes Kepler, Brahe's brilliant assistant, and some of the other local intellectuals are reading in the kabbalah and discussing it. Here in Prague Jews and Christians are arguing together over heretical ideas such as the planets revolving around the sun, and they are not being promptly forced to recant or being burned in the public square—not yet. But Thaddeus has his fierce duty to perform. He is a vessel through which the passion for what he holds as truth roars in torrents. Like Savonarola in Florence, who made a pyre of art he considered sensual and decadent, who burned all the Renaissance paintings he could lay hands on, Thaddeus is a fiery orator who stirs a crowd with ease. People in groups are the organ he likes to play. Above all, his hatred is sincere. He sees the Jews as a disease creeping through Europe the way two hundred and fifty years earlier Jews had been blamed for the Black Plague. It is an intellectual plague he sees running rampant in Prague. Dangerous thought is a disease that rots souls.

The public debate is held on a Sunday before a large crowd. What Judah has to do is try for a tie in front of a hostile and rabid audience. This is exactly what he achieves, by a fingernail's grace, counterpunching, attacking, but always breaking off the assault before victory. It is a long dance in the sun of the crowded square, a dance of swords and fire. A dance that becomes ever more technical, so that the crowd begins to dwindle as the Maharal coaxes Thaddeus from the perch of rhetoric into the gnarly labyrinth of philosophy, theory, quotation, arguments about translations. Thaddeus is seduced into quarrels about ever finer details propped by quotations and petty distinctions. By the time he pulls free, the time agreed upon is over. No one has won, and Thaddeus is furious, for too late he recognizes the Maharal's strategy—to entice him into technical arguments boring to a crowd that longs for blood, to entice him into academic argument that treats the Maharal as an equal rather than as Satan personified. The crowd came for a tournament and witnessed a seminar.

The Maharal has no time to rejoice in his muted victory. Easter is a dangerous time, and Easter is coming. Mobs often form at Easter and attack. At Easter prominent Jews may be seized and tortured till they confess or die.

Judah prays and he fasts and he aligns himself with the highest spheres according to the disciplines of the kabbalah, through the rungs of all the emanations toward the all that is nothingness, the Ein Sof. Thaddeus was angry and will find his revenge. In Judah the tzaddik—the righteous—and the hasid—the pious—come together. A mystic and a doer, active, passionate, driven, Judah can never close himself in his meditation and forget the community. He prays and fasts and fasts and prays for an answer to the danger he can smell, can taste.

Then on the seventh day of his fast, the Maharal falls asleep at his desk piled high with Hebrew pages, old and new books and fair-copied manuscripts from fifty scholars. He dreams he is standing in the Jewish cemetery, crammed with its tilted stones like the pages falling open of a fat book. Everywhere people are wailing and hastily digging graves. He sees a hill of pale bodies all flung on each other. He is facing the graceful Pinkas synagogue, and as he stares at its wall, a hand of light traces the word GOLEM. Right to left it keeps tracing that word. Then a voice that burns his ears calls his name once, twice. "Judah, you must make a golem of clay to rise and walk the ghetto and save your people. Do not falter. Rise and make a golem."

Yod, the ability to see visions is one of those human talents that flourishes when rewarded by a society and withers in most of us when punished by society. That is, whether the ability to see the hand of ha-Shem writing on the wall secures you pleasant notice for your religious and prophetic acumen, or whether it gets you locked up in the local nut bin, will determine how many people in a society form the habit of seeing what other people are wont to think is not really there. The Maharal has developed his ability to see visions, for they enable him to meditate, to clear his mind, to grasp what he considers higher truth. But like most Jews in his tradition, oftener he hears voices, and the voices instruct him on his duty.

What is the golem he hears the voice commanding him to make? A being in human form made not by ha-Shem but by another human through esoteric knowledge, particularly by the power of words and letters. The Sefer Yezirah, the mystical Book of Creation, is supposed to contain what you must master to form a golem with the power of the Names of G-d and the power of letters and numbers. Kabbalistic tradition tells us of many sages and saints who created a golem, not for any use but as a mystical rite. They would make and unmake these moving clay men, joining themselves to the power of creation, and, in the chanting and the act, achieve ecstasy. It is one of the crowns of glory a truly holy person might wear. We are also told of occasional sages who made a golem for some private use—running messages, cleaning the house—such as we use robots for, and these golem were both mute and stupid.

What is original is that Judah's golem isn't to be invented to prove the rabbi's mastery of esoteric knowledge. He believes himself commanded to create a golem to fight, to police, to save. Therefore this golem must be formed with intelligence and the power of speech. He is to become a one-man army. From the moment Judah first sees the hand writing "golem" and hears the voice calling to him to rise and create this creature, he asks himself, Am I really going to do this? Once he has framed the possibility, he knows that he must keep the project secret. He harbors no desire to be tortured as a sorcerer, always an open possibility for a polemical sharp-tongued rabbi.

As one who has been engaged in a secret project for the last two years, I identify with his hesitations. At any moment in history, certain directions are forbidden that lie open to the inquiring mind and the experimental hand. Not always is the knowledge forbidden because dangerous: governments will spend billions on weapons and forbid small sects the peyote of their ecstasy. What we are forbidden to know can be—or seem—what we most need to know.

Further, for a human being to make another is to usurp the power of ha-Shem, to risk frightening self-aggrandizement. It is to push yourself beyond the human. It is dangerous to the soul, dangerous to the world. As soon as the mind conceives of a possibility, it wants the possible to be actualized. It wants to be doing, no matter what the cost or the damage. The Maharal is preconsciously aware of human frailty. He does not sleep and scarcely drinks a little water. He cannot decide wherein lies the correct path: is his vision from ha-Shem or from his own ego, his desire to prove himself as learned, as holy, as powerful as the rabbis before him who had created golems?

The Maharal goes on debating inside himself for an entire week whether the vision that had come to him is a temptation or true instruction, a real mitzvah to be carried out. He wavers. Never before has such a febrile indecision burned him. He is afraid to act. He keeps finding reasons to preserve his skepticism.

Once years ago I met my daughter Riva secretly in the depths of the Glop, that jammed fetid slum where most people live. She spoke to me then, huddled in that loft full of damaged and abandoned machinery, about the temptation of danger: how sometimes the near impossibility of carrying out an action makes it irresistible. She must do it because she cannot do it, because it is both forbidden and held to be unachievable. That was when she began to move from pure data piracy toward something more political and even more dangerous. It was then she began her crusade of liberating information from the multis. The Maharal, lying awake as I lie awake, is fearful, as afraid of the remedy he imagines risking his life to carry out as he is afraid of the danger gathering for those who live in his care. Unable to decide, he lies supine to the night and the event, awaiting a further sign.

four

THROUGH THE BURNING LABYRINTH

On April Fools' Day, Shira, incongruous in her backless suit, joined the hundred thousand day laborers taking the eastbound tube. The escalators to the tube station were twelve across right outside the dome, where the blast of five o'clock heat leaned its scorching weight on her as she shuffled in line. She was wearing a white suit because she had had to check out of Y-S officially. Inbound night workers were lined up out in the still dangerous late sun to pass into the dome by palming the ID plates, but there was no ID required to leave. If you wanted to pass out of safety into hell, it was your business. No one could walk away into the Nebraska desert.

Shira was taking the tube across the country, jammed in a hot crowded car. She only hoped her luggage would arrive eventually, but the chances were, thieves would grab it en route. Her hands clutched the harness holding her into her seat. The tube car was windowless, as there was nothing whatsoever to see underground. She traveled for two hours before she changed at Chicago; she spent the night locked in an eight-by-six cube in the Chicago tube station, for she'd never make it safely across the Glop after dark.

The next morning she had two more hours to Boston. She did not want to think about Ari on a platform one third of the way to the moon with his father. Crying? Still wondering where she was, why she had not come, if she would ever come for him? She felt torn open. Would Josh watch out for early signs of ear infection? She had tried to call Pacifica, but Josh had refused a link.

She could not imagine what it would be like working with Avram, she could not imagine what it would be like returning to live with her grandmother. She had left home at seventeen, and a week was the longest she had visited since. Then she had been delivered from corporate enclave to free town by zipplane, from total fortress security to fragile peace in just over an hour, avoiding the densely inhabited slum of the Glop. Now her life felt like a crystalline structure shattered into bright dangerous shards that left her bleeding. Everything she had worked to create and sustain, everything into which she had poured her perhaps too abundant energy—her marriage, Ari, her work—was smashed or stolen from her. The temperature in the tube hovered near forty. She gasped for breath in the bad air.

Shira stumbled out of the tube exhausted and suffering from lack of oxygen. The small of her back hurt, and her sinuses burned. She had a headache that blistered her skull. Here she was in the Glop and there was no time to worry about small pain if she was to stay alive and intact. She pulled over her backless business suit the thin black covering almost all women and old people and many men wore in the streets. It covered age, class, sex, and made all look roughly the same size. She had not worn it in her years at Y-S, for there were no gangs in the multi enclaves. She pulled on metal woven gloves to cover her hands, though she was perfectly aware that although they might discourage a casual slasher with only a sticker, any real hand-hacker could laser right through the protective mesh. If only she could wear a sign indicating how low her credit was, she would be safe. Her hand was almost worthless today. Malkah would have transferred enough to help her home; otherwise she was flat.

Day workers and gang niños and the unemployed lived in the Glop— the great majority of people on the continent. Most of the remainder were citizens of some multi enclave. The free towns were exceptions, as were Rural Zones. Most people who lived in free towns like the one she had grown up in could have sold themselves to a multi directly, instead of contracting for specific jobs, but elected to stay outside the enclaves because of some personal choice: a minority religion, a sexual preference not condoned by a particular multi, perhaps simply an archaic desire for freedom.

The garment smelled stale as it billowed about her. It had deteriorated during its years of lying folded in the bottom of a storage cube, but she felt immediately safer in it as she joined the crowd on the movers, most wearing black cover-ups so they appeared like sinister nuns. She fumbled for her filter mask as she reached the upper levels of the station. Goggles, mask, cover-up, cooler: she had everything she needed to make herself ready for the street, helped by an edge of amphetamine from the capsule she stopped to buy from a vendor and popped as the mover chugged her along, once she had checked its content with her pocket scanner. It honed her paranoia enough to help her navigate the labyrinthine station where hundreds camped and slept in the filthy decaying passages that mumbled day and night of distant voices, muffled screams, drumming, zak music, running sewage, the hiss of leaking coolant. In some of the passages stores sold clothing, vat food, fast food, stimmies and spikes. Spikes were outlawed in the Y-S enclave. They were more vivid than stimmies. Instead of experiencing what an actor saw, felt, touched, was touched by, the user was projected into the drama and the sensations were more powerful—so she had heard. People told of kids found dead who had replayed favorite adventure or porn scenes until they starved to death.

Few multis permitted recreational drugs, unless issued by the company. In the Glop, every invented drug was sold by street vendors. In other corridors, vendors were hawking all the jetsam of the times: trash carted from the enclaves, junk of the last century turned into furniture, clothing, weapons, the wired-up skeletons of extinct exotica like robins and warblers, cannibalized parts built into makeshift robots. She noticed a knife made of an organic-based resin that would not show up on detection devices.

"How much betty for the sticker?"

"For you, duke?" Behind the metal mask, bloodshot eyes glittered. She winced. Duke was someone with money. She could not talk the Glop talk, and at once they identified her as a grud, a multi employee. "Cuarenta dos. Forty-two. This a sticker don't cry under rays."

"Treinta. Thirty." She let the knife drop back into the display.

They bargained ritually for another five minutes. She paid thirty-six. He had a regular credit box. Stripping the glove, she inserted her hand gingerly. He had his box rigged so that instead of just the amount and approval, her balance appeared.

"Hey, duke, hard times, eh? Flat, blat like a squashed cat. You sound como young meat. I run a good clean cheese shop—"

She slid the knife into the deep seam of her sleeve and strode on. Hot, it was hot, it was hot. Her brain was melting with the toxic fumes. She was both hungry and thirsty. She still had some water, and that would have to last her. She had no idea what diseases were running through the Glop at the moment, but there were always new types of typhoid and hepatitis, new viral scourges still colonizing from the tropics. She would simply have to endure her hunger. It did not do to imagine what the burgers or sushi were made of, animal, vegetable, mineral. Whether they had been alive in their previous incarnations or not, they were now surely swarming with local protozoa and bacteria. The smells of the cooking made her salivate, but she never slowed her pace. Walk fast but never trot. Old street rule. Some of the food was being charbroiled on hibachis or barbecue grills, some was being cooked on laser burners, some was simply turning over a fire built on the floor of the ancient building complex, the tunnels that had once been a subway system. Parts of the old system were flooded; the rest was occupied.

Most of the vendors, too, squatted in black cover-ups, although gang members distinguished themselves by their uniforms, paint, tattoos, by daring to show their arms, their legs, their faces and chests. They wore weapons visibly, everything from knives to laser rifles; officially weapons were outlawed, but the only laws that held here were turf laws of the gangs who controlled a piece of the Glop. The gangs met in raids, in treaty powwows, uneasily in public markets and common areas such as the tube stations, the clinics.

Sharp smell of urine and shit. A body. No, he was still alive. Around the body with its chest torn open and the arterial blood spurting out, stood a chanting circle of gang niños, all wearing cutoff jackets in purple and gold with a snarling rat emblazoned on the back, lightning shooting from his eyes, body pulsating, in constant movement caught in midleap, over and over again. They were chanting their killing song. She paused, kept moving. She could be lying there five minutes later. Everywhere the signs of two gangs warred, lasered into the pavement, splashed on the walls. Disputed turf was dangerous territory, a war zone.

She saw a stairway ahead. A toll had been set up across it, manned by a group dressed like the downed kid. They had an old jury-rigged hand box, and the line shuffled past it. She read off the stairway tolls and passed through their security, paid and climbed out into the raw. Parts of the Glop were under domes, but the system had not been completed before government stopped functioning. There were still elections, every two years, but they were just highly bet-on sporting events. All politicians did was run for office. Every quadrant was managed by the remains of the old UN, the eco-police. After the two billion died in the Great Famine and the plagues, they had authority over earth, water, air outside domes and wraps. Otherwise the multis ruled their enclaves, the free towns defended themselves as they could, and the Glop rotted under the poisonous sky, ruled by feuding gangs and overlords.

Outside, she adjusted her goggles and looked for transport. Short-distance pedicabs would not get her out of the Glop. She was near the northern fade-out. She needed a float car for hire. She heard a warning high pitch and threw herself into a building mouth before the flotilla of dust riders came tearing through the plaza in a blur of speed and flashing metal. Not everyone was quick enough. Blood sprayed out of the dust cloud. When they had passed, parts of two bodies were strewn across the broken pavement. She made her way past a gang fight of dogs quarreling over the flesh, toward the float cars tethered at the north end of the plaza. A cargo hold had pulled up on the east end of the plaza, and a recorded voice was calling for harvesters and vat boys. Out of the crumbling buildings, densely occupied to the last cubicle, a crowd of unemployed pushed toward the hold.

At the float car enclosure she put her hand into the box, and the monitor let her enter. The car boss set the coordinates. If she tried to change them, the car would simply land. When she arrived, it would automatically return. She paid in advance. Her credit was running low, but she hoped to be home in an hour. The float car ran on a cushion of air, following the old broken roads. It could fly for brief periods at a low altitude, frequently necessary to cross a river or a ravine where a bridge had collapsed. It was solar powered, quiet and not particularly fast. It could also move over water, which was important because when you had not taken a route in a while, you never knew how the ocean and estuaries might have advanced over the land, flooding low-lying sections. What had been terra firma three years before might be under the waves, for with the polar caps rapidly melting, the oceans rose and rose. Float cars were vehicles of the multi gruds and the free towns. Fast tanks moved as well over broken terrain, and they were armored. Corporate travel was usually by zip.

Driving a hired float car was undemanding. She need not do anything except steer it around or over obstacles. It had the coordinates of her destination and proceeded on its own. Overhead a vast helix of vultures circled. They had evolved to withstand UV radiation. They could live in the raw, as could most bugs, as could gulls and rats and raccoons. Not people. Not songbirds, all dead, so the insects flourished and moved in waves over the land, eating the hills to desert. The hills were deeply eroded. Scrub trees like pitch pine, wild cherry and bear oak had replaced sugar maples and white pines. Brambles and multiflora rose grew in impenetrable thickets she detoured around.

The car automatically cut east, toward the ocean, to miss the near corner of the Cybernaut enclave. Multis did not permit private or hired cars to pass through. Once the car had detoured the enclave with its green parklands under the dome, its coruscating city, she came into the area of free towns bordering the ocean. The road she was following ran straight into the sea, for low-lying coastal towns had been destroyed in the Great Hurricane of '29. The wrap on St. Marystown glistened under the amber sun. She was close enough to the waves to smell petroleum and salt. Now she could see rising from the waters the hill on which her own town, Tikva, was built, its wrap floating over it on its supports like a shining cloud. She steered the car ashore and up the hill toward Tikva. She put down before the gate that faced the sea, got out and let the car turn and veer off.

She stood with her pack outside the gate and only then remembered to take off the black cover-up. Nothing remained but to return where she had been nurtured as a child. Would it serve as a safe haven? Gadi might still be here. They were friends by electronic transmission, but Gadi in the flesh was more than she wanted to face. She could probably slip into town, as she used to do with Gadi when she was growing up, but she had no reason to. Slowly she approached the monitor. Would it still recognize her hand print? It did. The male voice that was the town computer greeted her by name. "Shira, Malkah Shipman expects you. Avram Stein expects you. Welcome."

She was embarrassed to find her eyes flushed with tears as she stuffed the cover-up into her shoulder pack. She was glad a moment later she had not tried to slip in, because she met two young people on guard duty. As official security, they bore dart guns with paralyzing capability. They had heard the monitor greet her and nodded her by. This must be a tense period, for there to be human guards on the perimeter. The free towns were not supposed to be able to buy laser weapons, although from the black market they sometimes did. They relied on shock or tranquilizers mostly, or on sonic weapons.

Walking under a wrap was different from being under a dome. The wrap was more permeable to light and weather; basically it shielded from UV. Inside temperature was only a little higher than outside. The perimeters were monitored by computer; a person crossing the barrier would set off an alarm. The gates, with recognition plates, faced each cardinal direction. When a hurricane struck, as it often did nowadays, the wrap could be furled to protect it. Basically the free towns had sprung up along the ocean because such a location was vulnerable and considered dangerous; no multi would risk inundation. The free towns flourished on that unclaimed margin.

Shira loitered through the streets. The buildings were all different, although none could be higher than four stories here. Some houses were made of wood, some of brick, some of the new resins, some of polymers, some of stone. She was tickled by the consonances and dissonances—little Spanish haciendas, stern Greek Revival houses, shingled saltboxes, an imitation of Fernandez' famous dancing house on its pedestal, jostled shoulders on the same block. After the uniformity of the Y-S enclave, the colors, the textures, the sounds and smells provoked her into a state of ecstasy until she found herself walking more and more slowly, her head whipping around like an idiot. Why had she ever left?

It was strange, too, to see things that were old, cracked, worn, houses that needed paint, a boarded-up window, a broken railing. People here carried out their own repairs in their own good time. Anarchic little plots of tulips and baby tomato plants, bean seedlings about to mount their poles lined the streets. At fourteen-thirty, almost everyone was at work. A robot cleaner puttered along the street, picking up the occasional bit of trash and sweeping madly. The sound of someone practicing violin, playing over and over a passage of Wieniawski, came through an open window. She wondered why that seemed startling until she realized that in Y-S, windows were not usually opened. The occasional passerby was casually dressed: open-throated shirts, pants, a full skirt, shorts, for the day was seasonally mild. She felt like a freak in her standard Y-S suit, now streaked with grime and soot. A couple passed her arguing loudly about somebody's mother, their voices raised unselfconsciously. Behind a hedge, a dog was barking at a rabbit in a hutch. In little yards, chickens were stalking about, and in one, speckled turkeys strutted. Ari would be crazy with excitement to see live animals. The smells assaulted her: animal smells, vegetable smells, the scent of yellow tulips, the heavier scent of narcissus, cooking odors, a tang of manure, the salty breath of the sea. Everything felt . . . unregulated. How unstimulated her senses had been all those Y-S years. How cold and inert that corporate Shira seemed as she felt herself loosening.

The house of her childhood: from the street a stolid square clapboard house, two stories offering a row of large multipaned windows. It hid its secret, that it was built around a courtyard like the synagogue she had always gone to, the one called the Synagogue of Water. No one before the twenty-first century had ever loved flowers and fruiting trees and little birds and the simple beauty of green leaves as did those who lived after the Famine, for whom they were precious and rare and always endangered. Shira had been born since the Famine, after the rising oceans had drowned much of the rice and breadbaskets of the world, after the rising temperatures had shifted the ocean and air currents, leaving former farmlands scrubland or desert, after the end of abundant oil had finished agribusiness on land; yet the consequences and tales of the Famine had shaped her childhood too.

Malkah was waiting in the courtyard. "Ah, Shira, you're home at last."

"Since Ari was born, I've wanted to bring him here and let you get to know each other. Here I am but without my son. What good is it?"

"Time for you to come home. But it's dangerous here. We're under siege. We'll talk about it later. Now come and let me hold you."

Malkah felt smaller to her, far more fragile, and yet solid enough. The yellow rose still twined on the wall, the courtyard was still planted with peach and plum trees, grapevines and cosmos and tulips, squash and tomato vines, a garden of almost Eden. Shira held Malkah close, feeling a sense at once of her grandmother's strength and age. Malkah had always seemed old to Shira, because Malkah was Bubeh and grandmothers were old, but Shira recognized in retrospect that Malkah had been a young and extremely vigorous grandmother. Malkah was born in 1987, so she would be seventy-two now.

Shira felt a lightening all through her as if tension so long-standing she had not even recognized it as tension had eased suddenly, a high-pitched background whine of machinery suddenly cutting off so that a blessed and startlingly rich inner silence flowed through her. This was the home she had fled, not from an unhappy childhood but from too early and too intense love, paradise torn.

five

FIFTEEN YEARS BEFORE: THE DAY OF ALEF

At thirteen, Shira loved passionately and secretively and was loved in return. However, she also knew this to be a state outlawed and demeaned by everyone except Gadi and herself.

She did not love Gadi alone, only most fiercely. She also loved her grandmother Malkah and her big sleek brown cat, Hermes. Hermes had been hers since she had found him as a kitten abandoned in the raw, where he would have died, for he was not adapted to survive out there. He was valuable, because the town was plagued with mice. Mice and mosquitoes liked life under the wrap. He was precious to her because he loved her uncritically, undemandingly, unendingly. Malkah's love was strong but abrasive, scrubbing her clean. Gadi's love bore both roses and thorns, like the immense climber outside her bedroom window, swarming all the way up the courtyard wall.

Her grandmother had raised her, as was the custom with women of her family. Malkah told her that when a woman had a baby, it was of her line. Men came, men went, but she should remember that her first baby belonged to her mother and to her but never to the father. Malkah said love was mostly nonsense and self-hypnosis, and men were by and large fine to work with and fun in bed, but never expect much otherwise. Of her Malkah expected much. She was the daughter of the line.

Shira knew better. At thirteen, she knew much more about love than Malkah. Malkah might say men were transitory, but Gadi was not. Gadi had been hers since they met in second grade, when his family moved here. Gadi said they were fated, they were bound. Other people wandered the earth their whole lives looking for their twin, their lover, their other self who would complete them and answer their deepest hungers, but Gadi and she had found each other so early that no one could ever slip between them. Still, it was not easy, loving him as intensely as she did. He was not easy. The world thought of them as children, refusing to recognize their bond—for whenever it became visible, they were in trouble. Nothing felt as intense as the times when they seized hands and charged off into their own private world. At once colors gleamed. Lights grew more intense, and shadows lurked darker and scarier and more enticing. Feelings pierced her, sweet and sour as the grapefruit shipped up every winter from South Carolina.

"Let's travel," Gadi would say to her, and Shira would answer, "Let's go."

Of course he did not mean traveling really, although they planned to wander all around the world and under the sea and up to the satellite cities. They had been to those places by stimmie, but Shira was stubborn: what she hadn't done in her own body didn't really count. She was old-fashioned that way, as Malkah had raised her. They were just exploring their little world and pretending.

But pretend with Gadi was more real than school or stimmies or her own thoughts. In school they rarely exchanged a word, for they had evolved a body language, signals and glances quicker than others could catch on to. Since Shira was halfway through childhood, they had protected their friendship with secrecy. Boys were supposed to play with boys and girls with girls. Her best friend ought to be some creature from her class, like Hannah, who giggled constantly, or Zee, who told her mother whatever she or her friends did, idiot. No one had ever said, Gadi and Shira cannot be close, it is forbidden, but they learned to watch out for the gaze of others, their jokes, their comments, their curiosity, sticky and soiling. Even those who meant well treated their bond as cute or transitory.

For years they had concealed nothing more than that they liked to play cards together, to work on puzzles, to act out stories of heroism and rescue. It was not exactly forbidden again, but neither was it encouraged, to explore the hidden levels of the town, the old abandoned streets, the empty houses and basements, the forgotten upper stories. There they played out their dramas, their dreams, stories from the stimmies. For years she had had this magic circle they could weave about themselves, luminous with Gadi's imagination, the place where she could never be lonely or bored. In that private world of play more intense, far more real than reality, she was whatever she longed for. Fear was a kind of background noise to growing up. They could not play in abandoned dwellings without remembering once there had been many more people in the world, too many, before the Famine, the plagues, local wars.

They both had old sec skins they kept in a shed. Some days they rushed out into the raw, beyond the wrap that kept off the poisonous rays of the sun, to walk with the thin coat of firmgel protecting them under the mustard sky. They would hike to the flooded city with its old-fashioned tall buildings, where the tide washed through marble lobbies and lapped at the broken elevators and the stairs that rose up and up. The wood and metal had been scavenged years ago. Their adventuring into the ruined city was truly forbidden and dangerous, because they never knew who or what they might meet there: roving gangs, organ scavengers who didn't mind at all if the body they found was still moving. She loved the ocean. For years they had swum there, in spite of undertow and sharks, not always having the grease worn in the water in place of sec skins to protect against the sun's radiation. They enjoyed undressing together, secretly, then slipping into the warm caress of the salt water. Shira swam well, and the sea braced and comforted her. In the water they were equally strong. Often she told Gadi they were both children of the sea. Gadi liked the idea of being anybody's son except Avram's. Gadi felt he couldn't please his father, no matter what he did. Avram wanted a son more like himself: one with a scientific bent, disciplined, scholarly, brilliant in a narrow intense range. The more Gadi was himself, the more his father despaired of him. Gadi could only satisfy Avram by acting like somebody else, and that could never last.

Today, after school—they were both just starting high school now, for Gadi was fourteen and Shira seven months and two days younger—they told their separate stories. Shira left a message with the house that she was studying for a history test with Zee. She would be sure to get home before Malkah; however, if she didn't, Malkah could not stand Zee's family and would never call them. Malkah sometimes worked at home and sometimes at the Base office. The Base was the gold mine of the town, where the systems were created that were the town's main export. Both Malkah and Avram were Base Overseers, among the most respected scientists (or, as Malkah preferred to be called, designers) in their fields. The products and systems they developed for several multis were the foundation of the town's independence.

Sometimes when Shira lied to the house, she felt as if the computer could tell. Like most houses, it had a female voice and a warm affect. She had always imagined it as being perhaps ten years younger than Malkah. When she was little, very little, of course, she had thought of it as alive, and sometimes still it was hard not to, for it knew so much about her and it freely uttered opinions and judgments. Malkah had enhanced it beyond the capabilities of the house computers of any of her friends. Shira did not know what Gadi told his mother. Sara was an invalid, suffering from a newly mutated virus that could not be treated. Her bones were slowly dissolving. She lived in a haze of medication, and Gadi could pass off any lame excuse on her.

As for Avram, Gadi's father was working in the lab as usual, putting in a twelve-hour day. Neither Shira nor Gadi could remember whether Avram had worked such long hours before his wife had begun dying, but both Avram's long hours and Sara's illness had been going on for five years.

Today there was a storm outside the wrap, the shallow waves of the bay lashing into muddy froth, slamming on the shore. They went instead to their secret place. Avram's lab occupied the second floor of the house where Gadi lived—along with six other families on the ground floor. Gadi said it had been a hotel, when the town was a resort. It was longish, squat, made of yellow bricks under a roof of red tiles, left over from when there had been weather falling on it. Across the front a wide veranda had once offered a place to sit, but all the wood had been scavenged and now the many doors had their own jerry-built stairs leading to the ground.

They crept up the old fire escape to the top floor of many small, unused rooms. "Imagine the maids," Gadi said. "Like slaves."

"They weren't slaves." Shira frowned at him. He always liked to dramatize everything. "They were paid."

"Paper money," Gadi said solemnly. He slid the window up. They had rubbed soap on it to make it slide better. He stepped in easily, gracefully, and reached to help her. Gadi had been growing fast for the last year and a half; now he was eight centimeters taller than Shira. She despaired of growing more. She was resigned to being short like Malkah. Malkah told her that for generations everyone had been taller than their parents, but no longer. In Tikva, they ate real food, but most people ate vat food, made of algae and yeasts. She had tasted it on a school trip; it was disgusting. Their teacher lectured them when they gagged on it, about two billion people who had starved to death in the Famine, when the ocean rose over rice paddies and breadbaskets of the delta countries like Bangladesh and Egypt, when the Great Plains dried up and blew away in dust storms that darkened the skies and brought early winter, when the deserts of Africa and the new desert of the Amazon spread month by month. Without vat food, most of the world would starve, as huge numbers had done in the twenties and thirties.

They climbed into the hall and took off their shoes before they crept along the dusty passageway. "Where are we going?"

"The blue room."

It was the nicest of the rooms that still had furniture. The walls were the same faded dun as the other rooms, but on the floor was a pale blue rug; on the old metal bed, a raggedy cotton bedspread offered homely comfort. The rooms up here were barely big enough for a double or single bed, a dresser, a chair. At home she could never bring Gadi up to her room, any more than he could bring her to his. When they were younger, they had played in each other's rooms, but now if they shut the door, their families would ask why. Like every other girl in Tikva, she had been given an implant at puberty to prevent pregnancy, but kids their age were simply not supposed to be interested in sex, and yet every kid was, in a nervous silly way.

Gadi sat down lotus position on the bed, and she sat the same way facing him. The light from the window turned his fine curly hair into a halo of down. "What do we have to eat?"

She pulled half a round loaf of rye from her bag. "Rye from the bakery and the usual." Telapia was a staple of life in the town, part of their meekro—fish farming, growing cukes, tomatoes, peppers, all part of the same self-contained system under the wrap. They had grown up eating fish at least five days a week: the same fish.

Gadi groaned, but he reached for the food. He was always hungry. Meals in his house were haphazard. He ate at Malkah's a couple of times a week—somehow his presence at the dinner table was acceptable, unremarkable. Shira nibbled, keeping him company. From below came the quiver of machinery, a high-frequency whine, voices raised and then lowered. The building was solidly made and gave them sufficient privacy if they were careful. Avram was downstairs in his lab. She could vaguely remember when Sara had worked in the lab with him. Now he had a young assistant, David.

They cuddled, Gadi putting his long arm around her, their legs tangled in the quilt. "Rabbi Berger didn't have to talk to you that way," Gadi said. "You were right, he just didn't like the way you said it."

She shrugged, pressing closer. "He says I have a bad attitude."

"Good. Keep it up."

"He's so bony. Do you think he rattles when he runs down the steps?"

"Am I too skinny?"

"You aren't too anything, Gadi."

"You say that now. Do you think we'll be like other married couples? Fighting and jabbing at each other. My parents weren't like that, if I really remember how it was. They used to speak their own language, top speed. They'd work together all day, and then at night they'd talk nonstop as if they hadn't seen each other for weeks."

Gadi's home smelled like a clinic. It was unnaturally quiet. She was used to a more cheerful and pragmatic atmosphere. Malkah believed in the creature comforts: good food, pretty dishes, curtains on the windows, comfortable healthy posture in front of the computers, the plugs kept polished, sterilized. "I wish we could live in my house."

Gadi kissed her lightly, just a brushing of the lips. "Your house is the good place of my dreams. It's always been that."

"Because of the courtyard. It's like the synagogue." A whole meekro within the walls of her house, all green and flowering, like paradise itself. "I wish we dared be there right now."

"We'll have it someday. We'll take off all our clothes and lie on the grass under the peach tree. You're my peach. I could eat you all up."

He was kissing her again, harder now, their lips soft and moist and avid, snatching at each other, sucking, their tongues entwined. Lately their bodies created a fierce intense place between them. For years they had been holding each other and sometimes kissing, but that part was growing stronger and more powerful. He pushed her sweater up to touch her breasts. They were growing, and he liked to play with them. It made her feel molten and as if the weight in her were shifting downward. Kissing used to be part of pretend, part of the games, but lately it was its own thing.

He fell back from her, smiling now. "Close your eyes, Shira. Close them tight. I'm closing mine. Now feel. We're blind. We're going to be eyeless. We're two blind creatures meeting to explore each other. And we speak different languages, so we can't talk. We can only touch and make noises."

Slowly, slowly, she built his body out of the ruddy darkness of her pinched lids. The buttons of his shirt felt huge. The closure on his pants was prickly and rough to her grazing fingers. It took them what felt like hours to undress each other until they were sleekly, hotly naked together. Her breath pushed in and out of her quickly. She could feel his heart racing against her cheek. Hot and cool, curly and sleek, firm and silky, wiry, metallic. His body was a city, vast, filling her head.

His hand came between her legs, touching her there where he had the week before when they were in the warm shallow water of the bay, dangerously swimming in defiance of sharks, finny and human, who hunted for flesh. They were defiantly swimming without protective grease, naked to the poisonous sun and the poisonous air. Then she had kicked him in surprise. Now she burned and her flesh roared around him like a fire gone wild in the wind. She pressed against his hand. He unclenched her fingers from his penis and began sliding it against her. At first he could not get in. She was frightened but she could not break the game, she did not ask what he was doing or protest. She never broke the game. It was a charm. This was where they had been leading, they both knew it.

He groaned. It was hurting both of them. They ground their bodies together in grim concentration, trying. At length he managed to push most of the way in, but then she cried out in pain and he went limp inside her. He slid out. They both laughed, holding each other.

"It's not as easy as it feels in the stimmies."

She snorted. "How would you know? Your parents have yours coded, same as Malkah does."

"I reprogrammed it. I can have any cast that comes through."

"Do I feel as good as those actresses?"

He laughed. "Only you know how you feel. I didn't mean to hurt you."

"It's not serious pain. Do you want to try again?"

He had pushed about halfway in and they were kissing passionately when a loud noise broke them apart, startled. "What is it?" she asked softly.

"Shh! Someone in the hall?" He leapt up and began dressing. After listening sharply—no one seemed to be up here, that wasn't what had scared them—she jumped out of bed and reached for her things.

Then they heard it again, someone screaming below. A great crash followed and then, unmistakably, the sound of an illegal laser weapon. Gadi flung open the door and ran for the stairway, never minding concealment now. She stopped only to get her shoes on, then chased after him still buttoning her shirt, closing the fly on her pants.

No one was in the hall when Gadi opened the door from the attic. As he rushed toward the lab, she took the time to close it. She did not want Avram guessing how often Gadi and she used the top floor. Should she follow him or just slip out? Then she heard Gadi shout from down the hall and began to run to him. She remembered the sound of the weapon.

She called out his name and ran faster. It had been relatively peaceful lately. She could remember learning in school about the last nasty little local war, in which almost a quarter of the town had been killed before Cybernaut imposed peace on the warring free towns, several of which supplied it with fish, seaweed, programs, chimeras, medicines from the sea. The multis insisted on peace.

Gadi was not in the outer room, but had passed inside. Avram was working on a project for a multi, Olivacon. Unlike Malkah, who dealt with misinformation, pseudoprograms, falsified data, the creation of the structures that protected Bases by misdirection and were called as a class chimera (a term Malkah herself had invented thirty years before), Avram worked with artificial intelligence. He built defense systems to defeat penetration into a multi or town base; corporations were always raiding each other, and information pirates stole and sold data and systems. The easiest way to assassinate anyone was to catch them plugged in and burn them brain dead. However, what she saw when she ran toward Gadi's voice through the next two rooms, to a part of the lab she had never entered, was Avram bending over his assistant, David, who was crumpled against the far wall. Another body lay on the floor, someone she had never seen before. David seemed to be unconscious, although his lids were fluttering. Gadi leaned uncertainly over his father, who was holding David, speaking to him. A bench and a rack of tools had been overturned and scattered amid madly blinking and buzzing instruments.

She stopped over the body. He was dead, obviously. No. She stared. Part of his head had been shot open, but she saw no blood, no brains. It was a machine. It had been shot twice, once through the body, in the area of the human chest, and once through the head. A milky fluid leaked from it instead of blood. It seemed to be part machine and part created biological construct.

David groaned and opened his eyes. Avram noticed Gadi and Shira for the first time. "What are you kids doing here?"

"We heard screaming. And laser noise," Gadi said. "Who is this guy?"

"It's a robot," Shira said. She was shocked, because robots were always obviously mechanical, in the form of the machines they were replacing. Artificial intelligence was the province of bodiless computers, not of the robots that labored everywhere. Computer intelligences were vast, but robots had only enough intelligence to be programmed for simple functions: cleaning, repairing, mining, manufacturing.

Avram let David droop against the wall and jumped to his feet, grabbing her arm. He was hurting her, but she was too frightened to complain. Avram had a shock of hair kept blazingly white. His fierce pale blue eyes glittered like chips of broken glass. "You didn't see it."

"What's going on?" Gadi said, stepping close to his father. "Shira didn't do anything wrong. We heard the weapon. Where did you get it?"

"That isn't either of your business. None of this is. It's simply an unsuccessful experiment. We'll all forget about it."

"What's wrong?" Shira frowned, trying to free her arm surreptitiously. Robots cleaned streets and the houses of those who could afford them, fixed everything from pipes to vehicles, did the general dirty work. Middle-class kids grew up with at least one toy robot, and rich kids had fancy ones to ride on or play with, but this was a strange humanoid robot.

"Nothing," Avram said. "This one cannot be fixed."

"Why did you destroy it?" Gadi asked. "Where did you get a weapon?"

Only corporate security and the eco-police had legal weapons. Anybody else had to get arms on the extensive black market or seize them in raids.

"David fell and hurt himself. It's more important to get a medical team here than to stand around gossiping." But what Avram did was to motion to Gadi and Shira to help him lift the robot onto the table, where he began rapidly dismantling it. It was much heavier than a person would have been. She had never seen a robot shaped like a person. It was illegal to make one that way, just as it was illegal to create robots with human-level intelligence. The top of the face has been crushed, but it had a human chin. Its surface felt like skin but drier. It was dead. No, a machine couldn't die. Machines simply broke.

Avram snapped off the left arm at the elbow and then at the shoulder, did the same to the right arm. "I'm sorry I sounded cross with you, Shira, but this is very important to me."

"I won't tell anybody." She was always trying to make Avram like her. Sometimes she thought he did, and sometimes he seemed to look right through her. Sometimes her very presence struck him into irritated anger.

"Gadi, go for help now. Tell them David fell off a ladder and hit his head. Shira, you should leave. Malkah will be coming home. I want you to promise me you won't tell any of this to Malkah." His light eyes stared into hers.

"I promise! I won't say a word."

He swung back to fix her with a glare. "Good. Because if I hear that you've told this to Malkah or anyone else, you're in trouble with me. I'll make sure you and Gadi have nothing to do with each other, and I mean *nothing*. I'll send him away to school." Avram ushered them to the stairs down.

Avram was always threatening to send Gadi to a strict school that was supposed to teach him discipline. Shira nodded her head fervently to signal agreement. When Avram went on glaring, she said, "I won't say a word to anyone, I promise. I don't understand anyhow."

"Of course you don't. . . . Sara! What are you doing out of bed?"

She was standing at the foot of the stairs, thin, girlish in her blue robe with her long brown hair loose. "I heard . . . screaming. Laser fire. I was afraid for you." She stumbled, and Avram flung himself down the steps to take her in his arms and guide her into their apartment.

"It was nothing, nothing," he said. "Don't be disturbed." He shut the door behind them.

Outside in the street, she said to Gadi, "Avram could have summoned a medic on the com-con. Sending us is a waste of time."

"He's going to hide that thing away. What kind of a robot could injure a person? They're all programmed to self-destruct before they hurt anyone." Gadi shook his head. "Something really strange is going on."

"How could it hurt David? Maybe your father and David had a fight."

"With a laser rifle?" Gadi rolled his eyes up.

"It makes no sense."

"It has to," Gadi said. "Father always makes sense, even if he's wrong. He doesn't get into random fights. Don't you tell Malkah." Gadi stopped just before the street that led to the clinic and seized her by the shoulders. "He will send me away, Shira, he will."

"I won't tell her anything. I told the house I was going to be with Zee. Malkah hates when I lie—I mean, when she catches me."

She left him at the corner and went on to her house, at the end of the row and just across an old lane. She hoped Malkah would not be home yet, before she had had time to brood about what had just happened. Then she remembered that she was no longer a virgin, and that made her smile for a moment, uncertainly, as she lingered before identifying herself. It was not a big thing, but it was something, like her bat mitzvah, both rites of becoming a woman. She had not bled, but she was sore. She put her hand to the plate, and the door swung open as the house greeted her: "Come in, Shira. Malkah is not home yet. She wants you to go and pick up supper at the Commons. Then make a salad from the garden."

She shut the door without answering, but instead of going to the kitchen, she went slowly to her room to look in her mirror. "I love Gadi," she told her mirror, as she had hundreds of times before.

The house, listening as usual, responded to her. "Love is important, Shira, in its place in a balanced life, but at your age, the love of your family is most important. You don't want to annoy Malkah by failing to pick up supper and make that salad."

Now a computer was giving her advice on love: a bodiless computer, or rather one whose body she inhabited, whose body was the house itself. "Now more than ever we belong to each other," she said to the mirror but silently, so the house would not ask her to explain what she meant by "belonging" to another person. Instead she asked out loud, "Why is it a worldwide covenant that robots not resemble people? I've heard that since I started school. Why do robots have to be simpleminded machines?"

"When robots were created with sufficient artificial intelligence to carry out complex tasks, a movement started in opposition, Shira, circa 2040. Malkah has instructed me that people found the first humanoid robots cute, fascinating and then quickly disturbing. Riots and Luddite outbreaks of machine bashing occurred. People were afraid that machines would replace them, not in dangerous jobs but in well-paid and comfortable jobs. Robots were sabotaged, and destructive riots broke out even in the corporate enclaves—"

"I understand. But I think it's silly." She smiled into the mirror.

"People sometimes fear intelligent machines, Shira, particularly people who have not grown up with a sophisticated computer. Or they don't mind a stationary computer but are afraid of one that has a body and can move around. I consider such laws important to make people feel secure."

"But, house, what happens to someone who breaks that law?"

"It's not exactly law, Shira, but a corporate covenant with more than the force of law. Artificial intelligence of a high order is confined to the Net and Bases, to stationary computers such as myself. Mobile robots are to be obviously identifiable as machines and supplied only with sufficient intelligence for their rote tasks. The penalty is immediate blacklisting and death."

"Death?" Shira swung around, thinking of Avram's rifle. "Are you sure?" That was a silly thing to ask a computer. "I mean, death, I can hardly believe that. Who would kill you if you built an illegal robot that was very smart and shaped like a person? The eco-police?"

"That isn't under their jurisdiction. Professional assassins work in the security corps of multis, Shira. There also exist highly paid free-lancers, operating from the megalopolis or from offshore free towns. Does this information pertain to your schoolwork? Do you wish me to bring up on your terminal a chart of the location of the offshore free towns that are pirate or assassin enclaves? I am programmed with details of corporate covenants and of the history of the cyber-riot period in question, if you would like to study any aspect of those events." The computer sounded hopeful. "I also can offer instruction in elementary robotics."

"Don't bother. I was just curious," Shira said, wondering what it all meant. "It's one of those things people say all the time: Robots can't be shaped like humans—and then one day you wonder why."

"If I were mobile, I could cook and run errands for you, but now you understand why this is quite impossible. Isn't it time for you to go and pick up supper from the Commons?"

six

WE KNOW TOO MUCH AND TOO LITTLE

Two days before her seventeenth birthday, the house told Shira she had a barred message waiting—coded only for her. It was Regional Edcom, announcing the results of her auction. Students who passed the Grand Exam in the highest two percentiles were bid for by universities. Fourteen schools had offered for her. Right away she edited out all those she wouldn't attend no matter what they paid her. Then she printed out the list and leapt up to find Gadi. He must have been sent his results too. General acceptances went out at the same time as auction results. They had to coordinate their choices.

He had told her he had to help Avram. Since they had accidentally stumbled into the first cyborg experiment, Alef, who had proved violent, Avram trusted them to keep his secrets and called on them when he needed help. Bet had been the cyborg equivalent of autistic and had been dismantled. Gimel was functioning in the lab, but Avram found it short on intelligence.

Identifying herself to the newly enhanced lab door, which announced her to Avram and then, obviously at his command, admitted her, she saw Gimel sitting on a lab stool, stiffly upright. If it had been a real person, she would have said it had a broom up its ass, like her Portuguese teacher. Gimel had the same bland amiable features that Bet and Alef had shared. So far Avram had not had to destroy Gimel. It appeared docile, the cyborg equivalent of slow. "I have finished the connections in the right knee joint," it said in a deep male voice with less affect than her own house voice. "So connect the left joint," Avram snapped. She waited for Avram to look up from the shell of an arm, in which he was building a network of sensors. She knew better than to interrupt him. She wished for a moment he would ask her to work on the knee with Gimel or on the arm with him. She liked the work of the lab. In school this year she had built a robot diver. Gadi hated to work closely with Avram, but she actually enjoyed it when Avram commandeered their assistance.

Finally Avram turned to her. His eyes fixed on the tunic she had worn to school. "Little Shira," he said, smiling. "If you're looking for Gadi, he's upstairs. Why do you put up with my demanding son?"

"Gadi's . . . wonderful, sir. He's bright and—"

"If he's bright, why doesn't he demonstrate it in school, where it counts? The results came out today, didn't they? How many colleges are bidding for you?"

She showed him the list. "Good girl. I wish you were my daughter, Shira. Malkah spits pride when she talks about you."

"She does?" She couldn't imagine Malkah making that kind of fuss.

Thanking him, she ran out, with Gimel following to secure the door behind her. Gadi must be studying upstairs. Avram had long ago figured out that Gadi and she used the old staff bedrooms, but Shira felt an unspoken agreement. Avram would pretend he did not know what they were doing, and they would never mention to anyone his illegal work with human-featured cyborgs. Avram was a man in a hurry always, a driven man, but she was aware that he had come to like her. Perhaps he considered her a steadying influence on Gadi. She wished she were.

As she climbed, she moved ever more slowly. She hoped, she prayed, as she crept up the steps that Gadi would have been bid on (or at least accepted) to at least one college she could consider. He had not prepared as she had. He was fighting with Avram. Since Sara's death, the house had disintegrated. Of course they took meals at the Commons, and a cleaning robot that looked like a cross between a dachshund and an old-fashioned vacuum cleaner kept the house usable, but their flat had the air of a maintained but impersonal public room, a hotel or rest quarters. Over Sara's dying body, father and son had assumed postures of mutual recrimination; now, a year later, they could not relinquish those poses of offense and defense just because the excuse had been buried. The house was strange, a sort of museum of antique toys that Avram had begun to collect recently. Machines ate obsolete coins, and you pushed a ball around a blinking maze; in hand-held games, tiny silver balls floated over holes on cartoon faces and scenes. Little pieces assembled to make paintings. It was as if Sara's death had freed Avram for a second sedate childhood of games.

Gadi was restless, irritable. Bored. He charmed their female teachers
and he got on with a couple of the younger men, but he was at war with
the older male faculty, in whom he saw Avram replicated. She knew him
as well as she knew her own body, her own room with the climbing rose
dividing around her window, but that did not mean she could help him.
She drifted along the hall in a haze of uncertainty, the printout of schools
clutched in her left hand. The silence of the hotel, their old habit of being
quiet and secretive up here, kept her from calling out his name.

Then she heard his voice from their blue room. Why was he talking
to himself? He must be studying: good. He had trouble with languages, for
he hated feeling like a child, unable to express himself. He might be
studying Chinese or Portuguese, for he needed a high pass in both of them.
More likely he was working at his computer. In design class he had been
creating dazzling airy bridges of thin metals, spiderwebs of light and space.
He stole time away from other studies to work on them. She could
scarcely blame him. They were beautiful. They stilled the mind to contem-
plation.

At the door she knocked softly, that brush against the door each of
them used with the other, and then she immediately opened it. "Gadi?"
She stopped two steps into the room, staring. For a moment she felt
nothing at all, because she simply did not believe what she saw. It was
impossible. It was not even the stuff of nightmare, because she had never
imagined this scene.

Gadi was naked on the cot where they had lain together hundreds of
times, but twined with him was another body instead of her own, which
she almost expected to see there, because with Gadi must be Shira. No,
the naked girl sprawled under him was Hannah, who gave a sharp outcry
like cloth tearing, and then began, as she always did, to giggle.

Gadi . . . Gadi glared at her. "Are you spying on me?"

She could not speak. Her throat closed. She could not cry out or
breathe. Instead she stumbled down the hall, rebounding off walls, down
the steps like a box falling, slipping and sliding, breaking into pieces. She
must have made so much noise that Avram heard her, for he stood in the
hall. "Quiet," he said, taking her arm hard. "Who is he up there with?"

"Hannah Leibling," she choked out and pulled free of him.

"I won't have anyone else up there," Avram said, shoving his hands
in the pockets of his smock. He seemed to be trying to comfort her. "I'll
get rid of her for you, little Shira." She began to cry then, the tears choking
her. "Then you go to a good university and forget my useless son. He's

not worth your care, Shira. The best universities are in Europa. Go and enjoy."

She was sobbing too hard to breathe. She could not stand for anyone to see her. She ran past him and down the steps to the street.

After her Avram called, his voice sharp with concern, "Shira, be calm! Be calm! It doesn't mean anything to him."

She ran on to the shed where they kept their old sec skins. Pulling hers on, she headed out into the raw. She did not go far. She climbed a dune and fell on the warm sand. On one side the vast shallow bay stretched, the ruins of the destroyed city poking from the eddies of the waves. Turning south, she could see over the robot desalinization plant to the sea beyond. The cooler in her sec skin hummed on. She could read the little red line in the corner of her face plate that gave her the temperature. It was twenty-eight degrees centigrade, a slow oven, a typical late May day in New England.

She thought perhaps she had died, for a great numbness overcame her. But it was only the trough of the wave of pain that slammed her a moment later. She did not know what to do with herself. She felt like a mangled thing, a rabbit that had run into a fan.

How could Gadi make love to that vulgar twit? They had always laughed at Hannah. Hannah had been making eyes at Gadi for years. Shira could hear her loud giggle, a glottal stop like water sucking down a drain. How could Gadi? She wanted to feel anger at him, but the pain drowned it utterly.

She would take off her sec suit and expose herself to the murderous sun, whose radiation would kill her. She would die, and Gadi would understand how much she had loved him and how his betrayal had wounded her. She saw herself lying peacefully on a board. She saw the simple cairn that would mark her grave. Gadi would come to mourn there.

That was a slow death, heat and dehydration. Radiation took months to kill. She would not remove her suit, no matter how much she felt like dying. Malkah had made her too pragmatic. Moreover, she could not stand the idea of Hannah telling the other girls, Oh, don't you know, I feel so terrible. Shira killed herself over Gadi and me. He just couldn't stay away from me, and the poor girl was consumed with jealousy. Shira rose to her knees, then to her feet. Jealousy was ugly, embarrassing, disgusting. She stumbled back. The wrap glittered like false hope floating over the town.

She went home without remembering as she spoke to the door how she got there. Hermes was lying in the courtyard, sunning himself—the sun that came through the wrap was filtered, safe, warm but not searing. He was in middle age now, twelve years old and as big as ever, not fat but hefty, more serious and more placid than he had been. She flung herself down on the warm tiles, pillowing her face in his hot brown flank, and freely wept.

"Are you in pain, Shira?" the house asked gently. "Should I call Malkah? Do you need assistance?"

"I want to be left alone!"

"Tell me. You know I keep your secrets. What's wrong?" The house knew how to coax. It had been her other mother. Did it really keep secrets from Malkah, who had programmed it?

"Just leave me alone!"

She did not hear Malkah come in, becoming aware of her only when Malkah said very softly, squatting on her heels, "I'm making schav, little one. Sometimes something so sour can help."

For a moment she was pierced by the suspicion that Malkah knew, everyone knew; then her pragmatism won, and she realized that her position gave away her state. "I'm not hungry."

"So eat to please me. A little soup, how hungry do you have to be?"

Sensing the indignity of her sprawl facedown on the tiles, Shira sat up. Malkah called her "little one" but was the same size, except a few pounds fleshier. They had the same dark hair, black in lamplight, red-tinted in the sun; the same large very dark eyes, big in their heart-shaped faces; but Malkah of course was an old woman, sixty-one years old. She wore her dark hair braided around her head and fixed on top with a silver ornament in the form of a dolphin. A salvage diver had given it to her. Only recently had Shira realized he had probably been Malkah's lover. Shira had been too young to understand then, nine, then ten; and Malkah had been discreet. No man had ever lived in this house. Malkah had never married. If you married and a man hurt you, Shira realized, you had no place to run home to, no place to hide and nurse your pain.

Malkah handed her a big handkerchief. "I have to go see to my soup. Did you feed your friend there?"

"Not yet." She had forgotten, and Hermes had not reminded her. Now he rose, stretched, stretched again and started for the kitchen, looking back for her expectantly.

She daubed at her face. How could she live with so much pain? She could not imagine how she would continue.

She did eat the soup. Malkah was right: it was soothing in a minor way. She was glad Malkah had decided to cook tonight. Most evenings one of them picked up supper at the Commons; sometimes they ate there with half the town. Other nights Malkah cooked, and once in a while she would have the house ask Shira to cook that night. Malkah sometimes did that when she knew Gadi was coming to supper. Another part of Shira's life laid waste, as spoiled as the vast tracts of dead trees that had been maples on the mountains before acid rain, before the climate got too warm for them. Would Hannah take him home to supper now? How could he choose Hannah?

"Didn't your auction results come today?"

"Oh." Shira blinked hard. "What did I do with them? I had them with me when I . . . I'll get them. I dropped them in the courtyard." She rose from the table and ran to look for the printout.

Malkah took it from her, scanned it. "Obviously this is not what upset you."

Shira looked into her empty soup bowl. "I'm fine now."

"Your young man, then."

"He isn't mine! Not anymore."

"Shira, you're too young to be plastered together for life. You've never listened to me about Gadi, and you're not about to start now, I'm sure. I couldn't stop you. No one can stop children in love unless by exile. But you'll never grow up if you don't let go of each other."

"I don't want to talk about it." Shira rose. "I'll clear now if you're finished eating."

"Still, we must talk at some point." Malkah fixed her with her dark gaze, like a beam of energy and will. "We must also decide about this auction."

"What do I care about that anymore?"

"Gadi was never going to get into the same universities you're sought by, Shira. You'll be paid to go. Avram will have to pay for him."

"He's bright! He's as smart as I am."

"But lazier. And scattered."

"But he's more talented than any of us. . . . No, I don't want to defend him anymore, I don't want to explain him. I hate him!" Shira began clearing.

"You love too hard. It occupies the center and squeezes out your strength. If you work in the center and love to the side, you will love better in the long run, Shira. You will give more gracefully, without counting, and what you get, you will enjoy."

Malkah did not know what love was. Shira refused to argue.

After supper the two of them sat in silence in the late ivory twilight of the court. Malkah was accessing the Net, plugged in in full projection. Everyone in Tikva was equipped with interface. They did not have the lavish stimmie spectacles other towns went in for, they did not have fast foils or wind cars, but every child born to the town was equipped to access the Net directly, heir to all the knowledge of the ages.

The Net was a public utility to which communities, multis, towns, even individuals subscribed. It contained the mutual information of the world, living languages and many dead ones. It indexed available libraries and offered either the complete text or précis of books and articles. It was the standard way people communicated, accepting visuals, code or voice. It was also a playing field, a maze of games and nodes of special interest, a great clubhouse with thousands of rooms, a place where people met without ever seeing one another unless they chose to present a visible image—which might or might not be how they actually looked.

Shira had her eyes closed too. Hermes lay in her lap awkwardly, for he more than overlapped, while she pretended to be studying. Instead she was tuned in to a program in the Net of lights and shapes that formed on her closed eyes, vaguely watery, shimmering grays, greens, bronzes. She was not fully projected but detached, watching from without, letting her pain fill her lightly now as flowing water.

Suddenly, at half past twenty, the house announced Gadi. Shira jerked to her feet, displacing the cat. The jack wrenched from the socket in her temple, leaving her nauseated at the sudden disconnection. The house had been programmed for years to recognize and admit Gadi, so it had simply opened to him and spoken to them. Stupid house!

Shira resolved to stand there in a dignified silence and wait him out. But the moment he came ambling with his loose long gait into the courtyard, she burst out, "What are you doing here? Why aren't you with her?"

Malkah was present but not conscious, blind and deaf, fully projected into the Net. Gadi glanced at her, recognized her state, and they both proceeded as if she were a piece of furniture.

"Come on, that didn't mean anything," Gadi began in a voice that suggested he was cosseting a child in a tantrum. "Here I am, with you as usual. If you hadn't come barging in today, you wouldn't be upset at all."

"Oh, you can do anything, and it's my fault if I find out!"

"Are we married? That's how you act. We've been married since we were seven, and it's a damned prison."

"If you think I'm keeping you in prison, escape! The door's open. Use it."

"I intend to. I have a right to live, to know other people, to find out who I am and who they are."

"Oh, was it a transcendent experience, finding out about Hannah's twat?"

"Shira, we're seventeen years old. Ask Malkah if we shouldn't be open to knowing other people."

They both glanced at Malkah, oblivious, eyes shut. She might be researching something, she might be involved in a seminar with twenty other projected minds, she might be carrying on a flirtation or a debate.

Shira vibrated with outrage. "Now all of a sudden common sense rules, adults are right, let's forget we love each other and play at being cartoon teenagers."

"Why did you come charging over there anyhow? Because you got your auction results. Right?"

"I wanted to talk about what we were going to do about college."

"We? Show me your auction results. Come on, show it to me."

"I don't want to show you anything."

"They're fighting over you, aren't they? They think they can make money off you. Just keep bashing away for four more years, and they'll get a good price when multis bid on you. Who wants an artist? Old Avram's going to have to pay to get me into college, tough on him. You see, we don't have the same options, do we?" He stepped close, his face twisted with anger.

"Not if your option is to fuck Hannah in the same bed we shared."

"It's my house and my room."

"You wanted me to walk in. You knew the same as I did the results were coming this afternoon. You're punishing me because you didn't do as well. But that doesn't matter, Gadi, it doesn't! I believe in you."

He walked away from her to stand in the center of the courtyard, looking around warily as if the house might attack him. He was as uneasy as if he were hitting her. The house of course would attack with sonics if he were doing physical damage. "I've got to get out, Shira. We're dying, the two of us. We're dying together. Don't you feel it?"

She stared at him as he stood braced, seeming taller than he ever had, or perhaps her knees were buckling. He was lost to her. She wanted to die. There was no more Shira, only bleeding meat, a roaring vacuum. Couldn't he see he was killing both of them? They were a double organism, one being. "All I feel now is pain." She would put an ocean between them. She would punish Malkah for insulting her love and Gadi for betraying it; she would go far, far from both of them, to Europa. She would take Avram's advice and remove herself to Paris, to Prague, to Edinburgh. Anywhere far away from here.

seven

UNDER NO MOON

The Maharal is speared through by what he has conceived, a task he can neither persuade himself to proceed with nor allow himself to abandon. Is this unbridled ambition? He quizzes himself incessantly. Making a golem stands as the masterwork of a true practitioner of kabbalah. Does he fear that he might fail? Is he afraid to risk himself in that ultimate attempt to harness the power of the Word in creation? Is he afraid to fail, or is he afraid to succeed? He has been a man of peace, a rabbi, a teacher, a sage whose influence is exerted through the power of the law, the force of intellect, the charisma of a strong character. This contemplated manu-facture of a weapon would be a commitment to taking action in the world. He is halfway to making a force capable of violence. Is that not a negation of the values by which he has lived—study and prayer and good works?

He tries to think to whom he can turn. His wife? The rebitzin, Perl, is four years older than her husband and wise in entirely other ways: she has learned through the years how to run a household on hope, how to cook feasts out of not much, how to hide money from a man who would give the last cent away, how to intercede between Judah and his children, who were expected to be far holier than they desired. Judah and Perl had been engaged for ten years before the rabbi had enough money to marry her. Her own father had lost all his money (which had never amounted to much except in his reminiscences) when his business failed. She had waited all that time, running a bakery and saving for the day when they would finally be together as husband and wife.

When she was thirty and he was twenty-six, they finally married. Perl gave birth to six daughters and to one son, of all those children who lived beyond infancy. She started late and she continued late. She bore her last daughter when she was fifty-two and her oldest daughter was also pregnant.

To say that Perl adores Judah would be true; to say she worships him would not. She is perhaps the only person who knows Judah well but does not fear his temper, for she has one of her own. She is used to giving orders, to managing a bakery, to keeping track of details and pennies. She is a big woman with a still handsome ruddy face. She had been zoftik in her middle years, but age has whittled at her so that her bones are more obvious now than her flesh. She has strong hands, big enough to engulf the slender shapely hands of Judah. Her pelt of white hair is kept clipped to ringlets that look like lamb fleece under the henna-red wig she wears as a respectable wife whose hair might tempt the angels.

All the daughters married, two of them to the same Itzak Cohen, for after his young bride Leah died of pneumonia from a cold that should have passed off easily, he married the next sister, Vogele. Three of her own children Perl has outlived, two daughters and her only son; she does not want to survive the others. Let them bury me and not otherwise, she prays to the Eternal. She prays in Yiddish, for like most women, she never learned Hebrew.

Judah knows what she would advise him. Forget this nonsense. Pay attention to your grandchildren, who are growing up too fast, pay attention to your congregation, for there are two adulterous couples I know about already. No, Perl would rail against such a dangerous experiment.

Chava would understand, but it does not seem appropriate to consult with his own granddaughter. The year before, Itzak's daughter Chava had come back to live with them. Chava had married young and been widowed young. She is content to be the Widow Bachrach.

Chava is attractive and learned and always has suitors. Perl is in no hurry to see Chava married again, because Chava is a great help to her. Perl is slowing down with arthritis. She does not want to be left at home alone with the Maharal, who knows himself to be poor company to a woman. Chava works as a midwife in the ghetto, and she has taken over her father Itzak's duties as the Maharal's secretary.

The Maharal, too, feels in no hurry to find her a second husband, although he would have leaned hard on any of his flock who behaved as he is behaving. He has often remarked and still believes it: Chava is his smartest child. She has the drive that his own son lacked. How he tried to push Bezalel, to train his son's intellect to surpass his own. He pushed too hard. He pushed his son away. Now Bezalel is dead, and there are no second chances.

He himself taught Chava Hebrew and even Aramaic, like a son. She helps him in his researches, she fair-copies his sermons and his writings for him in her beautiful Hebrew script and she sees his books through the Gersonides press, the Hebrew printing press of Prague. No, he does not want to lose her to some dolt of a husband who will wear her out with childbearing. Of course she must bear more children beside the son her in-laws kept; she must be fruitful and multiply with the right husband, but Perl did not marry till she was thirty and did not bear her first child till she was thirty-one, and she was healthy and strong to this day, bar a little arthritis of late. Plenty of time.

Chava for her part shows little interest in young men, even the pious ones the Maharal briefly considers for her. She likes working as a midwife, earning her living. Judah has heard her say to Perl, I deal with babies all day and all night. All the babies born here are mine. I have a huge family already.

Why does he suspect that Chava will see the creation of the golem, supposing he really were to risk it, as usurping not only the power of the Eternal but the power of women, to give birth, to give life. No, to discuss something this holy with a woman, he cannot do it.

The Maharal and his family live on the second floor, the third daughter, Yentel, and her husband and children upstairs, and downstairs, Samuel, a tailor who also deals in secondhand clothing. The three-story house was built with a doorway leading through to the courtyard and another house, the way things are slammed together in the ghetto, in any slot that stands empty, narrow houses craning toward the sky like saplings growing up starved from insufficient light. In the courtyard lives the astronomer and historian David Gans, in his brother's narrow house. From the window of the Maharal's parlor, Perl can speak across the few feet between the buildings. "Come and share our little supper tonight, Duvey." She addresses him as a son although he is in his fifties; he seems younger than he is because he is spry and curious.

David is bright but pragmatic and dislikes conflict. He has modern ideas about astronomy. He is welcome in the observatory Tycho Brahe built under Rudolf's patronage, the finest and most accurate observatory in all Europe. His work popularizing new discoveries in geography includes the best maps anybody has put together of the New World. But

David Gans is no kabbalist. About matters of the spirit he is timid. He loves to discuss ideas, but those concerning what he considers the real world, that of matter.

Shall Judah consult his ex-secretary and son-in-law, Itzak Cohen? Itzak is a good man, a bright man, but he follows the Maharal's lead. What he would strive to understand if the proposition were set to him is what Judah wants him to say. He is doubly precious to Judah because he married first Leah, then, after her death, Vogele, and because he fathered Chava, dearest of all to Judah, but to consult Itzak's opinions is to look into a watery mirror.

Itzak Cohen is in his early fifties, with his beard bushy and white. Out in the world, he is a famous scholar, a man other people consult, considered both wise and also able in his business matters, a rare combination. As soon as he is with the Maharal, however, his awe for his teacher takes over. His voice rises slightly. He seems smaller. He is a boy again.

Perhaps he might fill the role of surrogate son had his own father been less in evidence. With his real father, Itzak is firm, generous, forgiving: he fathers his own hapless sire, whom he has taken into his house to support. The elder Cohen is a born mark, fleeced by one confidence man after another.

How about Judah's brightest disciple, Yakov Sassoon ha-Levi? Yakov is twenty years younger than Itzak; he has come to brighten the rabbi's old age with his first-rate mind. He is undisciplined; in him the Maharal recognizes his own love of verbal combat. Judah seeks to temper that fire with wisdom and judgment. No, Yakov would immediately want to create a golem simply because it's dangerous and on the verge of blasphemy. He has still a great need to prove himself, does Yakov Sassoon.

Yakov Sassoon is a lean leathery tall man, recently widowed. He has been left with three children, all sons, and he is looking for a wife. He has already indicated his interest in Chava, who declined politely but fervently. Yakov is stubborn, sure he can persuade her. He wants to marry into the Maharal's family more than he wants to marry Chava, but she is attractive and bright. Yakov walks with a slight limp from a street brawl with a Christian gang in his adolescence. He has a fine strong deep voice, and he often sings for company, not only religious songs but Yiddish songs about wonder-working rabbis and lovesick adolescents and marriages and deaths. Music transports him till his eyes shine in his long thin face. Judah is fond of him, would not mind too much if Chava chose him, but his judgment needs tempering with experience and more wisdom.

Yakov lives nearby, in a house owned by Chaim the Silversmith, who has been doing very well and who is making for the Altneushul a beautiful silver crown for the Torah scroll, to be ready by Rosh Hashanah. It is his own gift. The various synagogues already have lavers and candelabra Chaim made, but they have been paid for by rich patrons like Mordecai Maisl. This is the first time Chaim has felt he could make such a contribution himself, out of his own workshops and his own pockets. The Maharal has spent several nights with Chaim working on the design of the crown, which is to apply to silver a method often used in calligraphic drawings, of using many small Hebrew letters to make up objects such as flowers and leaves.

Events decide for Judah. What makes up his mind is the arrest of Chaim the Silversmith, accused of consorting with the Turks and passing military secrets but in trouble for having quietly begun making fine candelabra and ceremonial objects of an original and striking design, competing with the Christian silversmiths. He is being tortured in the prison, and no amount of bribery on the part of his wife or his family seems able to get him free short of death. The Maharal goes on foot to the town hall, to the emperor's representative. He goes to see Father Jiri, with whom he is guardedly friendly. All the intercessions run into a wall of iron.

That the silversmith had been seized on such a trumped-up charge is a clear warning to the Maharal that he is reading the weather signs accurately and a blood storm is gathering. On the day bailiffs come into the ghetto with pikemen to seize the assets of the silversmith and turn his family out into the street, the Maharal tells Itzak and Yakov to come to him quietly, secretly and without speaking to anyone. "Begin a fast. Go the baths tonight and purify yourselves. Then come at midnight to the Altneushul. I will be there." It is Rosh Hodesh, the new moon.

He has decided to take only Itzak and Yakov with him. He thought of taking David also, then speedily discarded him. David would be wanting to ask questions constantly and take notes. Further, the Maharal suspects that it would be hard for David not to view the evening's planned activities as a physics experiment and impossible to keep him from writing up that experiment in copious notes with proffered explanations. No, only Itzak and Yakov may accompany him.

At midnight he stands in the doorway to the Altneushul, where I myself have stood, although never at midnight. It is a small but powerful Gothic building, with the front wall shaped like a jagged menorah. The oldest synagogue in Europe, it is at the farthest end of ostentation from a cathedral, being small, narrow and yet of a penetrating simple grandeur. You step down into it, and then your eyes rise to the narrow windows slitting the tall white walls. From the Altneushul the Maharal removes a Torah, wrapping it carefully in a cloak and then in another, larger cloak over that one, against the damp wind of March that slithers between buildings, down the twisted filthy streets, and then unfurls in the cemetery beyond the synagogue. The Maharal leads his helpers into the cemetery, seeing the glances of apprehension they exchange. What is he doing in the cemetery in the middle of the night? Has a dybbuk seized one of their own, or does a ghost rise because of some impropriety in the burial?

"Take each a shovel." He opens the caretaker's little shed.

Every night in Prague, the gates of the ghetto are locked, the Jews penned up inside for the night, the Christians supposedly fenced out: just as we are hidden behind our electronic walls, our surveillance devices, our amateur guards, seeking to survive. But a wall can be climbed over or tunneled under, or a few strategic stones can be quietly loosened. The Maharal knows the ghetto's every brick. It's tight living, everyone smelling everybody else's supper and hearing everybody's quarrels. Privacy, are you joking? In Prague in the Jewish cemetery, even the dead are crowded, buried on top of each other, the stones rammed crazily together like crooked teeth. The dead cannot be moved, it would be lacking in respect, but Jews are not allowed to bury their dead outside the ghetto. Therefore a fresh layer of soil is shoveled over the graves periodically, the tombstones are moved up to the new surface, a new grave dug in and one more tombstone added to the crowd, like rush hour on the tubes leaving a corporate enclave.

The Maharal walks in the lead with the Torah and a dark lantern swinging. Behind, Itzak trots, short and heavyset, with his white beard shining against the darkness of his cloak, and on his left side Yakov, tall as the Maharal, skinny, taking one slightly lopsided stride to every two of Itzak's, both of them with shovels over their shoulders like pikemen going into battle and Yakov carrying also a large but light wooden frame, which the Maharal gave him.

They are frightened, but they trust him and they obey him. At the end of the street of the willows, where no trees at all grow but tradition says there once flowed a stream that still wanders through cellars, Judah knows of a weak spot in the ghetto wall. The same stream that creeps like a ghost through the earth of the ghetto flows out to the Vltava. Here one can crawl out of the ghetto under the cover of darkness. They flit through the forbidden Christian streets, keeping silent, and into open country.

In the woods on the banks of the river, it is a cold clammy night with no light but that of the dark lantern, its feeble rays glimmering, and the river beyond like black shot silk mumbling over its stones. The leaves have not even begun to split their buds. The bare branches of winter rub together in the brisk wind. Somewhere an owl is calling as it hunts.

They set to work digging clay from the bank while the Maharal chants in a low singsong, praying all the while he, an old, old man, is working furiously, taking the shovel from first Itzak and then Yakov, digging faster than they can. They stare at him in great fear, fear he will suddenly die, because how can an eighty-one-year-old man stoop and lift, stoop and lift and haul like an eighteen-year-old? Fear because what are they doing, what vast grave are they excavating?

At last the Maharal is satisfied they have dug enough clay, and he lays down the wooden form. They see it is shaped like a man. They begin to pack the clay over the shape, to mold it into a body. Again, over the head of the muttering rabbi, Itzak and Yakov exchange glances of wonder and fear. Has the Maharal gone crazy? Is he suddenly senile? The death of his only son cast him into a deep depression, but this is madness. What are they doing, illegally out of the ghetto, prancing around the riverbank at the new moon, making a huge mud pie in the shape of a man?

The form the Maharal has laid down on the soil is larger than a normal man, as tall and broad as the strongest soldier. The Maharal stoops and works on the features of the clay doll. He molds the hair, the face, the organs. The huge clay doll lies there naked and ominous. Then the Maharal begins to pray, with his arms raised over his head. The wind has slithered away, and mist is rising from the silvered blackness of the river. His arms outspread, he begins to pray louder, rocking, davening, chanting. The hair rises on the nape of Itzak, and he turns to Yakov for comfort, but Yakov's mouth has fallen open and he, too, is praying strange words that seem to coalesce in the air between the men like a cloud of oily smoke.

The face of the Maharal is pale with ecstasy. He feels the power coming through him. It is the power of creation. It is always dangerous, it is lightning striking the tower and the world set on end. It is always the entrance of the Word into Matter and everything is born again. He feels the energy of something strange and new and terrible and focused to a spear piercing through him and into the clay before him. He sees his own hands shining with a blue-white radiance. His hands are crackling. His hair stands up with electricity.

All the combinations of letters and vowels he chants, and the hidden names of G-d he speaks, and the sacred numbers that built the atoms of the universe. He has become transparent with power that is pouring through him. His flesh is blackened like glass that has stood in a fire. His eyes are silver as the moon, without pupils or iris. He knows in that moment more than he has ever known in his life and more than he will know in five minutes.

Blue fire crackles over the clay doll as if rivulets of mercury ran over the surface and then sank inside. The clay begins to smoke and to heat dull red and then brighter and brighter. It is red as a heart ripped open when arterial blood spurts out; now it is orange and now burning yellow and now a white they cannot stare at. Itzak and Yakov shrink back. They are blinded. When their eyes stop tearing and they rub at their lids and then hope they can see again, the doll is cooling from orange to red and then dulling to almost the color of their skin. It is no longer clay but flesh at which they stare.

Now from the raised arms of the Maharal rises a fresh cold wind bearing rain. Right on their heads a small storm descends, the wind whipping at their garments and their hair and beards, rattling then breaking off the bare branches of the trees. For a moment the rain is everything, a solid wall of water, a drenching in which they almost cannot breathe. Then the rain subsides, the wind falls and the doll lies there, a man of flesh who now sprouts hair of a dull reddish color and reddish pubic hair about the flaccid organ that lolls against a massive thigh, who has new nails and eyelashes and ruddy lips, who is, although huge, as perfectly formed as any of them.

Itzak looks at Yakov, and Yakov looks back at him. Itzak mouths, "A golem?" and Yakov nods, his mouth still open. They are soaked to the skin and shivering with fear. They clutch hands, and each knows the other, too, would like to bolt.

Now the Maharal turns to Yakov and whispers in his ear what he is to chant and sends him marching seven times left to right around the body. He whispers to Itzak and compels him also, chanting and circling, a solemn dance round and round. Then he begins chanting, his beard and head hairs all bristling and bright, his eyes silvery, round and round, chanting in a voice as sonorous and uncanny as the howling of a wolf. As the Maharal circles, the chest of the Golem begins to heave slowly. His lips part. A breath that is a deep long groan issues from him and then another, and the man of clay begins to stir. The eyes flick open, but they are glazed, unseeing. The Maharal seizes the Torah scroll he has brought, and seven times he circles, dancing as if it were Simchat Torah. Breath shudders faster through the frame of the Golem. He moans loudly. He blinks his gray eyes and now he sees, he looks and sees them. He stares all around, lifting his head and looking from side to side like a big snapping turtle putting its head out of the river. He is alive, he is a living man, and yet there is something massive, inert, prehistoric in him. He is a lizard-man, Itzak thinks, he is a man of shale.

Itzak and Yakov instinctively draw back from him, frightened. The Maharal flinches back also, but then he gathers himself and comes forward to stand over the man who had been clay, the man he has made.

I lie in my high antique bed hearing the unfamiliar sounds of Shira in her room, finally, finally back with me. It is a precious ingathering. She suffers the loss of her son and perhaps even the loss of her useless husband, but she is returned to me. She used to object at this point in the story: how could a man of clay come alive? She has always been on the literal side in her thinking. Like you, in fact, my dear Yod. You should communicate well on that level. She will learn quickly to reach you, wait and see.

I remember that I spoke to her about the power of naming. What we cannot name, I said, we cannot talk about. When we give a name to something in our lives, we may empower that something, as when we call an itch love, or when we call our envy righteousness; or we may empower ourselves because now we can think about and talk about what is hurting us, we may come together with others who have felt this same pain, and thus we can begin to try to do something about it.

But I was talking in that partial way one does to children. That stage of life is full of little truths that do not quite fit together. I know what the Maharal felt, for in all creation, in science and in art, and in the fields like mine where science and art meet and blend, in the creating of chimeras of pseudodata, interior worlds of fantasy and disinformation, there is a real making new. We partake in creation with ha-Shem, the Name, the Word that speaks us, the breath that sings life through us. We are tool and vessel and will. We connect with powers beyond our own fractional consciousness to the rest of the living being we all make up together. The power flows through us just as it does through the tiger and through the oak and through the river breaking over its rocks, and we know in our core the fire that fuels the sun.

I understand what Avram, my old lover, felt when he created a person in his laboratory as truly as when he put his prick into Sara and they made Gadi together. As truly as when I gave birth to Riva and she lay beside me real and red and screaming. Every life is new. Every word is constantly speaking itself for the first time: birth, love, pain, want, loss. Every mother shapes clay into Caesar or Madame Curie or Jack the Ripper, unknowing, in blind hope. But every artist creates with open eyes what she sees in her dream.

Malkah

I have stood on Rosh Hodesh in the darkness of the wood by the whispering river, and I have called powers through me to blast into life what has never before been. That is what I should honestly have told Gadi and Shira when they sat at my feet in the courtyard by the blooming peach with its pink blossoms and I told them this story. I should have said I am the Maharal and I make the Golem with my whole life's best and most potent moments, and so does Avram, and so, perhaps, my darlings, may you. Creation is always perilous, for it gives true life to what has been inchoate and voice to what has been dumb. It makes known what has been unknown, that perhaps we were more comfortable not knowing. The new is necessarily dangerous. You, too, must come to accept that of your nature, Yod, for you are truly new under the sun.

eight

HOW SHALL I ADDRESS YOU?

As Shira was admitted to Avram's old laboratory on the second floor of the former hotel, she wanted to know: Is Gadi still around? She wished she could just walk in and ask Avram outright, for she would concentrate ever so much more freely with that taken care of. The building disquieted her. Her stomach clenched on itself as her hands balled into damp fists at her sides. She felt as if she were seventeen again, ignorant, fearful, a creature all gusty emotions and pain.

A standard service robot, walking upright but with a face plate and four metallic hands, let her in. "I am Gimel. Follow, please." The voice was affectless as an elevator or a food dispenser. Gimel was the dim-witted robot Avram had built her last year home. His face and hands were no longer covered in artificial skin. Perhaps Avram had given up building illegal cyborgs that resembled people. She was kept waiting in the outer lab while Gimel communicated with the locked inner lab.

Gimel led her through a set of security latches. When the door finally opened, a dark-haired man was standing on the other side, of medium height, with a solid compact build—obviously a security guard, as he was crouching just inside the door in a defensive stance, with his hands held to strike. She had been around enough wired-to-the-max, edgy security apes to come to a full stop, holding her breath involuntarily, keeping her hands completely still and visible. The last time she had faced an ape was when she had gone to complain about Ari's being moved to Pacifica Platform. Dr. Yatsuko, the portly head of the Artificial Intelligence section, had seen her himself, for the first time since she arrived to work there. It was almost shocking to be brought before him, but she had been too crazed with grief to care. Two apes had flanked him during their four-minute exchange, as if her outraged mother love might cause her to attack him with her teeth and nails.

"Yod! There is no need to defend me." Avram came toward her, rubbing his hands briskly together. His hair was entirely white and his eyes glittered as hard and bright as she remembered them. "Welcome, Shira."

The guard backed up rapidly, moving to the wall. His eyes stayed on the door until it shut and the locks automatically reconnected. She sidled past him, still nervous. She hoped that Avram planned to dismiss the guard so that they could talk without his twitchy presence. Never had there been professional apes in Tikva when she was growing up. Most of the town stood guard duty, and the head of security was chosen at town meeting. She was disappointed that professional security had appeared here.

Avram took her elbow and steered her toward his desk. "Yakamura-Stichen's loss is my gain. I do need your expertise, Shira. I'll match what you were making there—I told you that."

"But what can I do for you . . . Dr. Stein?" She thought of him as Avram, but if she was working for him, she could not call him that.

"I read your papers on the field density shock syndrome in projection and on the erosion of time sense in fused users. As for what you can do here, you've already met my project. Yod: come forward!"

The guard was staring at her openly. His curiosity was so obvious in his face that she wondered if he was a bit simple. His stare was open, intense, wondering. The irises of his eyes were dark brown, green flecked, set against unusually porcelain-appearing whites. His hair was almost as dark as her own; his complexion, olive. He was in no way unusual among the many physical types who lived in the little town. He looked vaguely Mediterranean in background.

Avram stood between them and off to the side. "Shira, this is Yod."

"Yod? That's an odd name—" she began, and then stopped because she understood. Yod was the tenth letter of the Hebrew alphabet. Alef, Bet, Gimel . . . Yod. "A cyborg?"

"*The* cyborg," Avram corrected in a pleased tone. He gave Yod a slap on the back. "This is what I've been working toward. Finally. And just in time, as you'll learn. Our situation here is deproving radically. Our Base is under attack from information pirates."

She moved forward, leaning close to touch its cheek. The artificial skin felt warm, its surface very like human skin although drier. She could feel the cyborg tense under her fingers, which surprised her. It made her feel as if she were being rude, but that was absurd. You did not ask permission of a computer to log on; computers did not flinch when you touched them. "Are you going to sell it to Olivacon?"

Yod responded to this by turning to stare at Avram, looking shocked. Avram had done an excellent job building the equivalent of minute musculature into its face area, in order to deliver a simulacrum of human reactions. She was curious about the programming that enabled the cyborg to choose what reaction to produce in at least a semiappropriate manner. Malkah had been working with Avram; had this been the project? Obviously Avram had applied the elaborate technology of human implants and replacement organs and limbs to the creation of the cyborg, but he had gone beyond anything she was aware of. Of course with corporate secrecy, scientists could never know what was really going on in their field hidden away in another multi. Industrial espionage was an exceedingly lucrative career.

Avram took her arm firmly. "Yod is a secret project of my own. What does Olivacon need with him? They have their security, trigger-happy apes raised on steroids and adrenophine. Yod will be our security, our protector. If we can't have weapons, now we have a one-man army."

"But robots are programmed to self-destruct before they injure anyone. How can a robot fight?"

"Yod's a cyborg, not a robot—a mix of biological and machine components. He's programmed to protect us—our town, its inhabitants, our Base. That's his primary duty. But to perform it he cannot be as naive and awkward as he now is. That's where you come in."

"Avram, all my work has been with corporate and public megabrains. I don't really have any expertise to offer with less than human—"

"My storage capacity is in the range of the artificial brains you've worked with, and I interface with such computers far better than a human ever could," Yod said, crossing its arms. "I, too, have read your papers available in the Net." It had a pleasant moderately deep voice she doubted she could tell from a human voice. "Should I demonstrate my ability to interface now?"

"Later. Yod has extensive cybernetic, mathematical and systems analysis programming, probability theory, up-to-date scientific knowledge of an encyclopedic width. He's also programmed with general history, forty languages, Torah, Talmud, halakic law—we can't have security that offends people, after all. But you'll no doubt make your way through his programming in the next weeks."

Shira was astonished but skeptical. Yod was an enormous breakthrough, but Avram was claiming for his cyborg far more than she considered credible. "You call the cyborg 'he,' I notice. Isn't that anthropomorphizing? I would like us to agree to proceed objectively, not in terms of wish fulfillment."

Yod spoke again. "How shall I address you?"

"I told you, her name is Shira," Avram said. "It isn't possible for you to forget."

"I've noticed variant forms of address. She called you first Dr. Stein and then Avram. That leaves the question of how she wishes me to address her. I believe we should explain to her that referring to me as 'him' is correct. I am not a robot, as Gimel now is. I'm a fusion of machine and lab-created biological components—much as humans frequently are fusions of flesh and machine. One of us should also explain that I am anatomically male, as you created me." The cyborg almost seemed to be addressing Avram in pique. It had turned away from her. She was going to have as much difficulty as Avram obviously did in remembering that human form did not make a human creature.

"Really? Why did you do that?" she asked Avram. In fact what did it mean to speak of a machine as having a sex at all? Surely it did not urinate through its penis, and what would it want to have sex with, presuming a machine could want, which she was not about to assume. Machines behaved with varying overrides and prerogatives. They had major and minor goals and would attempt to carry them out. But "want" was a word based in biology, in the need for food, water, sleep, the reproductive drive, the desire for sexual pleasure.

Avram looked slightly embarrassed. He did not look at Yod or at her but at the ceiling, his hands joining behind his back. "I felt the more closely he resembled a human being, the less likely he would be detected. It will be necessary for him to pass time with humans, and he must seem as much like them as possible. I frequently had to sacrifice efficiency to a convincing facade and behavior. I could see no reason to create him . . . mutilated."

"You didn't answer my question," Yod said. Its voice sounded offended.

"If we're going to work together, you might as well call me Shira. That's what my house calls me."

"Shira. That means Song."

"You have a knowledge of Hebrew?"

"Of course." It said that exactly as Avram would have. His inflection.

"It is that very point," Avram said, stepping between them, "that I need your help with. He needs to be educated in how to speak to humans, how to behave socially, how to handle his functions. He must be able to pass, do you understand? I'm already desperately behind on my contract work for Cybernaut. I can work with him at most two or three hours a day. He doesn't sleep, and he must be put to work all the time, learning. When Gadi was here, I couldn't bring him downstairs at all—"

"He's left, then." Shira felt the room grow suddenly more spacious. Perhaps the work might have some interest, at least to occupy her while she began negotiating, probably first with Olivacon and Cybernaut. She would give herself a month to relax, and then she would start job hunting.

"Two days ago." Avram could not suppress a smile of relief. "I should be able to catch up on my contract work and still have a little time to spend working with Yod."

"Gadi doesn't know about the cyborg, then?"

"Of course not. Why should he need to know?"

"Who does know, then?"

"Malkah. I needed her help with the programming. She has a rare capacity for discretion, you know," he said, as if letting Shira in on a great secret about her grandmother. "Malkah talks too much, but she doesn't talk about what she doesn't want you to know. That's unusual in a woman."

"I should think it's unusual in a man. But what happened to David? Your assistant. He knows."

"David had an accident. He's no longer with us."

While they talked, Yod looked from one to the other, its head rotating as though watching a tennis match. It had been provided with an expression at rest of nervous, high-strung curiosity. Yod's features had been well and finely modeled. It did not resemble what she remembered of Gimel, when it had had a face, so she assumed Avram must have created a new mold at some point. It was dressed in loose hideous clothing of the sort worn by unathletic men when they decided to appear sporty or indicate they were on vacation, luridly colored in orange and chartreuse and dully shining. Whenever Yod moved, his pants made little rustling sounds, like a nest of mice. Perhaps the first thing she would do was pick out new clothes for it and teach it how to dress. She had had to do that for Josh. A cyborg could not have less clothes sense than her ex-husband. She wished she could have reprogrammed Josh.

"What happened to the models in between Gimel and this one?" She was assuming he had begun with Alef and worked his way through the Hebrew alphabet. Yod started at a sound from outside, leapt over the desk to the wall, pressed against it listening. Came slowly back, still listening. Yod's jumpiness was going to be hard to take. She wondered if Avram couldn't shut it off and turn down its energy source. A hyperactive cyborg. It reminded her of a young guard dog, an immature Doberman, except that it moved with surprising grace. It did not move like the other robot, Gimel, slowly and obviously following an algorithmic program for operating each finger. It moved like a huge cat, faster than human reaction but smoothly. That speed and grace was alarming in something mechanical, whatever components it was built from.

"They all malfunctioned," Avram said. "Several were uncontrollably violent. That's why I finally called in Malkah on the software. It was an expensive folly until I created Yod. So far he's working out."

Yod said, more softly than it had spoken before, "I am the first who can carry out the tasks of my father."

"Your father?"

Avram shrugged, looking embarrassed. "Since Yod began to study human social organization, he sometimes refers to me in that way. I did make him, after all, and I did a better job with him than with Gadi, I have to say. Too bad Gadi doesn't have one quarter Yod's ability to concentrate and learn."

"Well, I am not your mother," Shira said bluntly. "I have a son."

"Avram does also," Yod said. "Besides me. But I am not allowed to meet Gadi. Will I meet your son?" It was constantly surveying the room, acting as if it expected a chair to spring at them and attack.

"I wish it could be so," she said. "He's been taken from me."

"Malkah told me about that," Avram said. "It's disgraceful. But it brought you here, didn't it?"

"It brought me here." In a moment of intense despair, she turned away from both of them. When she was growing up, Avram had never felt to her like a real parent, like the fathers of her friends, but rather he was brilliant, strange, armored. She had never had a father. She had been determined that her child should have both parents, in the old-fashioned way. So much for that fantasy. Now the two of them were regarding her with identical bright curiosity, cold, intense but remote: the gaze of a hunting hawk. Still, if Yod was one tenth as intelligent as Avram rashly claimed, her work might prove interesting for a while. It would pass the time; it would occupy her. When she was dug in a bit, she could start looking for real work, with a new multi. She had two years to endure; two years in which to reposition herself to fight for Ari when he came back to earth again.

nine

REVISING THE FAMILY ALBUM

Shira was pleasantly surprised that Malkah welcomed her with a minimum of reproach. She had forgotten how many friends Malkah had, other women coming by with little presents, with stories, with problems, with gossip. She had thought of her grandmother as living alone, but Malkah was seldom alone unless she wished to be—and she did value her privacy. Malkah also engaged in elaborate group correspondences and played games inside the Net. Shira would see Malkah sitting in the filtered sun of the courtyard or under the peach tree in her favorite chair, eyes closed or half closed, and she would think the old woman was dozing until she realized Malkah was accessing the Net, was plugged in and roaming; or working in the Base, constructing the elaborate chimeras that were one of the export products of Tikva, sold to multi and town Bases for protection.

"I have all these flirtations going," Malkah said. "No one can see me unless I want them to."

"So you don't tell them your age?"

"Some I tell one thing, some another. Most don't ask. It's the congress of minds, not bodies."

"So you have mental boyfriends."

"Girlfriends too. Have you never changed your sex, not even for an evening, Shira? I have a woman friend I court in Foxdale, who thinks I am a man of forty-two. She would kill me if she met me, enemy to enemy, but in the interstices of the Net, we play together."

"With Ari, I played constantly. I was a child again." Shira held herself across her breasts. "A mother without her child is a cart trying to run on three wheels," she said to Malkah, who was sitting in her favorite deep chair, staring at Shira with a satisfied expression.

"So a three-wheeled cart is a wheelbarrow, and it works perfectly well. You'll get your son back. We will beat them in the end. In the meantime, you have the precious family fertility. Have another."

"I don't want another." She had tried again last night to reach him through the Net, but once again the call had been refused. "I want Ari."

"Did you ever consider having a child with your dybbuk?"

Shira knew at once that Malkah meant Gadi. "Oh, is Gadi dead that his spirit should possess me?"

"He's dead the same way you are, my Shira. He can't commit to any woman, and you can't really love any other man."

Shira winced. Harsh words of denial filled her mouth, and then she swallowed them. "Maybe the worst fate for a woman is getting the man she wants too early. We couldn't stay together—we were children. But I can't belong to anybody else, not the way I was with him."

"I never wanted to belong to anybody. I only wanted to borrow them for a while, for the fun of it, the tenderness, some laughs."

"How many lovers have you had?"

Malkah's eyes skimmed over. She was silent for a moment. "I don't know. I haven't counted them in years. I remember when I was much younger, I would go to sleep on nights when I had insomnia by counting them. And I would never finish because I would be trying to figure if that one I could barely remember was really my lover or not. I insisted I do it chronologically, so when I realized I had left someone out, I had to go back to the beginning. It always worked to put me to sleep."

She stared at her grandmother, trying to read in the squat woman with the braids wound round her head, a few hairs escaping at the nape and over the ears, a femme fatale who could not count her lovers. "Malkah, I've only had five. Altogether."

Malkah laughed and then covered her mouth, looking embarrassed. "I have to say, I had five before I was twenty. I always was curious about the taste of a new man, how he would be. I wanted to bite into him."

She was startled and a little shocked that her grandmother was speaking to her so frankly. Perhaps now that she had been married and had a baby, Malkah viewed her more as an equal. "So how many were there?" she pressed. "Twenty? Thirty? Two hundred?"

"Around fifty, I would guess. I'd have to add them up. I still have insomnia, but now I tell myself stories instead of counting men."

"But so many . . . Did you chase them? Did you go up and proposition them?"

Malkah laughed. "I was never a beauty. You're far prettier than I ever was. But I had a good body and a roving eye. They always came after me when I wanted them to. . . . Avram was quite a layabout before he fell in love with Sara, you know. Before he went off with her to California."

"Avram? I don't believe it." No, she couldn't. Cold, driven.

"He was simply gorgeous as a young man. I have to say when I look at Gadi, I see Avram the way he was."

"You never had anything to do with Avram, tell me you didn't."

"I can tell you I didn't. But I did. For all of one summer we used to meet in the vineyard and spread a blanket hidden between the vines. After he met Sara, he fell violently in love with her. I don't think he ever looked at another woman."

He has looked at me, Shira thought with some distaste. He is always looking at my body.

"When things withered between them because of her illness, I think sex died within him. Some people go on wanting it as long as they live, but other people, they let it go as if it were a garment that had worn out. I think they're fools." Malkah nodded vigorously for emphasis. "I'm full of joy that you're home with me, Shira. It's making me babble nonsense."

"It's going to be different between us now, isn't it?"

"Why should everything remain the same?" Malkah dragged her chair closer and leaned toward Shira, her brows raised. "So what did you think of Yod?"

"Avram is making outlandish claims for its intelligence and capacities."

"Yod is surprising. But naive. Oy, really naive. Your job is to teach him how to function with people. With his strength and intellect, he could do a great deal of damage without meaning to if he's not properly educated. I'm responsible for his interpersonal programming, but he's had no opportunity to try out those capacities."

"Educating a machine is not a concept that makes a great deal of sense to me. His— Now you've got me doing it. Call it 'he.' "

"He is a person, Shira. Not a human person, but a person."

"After a lifetime of working with artificial intelligence, how can you anthropomorphize a cyborg? You might as well believe the house is really a woman, the way little kids do. Or name your cleaning robot and talk to it. It's appropriate for a little boy like Ari to think his koala robot is a live pet and form an emotional attachment to it, but we're supposed to be adults."

"The great whales—we had just about killed off the last of them before we began to translate their epic and lyric poetry. Were they people? Were the apes who learned to communicate in sign language intelligent beings? Was Hermes a real presence?"

"He had a personality, certainly. A strong one. I felt so bad when you wrote me about him dying."

"He was an old cat, Shira. He lived to be twenty. In the end he had a brain tumor and he was too weak to operate on again."

"Malkah, you've worked with computers all your life. A good heuristical program can enable an artificial intelligence to make valid plans and plot strategy and tactics, but to modify goals or behavior, you must change the programming."

"With the Net and Base AIs, the type of programming and the extent of independence permitted are strictly limited. Avram has gone beyond that, and so, my dear one, have I. I consider Yod a person. I enjoy his company." Malkah gave her such a wicked grin that Shira was sure that her grandmother was putting her on. "Now that I am no longer a responsible adult raising a child, I can be reckless and wanton. There are some wild cards in his programming. Some even Avram has no idea are there."

"Malkah, you're trying to trick me into doing this job. Why? Why don't you socialize it yourself?" Shira's forehead crinkled with suspicion.

"I've given Yod what I have to give him. Moreover, I've given you everything I had to give, Shira." Malkah sighed, resting her hands on her knees. She looked almost grim. "Now that you are grown and have suffered a few blows, it may be your mother has something to give you."

"My mother? Riva?" Shira was startled and a little resentful. "I haven't seen her since I went to college. We don't even talk on the Net."

"She may be coming here. Unclear as yet but possible."

"Isn't she with Alharadek? Why would they send her here?"

"She's not with them." Malkah spoke with an irritating air of evasion.

"Is she coming because she expects to get Ari? Or to blame me for him?"

"No, no! I suspect you might find her an interesting woman, Shira. But let's see what happens. Don't talk about it to anyone."

"Why not? What's the mystery? Afraid another multi will kidnap her?"

"Oh, she's wanted all right. But not for hiring."

"You sound as if there's a price on her head."

Malkah nodded. "Riva is an information pirate, Shira. She finds hidden knowledge and liberates it."

"Riva?" Shira's memories of her mother were few. When she was little, her mother had come often. Then when she was bought by Alhadarek, she was transferred to Cape Town and they saw her only once a year, on Shira's or on Malkah's birthday. Her mother had sent regrets to her wedding. Shira had not seen Riva in ten years. Riva was a few inches taller than they were, but basically Shira remembered her as a fussy, rather fuzzy woman who always came with many presents, never wrapped, secreted in her luggage. That such a woman could be an information pirate was not credible. A certain amount of industrial espionage was part of the system, multi vs. multi, but the pirates were total outsiders, renegades, the standard villains in stimmies. First the cyborg was a person, and now this! Malkah was either teasing her or growing senile and no longer able to distinguish fantasy from reality.

Malkah grinned. "I'm not crazy, Shira. Look, I'll show you."

Shira followed her grandmother to the main terminal. Everyone in town took turns at guard duty, and in time of trouble, everyone bore, illegally, what few arms they had. Security information was open to all. Anyone could access that Net file, and Malkah did. While Shira was still brooding over Malkah's mental condition, a brief synopsis of the crimes of Riva Shipman appeared on the screen along with a warning about the dangers she posed to the established corporate order. She had infiltrated and pillaged the Bases of half the great multis. She was held responsible for the failure of the allevium market: allevium had proved effective against the newest form of the kisrami plague—the disease that had killed Malkah's own mother. Riva apparently had stolen the drug formula and inserted it in the Net for anyone to use. Every little region had begun manufacturing its own remedy.

"How long have you known about my mother?"

"I've known her since she was born, you know," Malkah said with the same wicked teasing grin. "I've been aware of what she was doing for years."

"Why didn't you ever tell me?"

"How would it have helped you to know?"

"How did it help me not to know?"

"It made you feel safer. It gave you leave to choose your own way."

"Now I'll always wonder if one of the reasons Y-S devalued me was because Riva is considered a dangerous criminal."

"Not unlikely. Although we never have open contact between us. I suspect we might not even recognize her when she comes—if she comes."

"Why do you think she might come now? Did she mean to come because she wanted Ari?"

"No, love, she was never going to take Ari. Her life is too dangerous for any child to run with her. When you were a child, I made up that little myth about our family to explain to you why you were being raised by me instead of your mother. So you wouldn't ask questions. Your mother is a political fugitive, and she lives by her wits and her connections."

Shira found herself staring with slack jaw. "Are you telling me you weren't raised by your grandmother, back to the tenth generation?"

"It was a good story, wasn't it?" Malkah said proudly. "I thought you enjoyed it."

But Shira felt as if all the rooms of her childhood had suddenly changed place. She was annoyed, even angry with Malkah for having lied to her, for making her feel foolish. In storybooks, bubehs made cookies and knitted; her grandmother danced like a prima ballerina through the webs of artificial intelligence and counted herself to sleep with worry beads of old lovers.

Shira lay in bed that night with fragments of the day swirling in her head. Now she understood her anomalous position with Y-S. At least it had not been based on her ability, her work record. She felt justified, redeemed by the information, but at the same time, it set her entire notion of her stranger mother on its head. If Riva was really about to appear, it might well mean Shira would never recover Ari. Indeed how could she really hope to extract him from Y-S? He was already testing brilliant. While he was still on Pacifica Platform, Y-S would begin training him, educating him, shaping him. On Pacifica Platform, it would be much harder for Josh to maintain his marrano identity. He would lose hold of Ari. Y-S would gobble Ari and turn him into one of their bland clones.

Why could she not have loved Josh? It was her old restlessness. It was the worm in her heart that ate every apple rotten. What Malkah rightfully called her dybbuk. She would live to be an old, old woman always dreaming of the life she had known at thirteen and always yearning back to a paradise she had grown out of as if it were a pretty childish patent-leather shoe half the size of her adult foot.

Malkah obviously wanted her here and was trying to tempt her by pretending to believe Avram's outlandish claims about his machine. Perhaps Malkah was lonelier than she seemed. Shira had noticed that Malkah had trouble seeing. The old woman tried to cover up her poor vision, but she moved far more quickly in good light and far more slowly in dim light. She did not always see objects that Shira had moved from their accustomed place. It was a matter to bring up soon, but tactfully. Avram and Malkah both kept alluding to danger, but Tikva did not seem a town under siege. She suspected them of being overly dramatic in order to engage her interest. Needless fuss; she had at the moment no place else to go.

ten

WAS THIS A GOOD THING TO DO?

When Riva was still quite small, she had already a formidable will. Even as a baby she would swell with anger, she would scream herself sick or hold her breath till I was frantic with fear. At two, she would say *No* at top volume. I can see her yet standing in the middle of the courtyard saying that one word until the walls rang and then going stone mute and refusing to speak at all. How did we come to be locked so early in a contest of wills?

She was like a cat in that she hated closed doors. A locked drawer, a sealed box, a protected program, a book hidden away turned her insatiable the way other children longed for candy or French fries. The hint that something was beyond her understanding would make her study any tome. She liked to creep up quietly when I was gossiping, just to overhear stories that could have meant nothing to her about people she scarcely knew. She was burrowing around in the Base by the time she was twelve, in and out of everybody's files, my little star-nosed mole. I would shriek at her, "Privacy is sacred! You can't just rummage through people's lives and secrets."

"It's what we don't know that makes us stupid," she would say in hunched defiance. She refused to be ashamed. We should all know everything.

When I think of myself in my twenties, I see a fervent scattered creature snatching at sensations, grabbing for ideas, impatient as my own baby for answers and gratification. I was always trying to argue her into doing things my way, trying to talk her into obedience. My words washed over her, trying to erode her granite cliffs. I talked and talked; she stood mute, glaring.

You, too, were reluctant to speak at first. Do you remember, Yod? Some say that Judah's Golem—which means "matter, lump"—could not speak, but this is an error based on other golems of legend. He does not chatter but is taciturn, as befits a man of clay. But as he opens his gray eyes on this night of Rosh Hodesh of the month of Adar he asks the Maharal, "Father, was this a good thing to do?"

"It was a necessary thing. And you should not call me Father." The Maharal had endured a stormy enough relationship with his only son, Bezalel. Bezalel's death still feels to the Maharal both bitter and unnatural. Therefore the Golem calling him Father is particularly galling. A son should bury his father, not the other way round. Bezalel died of a petty disease, a cold that moved into his lungs, just as Leah had. It was an absurd death, which still grieved the Maharal. Judah had attempted to get his son designated as his successor as High Rabbi of Prague, but he had been refused, and Bezalel had left in anger. This being he has summoned is not his son. "You should call me Rabbi. Your name will be Joseph."

The Maharal hands the Golem the cloak in which he wrapped the Torah, to cover his nakedness, for the three of them had formed him as a man. They had done so without thinking about it or discussing it. The Maharal would probably have said that he did not think he could improve on the design. They simply made a man of clay.

"Joseph," the Golem repeats obediently. He lumbers to his feet, sways and seems about to fall, while from each side the Maharal motions Itzak and Yakov forward to support him. They are obviously reluctant to touch him. "Can you walk, Joseph? Look, one foot and then the other. Just so." The Maharal patiently demonstrates. "We must hurry back to the ghetto before dawn. Come, we must help him. I can smell dawn coming. We must hasten, or we'll be caught by the watch."

But no one moves forward to touch the Golem. The Maharal himself experiences a reluctance to put his hand on that strange flesh. Would he be as cold as clay? Would he feel as if he were dead? The Maharal must set an example, and he puts his arm around the huge being.

The Golem sways forward, his mouth slightly open, his face screwed into concentration with the effort. He bends like an oak in a strong wind, towering over the Maharal. He has short wild reddish hair and a muddy complexion. The Maharal had not made him with an eye to handsomeness, but neither is he deformed. He is thick-necked, broad-shouldered, built squarely and with massive, slightly flattened features, a hint of the Tartar.

Joseph first takes a step that throws him off balance, and once again he must be propped up. Now finally Itzak and Yakov assume positions on either side, letting him hold on to them. The weight almost knocks them off their feet. Then he takes a baby step. That works. He takes another baby step. At this rate it will take them all night to get out of the woods. There is no question of carrying him, for he is bigger than any of them and, from the weight of his hand on their shoulders, both the younger men can tell he is heavy indeed. "A little faster, friend," Itzak gasps out, Joseph's weight straining him.

Finally Joseph steps free of them and, in an awkward, jerky manner, walks at last. A step at a time, he proceeds. Then he trips over a log. He topples forward, striking his chin on the ground with a great thud. As they try to haul him up and he strives to rise, he crashes backward.

It takes all three of them to get him up again and moving. Itzak asks, "Rabbi, what will we tell people when they ask where this huge man came from?"

"Say, from Galicia. People will believe anything of Galitzianers. His mother sent him away to keep him out of the army. I found him, a feebleminded beggar in the street. He will be the shamash at the synagogue." Recently their shamash has found the job too difficult. He is an old man, he wants his rest. The Maharal turns to the Golem. He speaks more coldly to Joseph than to Itzak and Yakov. "You will cut wood, draw water, light the fires, take out the ashes, sweep the floors in the Altneushul, our beautiful synagogue. Do you understand?"

"I will do what you say. How can clay understand?"

The Maharal is not sure if the Golem is mocking him, but he chooses to ignore his doubt. He turns and heads for the city, followed hastily by Itzak and more slowly by Yakov, who strolls just a short distance ahead of the Golem, acting out his lack of fear. Yakov has recovered his dignity and is concerned not to lose it again. The Golem treads heavily in the rear, gaping at every tree, every bush. The flight of an owl through the darkness brings him to a standstill, mouth open. The Maharal feels his eighty-one years, his fatigue. This night has drained his last energies. His head whines with fever. It is hard to stride on as if possessed of inner strength when he wants to lie down on the earth. He cannot even imagine sleep, for he has been insomniac too long, fretting, fussing, picking at his sore conscience. All he can hope is to rest and be warm and dry again.

The Golem has mastered walking now. He moves well and powerfully. From time to time he stops to thrust out his arms or raise one above his head, to shake his head like a dog throwing off water, to nod or to blink, to move his jaw as if masticating something. The Maharal realizes that Joseph is trying out various physical functions, exercising his small and large muscles, experimenting. He wriggles his ears and his nose like a rabbit. The Maharal has an urge to rebuke Joseph for his grimaces as he would a boy in cheder, but he stops himself. The Golem is a mere baby in the world. He will learn discipline as soon as the Maharal can begin his instruction, but they must be quiet so near the city.

When they arrive at the place in the wall where the creek sidles through, they see two men of the watch with their pikes, waiting to capture them. They may be hung; they may be tortured and then hung. Whatever is in store, it looks like grisly death in some form, unless the men can be bribed. The Maharal has a few coppers in his pocket, a fine belt with a gold buckle, but that's it. He does not think that will buy them off. They get a cut of the possessions of men they arrest.

"Joseph," he says softly to the creature towering over him. "We're in danger. Those two watchmen will not let us back into the ghetto. We will die unless you can disable them. They haven't seen us, and they don't know you yet. See if you can slip up and knock them on the head so they won't see us pass through the wall to safety."

"I obey," the Golem answers. Silently and swiftly he glides through the darkness. The watchmen turn to see him just before he sets upon them. They only have time to cry out once as he seizes both, one in each hand, and smashes their heads together. He lets them drop.

The Maharal runs forward to bend over their bodies. The skulls are crushed. Blood seeps out. "Joseph, you've killed them!"

"They broke so easily." Joseph frowns in puzzlement. "Did I do something wrong? Are you angry at me, Father Teacher?"

"Killing is wrong," the Maharal begins, but then the Golem had been created to protect. "You should use no more force than is necessary at any given time."

"But I did protect you. Now they can't talk of who came out of the ghetto tonight."

"But their bodies outside the wall will call attention to the secret exit. Jews will be blamed for the murder. The idea, Joseph, is to save us from trouble, not to get us into trouble."

"Let him take them to the river and throw them in. There will be nothing to connect them to us," Yakov says. "I'll go with him, Rabbi. Wait inside."

Itzak and the Maharal hide in the bushes, waiting. Already the sky is streaked with the pale gray of predawn, not as if light came but as if the darkness were wearing through. The wind picks at them more bitterly, knifing through their clothes. The Maharal feels faint. He leans against Itzak. His long fasts have caught up with him.

Itzak takes advantage of the Maharal's weakness to say, "Teacher, perhaps this was a mistake. We could easily return him to clay right now, and no one would ever know. No one but us has seen him."

"Except for the watchmen," Judah says quietly. The murders have shaken him deeply. Of course he has seen people executed in the square or set upon by ruffians and murdered; these are violent times, and no one with eyes can avoid seeing fresh corpses. But he feels implicated in this crime, and that is new and disturbing.

"Maharal, we can send him back to clay. As if he had never been."

Judah musters enough strength to pull himself upright. In a few moments he will collapse in his own warm bed and Perl will minister to him. Perl will be waiting, he knows. She will scold him for wearing himself out, for staying out all night, for starving himself. She will feed him warm soup, she will bring a warm brick to his bed and wrap him in a goose-down comforter. He will be warm, and he will sleep. "What I have done is proper. I was given a vision and told what to do. He is our defender. He'll learn. And he's obedient. We must simply be careful what we tell him to do—be precise, be careful exactly what we say. Because what we order, he will carry out."

The Maharal is unsure if he is truly glad to see the Golem striding out of the thinning darkness or if he had secretly hoped that the Golem had vanished into the night and only Yakov would return.

"Joseph," the Maharal begins as soon as they are safely inside. "Killing is wrong. You were created to keep the peace for us."

"I protected you. The way I must." The Golem stands there flat-footed, patient. He looks as if he could stand all day just staring at the walls, at the stones of the narrow twisty street. The houses of the poor are built of whole logs; the fancier houses of dressed timber or stone. Everything fascinates him: a cat slithering over a wall to safety, a few blades of grass pushing out between paving stones. "Why are you angry at me?"

"You must be more careful, Joseph. Your strength is great, but your mind is weak."

"Maybe it can grow, Teacher. Maybe my mind can be strong too. But I must keep you safe."

Thus begins the service of the Golem to the Jews of Prague, while the Maharal is filled with bitter doubt. What has he summoned to life? What violence has he loosed on the world? He is a man of peace. He wants only to protect his flock. All the violence of his life has been verbal. The prayers he leads in the synagogue speak constantly of peace—Shalom, Shalom—although for the Jews peace seldom lasts. What peace they know is the peace of the few without power or weapons surrounded by the many with both. Thaddeus is preaching against them every week. The powerful crafts guilds have already claimed one victim, Chaim the Silversmith, whose mangled body, every nail torn off, eye dangling on his smashed cheek, toothless gums, battered feet, he can close his eyes and see, unwillingly. No one leaving the ghetto misses experiencing insult and sometimes random attacks in the streets of the city. Something is seething, something that lives like a tick on warm fresh blood.

Judah has fought his rabbinical rivals with words. With words he demolishes their arguments, with words he slashes at their work of words, their books, their circulated manuscripts, their sermons and lectures. With words he created this golem. But this monster does not fight by throwing words.

eleven

HE, SHE AND IT

Yod's eyes were strange, she thought, although the color was ordinary enough, a brown lighter than her eyes with flecks of green in the large iris. But the eyes fixed her with an unblinking and piercingly curious stare, beady, hard, like that of a hawk. If the cyborg had been a large cat or a very large bird, she would have imagined it wondering if this thing that was her would be good to eat. While it was awaiting input, did it have thoughts in any sense a human could understand? Did it not rather simply sit vacant as any other machine before the command to start up?

Yod had a presence, perhaps what Malkah had meant by calling it a person. Gimel simply was, with no more impact than a cleaning robot or a beverage cart. Yod, however, created a set of demands simply by fixing her with those hungry eyes and expecting . . . what? Knowledge, attention, information to devour: after all, that was what she was here to impart. But she would not think of it as a kind of overgrown child to whom she was acting as governess.

She started, however, as she would have with a child, with a battery of tests. For the rest of the day she administered the common sets. By noon she was tired, although of course Yod was not. It would have sat and happily taken tests for a year, she suspected. Answering questions and summoning information was one of its functions, and it could do it forever. How Gadi had hated exams. Avram had in a sense created the student he had wanted and not gotten in his son: a learning machine. In some aspects of intellectual development and ability, Yod scored vastly above the human range; in others, it was well within ordinary human parameters. It was like a bright child, perhaps the sort of child Josh had been, forward in its command of the sciences and of mathematics but quite retarded in its grasp of human relationships and the subtler values. Metaphorical thinking seemed to stymie it. It tended to interpret discourse literally.

On their second day together, she began where she had left off: with metaphorical thinking, the ability to create analogies. She administered a simple test designed for very young children. His score was zero.

She tried on Yod the Robert Burns lyric:

> O, my luve is like a red, red rose
> that's newly sprung in June.
> O, my luve is like the melodie
> That's sweetly play'd in tune.

It was a washout. "He was a botanist? A musician?"

"Yod, think of a rose."

"A rose is a flower closely related to a number of edible fruits. Sometimes its hips are eaten as soup or jelly, but usually they were harvested in the past by birds. Roses are a common gift to show affection. They possess color, fragrance, form—"

"Have you ever seen a rose?"

"In the dictionary program."

"I mean a real rose."

"No." Yod managed to imitate regret in its deep voice.

"There are roses growing along the south side of this building, old pillar roses, red and pink. Haven't you ever noticed them?"

"I've never seen the outside of this building."

"You've never been out of the lab?"

"I've been in Avram's flat, before Gadi came to visit. Almost every night I go down to the basement, where Avram has set up a gym. There I practice my martial arts with Gimel. He's sufficient to give me a challenge I couldn't get from a human partner."

"But you've never been outside?"

"Never. Avram always says I am not ready. Can you make me ready?"

"I don't think you'll ever get ready if we stay in the lab. I'm going to take you out right now, to my house." It occurred to her that Avram would be furious, but she had to proceed in her own way. "Now, on the street we have only two blocks to walk—you know what a block is?"

"The plan of the town is in my memory."

"While we're outside, you walk beside me and keep your mouth shut."
Yod shut its mouth tightly, as if keeping a large mouthful inside.

"I don't mean that literally. I mean you should not speak to anyone beyond saying hello if anyone speaks directly to you. If I have to introduce you, your name is . . . Yod Oblensky. You're a cousin of Avram's. I'll do all the rest of the talking. Do you understand?"

It grinned so widely its face seemed to split open. "Thank you, Shira. I've longed to go outside. I think about it every day. I even considered going quietly on my own, but Avram locks me in and I'm not willing to break the lock."

"Could you? That's a very high-security lock."

"I could break it."

She was startled by Yod's confessing that it had thought of disobeying Avram. She had always understood that a robot could not disobey. After all, it had not done so, but that it could even frame such a possibility astonished her. She had to find out quickly how real its apparent ability to master new situations was and how much it was capable of learning that went beyond the collection and regurgitation of facts. Taking Yod out was the first procedure in her exploration of its true capacity.

As she had expected, at this time of the morning few people were on the streets. It was a third of the way into the average workday, and even people who worked a split shift or who went to work early or late were all on the job. Children were in day care or in school. Only a street-cleaning robot came rattling along the street, stopping to pick up trash and sweep.

As it came up level to them, it darted forward to spear a piece of debris. Instantly Yod flung himself upon it, seized it, smashed it against the curb. The curb cracked with the impact. "Yod! That's a street cleaner. Come. Quickly. I don't want to have to explain this."

Yod bent over the mangled mechanism. "It could have been a bomb. I see now. A cleaning mechanism?"

"How do you feel when you see such a mechanism? Do you feel a sense of kinship?" She must be losing her mind, asking a machine how it felt.

Yod rose to rejoin her. When it was not in its security mode, it moved with surprising grace. "Do you feel a sense of kinship when you eat telapia?"

"Why should I?"

"You're as closely related biologically to that fish as I am as a mechanism to that cleaning robot. Perhaps you're closer."

She glanced sideways at Yod. "Put me in my place, didn't you?"

"Your place?" Gingerly it took her by the shoulders. "Your place is at the end of the street, correct?"

"I was speaking metaphorically. Do not actually put me anyplace. Just walk on, please."

The cyborg was craning around, swinging suddenly to survey the street behind them. Suddenly it sprang into attack posture.

"You're going to have to learn to use metaphor and simile, Yod, if you're ever to sound halfway human. By the way, that's a dog. It is not an attack dog. It's called a spaniel, and it's friendly."

"This incessant comparing of unlike things in ways that imply some point of similarity is important puzzles me." Yod reluctantly left the dog wagging its tail. "How can you tell whether such an animal is friendly?"

"In here." The door opened as she touched it. "Attack dogs attack. They may growl first or just attack. Most dogs wag their tails and wait to see your intentions. We communicate mammal to mammal, but I don't know how you smell to a dog, frankly."

"Welcome, Shira," the house said. "What is the mechanism with you?"

"It's a cyborg named Yod. You are to treat it as a person. Protect it."

The house did not answer immediately. This was one of those times when she felt as if the personality of the house, constant since Shira's earliest memories, were not artificial but real. She could not help feeling that the house was disapproving of her request. Finally the house said, "Request noted, Shira."

"Thank you," Yod said. "That was kind of you. I can talk now?"

"House, don't let anyone in except Malkah. Yes, you can talk."

"The sky isn't blue. I had expected it to be blue from information I was given in my dictionary—"

"You see color, then."

"I assumed you looked at Avram's design specs."

"Yod, there's the equivalent of an encyclopedia of material there. I hit a few highlights."

"I could read through it in a matter of hours. Yes, I see color as you do, although I can alter my vision to pick up infrared or ultraviolet if required—for instance, in a surveillance situation."

"The sky is not blue because of the greenhouse effect. We hope someday the sky will be blue again. . . . Were you disappointed?" she asked as an experiment. She wanted to see if the cyborg understood the concept.

"It wasn't as I expected it." Yod paused, frowning. It had been given complex programming to reproduce the equivalent of human facial expressions, and at times she found its artificial responsiveness disconcerting. "I suppose it's correct to say that I am disappointed, if disappointment implies that something did not meet my expectations."

She led him straight through to the courtyard. "Look. Now, that's a rose."

Yod strode toward it and reached out to examine a flower. Then with an exclamation it yanked its hand back. "It is armed." It seized the enormous old climbing rose and ripped it from the wall, trellis and staples and all, twisting it so that it uprooted.

"Yod! What have you done!" She struck the cyborg before she thought, in fury. Hitting him felt very like hitting a person except that he did not flinch. "That rosebush was sixty years old. I loved those roses!"

It stood looking at the enormous vine yanked from the courtyard wall. "I've angered you."

"Yod, I should not have hit you." It didn't know any better.

"I don't want to make you angry and unhappy. Shira, I never understood why humans apologize, but now I feel a need to do so. They're trying to get rid of this feeling of being in the wrong. They're expressing a wish to undo what they have done, but it is done, and regret is senseless. What can I do to fix this?" It began scraping at the dirt and replanted the roots ripped from the soil. "Please, Shira, tell me what to do, if there's a way to put back what I've spoiled?"

"I doubt if it will live, but we'll cut it back and try." She fetched a shovel from the garden closet. "Why did you attack it?"

"It attacked me first, Shira. . . . That was a thorn?"

"Do you experience pain? Is that possible?"

"I was built with pleasure and pain centers. I surmise that's how Avram planned to control me and how I am motivated, besides my primary programming for protection, survival and acquiring information."

"I brought you to experience the rose. What's left of it." She sighed and with the clippers with which she had cut back the ancient climber, detached from the pile of lopped-off branches a spray of yellow blossoms.

Yod extended a hand gingerly. It took hold of one rose and deftly plucked it, bringing it toward its face. "It has color, fragrance and form, just as my memory instructed me. But it also has a curiously pleasant tactile quality. I think you might describe it as . . . like velvet, perhaps? Am I using a simile correctly?"

"Excellent, Yod." She caught herself smiling at it. Smiling felt odd; how little she had had to smile at in her recent past.

"However, I have to comment that the velvet analogy is highly imperfect. I can distinguish the individual components of the nap of velvet—I experienced the material in the draperies in the living room of Avram's flat. In the case of the tactile experience of the rose, the smoothness is unbroken by nap and there is more dampness."

"Nevertheless, do you recall the Robert Burns poem?"

Yod recited it with a perfect imitation of her inflection.

"Now, what did he mean?"

"He meant that the woman was beautiful, like this flower, and that she smelled of perfume, perhaps."

"How do you know the rose is beautiful?"

"My base tells me it's so regarded by humans: that flowers are beautiful, although it seems, too, that humans often disagree about who or what is beautiful and that every era has different opinions. Beauty isn't a concept I find useful. I don't understand what it means, except as elegance in design."

"There's more implied in the poem. Do you know how long roses last?"

"No." Yod cocked its head and waited.

"Flowers are mostly creatures of a moment. That rose is already beginning to wilt. If you put its stem in water, it will last a couple of days."

"Therefore a flower comparison implies short duration."

"Correct."

It frowned. "Then it's a sad poem."

"Not exactly. But there's an undertone of mortality. With us there is often an undertone of mortality."

"I am mortal too, Shira. I can be turned off, decommissioned, destroyed."

"And you can feel pain, which surprises me. But how fragile are you?"

"I am not fragile at all. Humans are surprisingly fragile, if I understand your specs correctly."

"Now, the idea of design specifications for humans is metaphorical language, Yod, since we are not engineered or built but rather born."

"I am trying to understand the bonding created by the birthing process. It's quite strong?"

"There's no stronger bond."

"I can tell from your face that my reference to motherhood upset you."

"It's not a topic I can deal with at all objectively, not yet, perhaps never. I'm trying all the time not to think about my son."

"I want to express sympathy—is that the right phrase?—but I don't know how to do so without reminding you further of what you want to forget."

"I'm not about to forget, Yod, but thank you." Why was she telling a machine about her pain? It was like crying to the house when she was a very little girl and did not understand the house was not alive. "We should return to the lab."

"But the poem you taught me is ambiguous. How do you know he is speaking of the woman? 'My love is like a red, red rose' could mean his own feelings for her. They could be what he is praising as beautiful and announcing as transitory." He raised an eyebrow at her and waited, smiling slightly.

"I never thought of that." She stopped and stared at Yod. "Frankly, I'd like the poem less if I thought that was what Burns meant. That probably was true of that relationship, the way it is of most, but not a cause for celebration. You changed the subject. We should return."

"Must we? I'd like to see all of your house. The trees, too, interest me. I've seen them from Avram's windows, but I've never been close to them before." He behaved differently here with her than he had in the lab with Avram. He was a little less jumpy and far more expressive. He had become animated with her ever since they had arrived at the house. "The leaves are different on each of them. Is this . . . fruit?"

"Those are unripe peaches."

There was a pause while Yod accessed what a peach was. She was about to warn him as he examined the fruit not to detach it, but she observed then how very precisely and carefully he employed his hands. She was growing used to the slightly perplexed frown of concentration that came over him when he was retrieving some piece of unfamiliar information from his data bases. "Do you have a room here? Gadi has a room in Avram's flat. Avram has a room also that is only his. In addition, there are common rooms, such as a kitchen, where food is prepared—"

"That's standard. Yes, although I left home years ago, Malkah kept my room for me, just as I left it. Before the kisrami plague of '22, I'm told, several families lived in this house, but now there's just the two of us."

He turned back one last time to the climbing rose. "Creature of an hour. Yet my predecessors, too, were mostly creatures of an hour. Except for Gimel. He will likely outlast me. But he is not alive."

"Do you consider yourself alive?"

"I'm conscious of my existence. I think, I plan, I feel, I react. I consume nutrients and extract energy from them. I grow mentally, if not physically, but does the inability to become obese make me less alive? I feel the desire for companionship. If I can't reproduce, neither can many humans. Doesn't infertility afflict half your population?"

She decided not to proceed further down that road with him. Instead she led him into the kitchen. "What do you mean, your predecessors were creatures of an hour?"

"I'm not using the figurative language correctly?"

"I can't tell until you explain further."

"You know the fate of Alef. You were present, weren't you?"

"Avram told you about that?"

Yod stopped and faced her. His eyes stared into her. "Avram told me nothing. I accessed his notes. Except for Gimel, who could quite honestly be called retarded, Avram destroyed every one of my brothers."

"All the cyborgs who preceded you, you mean."

"They were all conscious, Shira, except for Gimel. Fully alive minds."

"That upsets you."

"If your mother had killed eight siblings of yours before your birth because they didn't measure up to her ideas of what she wanted, wouldn't you be alarmed?"

"You fear he'll destroy you also?"

"I'd be foolish if that fear didn't occur to me." He smiled then, with a melancholy air. "That's why I address him as *Father.*"

"Could we run through that one again?"

"It's a feeble attempt to establish a bond that may preserve me. How do I know he won't decide to scrap me? . . . Show me the house, then."

"Why are you interested?" she asked, nonetheless leading him into the central computer archive, Malkah's office at home and the brain of the house. She was aware he had tactfully changed the subject twice, and she further realized she was thinking the pronoun "he."

He sat down at the computer and rapidly interfaced. She nodded at him that he could use her plug. After all, Yod was not about to spread germs to her. She doubted if bacteria could thrive in him; he would not prove a fertile environment. "Even in her programs," he remarked a few minutes later, as he disengaged, "one receives a strong impression of Malkah's personality, have you noticed that?"

"I think that's always true of more creative systems."

He was waiting for her to lead the way, so she did, through the living room, then upstairs to the second ring of rooms. However, just as they reached the upper hall, which ran as a balcony around the second floor, the house announced Malkah. Yod leaned over the balcony and waved.

"Malkah! Look, I'm visiting. Shira brought me." At once he stepped over the balcony and dropped like a cat onto the tiles below. Shira leaned after him. "Yod! Are you all right?"

"Perfectly." He sounded puzzled. He was hurrying toward Malkah, who held out her arms to him so that they could embrace. Shira groaned, slowly descending the stairway. Malkah might be right to an extent that Yod had to be treated as some kind of entity, a machine with consciousness, but hugging him seemed beyond bizarre.

By the time she reached them, Malkah had sat down in her usual chair and Yod was kneeling before her, talking far more rapidly than she had ever heard him speak, words tumbling out. ". . . how much I have missed you. Communicating through the com link is not the same as seeing you, I understand that now."

"Avram decided I was a bad influence on Yod, so he shut me out."

"A bad influence?" Shira asked.

"I'm responsible for some of Yod's programming. Avram brought me in as a last desperate gamble to save the project."

"Malkah, I've done something bad here today. I destroyed your climbing rose." He explained rapidly.

"Yod, you can't help your violent urges, but I tried to introduce a counterweight. In time you may learn to use your strength more wisely."

"Malkah is my friend. The only one who treats me as a person and not as a tool." He beamed at both of them, a wide innocent smile of delight. "But you have made me more of a person today by taking me out into the world."

"But, Malkah, what made you come home so early?" Shira read the time from her inner clock. It was 14:35:11. Soon she should return Yod to the lab.

Malkah was leaning back in her chair, exhausted or depressed about something. "Yod informed me on the com link he was here."

"You're very fast," Shira said to him. She had been entirely unaware.

He nodded, still beaming. "The fastest."

"We had another casualty this morning," Malkah said, rubbing her eyes hard. "Aviva Emet." She sighed, her hands clenching the arms of her chair.

"What do you mean, another casualty?" Shira asked.

"We've had five programmers killed and another two reduced to vegetables in the last year. It happens while they're plugged into our Base and working. Further, our stuff is being stolen. We assume it's pirates. They kill, and then they steal."

Suddenly Shira understood. "And Yod is to be prepared to enter the Base and fight this menace?"

Malkah nodded. "That's part of it."

"I never knew Aviva Emet. Was she a friend?"

"She was younger than you are, Shira, and very bright. She came here last fall and apprenticed herself. What they killed her to steal was something we intended to sell at a very good price. It wasn't completed enough to sell, but it obviously was sufficient to be worth stealing."

Shira asked Yod, "Do you understand what they plan to do with you?"

"I was created to serve." Yod shrugged. "I am more capable of investigating these assaults than anyone else. Perhaps soon." He rose and looked for something to sit down on. Lacking a convenient chair, he picked up a block of granite, an old horse trough that stood in the garden, and casually moved it close to Malkah's chair, in a conversational grouping. Malkah threw Shira a look of amusement. She was pulling herself together visibly, as she always did after an emotional shock. Malkah had raised Shira in the belief that the proper response to a blow was to draw oneself up straight and proceed. If Malkah had been close to the woman killed, Shira would only find out gradually, for Malkah would grieve slowly and in odd moments.

Shira was still observing Malkah's manner with Yod. It was almost flirtatious. It shocked her slightly. Definitely Malkah responded to Yod as a male being. Shira had known Malkah to flirt with tomcats, but a machine?

AS SHIRA HAD SUSPECTED, Avram was furious. He ordered Yod into the inner laboratory, but Yod sat down quietly in the corner.

"I ordered you to leave."

"But it wouldn't be rational for me to do so. This concerns me, Father."

Avram's eyes glittered with anger. There are people who swell with anger, Shira thought, but Avram seemed to brighten with it. "How dare you take him out of the lab?"

She forced herself not to cringe, to try to sound calm. "He needs more experience, more stimulation than he's receiving confined here. It's time for him to mix with people. He has to learn how to operate in society. Avram, we must start somewhere. If we're together, most people will be paying attention to my being back and what gossip they've heard. Yod will be a little protected."

"Where did you take him?"

"Just to my house and then back."

"We saw Malkah," Yod volunteered. "She came home. I was very glad to talk with her."

Shira noticed that he did not mention that he had summoned Malkah.

Avram swung back to her. "Did you leave them alone?"

"No," she said. "I was with Yod the entire time. What are you afraid of?"

"Just don't leave them alone together. I don't trust Malkah."

"I do," Yod said softly. "She's my friend."

Avram snorted. "However, I agree that already he's improving. But be extremely careful. Don't let him talk with anyone yet, and don't give complicated explanations. Shall we agree on a cover story? We'll say he's my cousin, as you suggested, and he has come to work as my lab assistant. Everybody knows I haven't had one since David's accident."

She was relieved that Avram's anger had been mollified. It made her feel more confident that she could work with him. Behind Avram's back, Yod inscribed on the air the Hebrew letter *chet:* the nature of David's fatal accident.

twelve

A SEA CHANGE

Shira stood in the lab, about a foot from Yod, who shot her a look she could read only as complicity. They shared a sense of alarm. She was no longer surprised that she credited him with reactions: they might be simulacra of human emotions, but something went on in him that was analogous to her own responses, and making the constant distinction was a waste of energy.

Before them Avram was pacing. With the back of his hand he swept a pile of books and memory crystals to the floor. Automatically Gimel slipped past and was darting in and back restoring order as Avram paced. "Is he really my son? I wonder sometimes! Oh, I know Sara was faithful to me, but in the hospital, they could have made a mistake. You hear of it. If you don't check the gene print. But I did. Something went wrong. Something went awry, and I swear he should be scrapped the way you scrap an experiment that you have poured years and credits into and finally you cut your losses!"

Even now her instinct was to protect Gadi, to defend him. She forced herself to sound barely interested. "What has Gadi done now?"

"He's got into trouble again. Bad trouble."

"What kind?" Shira asked cautiously. She was not sure she wanted to know, but she had little choice. Nothing was going to happen today until she had calmed Avram, until he got out of the way and let them work. Trying to teach Yod how to pass for human was a more than full-time job but often amusing, as they acted scenes together like bright children, playing at the interactions he soon must carry out in earnest with people of the town. His questions startled her. "What does 'excuse me' mean? Excuse me from what? If I shouldn't do something, why do it? If it's permissible, why apologize?"

How little time it had taken, the six weeks they had been working together, for the two of them to close ranks against Avram, quietly, almost secretively, trusting each other more than they could their boss. Yod was holding himself together, but Avram's tension obviously aroused his need to defend, so that he kept clenching and unclenching his fists. He quivered with what in a human would have been anxiety. In Yod she suspected it was the unfulfilled need to take action: move out, defend, attack. Inadvertently his hand closed on the edge of the table and broke off a piece of the metal rim. He looked embarrassed and slipped it in the pocket of the shorts she had bought him.

Avram stopped pacing and turned to face them. "This must go no farther than this room, although we may not be able to keep it quiet. Gadi has . . . He has become sexually involved with a fifteen-year-old."

"A male or a female?" Yod asked blandly.

"A girl. My son's a flaming dandy, but he's monotonously heterosexual."

Sexuality was one of those areas that changed utterly from multi to multi, town to town. What was the norm in one place was forbidden in another. In Uni-Par, Gadi's multi, the commonest marriage was a triad. She felt a roiling hot mixture of emotions, like a pot of thick fudge about to boil over, but there was no sweetness in it, only resentment, guilt, complicity. Was Gadi still trying to recreate that lost and secret place of pure sugar intensity, fused bodies and hearts? For a while she knew he had sought that lost ecstasy in drugs, but it eluded him. "Where did this happen?"

"Azerbaijan. He's lucky to get out with his neck. He was publicly flogged. If he wasn't so overvalued by Uni-Par, his corpse would be fueling a waste power plant now. Because of his virons, they negotiated a flogging and they'll be shipping him out by closed zip."

"He creates the imaginary worlds of the stimmies?" Yod asked. "And people value the experience of exotic landscapes?"

Both Shira and Avram nodded without looking at Yod. Shira asked, her voice betraying her by quavering, "Shipped where?"

"Here. He's in disgrace. Oh, they'll recall him. No one in Uni-Par has a memory longer than six months."

She felt trapped. She had to get out. She couldn't. She found herself breathing quickly. Yod, whose hearing was abnormally sensitive, was about to speak, when she made a gesture asking him to keep silent. He understood.

"I want you to know, Shira, I did not invite him here. I found his last visit taxing enough, and that was only a long weekend. How my son and I will survive six months under the same roof is more than I can fathom. How could he be such a complete schmuck? He acts without thinking, just as he did when he was a child. He has never grown up, never!"

She found she could form only short sentences and still control her voice, her rising panic. "When is he coming?"

"Tomorrow."

"So soon . . ."

"Isn't it." Avram looked hard at her. "You're not looking forward to him any more than I am."

"I'm comfortable talking to him image-to-image. That nice electronic remove makes it safe."

"This is going to be awkward indeed. And just when we were making some headway. Yod has developed daily since you've been working with him. His progress is measuring consistently above my projected curve."

Yod threw her a veiled look of gratitude. She forced a weak smile at Avram. "I agree, we're making progress."

When Avram finally left them, Shira tried to administer one of the cognitive tests, but she found herself pulling the plug from her temple and crashing the program abruptly. "Yod, I have to go out. Outside the wrap. Do you have a sec skin, or should I go alone?"

"You mean into what's called the raw? The unprotected light and air? I don't require a sec skin. I was built to endure the raw without protection."

"Nonetheless, we'll find one for you. We can't let anyone discover your unique properties. I bet Gadi's old suit is still where he used to keep it." It was. She ran home to fetch hers and then returned for Yod.

The perimeter was more tightly guarded than it used to be, so Shira left officially. She walked fast. The bay. She wanted the comfort of the sea. She had not been swimming since she had been back; she had not been swimming all her years at Y-S. Yod strode beside her easily, his head bobbing in constant surveillance. "What is that?" He assumed a defensive posture.

"A vulture." It had found a dead rabbit. Rabbits had survived UV radiation by becoming nocturnal. "They're birds that can live in the raw. Ignore it." She hurried them over the dunes and through little boggy hollows of cranberries and drifts of beach plum in blossom. The air smelled salty. In the dunes it was hot indeed. Under the firmgel she was sweating freely. She headed into the drowned town below. The tide was out, so some of the old streets were dry, seaweed lodged between the tilted slabs of century-old cement. They had to hike and then wade through several ruined blocks before they came to a good swimming beach. With the bay risen over drowned marshes, seaside houses, roads, with the massive hurricanes they experienced yearly, which left wreckage of buildings, vehicles, machinery under water, a good beach was one where she could hope to swim without being maimed or impaled on some hidden wreck.

They squatted on a broken wall, what had been the lower story of a house now washed away and half buried. She peeled off her sec skin, reached for the waterproof grease that was supposed to protect her, then hesitated at stripping further before Yod. In Tikva, children were not instilled with nudity taboos. Nobody under twelve hesitated about tossing off their clothes, with the result that nobody over the age of twelve was ever naturally modest.

She had since lived in cultures, like Y-S, that had fierce injunctions concerning what parts of the human body should be displayed in what circumstances. It went with rigid sex roles—not at work, of course, for no one could afford such nonsense, but in every other sector of living. Women dressing for dinner often bared their breasts at Y-S functions, but the legs were always modestly covered to midcalf. The back was usually bare; the standard business suit, with its deeply cut back, was designed to show both men's and women's musculature and fitness. However, it was the custom to keep ears and nape covered for women, who were required to wear their hair at least shoulder length, often artificially straightened. Malkah had cut Shira's to a sleek cap just last week. At Uni-Par, Gadi's multi, nudity was a sign of status. The higher you were on the pyramid, the less you wore, the better to show off the results of the newest cosmetic surgery performed on your body. At Aramco-Ford, women wore yards of material and short transparent symbolic veils.

She had never owned a bathing suit, and she wanted to swim. She wanted to feel the salt water stinging all the small cuts and abrasions of her body like benign sandpaper; she longed to feel salt-cured, wet on the surface and dry at the bone. She needed to lose herself in swimming. Why was she hesitating to strip before a machine?

"Do you know how to swim, Yod?"

"Yes, although that's a skill I've never before accessed. I'm programmed to enjoy exercising all my functions. Do we swim in this moving water?"

"This is Massachusetts Bay, and yes, we swim in it." She was still squatting there in her briefs and shirt. Finally she pulled off her tank top, left on her brassiere and briefs, sliding the resin knife into the seam, rubbed herself all over with protective grease and waded into the water. Even more quickly, Yod undressed. He stood on the edge of the crumbling wall, looking doubtful. He was drawing in air in long sharp breaths as his midsection inflated strangely. Of course; he was heavier than a human of the same size. He had to create added mass to avoid sinking. "Come on in," she called.

"This water is radioactive and highly polluted with toxic chemicals, including petrocarbons, acetic acid, chloroform—"

"This is the only ocean we have in our backyard. It will have to do."

She glanced at him, poised uncertainly on the water's edge. His body was exactly the same color all over, a rich olive. He had pubic hair, although almost no chest hair. He had been given a navel, absurdly, and also a penis, which she quickly looked away from. He looked bloated, puffed with air. "If you aren't coming, wait for me here."

"Shira, this is dangerous. Wait." She heard a large splash and then a loud churning of the waters.

She treaded water, waiting. He had not quite got the knack of his programming yet. He was splashing in all directions, sputtering, thrashing and kicking. She swam back toward him. She felt efficient, sleek in the water. As long as it had been since she had swum, she was at once at home in the water. It was strange she should want to swim today, for it was something she had always done with Gadi or, when she was much younger, with Malkah, who had not been at all reluctant to slip out to the bay, in an era when it had not been as dangerous as it was now. The higher the water rose, the more hidden traps lay underneath, and organ pirates had multiplied. The sea had always been the great escape from school, from home, from tension.

"I'm programmed to watch for sharks. I have an image I can call up on my retina of a shark, but I see none."

"This isn't their preferred hunting grounds, but keep an eye out anyhow. There can be a first time."

"Often people speak in tautologies, Shira, even yourself." He straightened out in the water and began to cleave it with his strong arms, heading toward her. His perfect coordination had taken over. She realized he could probably swim across the ocean to Europa, steadily churning through storm and calm alike; except that he did require nourishment every day or two. Perhaps he could convert sea water to energy, like the fusion plant whose stacks she could see sticking up on the next inlet. He slowed to her pace. "This is most interesting and novel to me, but I don't understand how swimming relates to the great sense of distress you demonstrated in the lab."

"I don't know if I can explain."

"Why don't you wish Gadi to come?"

"I'm afraid."

"Of him? In what way? I can defend against any threat to you."

"How am I going to explain this? What do I fear? Remembering. Gadi and I loved each other when we were children, but not what they call puppy love."

"The love for domesticated animals is common—"

"I mean we loved as intensely as adults love, perhaps more so." She had stopped swimming, and she found herself sinking as she spoke. She let herself go down and then arced toward the surface again. Yod seized her by the shoulder and hauled her up.

"I don't need rescuing, thank you."

"You're welcome," he said blandly, swimming circles around her. "I don't understand what you fear."

"He ended it. I still remember the pain. I'm afraid it's inside me, waiting to break out."

"Doesn't human memory have a tendency to fade, to lose intensity?"

"Yours doesn't?"

"I can play back events, fast, slow, stopping at will."

"I'd lie down and die if I had that ability."

"I study every interaction between us. I learn about human behavior from this replay, and above all, I understand you better."

"Every interaction?"

He nodded.

"Would you mind editing out my getting undressed?"

"Why?"

"Never mind."

"That's an expression I don't understand. To return to Gadi, you fear the pain of remembering, but you remember anyhow."

"I fear wanting him back when there is no back. No way to return to the place where we both knew love. Neither of us can love anyone, Yod. I know to you that must seem no more than as if I said I can't fly, but it matters to me."

"I understand, theoretically speaking, the value of love in human intercourse. But you love Malkah. Obviously you love your son."

"Love is an ambiguous word. We speak of loving roast turkey or swimming. I don't mean that I can't feel affection. But my capacity for bonding in passionate love with a man seems to have been burned out at age seventeen."

"You see in Gadi this same problem. In the fifteen-year-old he is seeking you at fifteen, since this is not the first event of this nature."

How did he know that? That was Malkah speaking, she knew it, that was Malkah's analysis. She let herself sink for a moment, then bobbed up, angry. "Have you been discussing me with Malkah?"

"I haven't seen Malkah since that day in your house."

"You eel! You and Malkah chatter on the com-con nightly." That was the internal communication of Tikva, used by its inhabitants, computer to computer, house to house, from the time they could talk. Could he actually lie?

"I've made you angry?" He cocked his head, marveling. "And this time I didn't break or ruin anything."

"You have a strong will to survive."

He nodded. "It's a primary part of my programming. As of yours."

"Then do not, do not, do not discuss me behind my back with my grandmother, ever again."

"What are you threatening me with?"

"My displeasure, Yod, nothing more. I have no power, over you or over anyone in the whole entire world."

"But you do have power over me, the strength of my desire to please you. Gadi's important to you because he came early into your life, as you've arrived early in mine. You don't like to hurt anyone, so I'm not afraid of you as I'm afraid of Avram. When I discuss you with Malkah, it's to learn."

"Yod, you're supposed to be learning about the world and how to behave with others so you appear human, you're not supposed to be studying me."

"I can create my own goals. Shira, when you talk to me freely and openly about yourself as you just did, I don't need Malkah to explain you to me."

"I already communicate with you better than I did with my husband. Oh, shit!" She turned in the water and began swimming off furiously. It was horribly true. She enjoyed better rapport with a machine than she had with Josh. In fact she had always found computers easier to communicate with than Josh. He had all their literal-mindedness but was capable of displaying acidic resentment and of simply ignoring her, as no machine intelligence could.

When Josh finished at Pacifica, she would have to return to him, if she could get him to agree. She would have to truncate herself to fit into his notions of wife and mother, for that was the only way she would ever get Ari back. Tears blinded her till she stopped to tread water.

Yod was churning along at her shoulder. "Shira, is that a boat? I'm not familiar with that mechanism." He rose in the water to point, just as a net shot over them.

How could she have been so stupid? Organ scavengers. She was being drawn under by the weight of the net. She kicked at it, panicked. It was dragging them toward the boat, yanking them underwater with no way to rise and take a breath. She told herself to stay calm, to think. She remembered the knife. She groped for it, worked it out of the seam of her briefs and began sawing at the coarse mesh. Already she needed oxygen. Her lungs burned. The precious air trickled out of her mouth in bubbles and rose to the surface, silvery above them. The cords were tough. She had to breathe, she had to. She slashed at them, wanting to cry out, to scream. She hacked and hacked at the cords but could only dent them. Her sight was speckling out. She was going to breathe water soon and drown; she would lose control. She sawed hopelessly, frantically.

Yod observed her. He tried to speak, but water flowed in and he grimaced, sputtering. Then he seized the cords of the net in his hands. Slowly he pulled; gradually the cords stretched a little, stretched more and then finally ripped asunder. The net parted in his hands like a spiderweb. He seized her under the arms and bore her to the surface, where she gasped for breath, coughing out water. Yod was still grasping her as he turned in the water. He began swimming much faster bearing her than she could have done alone, back toward the broken wall where they had entered the water. They had come perhaps a hundred meters.

She heard cries, the whir of an engine, and twisted in Yod's grasp to stare back. The organ hunters' skimmer was bearing down on them, a fast hovercraft settled now in the water for capture. It was a small boat with a low cabin, mostly refrigerator hold. She had seen them before, but never almost on top of her. No one growing up on these shores could avoid seeing the hunting boats in the distance. People didn't survive seeing them close.

Two men, fully filtered and masked, were wielding dart guns. Paralyzer was volatile and wouldn't affect the quality of the organs; scavengers never shot prey with projectiles or lasers. A third man was readying the scoop net to pick up their bodies at once. The masks were the color of ivory, rigid, beaky, giving the three men on deck the appearance of the tops of totem poles. Although they shouted each other on, the masks were expressionless. They would tear her apart with their knives. They would rip the heart out of her and her eyes and her womb and her liver and kidneys, all would be packed away into vats of gel. She would be paralyzed, but she would feel them cutting her to ribbons. She hoped they took her heart first. Yod turned to look at them. He let her go. She realized he had been hit. He plucked a dart from the skin of his shoulder to squint at it.

"Paralyzer," she gasped. He should be reacting already. The poison was instantaneous.

"Dive. Take cover." He went down like an anchor released. She swam furiously underwater until she had to rise just enough for a breath. She peered around quickly for shelter. Then she dodged past the wreck of a broken and abandoned dredge, keeping it between her and the skimmer. She treaded water in the lee of the dredge, peeking through a crack in the metal. She could not hope to escape by swimming. Yod must have sunk to the bottom. She felt a pang of loss for the cyborg. She had grown used to his company. He had become her job. If she could stay under the dredge, she did not think they could get her; but how long could she play hide-and-seek with them? It was all her fault, brooding instead of paying attention. At least Yod had died quickly. Her own chances were dim.

The skimmer was coming slowly to enable the hunters to aim their dart guns. Abruptly it stopped and began to rock in the water. It tipped violently to the left, again, again. A great crunch sounded, as if it had hit a rock or a building. Over it went, spilling the three hunters, the driver crying out from the wheelhouse. It happened so quickly she went on staring. Her body still screeched fight or flight. They must have struck an old wreck or a building that did not break the surface. The driver had forgotten to watch the underwater plotter. These waters were full of hazards, but all boats bigger than dinghies were equipped with sonar.

She had begun swimming again toward the shore when she heard splashing behind her. She still had the knife gripped in her hand. She turned in the water to face her pursuer. She was just in time to see the last of the swimming hunters disappear underwater. He never came up. What stuck its head out a moment later was Yod coming toward her in a powerful crawl.

"I thought you had drowned." Then she wondered if he could.

"The paralyzer didn't affect me."

He let her swim on her own. Behind them when she glanced back, the bay was empty except for the capsized boat, slowly filling with water. While she watched, it went down. Four men dead. She could hardly mourn them. They made a living by stealing people and selling the organs to the multi labs that provided implants for execs, talent and security. Artificial replacements for every organ in the body were available, but they could be damaged by certain frequencies: therefore the highly placed, the wealthy wanted the safety of real organs to defy assassins who could attack from a distance. Regular corporate gruds and people in the free towns depended on artificial implants, of the kind Malkah and Shira had in their eyes.

When she and Yod hauled up on shore, Shira would have liked to rest, but the hunters might have a partner boat. She pulled on her sec skin, motioning for Yod to do the same. Then she led the way toward the wrap at a dogged weary trot. Yod was frowning. He was not tired and had no trouble talking while he jogged. "Shira, I must tell you something. This is the first time I have truly defended. It was highly pleasurable. Yet my philosophical and theological programming informs me I've committed a wrong. I liked killing them, do you understand? Is that how it should be? Is that right?"

She was startled and took several moments to formulate an answer. "Yod, your programming creates your reactions. You didn't choose to enjoy it."

"Killing them was as enjoyable as anything I've ever experienced. I think I must be programmed to find killing as intense as sexual pleasure or mastering a new skill. It was that strong."

"What does it mean for you to feel pleasure?"

"How can I answer that? What does it mean to you? I know that it's entirely mental with me, but mammals, too, have a pleasure center in their brains. You're programmed to like sweet tastes and avoid bitter ones. I'm programmed to find some things pleasurable and others painful."

She could think of nothing to say; she found his statements frightening. Probably when she felt less exhausted emotionally and physically, she would find his revelation even more disturbing. Yod had not been given knowledge of the organ trade, so she briefed him as they went. Under the sec skin her body was clammy, itchy. She would drop Yod at the lab and head home for a bath and a nap. "Are you impervious to poison of all kinds?"

"No. Most acids would burn me also. But a neural paralyzer designed for a mammalian system is ineffective against me."

"A laser would injure you." She was remembering the broken cyborg Alef, its head blasted open.

"Any explosive or laser device would injure or kill me, Shira, the same as yourself."

"I was careless today. My past welled up and clouded my judgment."

"I was careless too. I should have detected the boat, but I didn't understand what it was. I need to learn more. I need to know far more to protect you adequately. I'm ashamed I didn't stop them before they frightened you. Never should you be frightened."

"Yod, I'm not your child any more than you're mine. This is a frightening world, and it's best not to forget that, the way we both did this afternoon."

"Is this outing something I should mention to Avram?"

"Just say that we went out into the raw for a lesson." Shira smiled and tapped his arm in the sec skin. "You're learning certain human behaviors rather quickly. Such as discretion."

"It was a provocative lesson today. Much to reflect on. Tonight, instead of practicing with Gimel, I'll play this back many times."

A kid standing guard released the gate to them. Tomorrow she would have guard duty for the first time, fitted back into the self-running of the town: every citizen owed the town eight hours of labor a week. Fortunately Yod did not seem to demand gratitude from her. She was too wrung out to force much response. She longed to be alone and quiet and numb. Then she thought, Why did he compare killing to sex? When did he ever experience sex? Would a cyborg masturbate? That was too bizarre. Could a cyborg enjoy a stimmie? She did not want to speculate about his remark, but it disquieted her. As the old hotel came into view, she realized she had not thought of Gadi in an entire hour. Great therapy. Perhaps she should find a little war to join and dangle her life for bait. The danger would serve to keep Gadi out of her mind.

thirteen

A DOUBLE MIDWIVING

The Maharal is exhausted, but still he rises by midmorning, with Perl scolding him for his passion to make himself sick. He must conceal the origins of the Golem, quickly. From Samuel the tailor and dealer in secondhand clothes the Maharal buys the biggest pants and the biggest shirt and the biggest of everything in the shop. Nothing matches. The Golem looks at himself in the mirror with sullen curiosity. Why do I imagine he is thinking and feeling? the Maharal asks himself. Because it looks more or less like a man, I think of it as a man. But it is a tool. A clumsy and dangerous tool that must be carefully controlled.

"Whose pants were these?" the Golem asks Samuel. His voice is very deep, Judah thinks: the bass befits a creature of his size, as the longer organ pipes have the deeper pitch.

Samuel scratches his head. "They were the pants of Chaim the Silversmith, may he rest in peace."

"And this shirt?"

"The widow of Gershom brought that in."

"I'm a walking cemetery of clothes," the Golem says to the Maharal as they cross the narrow street with the houses leaning over it. "Today the widows of the constables are gathering up their old clothes. I have been thinking about murder. I still think what I did was correct. I am to protect." Then Joseph stops stark in his tracks, his mouth falling open, to watch a pigeon beat from roof to roof on whistling wings.

The Maharal must take Joseph's elbow and hustle him along, as every object in the street fascinates him. He peers at everyone. He is so big and impassive, he frightens some. Judah gives him a brief lecture on the rudeness of staring.

"But how can I see if I don't look?"

"You don't need to look at people so hard. It frightens them."

"But you don't want me to be stupid. I'm trying to learn, Teacher. Teach me."

"I'm going to teach you how to be shamash at the synagogue. That should occupy you and keep you out of trouble."

The Altneushul is a building that has never ceased to move the Maharal, from the day he arrived in Prague when he was forty, as it never ceased to awe me when I was studying at the university. I have never seen a small building with greater dignity. It has a presence of holiness and of concentrated history. It is not tall outside. Instead, when you enter the Altneushul you step down, for the height of the interior was gotten by going down as well as up. It has a sharply pitched A of roof, with a single row of crenellations like teeth in the shape of a menorah to decorate its simplicity. It looks strong, ancient, of and from the earth. Inside, while there are individual splendors of decoration—the Torah curtain, the metal screens—the overall effect is austere. It is a place to lift your eyes, pray from your spine.

Now the Maharal shows the Golem his duties. "Avoid gossip. Avoid chattering with the old men and the old women who will come pestering you. Keep your mouth shut and work hard."

Joseph obeys, for he wants to please Judah; perhaps this was the source of the tradition that the Golem was mute. As shamash of the synagogue, Joseph works hard and cheerfully. He takes his meals at the rabbi's table. At first he lowers his face into the soup and begins to lap it up like a dog he saw eating in the courtyard. When he finishes the soup, he bites into the bowl. He has ground a large mouthful of china between his powerful teeth before the Maharal can stop him. But he does not choke. Instead he chews the china and swallows it just as if it were a piece of challeh.

Judah says hastily, into the stunned faces of his family, "He's an orphan. We must teach him manners. He has been living among beggars and lunatics."

By the end of the week, Joseph has learned to eat with utensils, although sometimes he still mistakes what to eat. Given a chicken for the first time, he seizes a drumstick and eats it entire, bones and all. Once, in the courtyard, the Maharal sees Joseph pick up a brick, bite off the end and chew it thoughtfully. Judah groans and covers his face. How to explain to the Golem what is edible and what is not? It is all one to him. Whatever is inside him processes it all. A brick is the same as a potato. Perhaps he finds it tastier like a man eating meat, the stuff of which he is made, the Maharal wonders in despair.

Now that Joseph has learned at least minimally how to comport himself so that others will think him simple but not—usually—dangerous, the Maharal decides it is time for the Golem to take on the duties for which he was created. As the weather slowly turns mild, danger grows. Young men of the town like to break into the ghetto and commit mayhem. It gives them something to do on a fine spring night. There is a rising whine of violence barely suppressed in the city. The Turk has won some recent victories; the price of bread is up; more peasants have been forced off their land. Thaddeus is preaching to big enthusiastic crowds. He has started a young men's society of knights and ambitious guildsmen dedicated to driving out infidels, heretics, Jews, to cleansing the city and reestablishing the clean simple living each generation likes to imagine characterized their grandparents.

"Every night, Joseph, I want you to go out and patrol the ghetto for danger." The Maharal has learned that Joseph eats but does not sleep.

"What should I watch for? What should I do?"

Everything must be explained. For instance, the Maharal tells Joseph to seize anyone he finds suspicious and take him to the watch or bring him directly to the Maharal. On one of his patrols he seizes an old scholar who sleeps little and walks while he ponders, perhaps falsely secure in the belief that he is so obviously a poor old man, nobody would bother to rob him. Why does he seize this harmless old man? Because when he asks the old scholar what he is doing out, the man replies, "What are *you* doing? I have a suspicious nature myself." Therefore Joseph seizes him and drags him before the Maharal on the charge of being suspicious.

Joseph is obedient but more literal than any child. He does exactly to the letter what he is told, rather than what the Maharal may have meant. Judah finds himself thinking a great deal about the need for precision in language. Still, Joseph learns quickly. He asks as many questions as Judah remembers his children asking, perhaps more. They are not the same questions. Where did I come from? Why is grass green? Where does the sun go when it goes down? Judah can hear Bezalel's reedy childhood voice. Joseph asks none of these. Once he has begun to learn to distinguish between the natural world and the artificial world of human artifacts, he loses interest in birds and trees. His questions concern people and their doings.

Why do parents love their children? How does a man pick a wife? Why do people laugh? How does someone know what work to do in the world? What do the blind see? Why do men get drunk? Why do men play with cards and dice when they lose more than they win? Why do people call each other momser—bastard—when they are angry and then again when they are loving? You little momser. Why do people say one thing and do another? Why do people make promises and then break them? What does it mean to mourn?

Sometimes Judah feels as if he has acquired an immense five-year-old who wants nothing more than to follow him around and ask him questions. He must turn on Joseph again and again and tell him to go and sweep the floor, to polish the silver in the Altneushul, to trim the candles and the lamps. He is always having to deny his attention to Joseph, who would gladly absorb all of his time as a tutor in human behavior and general learning.

Every night Joseph trots tirelessly through the narrow dark ill-smelling streets with sewers running down the middle, runs fearlessly through the shadows. He lifts the drunkard on his shoulders and deposits him inside the door of his home. If Jews are quarreling in the streets, he separates them, gently but inexorably. He is learning how to use his strength, but sometimes he forgets. He has become the unofficial policeman of the night, a solitary patrol of peace. This task he carries out cheerfully, quietly. Now when he has an errand to run for the Maharal, people greet him. The wife whose husband he lugged home, the man whose purse he saved, they address him respectfully. Although Joseph cannot smile, he can nod, and his voice in answer shows his pleasure at the friendly greetings. Sometimes the Maharal notices him lingering in the street to enjoy the pleasantries. Then the Maharal frowns and steps out to call Joseph to his duties in the synagogue.

But Passover is coming, and close on its heels will arrive Easter, the holiday always feared by the Jews of Prague. Thaddeus is preaching they are murderers of God. Rocks, garbage, excrement are tossed at the gates of the ghetto, and any Jew returning close to dark is apt to be set upon. In the mild nights of April, with the scent of narcissus in the air and the willows already chartreuse along the river, gangs of youth climb over the wall and look for trouble.

One overcast April night with the feel of rain in the air, voices and scents magnified by a light fog, an expectant mother calls for Chava to deliver her. The messenger is the ten-year-old son, and together they start back. But a party of rowdy knights from the town has broken into the

ghetto and accosts Chava at the corner of two streets. They throw her
down on the damp pavement, two of them pinning her head and shoulders
into the dirty stones of the street while she bucks and bites at the hand
that is clapped across her mouth and covers her nostrils so that she is
choking and cannot draw breath. Two of them are prying her legs apart
as she tries to fight the crowd of them, futilely. The ten-year-old lies
bleeding from his skull. Then Joseph on his rounds comes running. He
tears their swords from their hands. One by one he casts the men into the
buildings like a dog tossing water from his coat. Their blows are feathers
tickling his shoulders. They break their knuckles against him. One dagger
scratches him and he bleeds, blood that in the darkness looks black.

Chava picks herself up, grabs a fallen sword, pulls her skirt and
petticoat down. The sword is heavy for her and she grasps it in both hands,
hilt against her belly for support. One of the knights is about to skewer
the Golem from the back when she runs him through instead. Finally
Joseph stands panting among the dead. Joseph and Chava look at each
other. "I must take you home," he says.

"Let me see that cut. It's already stopped bleeding. You heal quickly."

"They can't hurt me." Joseph snorts his contempt.

"Oh?" Chava smiles sarcastically, but the hand she rests on his arm
is kindly. "You aren't mortal, maybe?"

"Go home now. I'll take you."

"Simcha Roth is still in need. Babies wait for nobody. You can walk
with me, quickly. Then take that poor boy to the doctor and throw these
bodies over the wall."

"All of that I will do. . . . You killed a man, too, tonight." Joseph
matches his pace to hers. "Does that bother you?"

"Let's never speak of it to anyone. Particularly, Joseph, don't mention
this to my grandfather or my father, Itzak. I deal with life and death every
time a baby must come from its mother. Those men meant to shame me
first and then to kill me. I'm grateful to you, Joseph."

The next morning a storm blows, and there are only nine men at
prayers. "Joseph, make a minyon with us," Samuel the tailor begs him.

Joseph takes his place with them. When the Maharal sees what has
happened, he glares at Joseph, but he can say nothing till afterward. Then
he scolds him. "You are not a man. You cannot make a minyon."

"I am not a man, but I am a Jew. Thus you made me. It takes ten Jews.
If I was an angel, would you tell me I could not make up a minyon?"

After the rabbi has gone off to hold his court, to work as a judge,
another of his hundred duties, Chava comes out of the study, where she

has been copying the rabbi's new treatise on education. "They tell me I'm a Jew but that I can't make up a minyon either," she tells Joseph. "Whatever you are, you are not less than a man."

"Chava, if you mean that, teach me to read. I know only what I hear."

She is moved by his desire. Most women were illiterate then, although less often among the Jews than among the Christians. Frequently, learned men taught their daughters. But Chava is aware that to be able to read and write sets her off from the great majority of women, who are blind to the words and the knowledge of books. A terrible blindness. "I'd be happy to teach you."

Chava finds Joseph strange, observing that he patrols the ghetto and never sleeps, that he has more than human strength. She has read the kabbalah and the texts of Abulafia. She suspects what Joseph is, but she says nothing, not to Itzak, her father, not to Joseph, not to Perl, not to the Maharal. All children are made, she thinks, by a mother and father. So poor Joseph has only a father, one who does not cherish him. Am I to think the less of him for that? He may not be a man as men are, but he's alive, and he wants to learn. That is a beautiful hunger that should be fed. He saved my life and my pride; I value both. I value him.

From that moment on, Joseph loves Chava, but he is ashamed of his love. He is a golem of clay. How could any woman embrace him? He could not give her children. If he should touch her, he is terrified he would bruise her flesh that seems light as a petal to him. He would crush her as he crushed the narcissus he tried to pick on the bank of the Vltava. He knows that the Maharal, whom he always longs to please, whom he cannot help but consider his father, would never forgive him. He cannot bear to imagine the anger of the Maharal if he should ever touch Chava. But Chava is the sun of his day, his rose of light. Whenever she is called out for a birth, he walks with her and he waits outside, all night if necessary, until the dawn renders the ghetto as safe as it ever is.

People think of love as a human emotion, but I have seen dogs and cats and horses die for love, and never yet one person. I have seen women die *of* love in my youth, when childbirth was more dangerous and abortions not always safe, but not *for* love. Yod, you are capable of affection, so why cannot Joseph be? His simplicity makes him more vulnerable to the need to bestow and receive affection, not less so. Your capabilities, my dear, I worked long and hard to extend while working on your pleasure and pain centers and your capacity to imagine. In Freud's terms, that old marvelously creative humbug, that sculptor of urges, I balanced thanatos with eros. Avram should not have let me loose if he wanted a simple man-made cyborg, for you are also woman-made. My knowledge is in you. But nobody, my dear, gave you your infinite hunger to understand. That you gave yourself. Never, Yod, never believe anybody who tells you, not Avram, not even me, what you are and are not capable of. Find out for yourself. Be less humble than Joseph, my angel.

During this period, in spite of the Maharal's occasional anger, Joseph is happy. Chava teaches him the Hebrew alphabet and the German alphabet, which is used for Czech also, so he can make out signs, and soon he will be reading real words in real books. He sweeps the synagogue and patrols the ghetto. In the streets people speak to him, no matter how funny they think he looks. Seldom now do the boys throw stones at him or tease him. When he lumbers along the narrow streets, people make way for him. Some smile, others nod. He thinks, I belong here. Here is where I live. People like me. I have friends, and this is my home. Although he cannot smile or laugh, his eyes shine with the joy he feels. If there were cloud-gray jewels, they would be his eyes now briefly when he is alight with happiness.

fourteen

BY THE LIGHT OF THE UNYELLOW MOON

The next day, Shira braced for Gadi's return, but it was another week before he was shipped in. Then he was rushed immediately to the hospital, a building complex even older than the lab building. The flogging had been far more than a formality. His kidneys were injured—one must be replaced at once—and he had experienced a buildup of toxins. He was unconscious and would remain isolated for ten days to two weeks.

The next Shabbat, a message robot appeared at the gate, and Malkah and Shira went to fetch it. Message robots were small self-propelled wheeled vehicles; always a strident yellow, they resembled tiny cannons, barrels on treads. They rode a special car in the tube trains and then continued under their own power. They offered a secure way of delivering messages, since they could be blown up but not decided by anyone who did not have the correct DNA. This one was programmed only for Malkah's. She had to feed it an injection of her blood. It would only deliver its message if given living tissue. Hair did not work, nor nail clippings. Ironically, in a fully electronic society with everything on computers, the only fully secure channel that could not be hacked into was the little message robot.

Shira and Malkah squatted in front of the barrel, while it hummed to itself, verifying Malkah's DNA. Finally it spoke. "I am from Riva," it said in its affectless high-pitched drone. It sounded like a mechanical mouse. "I have been detained, but I am definitely coming. I am with a friend. We will be arriving as an old lady, your sister Dalia, and her nurse. Make the house as secure as possible. Arrange that no one exercises curiosity. I am a very dull and demanding old lady. I am programmed to repeat this message once. Are you ready for the second delivery?"

"Proceed." Malkah hugged herself in delight. The message robot repeated, then went into erasure mode, when it could not be touched without producing a shock. "I am programmed with the DNA of my sender. Do you have an answer?"

"It is I, Malkah, responding. I will make the house secure. Shira is here and knows you are coming. I look forward to seeing you, with whatever face. My sister Dalia was always a pain in the ass, and I will be sure everyone here knows that."

The robot repeated the message for corrections, then went into encoding mode. When the message had been secured, it trundled off. Shira accompanied it to the gate, watching until its bright yellow disappeared among the dunes. Message robots were seldom bothered, even by gangs in the Glop, since tampering with them never produced a message but did reliably provide a small messy explosion. They ambled around the world through the Glops, into multi enclaves, onto the tubes and the zips, far more freely and safely than people or animals could. Shira watched it wistfully. That was true freedom, she thought, something now available only to special machines.

It was a quiet day in Tikva; on Shabbat, only essential services continued. Most of the children of the town were out on the streets playing or at children's events in one or another synagogue, so that today it seemed almost a town of children instead of adults. As was the case everyplace, the leftover radiation from power plant residues and the stockpiles of toxic chemicals long since part of the water table had left most people infertile without heroic measures to conceive (and the credit and/or position to command those measures). Further, every pregnancy outside the Glop was monitored genetically and developmentally. Thus the ability to conceive and bear healthy children was both prized and viewed as somewhat primitive. That capacity, too, had set Shira apart at Y-S. Most educated young people of her generation thought out loud or secretly that infertility was Gaia's way of protecting her totality. People had gone too far in destroying the earth, and now the earth was diminishing the number of people. Perhaps when the earth had come back into balance, reproduction would become again the simple matter it seemed to have been for their ancestors.

When she arrived at the house, Gila, a tiny redhead who was manager of the telapia co-op, was drinking wine and eating melon with Malkah while they played chess, a never-ending battle of two nearly matched opponents that had gone on since Shira could remember. She went up to her room, turned on one of her holos of Ari—a day in the local park, Ari and herself sprawled on the grass watching robot birds, his eyes round, fists waving—and stared at it, eyes dripping. Then she sat down at her personal base and began going over more of Avram's interminable notes on Yod. She could hear Gila's high-pitched vibrato cries of victory or defeat—a tropical bird screeching in the patio—and Malkah's lower-pitched and lower-decibeled replies. Gila was excitable; Malkah liked to play against her friend by acting phlegmatic. She would play chess at half her normal speed to throw off Gila's timing.

Gila had brought the melons and the wine. Malkah cooked a light supper, that they ate in the courtyard, on the table under the plum tree. It was still dropping little green plums on the flagstones. At twilight they lit the braided havdalah candle, passed the spice box, recited the blessings and doused the candle in wine, formally ending the Sabbath. "It's full moon tonight," Malkah remarked. "All the young people run outside to fuck as if it's more fun if you pack sand into all your crevices."

"Malkah, you're getting old and crotchety," Gila said. "I wouldn't mind being in the dunes tonight with the right company."

Malkah and Gila went off to a string quartet that was playing, but Shira did not feel like sitting still in a crowded room listening to Haydn. She was restless in the long mauve twilight. She drifted up to her room and lay on her bed trying to think of someone she felt like chatting with on the com-con or reaching through the Net. She could feel Gadi's presence, a disquieting magnetic pull, so that she was sure that even if she were blindfolded, she would know in which direction the hospital lay. It had been a mistake to come back here; yet Malkah's company was good for her. She found working with Yod engaging. Damn Gadi. Damn him.

Then the house said, rather coldly, she thought, "The machine Yod wishes to enter."

"I told you he could come in." She rolled out of bed and turned on the light. His light swift steps crossed the stones below. She hung over the balcony. "Yod? What are you doing out alone?"

He stood diffidently at the bottom of the stairway. "I was bored."

She came down the steps to him. "You actually experience boredom?"

"Frequently. Avram's at the hospital. Shabbat felt interminable: you don't come to work with me. I worked for hours with the computer. Gimel and I can't fight until everybody has gone to bed. I read Stendhal's two novels—"

"You read novels? Why?"

"Malkah suggested that as a way to understand human interactions and responses. It's a key to people's interior life."

"Is that necessary for your defense functions?"

No lights had been turned on in the courtyard, but the pale oyster afterglow of eight o'clock in late May tinted the air. He stood rigidly still, with his hands behind him. "How can I know, Shira, if what occurs in me bears any resemblance to what you call boredom or pleasure? I use the words. What others are available to me? In understanding humans, I try to grasp my own inner life."

"If we'd talked earlier, we could have gone to a concert with Malkah and her friend Gila."

"Music doesn't engage me. I can analyze it, but it doesn't move me. I've watched Avram with his eyes shut and an expression of what appears intense pleasure on his face."

"Soon we should attend some public event where you aren't the focus. Where we can practice your blending in. Tomorrow we'll eat in the Commons."

"But not tonight . . . You can go outside without a sec skin at night?"

"Sure. With a sea breeze blowing, the air isn't too poisonous tonight. We can walk up on the hills. Our adventure didn't make you dislike excursions?"

"I told you, I enjoyed it all. Too much."

They were not the only people outside the wrap tonight. Couples were sharing blankets on the hill over town, but Shira and Yod kept to the path and she led the way higher, where it was faintly light still and they could turn and watch the mercurial bay climb more than halfway up the sky. The ground here was sandy and warm from the day. Tonight there were even stars to be seen. The sea breeze had shoved the usual clouds farther inland. Here and there light from a planet or star drilled through the omnipresent haze.

Yod put out his arm tentatively. "You can lean against me if that's comfortable. My arm won't tire."

He was pleasantly warm and compact. She turned slightly from him, propping her back against his shoulder. "This is fine."

Yod was watching a couple lost in darkness on the slope. She knew they were there only because she had heard them laughing as Yod and she passed them climbing up, but with Yod's infrared vision, he could see in the dark. "They are having sex. Is that an acceptable idiom?"

"Yes, but watching them isn't. Don't!"

"But it's interesting, and they have no idea I can see them."

"It's a private thing." She found herself disturbed, and then she was back on this slope on warm evenings with an old spread removed from a bed on the third story of the old hotel. She had lain on that spread with Gadi while they tangled their bodies together and their minds seemed to interpenetrate. Her body had opened to receive him, she had throbbed translucent and shining, turning in the medium of her pleasure like a brilliant pulsating jellyfish. Malkah had once told her sex got better as a woman grew older, but for Shira it had diminished to a simple act more concerned with giving pleasure to a husband than with transcendent liquid ecstasy.

Yod shrugged and turned to her. "I don't understand why my observing could do them harm, but I don't want to annoy you. . . . Look. There's a fire far out on the bay. A ship burning?"

"That's the moon coming up."

"But the moon isn't red . . . ?"

"It won't be red long."

In silence they watched it inch perceptibly from the water. She could feel Yod's excitement. As it swelled into a half circle over the water, huge, swollen, molten red, he began to recite its names in all the languages he knew, as if it were a chant: "Moon, levana, yarayach, la lune, luna . . ."

"Stop! You've never seen it before! Have you?"

"I have many images stored, but that isn't the same as knowing—although I used to think it was."

"How strange to be born knowing *of* so much and yet not knowing it." It was years since she had sat outside at night under the sky, feeling wind brush her skin, feeling wind tangle in her hair. Under a city dome, no one came and went as casually as in Tikva. She felt a powerful joy she labeled silly, irrational, but nonetheless felt percolating through her like a drug designed at once to stimulate and to relax. "I was reading more of Avram's lab notes today. You're two and a half years old."

"That's a meaningless comparison. You were right: there was no point in watching that couple. They did nothing interesting, and that only once."

"Do you remember your equivalent of birth?"

"The moment I came to consciousness, in the lab, everything began rushing in. I felt a sharp pain, terrible, searing. I cried out in terror."

She swung around to stare at him. "What kind of pain?"

"I wanted to sink back into unconsciousness, I wanted to feel nothing." Yod spoke vehemently over his own shoulder. "Everything assaulted me. Sound, sight, touch, all my sensors giving me huge amounts of data and all of it seeming equally important, equally loud. I was battered almost to senselessness. I understand why Alef and Dalet and Chet responded by becoming instantly violent and attacking anyone present."

"So like a human infant you came into the world protesting and angry."

"I experienced vast random streams of information forcing their way into my consciousness. I was flooded with internal readouts, temperature, distances from me to other objects, chemical analyses, reports on the temperature of various parts of my skin and of the atmosphere, definitions of words, calculated trajectories, trigonometric functions, algorithms, precise time, world and local history, forty languages. I experienced sensory overload that was intense and meaningless at once. I might have acted as vacant as Gimel or simply burned out and had half my functions turned off."

"You said you were frightened?"

"I was too confused and too invaded to sort out feelings. I didn't know what they were. I only knew I was in pain and I must get out of pain. I went forward."

Shira could feel him wrestling with language, trying to explain himself. She had an almost tactile sense of his grabbing at words and phrases, cobbling them together as if in a high wind. "One aspect of working with you, even of being with you, that I really appreciate is how hard you try to communicate. Human males don't often have that habit."

"They are not as alone, Shira. Only Malkah ever communicated with me as we do. For a long time I could not sort out what was important from what was trivial in the storm of details assaulting me. In a sense I was born knowing far too much to understand anything. All facts seemed equal to me, any sensory readings as important as any other. That my left foot was seventeen point three centimeters from the lab table appeared as important as my ability to interface with bases at a speed and facility surpassing any human intelligence."

"It fascinates me, what it must be like to be born an adult, to have no childhood."

"I have no mother or father. My only living sibling has the personality of one of those fish you showed me."

"So you really don't think of Avram as your father?"

"Of course not. My relationship with him is one of unequal power, which is like a father-son relationship in minority, as I understand it, but not nearly as complicated or compelling. He manufactured me. He chose to make me exist—but not me as an individual, not who I am, only some of what I can do. I can never dare reveal myself to him. He's more my judge than my father." He turned and stared again at the moon. "Now it's finally turning yellow. How often my stored information is partial. It says a banana is yellow when it is brown and black and yellow, and inside cream with brown flecks. It says the moon is yellow that rose from the bay red. The definitions of feelings I am programmed with are precise, orderly, but what I experience is sometimes sharper than I know how to endure."

"That you have what you call feelings astonishes me."

"What I feel most is loneliness, although for a being who is unique, one of a kind, to feel lonely must appear ironic. When we're together, I'm not lonely, but when you go home, it's worse than it was."

"When you're interfaced with the computer, do you feel lonely?"

"No. I feel engaged then. Inside a great artificial intelligence I can use functions simultaneously and to the max. But I have no sense of companionship there. For me, as for you, a computer's only a tool, not a friend."

"Do you think Avram should not have made you?"

His eyes reflected the moon, more like a cat's eyes than like a person's, shining with a greenish hue, but the effect was not unattractive. "I don't know yet. It took me eighteen months before I could begin to think critically. For a long time, the only comparisons I could make were mathematical or statistical."

"To be so unique has a painful side. I begin to understand a little."

"Ah, Shira, you understand a lot. See, I am beginning to use exclamations. Ah! Oh! Ow! Ai!" He was teasing now, imitating various voices he had heard. "Bless you. Salud. Bye-bye. For shame! Fuck you! Hey, baby! Hooey. Whazat! Wet shit!"

"Soon you can be as foul-mouthed as all the other three-year-old boys."

"I don't understand the concept of dirty words. Why is saying to have sex or to have intercourse acceptable and the word 'fuck,' which means the same thing more economically, a dirty or swear word? Why should a word that means giving and receiving pleasure be used to mean doing someone in, or used as a general insulting adjective? You fucking idiot, to quote Avram."

"It's not rational, but we seem to need words we think are bad. Yod, until you've mastered interactions with humans, I think you should lay off those words."

"Even with you?"

"With me it doesn't matter. Look, now the moon is ivory."

"The moon has no effect upon me except that I find it pleasant to be out here under it. But it affects you, doesn't it? The moon has a powerful influence upon biologically based life forms."

She laughed. "Do you expect me to howl at it like a hound dog?"

"Avram said that the moon had a strong effect on females."

"If you want to know about women, ask me, not Avram."

"I can also ask Malkah about women, if it doesn't concern you personally?"

"Sure." She suppressed a yawn, settling herself more comfortably.

"Are you sleepy?"

"No! Did I sound tired?" She was slightly insulted.

"I don't know how humans sound when they want to sleep, only that they do so at night. I've never seen anyone sleep. It seems mysterious. To be unconscious would be fatal to me. My functions would cease. I saw a dog sleeping once when we were together—you said he was sleeping—but when I bent over him, he lifted his head. I would like to see you sleep."

"Tough luck, Yod. I'm not sleepy. But probably we should go back before Avram becomes frantic. . . ." She began to gather herself to rise. "By the way, isn't he still locking you in the lab? How did you get out?"

Yod anticipated her move and was up and helping her before her first gesture was completed. " 'I picked the lock' is the phrase, I believe, although picking is not apropos, since the lock requires a code to open. I wanted to go out into the night and find you. And I did." He reached over his head and plucked something out of the air. "What's this?" He was holding a brown bat, which hissed and beat its wings in his grip.

"A bat." She gave him a moment to access his base. "Don't hurt it. We're overrun with insects since most birds died. Bats are protected worldwide."

He opened his hand and let the bat go. "It has external parasites."

"It eats insects, and insects eat it. Thank you for not hurting it."

"I didn't think it dangerous. And I'm happy tonight. It's strange. Mostly I like when I'm totally involved and don't feel. Feeling that isn't pain is new."

In the street near the gate, they were stopped by a young woman planting herself before them. "Shira, Shira, don't you recognize me? You're not still mad at me after all these years?" She burst into nervous laughter.

It was the laugh that Shira recognized. "Hannah! I didn't know you were living here."

"I was off in Tokyo studying medicine, but don't we all come back if we can? Even Gadi, I hear, has come home. . . . Aren't you going to introduce me?"

Shira prayed nothing would go wrong. She took Yod's hand in hers: slightly warmer, slightly drier than a human hand but close enough to fool someone who wasn't alerted to the difference, she supposed. She took his hand so that she could signal him if he began to respond oddly. His hand remained inert in hers for a moment and then clasped hers back. She was afraid he would inadvertently crush her hand, but he seemed able to control the pressure he was exerting. "Yod Oblensky, Hannah Leibling. I went to school here with Hannah, Yod. Yod is Avram's cousin. He's come to work with Avram, as I have. Yod is Avram's new lab assistant."

"Oh, you're related to Gadi too. But you don't look like him at all!" She giggled, making her eyes huge in her face.

Her laughter was making Yod uneasy. Too bad. Shira loved the idea of Hannah batting her eyes and sidling up to the cyborg.

"Yes, I'm living here now," Yod said. He was about half a beat off the conversation. But Hannah was only interested in flirting with him.

Shira must explain to him how to flirt back. That would be quite a task. She could see them practicing flirtation routines in the lab, and she almost laughed out loud, silly as Hannah. She tugged on Yod's hand. "We have to be getting back now. Avram's expecting us."

"Well, I just think it's going to be ever so much livelier and more fun around here, with Gadi back and now his cute cousin! Bye-bye!" She broke into a conniption of giggles. How could a woman of twenty-eight still giggle as she had when she was ten?

"Damned silly little twat!" Shira muttered, kicking at a loose stone.

"Twat? That word is not in my dictionary."

"Never mind, Yod. That's one of those dirty words. I don't like Hannah. Forget I said it."

"I can't forget anything. You spoke in a friendly manner, although I could tell you were upset. Your body became rigid. But I liked your taking my hand. That was pleasant. What did she find amusing? Was I behaving in an inappropriate way?"

"She giggles at everything, Yod. It's nothing personal. She was flirting with you, so we must assume she thought you were human."

"Flirting?" There was a pause. He was puzzling over the information, looking up definitions, preparing a query. "Did she wish to initiate a sexual encounter?"

"Flirting usually has little to do with sex: I don't care what your data base says. It's just social grease to make things move and please people. But Hannah would probably have sex with Gimel if given the chance, so don't be flattered."

There was another silence. "But Gimel is not capable of any kind of sexual act."

That makes two of us, she thought as she left Yod to handle Avram by himself. Gimel and me, the entities sex has left behind. "Oh, Yod," she called after him. "My disliking Hannah doesn't mean I need to be defended against her. Don't hurt her. She's no danger."

"I comprehend the difference between dislike and danger, Shira," Yod called back, sounding insulted. "I will not defend you against anchovies."

"You made a joke!" She strolled toward her house. Then she thought, I should have asked him what he would do if Hannah tries to get him into bed. Hannah is fully capable of pressing her luck. I'd better prepare him for dealing with her in a polite but offputting way. Too bad I couldn't have done the same for Gadi, all those years ago, taught him to say no gently but firmly. Cyborgs have certain advantages over people: they can be programmed.

fifteen

THE SAME AS ME

If Gadi was in disgrace, Shira thought, he did not seem to know it. As soon as he was conscious, he began holding court. Fame gilded misadventure. Few women condemn a man for pursuing another woman illegally or inconveniently, and Gadi's flogging seemed to have made him a martyr for sex among the young people of Tikva. The older people might judge him harshly, but he was one of Tikva's famous exports. Everybody was chattering about Gadi, Gadi, Gadi. Shira found herself constantly reminded of his presence, his charm, his aura, even before he summoned her.

If she did not go, everyone would gossip more. If she did not go, she would be revealing fear of him. She had married, borne a child, taken other lovers; did nothing successfully interpose? Was she still a child subject to his whims, vulnerable to smiles and frowns as if they were victories and defeats central to her existence? She dashed about her room, tossing dresses and undergarments to the floor. Half her earrings were strewn over the dark blue coverlet like fallen petals from some exotic tree stripped by the wind. She could not bear the thought of his finding her unattractive. She would appear before him and she would feel the same old pull, she would want him again, while he would be merely friendly. He lived in a world of high glamour, surrounded by reconstructed females, bodies constantly resculpted by scalpels, implants, gels, to the latest image of radiant beauty. She was a techie whose only operation had been retinal implants to correct hereditary myopia. She had borne a child. She would seem almost middle-aged to him. She was commonplace, banally human, as natural as seaweed and mud. She felt ashamed, as if her unaltered, unenhanced body were something gross.

Blue was her favorite color. It set off her skin, her dark hair, her dark eyes. She would feel safest in blue. But what blue? She should not appear too dressed up. She should not appear sloppy or ill-clad. Her clothes had finally arrived and she had a full closet, but many of her things were the style of Y-S, backless and long. She needed a woman friend. Malkah had dozens. "Malkah!" she bellowed. She was ashamed to be overwrought about visiting Gadi in the hospital, but she needed advice.

Malkah came up the steps. "So the prince has sent for you, and every piece of clothing you own is wrong."

"I have to wear something, Malkah. I can't go there naked."

"You'd look stunning. All right, you want a decision. Wear the bright blue sleeveless dress with the U neck and the flowered shawl. Put them on."

Shira obeyed, out of emotional fatigue. Then she clasped on her favorite lapis lazuli necklace, which her mother had given her when she graduated. "I want to look happy. I want to look successful. I want to look like anything but what I am, a twenty-eight-year-old miserable failure."

"Nobody at twenty-eight is a success or a failure. It's too early to figure out which way the tide's moving. . . . Take Yod with you."

"Why?"

"A strange man is the best accessory."

"But Yod isn't."

"Gadi won't guess that. Yet."

"I'd be worrying the whole time that Yod would decide to smash a doctor into the wall for giving an injection, or Gadi will say, Can you raise my bed a little, and Yod will pick up the whole apparatus."

"Good. That's exactly what you need for facing Gadi. Take a problem with you, and Gadi won't be your focus."

"Malkah, you're a genius. But I'll have to persuade Avram. He's beginning to prepare Yod for defense of our Base." She had gradually been introducing Yod into groups of people. Several times, Avram, Yod and she had dined in the Commons. Most evenings she walked Yod all over Tikva. Yesterday afternoon she had taken him to observe a teenage soccer game. He did not find soccer any more entertaining than she did, but he thought people fascinating. She tried, however, to avoid extended one-on-one conversation. She had outfitted Yod in the usual summer uniform of young men in Tikva: shorts or pullover—tee or tank—with a contrasting scarf.

She found Yod playing go with the computer while Avram critiqued his game and on another terminal kept up with his technical journals. Avram's first reaction was utter refusal, but Yod argued hard too. "Your biological son can't be kept from meeting me. When he comes home, you can't go back to locking me in the laboratory."

"Should have built you with an Off button," Avram mumbled. "Don't bet I can't design a security apparatus that will keep you in!"

"I doubt that, Father, but I must assume my duties soon anyhow. Locking me in will have to stop."

Yod spoke quite differently to Avram than he did to her or Malkah. He spoke more precisely, more coldly. Which was real? What did it mean to think of a real affect for a machine? Could Yod simply alter his style to please each of them in turn? Well, didn't people do the same? "This might be an ideal way to introduce them. It is likely Gadi will pay more attention to me than to Yod."

"Perhaps it has a use," Avram muttered. "I certainly don't want to introduce them. Beat the computer at go, Yod, and I'll let you. Otherwise Shira visits alone." He settled back in his chair with a little smile. She was reminded of the civil war between Gadi and Avram when Avram had tried to make him play chess or go. Gadi hated competitive games. All of Avram's attempts to teach Gadi chess ended in mutual temper tantrums, father and son glaring in silence like stuffed owls over the lopsided board.

So why wasn't Avram playing games with Yod? Because Yod could too easily beat him?

A look of manic concentration came over Yod's face. His eyes glittered. He bared his teeth slightly. He began playing twice as fast. Within fifteen minutes the computer conceded and he was free.

When they got outside, Yod assumed his usual position, on the street side as they walked. He liked to interpose himself between her and as much of the world as possible. At times he ducked around her to and fro like a large dog. "You're dressed differently tonight. For instance, when we go out, you do not wear such a dress that shines." He pinched the cloth between his fingers.

"Silk."

"What is the purpose of that object around your neck?"

"It's a necklace my mother gave me. Just to look good."

"Would I look better to you if I wore stones around my neck?"

"Men sometimes wear pendants—a single stone. It depends on the place."

"It depends on the neck, to be precise." He smiled. Perhaps he was making a joke. A weak pun. "Body covering has symbolic and aesthetic values that elude me. Clearly this climate in June is warm enough so that there's no real use to clothing."

"As an adult, when you strip, you make yourself vulnerable. Nakedness has a symbolic side also."

Yod was silent for the next two blocks. That was unusual enough for her to take his arm and ask, "Yod, what's wrong?"

"I'm trying to overcome a desire to attack Gadi as soon as I see him."

"Yod, if you're thinking of attacking him, you go straight home."

"I'm in control. I promise I am in control."

"Why do you want to attack him?"

"Both you and Avram perceive him as a threat."

"Not a threat like pirates or organ scavengers, who kill people. Just a source of discomfort." She held on to Yod's arm. "If you think you may attack, you must go home."

"I won't attack. I will be still. Keep holding on to me."

"I can't do that in the room, when we go in. Why do you want me to?"

"It helps me to keep control. Half of me wants to demolish him. Half of me is curious and wants to know him."

"Yod, could you be jealous of Gadi? Is that possible?"

"I don't know what jealousy is, precisely, as applied to myself. It's true, he's the biological son. I'm a weapon, a tool, but also designed to perform well at activities Gadi failed."

"Then he should be jealous of you."

"Why? I'm not even human. Half the time you don't think I'm real, not fully real, not as real as Gadi."

"Is anyone as real to me as Gadi? Only my son."

Gadi's room was in the recovery wing of the hospital, rooms that opened on an external corridor, rooms with trees in buckets and window boxes full of flowers. In his window box verbena grew. She had to pull her gaze away from the bright heads of flowers and make herself meet Gadi's cool stare. His room was full of toys, presents, objets d'art, fresh bouquets.

He was sitting up in bed, wearing purple into mauve translucent silk pajamas, with an amethyst band about his head, enhanced jewels, small but very reflective. He also wore one long amethyst earring and a large amethyst square-cut on his left-hand wedding ring finger. "Gadi, are you engaged?" she asked, pointing at the ring.

"To myself. 'Above all else to thine own self be true'? Isn't that the quote? Who's this?" He drew himself up in bed. She could tell he was not pleased. His gaze ran pointedly up and down Yod, who stood as close to her as he could get without actually squatting on her head.

"This is Yod Oblensky, Avram's cousin." Oh, shit, she thought, Gadi is going to know Avram doesn't have a cousin Yod. "His second cousin. He's working for Avram too, as you know I am now."

"One happy lab rat family," Gadi intoned, extending his hand.

"Gently," she muttered to Yod as he pounced on Gadi's hand.

"Yod Oblensky? I don't remember. . . . Family is one of those tedious subjects I have never bothered to keep up with. I suppose then we're second cousins once removed, whatever that means, although removing relatives does appear attractive." Gadi motioned Shira toward the bed. "Sit here."

Yod promptly sat on the bed between Shira and Gadi. "Thank you."

Shira had an abrupt desire to giggle. Gadi looked astounded. Yod was heavier than a person of his size would be, and the bed sagged alarmingly. Shira sat in the only chair. "How are you feeling?"

"How do you suppose I'm feeling? They had to replace a kidney. My poor body has been extensively processed by various machines, what else? I can't wait to get out. Boring! I must figure out what to do with myself for the next three to six months, until I'm redeemed, resurrected and can ascend again to the heights of stimmieland."

"Perhaps you could be knocked out till your time is up," Shira said. "That would eliminate the boredom."

"Don't be nasty. I'm delighted you're here. That puts a whole different cast on events. We can amuse each other."

"Perhaps so," Yod said. He intentionally moved into the line of sight between them. "What do you think you'll do?"

"I haven't been conscious long enough to slap plans together. I'll improvise and play with Shira. Annoy my father. See old friends. Maybe teach some bright local kids about stimmies, run a sort of school in the streets. Graduation prize being a chance back in Veecee Beecee. Maybe I'll make Shira the heroine of a fabulous adventure among the Green Fang People."

A suspicion took her, a cold sinking suspicion, that Gadi was assuming they would become reinvolved. He might well think that way: she was available, convenient, with the intervening years giving her a patina of novelty. It was hopeless. It could not work. It would be fatal. She would love him again, and he would not love her. It was a pit.

"Hannah is here," Yod said. "Perhaps you can play with her."

How did Yod know about Hannah and Gadi? Certainly Avram never told him. It had to be Malkah, conspiring with him again. How could she keep her grandmother from gossiping with her cyborg? Or had Hannah herself told him? "Yod, you're a terrible gossip. You love to collect old scandal."

"Everything about Shira interests me," Yod said blandly to Gadi.

"I can see that," Gadi said. Shira strained back in the chair so that she could catch a glimpse of Gadi around Yod. Gadi looked annoyed, his eyes slitted. Then he produced a broad smile. "Last time I was here I tried to go swimming at the white beach where we used to so many times, but it's drowned now. It's just an offshore island. And the fisherman's house where he used to stack his lobster pots to dry—remember he gave us a bag of lobsters once and we carried them home?"

"I'd forgotten." For a moment she warmed to him, remembering the pot Malkah had set to boil, the feast under the peach tree. "Who did you try to go swimming with?"

"I was thinking of you the whole time. . . ."

Two guys they had gone to school with ten years before arrived with three teenagers, all breathless about meeting the designer of Mala Tuni's last seven stims, the designer who had created Devora, Land of Endless Desire. Shira took the opportunity to slip out, tugging Yod along. He came semireluctantly. She could tell he was curious about the group and still eager to try to confront Gadi. When they were on the street, she felt herself sagging with relief. "I can't believe I got through that."

"With one blow I could smash his skull."

"Stop that. Do you want me to be afraid of you?"

"I exist to protect you. I would never let harm come to you. Never."

"No one can keep anyone else from all harm, Yod. I could be harboring a disease at this moment. I could be struck by a piece of a falling satellite. But you did make it easier for me to see him."

"He wants you. He wants to have you back."

"I doubt it," she said lightly, walking more quickly.

"Don't doubt it. He wants you."

"How would you know that?"

"I recognize it. It is the same as me."

"What?" But she had heard him, and she kept walking numbly, more slowly. "That can't be."

"It is. The wanting is the same."

How did I let this happen? she wondered. How *can* it happen? This is nonsense. This is absurd. I am not hearing what I think I am hearing. This walking computer cannot want to perforate me. "Yod, you're a very intelligent and able machine, but you're a machine. What does it mean to want a person?"

"I want to do with you exactly what he wants to. But I can do it better. I promise. I'm stronger than Gadi, more intelligent, more able in every way. I want to please you far more than he ever could."

This was a facsimile talking, a machine like a beverage dispenser, and it was spouting nonsense. Fused circuits? Overload? Malfunction? She did not want to confront Avram, but she would surely bring up this malfunction with Malkah. "Avram hired me to teach you social interactions. That doesn't include sexual initiation, frankly."

"I don't require initiation."

"You're telling me you've been with women sexually?"

"Only one. So far."

Had Hannah got to him so quickly? It would not astonish Shira. But then could Hannah be so stupid as to fail to observe he was not human? None of that speculation got her off the large hook on which she was dangling. However absurd she found being propositioned by a computer, she had to let him down gently as if he were a human male. "Yod, I don't want to become involved with anyone. I've told you I can't respond. I'm a kind of cripple. And it would be extremely inappropriate. I don't believe in complicating the teacher-student relationship, which ought to remain disinterested."

"I am not disinterested. It's an obvious equation. As Gadi is to you, so you are to me."

"If you can see how miserable my early fix on Gadi made me, can't you abort what is obviously a losing pattern?"

"If you're with me, you'll feel protected from him." They were walking along the street just outside the old hotel. In the shadow of a large maple that filtered the light from the antique streetlamps, Yod stepped in front of her. He bent forward and laid his hand gently along her cheek, fingers spread. Lightly, barely perceptibly, his fingers explored from cheekbone to chin.

Unbelievably, she felt a stir of response in herself. She stepped back, jerking away. "No, Yod. No. Can I trust you to listen to me?"

"You can always trust me." He dropped his hand and retreated a step, clasping his hands behind his back. "I obey." He went up the steps to the door. He took hold of the doorknob and then, with a twitch, crushed it. Slowly he entered, stopping to glance back at her where she stood under the maple. She hoped he would not entirely demolish Gimel in their martial arts routine that night.

sixteen

LITTLE GIRL LOST

Summer has landed; the heat is enervating. However, in Prague in 1600 it is April, season of buds unfurling and small persistent rains. The rain is pattering on the gray stone and the mustard and terra-cotta stucco, on the red tiles of the roofs, on the gray waters of the Vltava, on the hills and the winding alleys that climb them, streets that are steps worn by centuries of feet. The castle on its cliffs hangs like a mirage at the top of random ways. Old lindens bend over courtyards where four hundred years later I drank wine and ate traif, at inns marked by the signs that name them in the time of Rabbi Loew: a hunter and an elk, three swans, a bear dancing, two camels. Twilight and love affairs seem about to stretch on forever. I was younger than Shira is. No one born now will experience the world of gentle air we could walk through on impulse, without protection, winds and rain that caressed our skin, deep thick woods, grass like green hair growing thick from the moist earth. We were killing the world, but it was not yet dead. The world of my youth was still the earth of 1600, when the Maharal penned up in the ghetto seldom sees trees, either, but paces in his worrying and prays.

Now Passover approaches, time for anti-Semites to crank up the favorite fable of the time, the blood libel. (Lest we imagine, dear Yod, that this is a quaint medieval superstition, let me remark that in 1899 a Czech Jewish shoemaker was brought to trial on charges of ritual murder in which it was claimed the whole Jewish community of a village was involved. He was promptly convicted in the press and then in court and only saved from death by Tomáš Masaryk, later founder of the Czech republic.) Every night the Golem stalks the streets in feverish quest for troublemakers. Saturday of the week before Pesach, he catches two toughs carrying between them a burden wrapped in old carpeting. He lays one out with a blow, crushes the other under his foot while he unwraps the carpeting to expose the bruised body of a young boy whose head has been bashed in. He ties the two toughs to the body and carries them to the watch. Maybe they were just getting rid of the body and the ghetto seemed a likely place; maybe they were going to plant it to be discovered as proof of Jewish ritual murder.

In gentile Prague a story begins to circulate that shortly becomes a festering scandal: a maidservant from the household of a prominent knight has disappeared, vanished on the day she was sent to redeem a pledge from a Jewish moneylender. Maria is a sixteen-year-old who shines in all the reports ever more virginal and pure, more pious and more beautiful. Maria has disappeared, and the rumor circulates like a growing bad smell that the Jews have kidnapped and murdered her, for the Christian blood to make matzoh.

"Search," the Maharal tells the Golem. "I don't doubt she's been murdered. Find the corpse. I'm sure it is already secreted in the ghetto or about to be. They're going to plant her body on us, I know it."

Down the darkest back alleys, into cellars, old excavations, tunnels, buildings that have fallen in, the Golem roams, daytime and night, searching for the body of a girl he has never met. Maria has been briefly described to him: braided brown hair, blue eyes, wearing a red coarsely spun overskirt, a brown smock. Around her neck hung a necklace made of a single gold coin strung on a ribbon, and a second ribbon with a wooden cross on it. She is of medium height, with a scar on the back of her left hand. She was born to a family of servants who worked for the knight on his country estate. She had found favor and been brought to the city to work as a housemaid.

Nobody remembers seeing her, nobody remembers anybody bearing a suspicious burden into the ghetto. Joseph wonders if she exists, this adolescent he is vainly pursuing. Sometimes an image of her forms in his mind, but it keeps shifting. He realizes after a while he is using faces of women he has seen in the streets to make this girl more real, for he feels the futility of his search slowing him day after night after day.

Joseph has run out of places to search in the ghetto. He swears to the Maharal that the girl cannot be hidden within the walls. Joseph cannot find Maria, and now Isa the Deaf, who delivers kosher wine, has disappeared as well. Samuel the tailor provides Joseph with the clothes of a gentile drayman. So that Joseph can pass through the city freely, Judah gives him permission to remove the yellow badge they all must wear. The Maharal fills Joseph's pocket with coins, warning him about their use and display. Now Joseph must search in the large and strange world outside.

As he passes through the gates of the ghetto he knows now as well as any of the humans who live there, he feels a heady mixture of fear and exultation. He is escaping—from who he is. From the Maharal. From his many duties, although in the service of one of them. From observation. From accountability minute by minute. From the knowledge and potential knowledge of who and what he is. He is just a huge man jostled by others in the street. It occurs to him that he could run off from his fate and live as other men do, as it has occurred to Jews in every time to sneak out of being Jewish, to take on the coloration and the jargon of the prevailing culture—Christian, Islamic, corporate—and simply give up the prickly destiny, the treasure that so often kills. If he simply keeps walking, he could hire out his strength and live in pleasant obscurity, enjoying his daily bread and wine.

Out of the ghetto he goes, along the river to the square of the knights of the cross and the fortified tower entrance to the great stone bridge named after the emperor Charles, the Karl bridge. As he traverses the Vltava, he can see the towers and spires of the vast block where Hradcany Castle and the cathedral stand, but his way leads at once into the partly aristocratic Malá Strana, where he hopes to bring the mystery to ground. How many crosses stand everywhere. They seem to him sinister as swords drawn.

The knight's house is near the river, in a neighborhood dominated by a seminary and a brewery. Joseph's careful observation of human behavior provides him with an idea how to proceed. He finds a likely tavern near the house of the knight. He requires gossip, ordinary neighborhood gossip. He requires a sense of who is connected to whom.

He gets little in the first tavern, except an offer for an afternoon's work, which he takes to increase his credibility. He helps the man load a cart with barrels from the brewery, to which the tavern is attached, and then deliver them. In the course of the afternoon he learns that Maria was a house servant and seldom seen outside. Her parents only arrived in the city after her disappearance. Previously they had worked in a dairy at the knight's country estate. Stefan Zacek is the knight's name.

In the next tavern, where he spends the evening drinking and standing drinks, he learns that although Maria has rarely been glimpsed, all agree on her beauty, especially those who have never laid eyes on her. Her beauty, like her odor of sanctity, gathers interest and grows with the retelling. The wife of the knight is widely regarded as a much put upon woman, usually pregnant. She has borne the knight eight living children, nobody bothering with a count of miscarriages and stillbirths. She is pious and suffers from most complaints known to too often pregnant women, including early toothlessness.

Fortunately the Golem can pour alcohol into himself without consequence, except that after a while, his body being finite, it must pass on out. Water, wine, beer, brandy, milk: his body processes what energy it can from them, and one substance is like another. Still, he imitates the mannerisms of the men around him lest they notice how impervious he is. They admire his capacity, but he is careful to slur his words. When he tries to eat the local salami, the first bite burns his mouth as if it were corrosive. Then he understands. He can eat bricks, chew stones, eat crockery, but he cannot eat traif. He shakes his head sadly. His fantasies of disappearing into the world dwindle. How can a golem who eats bricks but not pork ever hope to pass in Bohemia?

The knight Stefan, the men say, some with admiration, others with contempt, is a gambler. He bets on everything from horse races to whether it will rain or snow, the outcome of fights and matches, how many balls a juggler can keep aloft. He has squandered his wife's dowry and much of his own inheritance in games of chance. When he wins, he thinks of his bounty as money from heaven and spends it fast, often on the higher class of prostitutes, sometimes on presents for his wife and many children. When he loses, he always imagines his misfortune temporary and borrows to pay off his gambling debts. Who does he borrow from? The Jews, of course, those bloodsucking sly greedy monsters; they lend him money.

Who in particular? Who lends money so easily to a gambler? Why, Maisl the Weasel. Not the richest man in the ghetto, Mordecai, but his less astute baby brother, Eli. That's the bloodsucker Stefan owes his ass to. Joseph has seen Eli in the synagogue. He resembles the weasel the gentiles call him only in his extreme thinness and his nervous habit of moving fast. His complexion is yellowish. He has stomach troubles. Otherwise he is a timid man of forty-five with a slight stammer and a history of having failed at the export-import business and several others. Mordecai, the greatest success the ghetto knows, who lends money to emperors and finances exploration and trading expeditions off the edge of charted lands, picks up his brother, dusts him off, gives him a few wise words to no avail, sets him on his feet and gives him a new business to fail at every few years.

After the tavern closes, Joseph, awash but still sober as a paving stone, stands in a doorway, contemplating the knight's house. In there must lie the answer. He hopes they are all asleep. As he circles the block of which the house is part, dodging from shadow to shadow, he listens. On the back side of the house, toward the river, he scales a low wall, dropping into a courtyard. How much more spacious the houses are here, wasting the land behind them in trees and a kitchen garden. A dog lunges at him, barking. The Golem stands still. The dog falls silent, hangs back, sniffing. This does not smell like a man. This smells like nothing but a wall. He comes tentatively forward to sniff again. Joseph does not even blink. The dog sidles closer yet. Joseph reaches out and breaks its neck in one blow. He feels the surprised life leaving the dog, and he has a moment of severe guilt. The dog, the men of the watch, they are the same, alive and now dead. Dead under his hands. He stands over the cooling body of the dog and prays for it. If it has no soul, whatever that is, presumably neither does he.

But he has been given his orders, and he knows the necessity. From the courtyard there is an entrance to a cellar. The wide double doors are locked, but he breaks the lock without hesitation, cautiously descending the broad steps where barrels of wine and beer, apples and cabbages, are carried down. It is dark and damp; it is the inside of a black and slightly rotten potato, perhaps one that has frozen and thawed. Mice scuttle away. Hams are hung from the ceiling, sausages cured in the fall. He has discovered that he cannot eat traif, so he dips out sauerkraut from a barrel to satisfy his hunger while he stumbles around looking for a body. He finds an old carpet, broken chairs, rusted weapons, stored grain and mice to eat it. As he chews thoughtfully on a piece of tile, he wonders what he is doing in this cellar, creeping around in the middle of the night. He helps himself to a supply of candles and a tinder to light them.

What he does find, after an intensive search of the wine cellar, the root cellar, the vault where ice is stored in straw, is a locked passage, which he unlocks with his hands. This is even darker. To find his way, he must light a candle. The air is poor and the candle flickers wildly, a small drooping flame as he passes from under the knight's house, on and on for what feels like miles but is probably a hundred yards. Finally he reaches the end of the passage, locked also but easily opened. He is now in another cellar, colder, just as dark, with a strong smell of fish and human piss. Water is dripping. He suspects he has approached the river. It seems to him he can feel the river flowing past the far wall.

A hoarse voice calls out in the darkness: "Let me out. Who is it? Vaclav? I'm hungry. Vaclav, where are you?"

He follows the voice to another locked door, which he breaks open, shattering the heavy wood with one blow. He raises his candle and stares at the woman cowering at the end of a chain running from her leg to a loop set in the wall. Her hair is matted and her face swollen. She shrinks from him, covering her face as if to make him vanish. "Who are you?" he asks.

"Maria," the woman says. "Pane, sir, are you going to kill me?"

"I'm Joseph. I'm here to get you out." He reaches for her arm.

She backs from him. "You're going to kill me! I know it. Pane Stefan sent you. This is his." She pats her belly. "Why should he care? Other men have bastards and take care of them."

"He does plan to have you killed, for he's put it out you were kidnapped." Joseph rips the chain from the wall, lifting the candle to examine her leg.

"Who'd kidnap me? Who wants a servant with her master's bastard in her belly? Not even my parents would take me back."

"Everyone in the city is saying the Jews took you for your blood."

"Are you a Jew? Are you going to kill me?"

"Don't scream. We don't kill, even when we should. I'm here to prove you're still alive. We're going to the town hall."

"How can I believe you? Vaclav said I was going to die today."

"Come on." Picking her up like a sack of potatoes, he slings her over his shoulder. She starts screaming. He tears off part of his shirt and binds her mouth. He finds another exit, but the steps lead to a door not only locked but wedged into place. He puts her down, holding her with one hand while he shoves at the door. With a loud clatter, stones roll, and then he can force it. They are indeed just off the quay. The moon is up, two days short of the full. Tomorrow the Passover matzoh will be baked. In the stable, horses wait in their stalls, and between the rows of stalls, a delivery cart stands loaded with kosher wine. That's Isa the Deaf's cart. What is it doing here? This is nowhere near the kosher winery. One empty barrel stands beside the cart. Over the seat are laid the clothes of the deliveryman, Isa the Deaf. On the overcoat Joseph notices a little blood. He doubts they will see Isa again.

He turns to pick her up. She has risen to her feet but is not running. She pulls the gag loose. Backed against the wall, she glares at him.

"Don't start screaming again," Joseph says wearily. "If you rouse one of them, the men who captured you, you'll end up in that barrel and I'll lie on the bottom of the river like the poor man whose clothes are spattered with his blood. I'm not rescuing you because I like you. I've been sent to save you for the good of my people. Now shut up and let me get you out of here."

"I can walk."

"You can't walk fast enough. You're too weak." He picks her up again over his shoulder. This time she does not scream but beats on his back.

"Don't carry me with my head down, you ox, you horse, you beast! The blood rushes to my head."

"How shall I carry you?" Joseph is trotting at a steady clip along an alley and then in the general direction of the town hall, uphill.

"In front, like a man is supposed to carry a woman."

Her head is thumping against his back, so he obeys her, finding a position she seems to like. She puts an arm around his neck. "This isn't so bad. Are we really going to the Malá Strana town hall?"

"Yes. You aren't frightened of me any longer?"

"Well, not so much. If you were going to kill me, you wouldn't carry me around in the streets for an hour first."

"I told you the truth. Shh." He takes refuge in a doorway, cupping his hands over her mouth.

She bites him, and he inadvertently draws his hand back. But she does not scream. She just pokes him and whispers, "We should crouch and cover our faces. They have torches. Skin picks up light—did you ever notice?"

Four men march along with a quasi-military step in the direction Joseph planned to take.

"Look, the town hall won't open till morning. We might as well take our time. You don't have to haul me around like a sack of potatoes." She has recovered her spirits. Beautiful she isn't, even in the soft light of the moon. Of course she is dirty and odorous from her captivity, her hair matted. But her features are sharp, pointy. "What's your name, giant?"

He let her walk and marches beside her. "I'm Joseph." Something seems to be happening farther up the hill. He is not certain what to do.

"Maria and Joseph and little baby in the womb, the son of the lord! Lord Stefan." She laughs mischievously, sliding her arm through his. Her laugh is deep and rowdy, making him want to laugh with her, only he does not ever laugh. He does not know how. "You smashed that door as if it was woven of reeds and you threw the stones away from the entrance to the cellar like cushions."

"The holy one made me strong."

"He sure did." She squeezes his arm. "You have muscles like rocks, Joe. Is that what they call you—Joe?"

"No . . . They just call me Joseph."

"Come on, take this chain off me. It weighs a ton, and my ankle is bleeding from it."

He kneels to bend the metal apart. Her ankle is bloody. He watches her carefully as he bends over the chain, but she does not try to play any tricks. When he stands, she takes his arm again, ready to walk on. She wraps the chain around her arm like a bracelet, swinging the end. He is worrying about the armed men who just passed them. A patrol? "I think we should go to the Old Town Hall, across the river. It might be safer."

"Stefan was really sweet to me at first. You know, you see your master all the time, drunk and sober and picking his nose, but when he starts paying attention to you, even though you know what he is really, it's like an angel speaking to you. Do you have a master?"

"I do. But he's never drunk."

"I figured you were a servant like me. Stefan, my master, he was all of the time giving me little presents, and he had nice ways. He gave me a brand-new white apron and a cap and a blue woolen shawl, and a gold coin I wore around my neck till Vaclav took it. He said I made him laugh."

"I believe it."

"I'm grown up for my age, Joe. Half the girls in the house, they don't know how men are made, but I was raised with animals and brothers. The minute I was carrying, I knew it. I thought he'd be happy. I thought, Now I've got my place for sure. He'll set me up and take good care of me. Ha! I still don't understand what hold his old fat wife has on him, but she does. I didn't know he'd be mad—after all, what did he expect, putting it to me every day? I surely never guessed he'd lock me in a cellar and give it out I was dead."

"You would have been, soon enough."

"I know that, Joe. Vaclav, who brought me my food, told me so. Vaclav always gave me sour looks. He said I wouldn't put out for him, so I deserved what I was getting."

The tower on the bridge is closed. They cannot cross until dawn. Joseph leads them to the stable of an inn next to the tower. "You can rest in the straw. I'll stand guard."

Instead she cleans herself up in the horse trough. "I don't want to look a complete mess at town hall. People are more likely to believe you if you look good—have you ever noticed?"

"Never," Joseph says. He squats with his back to her, watching the courtyard between the stable and the inn. He will be able to hear her if she tries to sneak up on him or to creep out.

Somewhat later he hears her coming up quietly behind him, and he swings about defensively, ready for an attack. Instead he sees her, quite naked, with her wet hair hanging down her back like a broad sleek ribbon, coming toward him with a little smile. She does not resemble the women he has accompanied Chava to, huge in the belly. She has only a slight swelling. If she had not told him, he would not know she is pregnant, but he supposes that Chava would know at once. Her body is rosy, small and high-waisted, broad-hipped, with pert breasts that seem to peer in different directions. She carries no weapon, and her smile only broadens as he looks at her.

"Joseph, have you never seen a naked woman before?"

"Never."

"You're fooling me. At your age?"

"I'm younger than I look," the Golem says honestly. He rises to his feet, keeping an ear tuned to the courtyard.

"Big men like you often seem older than they are. I'm sixteen. What are you?" She puts her hands on his shoulders.

"I'm no older than you are."

"I like that." She begins to rub her hips against him. "I'm grateful to you. Now they'll probably shove me in a convent. It doesn't count if I do it with you, because I'm already in the family way."

By now Joseph has figured out what she means. He stands very still, more frightened than desirous. "I don't know how."

"I didn't either, but Stefan showed me. Unless Jews are made differently? I heard you are." She tugs at his baggy pants, loosening them. "I figure you have to get children the same old way, right?"

Joseph finds himself with his pants down around his ankles and his penis standing up and out while her fingers run cleverly around it. "Well, it's different. But it looks as if it works the same way. Want me to show you the game Stefan taught me?"

Joseph jerks back. "Shh! Someone's coming." He grabs her, scoops up her pile of clothes. They creep into an empty stall. The light of a lantern shines into the stable. A horse whinnies recognition. The hostler has come to lead it out. "Come on, Mudjumper, we got a long way to go today. They'll be opening the bridge any moment." He leads the horse to the trough, but the horse shies at the water.

"Looks dirty to me too," the man says. "I'm going to say a nasty word to our landlord. They got such a good situation they think they can deal sloppy with us, hey, old girl?"

"Get dressed," Joseph whispers as the man leads the horse into the courtyard. "We'll go through behind him."

Dawn is just streaking the sky, clouds like smoke drifting low over the buildings, mist skeining the river. As they walk about twenty yards behind, waiting for the gates to open, Joseph feels a great relief. He was curious but frightened in the stable. He imagines his great weight crushing life from the girl, her fragile bones splintering in his massive grasp.

Still, he is quietly pleased that she thought he was a man like other men. Now he has nothing he must conceal from the Maharal. He has done his duty and nothing else. Still he wonders what it would have felt like, he wonders whether he should not have tried with her. She has abandoned the idea as quickly as she happened on it. Now she ambles by his side, limping slightly on her sore ankle, clutching his arm, looking all around and occasionally giving the chain a swing so that it clanks. With her hair drying loose and her face clean, she looks like a pleasant child. Trustingly she clings to his arm, letting him draw her along. What will become of her? That is not his business. He has not made it his business. He belongs to the Maharal and not to Maria. He thinks she will probably make her way; at least he hopes so. He wants to tell her that he likes her and wishes her well, but even this he does not know how to say.

seventeen

THE SON OF FRANKENSTEIN

Shira felt nervous when she came to work the next day, but Yod was in his cold Avram mode. It was as if nothing had been said between them under the maple tree. They playacted social scenarios all morning, giving him practice shopping, selecting food, interacting with guards, meeting people on the street and in the Commons. Avram watched and critiqued. "Too wooden, much too wooden." "No, he sounds like a recording."

Then Avram began working with Yod in simulated attacks while interfaced in the Tikva Base. Shira was free to leave. Malkah was working at home more and more, since she was expecting Riva. Today she was cooperating with Avram in Yod's exercises. When Shira walked in, Malkah was plugged in and did not notice her. People fully interfaced saw nothing except in their own mind. The computer-generated images assumed far greater reality than the stimulation of the optical nerves by actual sight. Shira considered plugging in to watch their war games, but she decided to putter around the courtyard, pruning, transplanting seedlings, deadheading flowers.

An hour later, Malkah withdrew. "Are they finished?" Shira asked.

"Not nearly, but I am. They can go on attacking, defending, but I have my new chimera to work on. It has wonderful little worms embedded throughout, infinite burnout loops. An intruder could destroy two thirds of their forces in penetration, never realizing it's only a chimera. I surpass myself. Let's have tea and muffins. Then I'll go back to work on it."

Both were coffee drinkers, so tea was a very occasional treat. They set up their table under the tree whose peaches were still swelling, its long languid leaves drooping over them. "Malkah, something disturbing happened last night. Yod expressed desire toward me."

"Well, you've been spending huge amounts of time together, Shira. I suppose you were shocked."

"What kind of programming did you give him? Is he going to attack me?"

"He has total inhibition blocks against sexual violence. You're safer with him than with any other male in Tikva. Or perhaps the world."

"He isn't a male. He's a machine."

"Avram made him male—entirely so. Avram thought that was the ideal: pure reason, pure logic, pure violence. The world has barely survived the males we have running around. I gave him a gentler side, starting with emphasizing his love for knowledge and extending it to emotional and personal knowledge, a need for connection. . . ."

"What Avram's notes lack is what differentiates Yod from the failures that preceded him. That's your work, right?"

Malkah nodded. "Have you accessed Avram's logs on Alef through Tet?"

"I've read his summaries, but the actual logs are sealed."

"Not to me." Malkah gave her a wide wicked grin. "I plundered them, realizing I needed more information than Avram was about to give me, when I got involved in programming Yod. I'll shunt it through to your private base right now, and you can study it at your leisure."

"Do that. I'll look at that material once I've got through Avram's notes. But, Malkah, I have Avram's notes and his log. Where are *your* crystals of that work? I want to load that too."

"Didn't I give them to Avram? They must be around someplace."

"Could you look for them?"

"Oh, sure. I'll look. I haven't used them in months."

Malkah plugged in and went back to work. Shira set out to slog through more of Avram's notes. She was convinced Malkah knew where her own crystals were, for it would be out of character for her to misplace anything. Malkah inhabited the house comfortably and totally, as if it were a favorite sweater. She knew exactly where she kept herb tea for a cold, the holos of Shira as a baby, crystals of work she had completed twenty years before. Malkah had some reason to hide her notes, instead of letting Shira see them.

They were sitting as so often, companionably, each plugged in, each in a favorite chair. Shira was only lightly connected, not projected into her personal base, just reading notes, stopping to make notes of her own.

Malkah was into the Tikva Base, fully projected. Moving in and out of large AI data bases was something taught all children in Tikva but an ability possessed by only the more educated in the Glop. The ability to access the world's information and resculpt it was the equivalent of the difference between the propertied and the landless in the past of lords and serfs. Keeping Tikva a free town was dependent on their Base and its maintained integrity. In the Base they built chimeras, systems, defenses to be sold to multis. Otherwise they'd be gobbled up by a multi and redone overnight. Only towns that sold something unique survived free, for the multis would just as soon end the trade. A town needed to be selling to several rival multis, as Tikva did, to maintain that fragile independence, so that one multi would not let another commandeer it.

The notes commanded her full attention. Yod's tactile senses were far finer than human. He also had the ability to measure distance precisely, using a subsonic echo, much as bats navigated; no wonder he'd been able to pluck the bat out of the night air. She smiled. He was equipped with sensor readouts of temperature, the same way her own retinal clock gave her a time readout whenever she thought the question. He could heft something and weigh it accurately in the palm of his hand. His hearing extended into the range of a dog's; his normal sight in dark rooms was equal to a house cat's, but he also had infrared on call. "They didn't do anything interesting, and they only did that once." He was incorrigible. Stubborn as a human being. No matter what Avram said and Yod promised, he did not always obey. He obeyed sometimes, but at other times he did exactly what he pleased.

She heard a scream, saved and exited, rising to her feet. Malkah had fallen from her chair. The plug had slid free. Shira ran to her, clenched in fright. Had Malkah been attacked? Five dead, two others vegetables. "I activated an emergency call," the house said. "Medics. Do we need security?"

"Medics, yes. Wait for security decision." Shira knelt over Malkah, who lay crumpled. She felt for a pulse in the wrist; nothing discernible. In the temple. Ah, there. Erratic, weak. A heart attack? Malkah's lids fluttered. Please, please, please, Shira thought, although she did not believe in personal prayer. It was irrational to suppose a holy force could be petitioned to do or not to do something. Please, I can't lose her, I can't. She chafed Malkah's temples as if that could bring her back. I can't lose Ari and her. "Malkah, please come back. Please. Open your eyes. Please."

Embedded in a base, plugged in, a person was vulnerable to mental warfare. The very neural pathways that the impulses from the machine traveled into the brain could be burned out, the brain rendered passive as a sponge. The mind could be forced into a catatonic loop. A program could be launched that froze the ability to breathe. The brain could be simply shocked to death like an electrocuted rat. If information pirates, if raiders or assassins broke into a base, they could set traps, they could ambush and kill as well as steal the artifacts created there. There were multi raiders and free-lance pirates.

Malkah opened her eyes. They closed again immediately, and she went limp. Shira chafed her hands. She slapped Malkah's cheeks. She listened to her heart, resting her cheek against Malkah's chest and smelling sandalwood. Finally the medics arrived. Three of them squatted around Malkah and began working on her. Shira hovered, feeling in the way, frightened, wanting to pester them to know Malkah's condition but aware that she must let them work. The house said, "Shira, you have an incoming message from Avram."

"Avram, Malkah has just been attacked."

"Yod said something had happened. He suddenly pulled out of the simulation and disappeared. He was able to break off their attack, but he couldn't tell if Malkah was injured."

One of the medics sat back. Now Shira recognized her as Hannah. "How is my grandmother?"

"She's weak, but she's conscious. You can speak to her." In her work role, Hannah did not giggle. She was businesslike, her hands moving deftly among the devices and their readouts.

"Malkah, you were attacked in the Base?"

"Yes," Malkah answered weakly. She looked and sounded like an old lady. Her voice was feeble. Her eyes would not open all the way.

"Is she going to be all right? Is there neural damage?"

"Not like we've seen on the others," Hannah said. "We'll take her into the hospital to run some tests. But that she can speak is astonishing."

She prepared to leave with them. "Avram, you heard that? I'll be in touch later."

MALKAH CAME HOME the next day, going straight to bed. She was drained and shaken, but essentially undamaged. "Yod saved my life," she said, lying in her high old carved bed, a massive piece of furniture made by a great-granduncle who had been a back-to-the-earth artisan in the days when trees had grown in abundance and wood had been common instead of precious. One bedpost was carved with the date 1979. Their wooden furniture, Malkah had often told Shira, was worth a fortune, but she would never sell it off.

"Yod was able to sense the attack, even though he wasn't in touch with you? How?"

"He interfaces with computer intelligence in a way qualitatively different from the way we do. With part of his mind he's in touch with what he's doing, but another part is constantly surveying the background of other activity." Malkah awkwardly groped toward a cup of herb tea. Shira placed it in Malkah's hand, which dipped alarmingly. Malkah sipped it, put it down with a thud as if the cup were heavy.

"Of course. He has multi-tasking ability, like any other computer."

"A computer, Shira, could not have saved me."

Shira bowed her head. "I know that. And I'm grateful. You're all I really have in the world. You're my grandmother, for all purposes my real mother, and my best friend."

Malkah smiled weakly. "Besides Yod, my artificing, my fabling saved me. You see, my medical file is a chimera. It says I have an artificial heart, but as you know, I don't. They were aiming to stop it. The medics have my real files on paper, I insist on that, but I am always sneaking in and playing with the files that are in the Base."

"That's the real reason you never married, Malkah."

"Why?" Malkah whispered, fallen back against the pillows.

"You'd have had to remain only one person, when you like to be changing and multiple. Spouses insist you be the person they think you are."

"Children try to do that too," Malkah whispered. "But they never know who you are. Until much later."

AVRAM FORCED HER to plod upstairs to where Gadi had launched a building project. Reluctantly she inched up the old narrow staircase, feeling herself growing younger and blurred. A blast of sound enveloped her.

Gadi had changed out of his media gear into a smartened-up version of the local dress. He was having part of the third floor remodeled in a great hurry for an apartment, working with a young crew—a few of their old schoolmates and their younger brothers and sisters. The music blared till the room shimmered with sound. He had set up little local virons, so that she walked first into a lavender cloud dripping crystalline stalactites, smelling of lilacs and uttering Chu's latest opera, then into a throbbing

room-sized heart reeking of musk and wine while it shrieked the latest
nerve-rock hits. She had been sent in search of Gadi, for he was to be read
in today. Avram was terrified that Gadi would figure out what was going
on before he had been briefed, and would say something publicly.

She drew him aside. "We have to talk."

"My view exactly. How about tonight?"

"This isn't a personal conversation. Avram and I must discuss with
you the project we're working on."

"Merde, Ugi. What do I care about lab blab?"

Ugiah—cookie—had been an old affectionate name he called her by.
Even now it made her smile. "You'll care about this. It concerns Yod."

"Your weird boyfriend. I'm all ears. Let me get the crew properly
launched on knocking out the right and not the wrong walls, and I'll join
you in labland in twenty minutes." He stopped, swung on his heel to say,
"Really, you can do much better. He isn't couth, Ugi. He sits and glares
like a demented antique clock."

"I'll see you downstairs."

"I thought your marriage had exhausted your unbaked predilection
for techies with two left hands. Now yet another?"

"Gadi, you never met Josh. You have no idea what he's like."

"Can you really believe that?" Gadi stepped very close to put his finger
in the indentation between her nose and and upper lip. Irrelevantly she
remembered Malkah telling her when she was little that an angel had
touched her there before birth and made her forget everything she knew
as a wise soul. Gadi said in an amused silky voice, "I bought his life file
from an info pirate. I probably know more about old Josh than you do."

She knew as she hurried downstairs that Gadi had not yet forgiven her
for marrying. She did not judge him for that resentment, for if he married,
she would feel bitter. As long as both were equally crippled, they shared
a camaraderie of those inept at committing.

Avram paced. Yod stood in a corner. She had not seen him without
Avram since their unfortunate pas de deux on the street; she could not tell
if he was being machine-like and cold because of Avram's constant presence or because of her rejection. Now the coming explanation to Gadi was
making them all anxious. Yod started at sounds, swung around to glare at
the wall, the ceiling. She could not help but feel he would like to pulverize
something. At moments like this he reminded her of an attack dog more
than a computer. He built up a charge that wanted to leap out in action.
His dark bushy hair seemed to stand on end. His hazel eyes reflected every
light.

Yet he had saved Malkah when no one else could have. If he had not been monitoring the entire Tikva Base in a way she could not even imagine, Malkah would be dead. She wanted to express that gratitude less woodenly than she had so far been able to in Avram's presence, which inhibited her also. Today no hints of complicity linked them in a conspiracy of underlings. Yod did not glance at her, for he was occupied with that automatic three-hundred-and-sixty-degree surveillance never so blatantly displayed since the first week they had worked together.

Gadi came in arm in arm with Gimel, whom he had seized upon. "I've made a new friend."

"A simple robot," Avram said. "As you know, I've been working on cyborgs since you were a child."

"I remember one that was clearly illegal."

"They're all illegal. But necessary to defend Tikva as a free town. Yod is just as illegal as the others. More so, since he works."

"Yod? Purple shit! I don't believe it." Gadi turned to stare at Yod, who looked back implacably. "A robot? You know, I've heard rumors about projects like that in the assassin ports." He ambled up to Yod and pinched the skin of his lower arm. "Feels real to me."

"I know other people are making attempts, but I've succeeded. You must keep this secret. I don't want to die by assassin tomorrow. He's a blend of lab-grown biological and electronic components."

"Well, call me the Son of Frankenstein! Things are wilder here than I'd have guessed." Gadi planted himself squarely in front of Yod, who was backed against a counter. "We haven't got anything like you in the industry. Forget Avram and come to Vancouver with me. I'll make you a star."

Shira realized that Yod was feeling what she could only describe to herself as deeply embarrassed, perhaps humiliated. He stood like Gimel, his hands clenched at his sides, staring off into space now, avoiding Gadi's gaze, as he could not avoid Gadi's curious examination.

"Gadi, I need your word," Avram said. "This is not a matter for jokes. If you cannot give me your word, I'll have to protect myself."

Yod's hands shot out. He lifted Gadi high into the air and held him flailing. "Avram requires that you promise. I can hold you like this all day and all week."

"Yod!" Shira cried out warningly. "Careful."

"I . . . promise," Gadi croaked out.

Yod set him down. Gadi rubbed his chest and his hip gingerly. "What happened to the good old built-in robotic inhibitions against violence? I've been half crushed. I'm barely out of the hospital."

"Who is Frankenstein?" Yod asked.

"He built a monster," Gadi said. "Like my father has."

"A monster?"

"I'll point you to the story. Mary Shelley wrote it first, but there have been plays and flat films and stimmies."

"No resemblance," Shira said firmly. "Gadi is teasing you, Yod. Forget it."

Avram pounded the counter impatiently. "The important thing, Gadi, is that for once you act responsibly and don't gossip about this experiment with anyone. It's dangerous. Malkah was just attacked. We're under siege here. Try to understand this is not a joke. Not something to gossip about. Not something to make use of."

"Well, the free towns are anachronisms. If you were part of a multi, you'd be protected."

"It's our choice, not yours," Avram said. "We pay for our choice every day. As do you."

"This time I paid a couple of quarts of blood and no little skin. You don't have to worry. I'm used to keeping people's secrets. I know things about stim stars the daily pops would kill to air."

As Shira was escorting him from the lab, he murmured, leaning to her ear, "To think I was jealous of a machine! I'm slipping. You put one over on me, Shira, you sly pussy. When I saw him in the hospital, I interpreted his stiffness as threatening posture. Now I see it's robot ineptitude." He did not press her again about seeing him that night.

She was relieved. The moment he did not perceive a rival, he slacked off. Why did she feel the faintest pique of disappointment?

eighteen

TO DIE IN THE BASE

"I hope I die in the Base," Yod said quietly. He sat before a terminal in Avram's lab. For four days he had spent at least twenty-two hours out of twenty-four patrolling Tikva Base, plugged in fully projected. He had not been willing to leave the lab. The last time she had seen him had been the day Gadi was read in. Shabbat had intervened; she had spent it with the convalescing Malkah. Sunday he had begun his immersion in the Base.

Today she had plugged in, made contact and insisted he disengage and eat. He did require nourishment and usually took food, although he had the capacity to metabolize any organic compound not poisonous to him, and a number of inorganic compounds as well. But the tray of food from the Commons she had brought to him sat untouched. He exhibited none of the physical slovenliness a human would have after working nonstop; his face was clean and beardless, his dark hair neat, his olive skin shone in its usual simulacrum of health.

"Why do you want to die? What's wrong?"

"That's assuming I'm alive. I read *Frankenstein* and then many other versions of this story, from novels to books of crudely drawn cartoons. I watched flat projections called films. Then I entered two stimmies."

"Yod, I told you to forget all that. What has a fantasy of the nineteenth century to do with you?"

"Dr. Frankenstein was a scientist who built a monster. I am, as Gadi said, just such a monster. Something unnatural."

How could a machine feel self-pity? Nonetheless she had to deal with this sulk. "Yod, we're all unnatural now. I have retinal implants. I have a plug set into my skull to interface with a computer. I read time by a corneal implant. Malkah has a subcutaneous unit that monitors and corrects blood pressure, and half her teeth are regrown. Her eyes have been rebuilt twice. Avram has an artificial heart and Gadi a kidney." She perched on the edge of the table, trying to get him to face her. "I couldn't begin to survive without my personal base: I wouldn't know who I was. We can't go unaided into what we haven't yet destroyed of 'nature.' Without a wrap, without sec skins and filters, we'd perish. We're all cyborgs, Yod. You're just a purer form of what we're all tending toward."

He looked her in the eyes for the first time, glaring, unblinking. "You don't even believe that. I disgust you."

"You've never disgusted me. Sometimes you scare me a little. Sometimes you confound me."

"When we were at the bay, when you saw my body, you looked away. I am ugly to you." He pushed his face into his hands. The gesture was awkward, as if he had seen it in a stimmie and was trying it out, but the miasma of pain emanating from him was palpable.

"It isn't polite to stare at someone's naked body if you're not involved. And women learn never to stare at men, because that can unleash violence."

"The monster tried to communicate. He tried to be with people. But he was violent, as I am. He could only arouse hatred and commit harm."

"Yod, you already saved Malkah's life. You were not created out of some mad ambition of Avram's to become a god. You're not cobbled out of human garbage. You were created to protect a vulnerable and endangered community."

"What were you created to do?"

"I see your point. But once we grow up, we all have purposes, goals, functions in a society."

"Set by yourself."

Shira hefted a quartz paperweight, put it down. "Not necessarily. When I worked for Y-S, I governed little in my life. I certainly didn't set my own goals at work, and I wasn't in control at home. And now? Avram set up this project, and he's my boss as much as he's yours."

Yod got to his feet, still fixing her with that implacable unblinking dark stare. Normally he made an effort to blink regularly, like a human. "Why are you arguing with me?"

"I don't want you to be in despair."

"Why not? Because you'd be out of a job? Avram will just build another cyborg." Yod took the paperweight in his hand, held it up to the light. Then he squeezed it in his hand until it shattered. "Perhaps one who is more obedient. Who has less need for human interaction, who won't go about like the monster, frightening and pestering humans."

"What a magnificent adolescent funk you're in. Now you're more like a person than ever, with internal problems, a feeling of inferiority, the capacity for depression. We all live with this busy murk of pain and doubt inside us. So will you." She walked away from him. Avram was a genius, he really was, she thought, to have built this quirky artificial person. Did Avram truly understand what he had created?

"Is this what you feel like, Shira? Because of your son, because of Gadi, do you carry this thing in you like an animal devouring you?"

She came to him, putting one hand lightly on his shoulder. "Just so."

"Then I'll endure it." With infinite care, he took her other hand in his and raised it toward his face. For an instant she thought he was going to kiss her hand, but instead, with a gesture such as Hermes used to make, he bowed his head and rubbed his cheek lightly against her palm. His cheek was smooth as a child's or another woman's face, beardless.

It was such an odd and catlike gesture, she smiled as she stepped clear. "I do think of you as my friend. And unlike the monster's friend in *Frankenstein,* I don't need to be blind to like you. You're not misshapen or monstrous. People generally take you for a human, don't they?"

He sat down and reached for the tray. "I'll eat what you brought. Thank you. A friend, that's good. *Good!*" he said, imitating the monster's inflection from the old flat film.

"It can't be 'Good!'" she said. "It got cold while we were arguing."

"It is the same material whether it is twenty degrees or thirty degrees."

"Some food is supposed to be hot, like most soups and regular coffee; some, like salad, is supposed to be cool; some, like ice cream, is supposed to be frozen."

He shrugged, eating quickly, methodically. "Humans make many distinctions that evade me. Tell Malkah I miss her. She has not been in the Base."

"No. She's still weak, and she's afraid to plug in."

"That's like a bird afraid to fly. How's that for a simile? Is my grasp of figurative language growing?"

"By leaps and bounds."

With a fleeting smile, he turned to finish the meal, then shoved the tray from him. "Now I'm plugging back in. I should not be disturbed until

I disengage. Tell Avram to leave me alone, and you too, Shira—don't return until I send a message or come to you. I must stay in the Base until my task is accomplished."

Shira found herself unnaturally free. In spite of what Yod had told her, she did stop by several times a day. His body sat inanimate, deserted. He could have been gutted already, he could be brain dead. She wanted to summon Avram to use his equipment on Yod to see if his mind was still alive, but Yod's injunction that he not be disturbed held her back. She felt a little guilty standing before him, staring at his slack body; she also felt an unexpected desire to touch him. His finely molded features offered the innocence of sleep. Her curiosity felt prurient and tacky. She fled.

She gravitated upstairs. Gadi had created a mood of party on the construction site, where more volunteers came and went than he needed. Some old friends just got in the way, but Gadi gave everyone a task. Most of his volunteers were teenagers or college students home for the summer. They had heard of Gadi for years, heard gossip about him, enjoyed his work, fantasized about his life in Veecee Beecee.

The work was going smoothly and rapidly. Once the pickup crew had knocked out walls in order to create a good-sized space, they had only to fit the modular units in to set up new walls, barriers, doors. He left the outer walls and the windows intact.

"Ugi, see, I'm incorporating our old room. I'll keep it as my inner sanctum. In Veecee I have a house with a tower, built for Rush Bobbin—you remember him, he was big in rapture stimmies a few years back. He could project high lust like nobody else. For a while. He burned out. They all do."

As he marched her over, arm around her shoulder, the blue room with its iron bedstead was just as it had been, rag rug on the floor, shade at half mast on the window. He obviously felt more nostalgia for this room than she did; it was marred for her by the last time she had seen it. Odd shrine. A room where they had blundered into love perfect and round and gleaming; a room where Gadi had broken that crystal artifact to bits, as Yod had crushed the paperweight. They could stand as now on the threshold together, but never could they enter the true room, embedded in the past like a bubble in glass. She had a moment of almost chokingly rich identification with Gadi, like a scent too heavy to breathe. Indeed, she could smell the slight tang of his sweat under a perfume he used, subtle but loaded with pheromones. It cost more an ounce than gold; she recognized it from stimmies, where both men and women often wore that scent. It was called Lust.

Meals were picnics among the chaos of construction. They all camped on rugs and blankets and pads in the middle of the opened-up rooms and shared whatever they had. Shira found herself sitting cross-legged on the floor giggling while she nibbled chicken wings, corn bread and cucumber salad. In Tikva, they had real food as in the multi enclaves. In the Glop, people ate mostly vat-grown foods made of algae—her college years had been spent eating that artificially flavored, dyed and textured stuff. With the drying up or drowning of the great breadbaskets of previous centuries, the world was always short on earth-grown food. It was a luxury now, but here they raised much of their own produce, fish and chicken. She felt herself suddenly fifteen, as if the intervening years had lifted like a suit of armor she had been wearing and here was Shira again, the real Shira, giddy, adolescent, joyful and simple as a bird singing—in a cage? She felt a sudden pang of wariness, as if a hot wire had pierced her.

Gadi dropped gracefully beside her. "How do you happen to be free of our oversized lab rat today?" He lolled on his elbow, speaking softly under the throbbing music.

"It was cruel to give him the Frankenstein material."

"I thought it rather apropos. And he was fascinated. He watches everything on superfast forward, you know. I'm beginning to enjoy him. Notice I follow polite local usage and call it 'him.' Shira, the Council has been after me to do something for the town—as if I'd *chosen* to vegetate here."

"You were talking about running a little school."

"I suppose I will have to carry through. Talking is so much easier. Wouldn't you like to help me? It could be fun. We'll create festivals and virons and all kinds of pretty games."

"I'm employed already," she said dryly. She noticed that sitting so near to Gadi, she was not breathing quite normally. She was holding her breath and then quietly, surreptitiously, gasping for air. The pheromones were affecting her; but so was Gadi himself, curled there in a graceful and languid sprawl with his gray eyes half shut, glittering at her. His face was a dark tan, almost café au lait, de rigueur this year in the media trades. They were all dipped. Against the dark skin, his eyes gleamed like mercury. He ate a wing fastidiously, sensually, watching her. He bit into a peach and then passed it to her. She shook her head no. She had a sense of being coaxed too fast. No, she was paranoid or projecting her own attraction. After they had parted, she forced herself to observe, Gadi had gone on growing. He was taller than Yod, taller than Josh, in fact. He kept himself slender and supple. She wondered defensively how much time and money went into his beauty.

"Gadi, I've been wondering if you understand why Avram made Yod. He says it's for defense of the town, but when he began with Alef, we weren't under much pressure, at least that I knew about."

"When I was little and we lived in the Bay Area, he got into trouble with robotics experiments." He stroked her cheek. "That's long before he ever considered coming here." He had a casual way of touching her as if they were lovers, as if he had every right, but never quite in a way she could challenge without playing the fool or the prude. It kept her off balance. "I was a test tube baby. I think those five years of trying made him think there had to be an easier way to create life—especially more obedient life."

"Yod isn't always as obedient as you imagine." She leaned away.

"Anybody can see I've been satisfactorily replaced. I'm sure Dr. Frankenstein had a son who wrote Byronic poetry, wore his hair halfway down his back, whined about the stink of chemicals and jacked all the maids."

She realized she was seriously tempted to tell him about Yod's approach; that desire to confide scared her. The impulse felt . . . half disloyal, half dangerous. He was licking his fingers, delicately as a cat. "I always gain weight here. The chickens taste better, did you ever notice? Remember how Malkah used to pot roast a chicken for us with carrots and onions and called it Gadi's treat? How we used to lie on the grass of your courtyard all full and happy as puppies and she'd tell us tall stories? No stim can ever be more magical. Remember, Shira?"

"I remember." The memory scared her. She excused herself, checked Yod—immobile as ever, dead as a plant stand—then rushed home to look in on Malkah. She mistrusted her own withdrawal. Why shouldn't she enjoy herself with a group of kids? Had Josh infected her with his inability to enjoy? Had she entered a premature middle age? After all, Gadi had done exactly nothing but act friendly.

In the two long blocks on the way to her house, five people stopped her to ask about Malkah. Each one had a different recipe for depression. The whole town knew that Malkah had taken to her bed, and it frightened them. "Exercise," Hannah urged. "Music is the best therapy," Zipporah said, pressing her arm. Shlomo, who had gone to school with them and was rushing off to visit Gadi, paused to shout, "Bake a chocolate cake! Chocolate'll do it."

Malkah was huddled in bed. Shira addressed her with tentative disapproval. "I thought you were going to get up today?"

"What for?" Malkah turned her face to the wall. She looked ten years older than she usually looked. Her face was puffy and waterlogged.

"Don't they expect you back at work?"

"What do I care what they expect? I've had a long and full career. The hell with them."

"But you don't have to lie in bed to stay out of work. We can enjoy your vacation together."

Two small tears trickled from Malkah's eyes, till she angrily blew her nose and frowned. "I'm nothing without the Base, nothing. I need my work, I need to feel in touch, I need to ride out and build and feel the power. But I can't do it any longer. I can't."

"The attack made you afraid?"

"Of course it did. It was aimed at me. Personally. It wasn't random, it was an ambush. I felt I recognized one of the razors. A familiar mind."

"Yod is patrolling the Base."

"I'll never meet him again there. Never."

"Malkah, I want you to get out of bed. You don't have to plug in. I want you to cook and work in the garden. I can't carry the house by myself." She sounded ridiculous. The cleaning robot cleaned, the house took care of itself, meals could be picked up at the Commons, and dirty clothes were dropped at the laundry. Cooking was purely recreational. In Tikva, everybody over fifteen worked. No one kept house.

However, Malkah went along with the pretense. With a great show of reluctance, she put on her purple velvet robe. She sat scowling while Shira brushed her glossy hair and put in a carved walnut barrette. "That belonged to my own mother," Malkah said, as she had many times before. "In getting married, you've broken a tradition started by her. Maybe getting divorced undoes the harm." She was being reproachful, as she had not been when Shira arrived.

But Shira was glad to have Malkah doing anything at all, just so she got out of bed. Her collapse was deeply disquieting. Malkah was always vital, strong, crackling with energy. For the first time, Shira wished her stranger mother would actually arrive, to distract Malkah and enliven her. Shira was not the only one worried about Malkah. A counselor arrived and spent a futile hour with her. At suppertime, Gila appeared with two kittens in a box, sleek shiny black kittens with enormous round copper eyes. She dumped them in Malkah's lap. "Ten weeks old." They were screaming. One immediately ran under the couch and had to be hauled out, hissing.

"What do I want with kittens? I like grown cats. A nuisance!" Malkah snorted. "I'm too old for kittens. They're too much work."

"Why, since you've retired, old woman, you can make yourself useful. They're orphaned. If you don't take them in, they'll be dumped in the raw."

Groaning as if every joint ached, Malkah carried the kittens into the kitchen and set out making a mash of egg and cereal for them. Hanging behind, Shira said to Gila, "Orphaned? Conveniently at ten weeks?" Shira had priced a kitten for Ari once. How he would love to have a real live pet.

Gila put a finger to her lips. "I paid a fortune for them. Sha! The counselor recommended she be given something alive to care for."

They gave Malkah some time alone in the kitchen. When they came in, the kittens were eating on the table and Malkah was sitting with her head tilted, making mother-cat noises in the back of her throat, that burbling French *r* sound, m-r-r-r-r-u-u-u-ah.

By the next day, Malkah carried the kittens about inside her dress, played with them with her belt or string, wrestled them gently so that soon the backs of her hands were crisscrossed with tiny claw marks. They had speedily decided she was their mother now and followed her when she put them down. When Malkah retired, she took them off with her into her bed.

Shira tried to read, but she was worried about Malkah. The kittens would offer distraction for a while. If Yod could not succeed, either Malkah would give up her work and wither; or she would enter the Base again, and sooner or later the raiders would kill her.

How were they breaking into the Base? Tikva defenses had always been extraordinarily secure. After all, antipenetration programs were their export. Malkah had said something strange to her: that she felt she had recognized one attacker. Shira slipped on her silk robe, sat at her terminal. She requested information from the Base but did not plug in. She was afraid, she admitted to herself. She requested a list of all those Malkah had worked with in the last ten years on Base security and their present whereabouts.

The Base Overseers were Avram, Malkah and their best hardware person, Sam Rossi. Malkah was most responsible for Base defenses. Shira requested copy and carried the list to bed with her. Seven people had worked with Malkah closely enough to know the Base defenses. Of those seven, five were still in town. The other two were working for multis. Unlikely pirates.

However the pirates had penetrated, the Base was no longer secure. What should she hope for? That Malkah refrain from her own creativity, the exercise of what could only be described as her art; or that Malkah risk her life and her sanity? Shira could only hope that Yod would succeed. No human could remain plugged in for longer than four or five hours. One of her best-received papers had been on the effects of overprojection. If and when Yod emerged, she must examine him carefully for signs of what she had named the fused user syndrome. With humans, much of the immediate trauma was to the body, but the lasting results were often an inability to relate in real time and real space. No consciousness she had ever heard of had remained projected for three days without pause. She wondered if Yod had simply committed suicide his own way, or if he could really still be patrolling, fully conscious?

nineteen

MALKAH'S BED SONG

Now comes the part in the story where the Golem is sent to uncover the truth behind blood libels and save the Jews, again and again. He becomes the world's first private detective and one-man clean-up squad, but I just can't focus on it. It seems as routine as going through diagnostics on the computer or my body. What's wrong this week? What minor or enormous catastrophe are we striving to stave off, or failing that, cleaning up after? Yet the teeth that grind us fine in the end are the slow deaths we cause through our greed, our carelessness, our insufficiency of imagination. The news is never given in full stimulation mode. None of us want to know that intimately about other people's problems. We want the remove of viewing a screen or reading print. We prefer not quite to believe until death grabs us, as I was seized by the nape.

My problem is that my despair dyes everything a sullen gray. I have always viewed despair as sinful self-indulgence; perhaps I truly believe that relinquishing hope is the inevitable result of sitting still. If I do not keep moving, if I do not have projects and the heady clamor of problems to be solved, I will subside into a state of near-fatal clarity in which I will begin to doubt the value of everything I normally do. The result is a personal ice age in which I lie embedded in my own glacier that is burying the landscape I usually love but to which I am now as indifferent as the ice I have exuded.

If only they had sent an assassin after me on the street, if only they had sent a fake message robot to blow up in my face. But to attack me in my work, that was a stroke of true genius. Now I fear my own creativity.

Never to move in the Base again, that's death. Plugged in, I leave the gathering infirmities of my body, my body that quietly fails me after being so good to me. I have enjoyed excellent health. I have been robust for a small woman, sensual, energetic. When other women lay about complaining of pains and malfunctions, I was immersed in my work, and when my day was finished, I went after my pleasure single-minded as a cat. I liked to eat. I never attained the shadow-thin neurasthenia much admired in my youth, but I never put on excessive flesh either, except for the two years after Riva's birth. Most of the time I've been what you might call firm but fleshy. Now I find myself a little too thin, for I have less appetite. The flesh is leaving me. I grow leaner and ascetic. The physical pleasures I have pursued with such avidity stand at a slight remove, smiling at me across a gradually widening gap, as of a boat slowly putting out from shore.

I lie here in my own bed, discharged from hospital feeling like a hartebeest or a gazelle attacked by a cheetah, mauled and then, the attack interrupted, left partially dismembered, hamstrung, bleeding.

I was projected in the Base that afternoon, working on my chimera. Suddenly I realized I was not alone. I perceived two of them coming at me. They were in the form of projectiles, but I could sense a male and a female presence, even as I threw up a wall of force and launched a counterattack. But they had had time to prepare, and I had not. They smashed through the structure I had been building, a chimera that is one of my masterworks. They bombed right through it, and my dismay at the destruction slowed my response. Yet even as I fought and knew myself to be outmaneuvered, I felt something familiar in one of the minds. I knew that person. I can't force myself to reenter that searing pain when they pierced my defenses and came at my mind. I don't want to remember! I was caught, about to be burned out, on the verge of brain death. Yod interjected himself. Abruptly I felt him there. They were killing me, and then he was between us.

Without Yod, would I have died or become a vegetable? The worst terror is to imagine being trapped in a catatonic state, in a loop of agony, reliving over and over again that attack, that entry of something metallic and hard driving into the brain, a cold burn of electricity, a deep shock that chars the cells. Now I am burned still and afraid. I fear even dreaming, and so I take Hannah's drugs that suck me to a dreamless sleep.

I sit up now, clutching my pillow, sweating cold and slippery in the heat of the afternoon. Outside in the courtyard, the small birds we saved, that must be caged every fall so they do not try to fly south, are cheeping and pecking in the remaining vines—minus the rose Yod, battleground of warring programs, yanked out. Sometimes I imagine I am dreaming in coma. I fear I am lying in a hospital bed while they argue over whether to turn off the respirator, and that I hallucinated Yod's rescue. He came out of nowhere briefly in his own form and then as an enormous tank interposed, smashing them away. They fled. He hesitated between impulses. Then he carried me until I was free of the Base. Afterward he turned and shot rocket-like in the direction of the two razors' flight. But of course they were long gone.

They were gone, but they will be back. We all know that. The Net is always secure, because it is the common information system of the world. An attack on anyone there is like an attack in one of the treaty areas, the open ports: all the multis would launch an investigation and punish whoever broke the peace of the Net. Bases are only as secure as those who set them up can make them, and naturally we are frequently under siege, not only from information pirates like my own daughter, like those who attacked me, but also from multis and sometimes other free towns. Our Base is our independence, our strength. We cannot survive free without economic integrity.

This is my own failure, for I have specialized for the last twenty years in security systems involving chimeras that hide the real base in false bases. That's what we sell; but the very best we keep for ourselves. My finest ideas are floating there, intricate beyond mapping. We have every one of us felt safe inside our Base because we had state-of-the-art obfuscation protecting us. I am a magician of chimeras, and now my magic is penetrated, undone.

Perhaps I am ashamed and chagrined too. I have been a defender of my people. I am a small woman who has stood tall. I have been independent. I have relished my own company, and when I let a man into my bed, it was for my enjoyment only and the pleasure of his company—not because I needed any more from him than that mutual zest and exploration that used to be my best means of recreation. I have been protected by others, certainly, excused guard duty; my town has revered and celebrated me because I helped us all to stay free. Now I must acknowledge that without Yod I would be dead or worse.

I didn't even thank him, and I have not let him come to see me. In my state of collapse and ruination, I prefer to sulk alone. What am I without the Base? I cannot build without using my mind in that linkage whose talent was first discovered when I was twenty-four. During those early attempts at plugging in, at projection, we had many casualties. We didn't understand what we were doing, or we would not have dared. But the freedom! To imagine algorithmically, logically and fully, to think forward, clear, loud thoughts permitting no distractions, no misgivings, a discipline of the inner life. I have indeed been a proud creature, running in the wind of my own mind, free and driven at once. It has been a rich and good life at a time when the lot for most people is grim, nasty, violent, a shrunken life in the garbage of previous generations, burrowing like rats in the trash heap as wide as the horizon. We are lucky here, and I have been among the luckiest.

Is it greedy to wish to be happy till the end, to be engaged, fulfilled, to go on working until I die of the kind of massive stroke that we are beginning to understand is an occupational hazard of the aging base-spinner? Would I have given up my earlier pleasure if a bargain had been offered me, an insurance salesman of a Mephistopheles willing to let me have it easier in my old age if I had relinquished those pleasures I grabbed with both hands for many years? Would I have bought his deferred annuity? I doubt it.

I cannot endure the thought of spending my leftover life puttering around the house, useless, adrift in ennui, weak and stalled in my fear. Yet my fear is quite real. It is a demon with sword of fire barring the gate back where I may not return, where I truly belong.

What is physical aging to a base-spinner? In the image world, I am the power of my thought, of my capacity to create. There is no sex in the Base or the Net, but there is sexuality, there is joining, there is the play of minds like the play of dolphins in surf. In a world parceled out by multis, it is one of the only empowered and sublimely personal activities remaining. I have always known I was exceptionally blessed to be able to revel in my work.

Now I am reduced to my aging body in my room, which is luxurious but insufficient as a world. At seventy-two, I knock against my limits constantly in the flesh. I cannot walk as far as I used to. My knees give way. I don't sleep soundly. My body creaks and groans. Worst of all is the slow leakage of light from my world, the darkness closing in. I cannot bear the thought of not being able to see the faces of those I love, of total physical dependence.

When I conceived of seducing Yod, it was a marvelously mischievous idea tickling me; besides, I have never grown out of the pleasure of teasing Avram. That summer we were involved, how I loved to turn him inside out like a glove. Even when he was young and so gorgeous it almost hurt to look at him, even when he was so driven by his sex that he ran about snapping at his own tail like a puppy, he always had a stuffy priggish side that offered me ample temptation and opportunity at once for setting him on edge.

I knew my seducing Yod would drive Avram into fits of indignation. Perhaps I was still sore from the time we tried to be lovers after Sara's death and he was impotent and then angry. He had shut down his sexuality for years, and it could not return overnight. Why weren't we more patient with each other? Why didn't we try more tenderly? . . . But I wanted to know if I had succeeded in giving Yod a viable sexual capacity. And I'm fond of Yod. It was not an idea that would have occurred to me during the first two years of his existence, but he has become more and more of a person and a presence as time has gone on. As he learned to master his vast store of information and his hugely different programming segments, he began to define his own desires, opinions, even values. He was emerging as an attractive entity, and I thought how wicked and delightful it would be to see what might happen.

Of course Yod has no prejudice against a woman because of age. He is not breaking any Oedipal taboos, for he was not born of woman. He was not born at all, and he does not sully his desire with fear or mistrust of women the way men raised by women do. He was delighted to be able to fulfill his programming, and he discovered he liked sex better than almost anything. Wrinkles, infirmities meant nothing to him. He wore me out. It was I who finally called a halt, by the gentle process (in order not to hurt Yod's feelings, because he has them in abundance) of allowing Avram to guess what was going on.

Why did I stop it? A fatigue with the flesh. It was a lovely way to end my sex life, for I found that not only were the physical demands and the drain on my energy considerable, but I simply did not want to put that much into a relationship with any lover, not even a cyborg programmed by me myself to satisfy. In many ways Yod was dear and even relaxing, without all the neuroses and complications of any human male; but he is still quite demanding in his own way, and my solitude and my energy are precious to me.

I did not know I was ready to relinquish that part of my life, for I had always believed that as long as I lived, I would be interested in love; in making love. My identity was fused with the notion of conquest, perhaps. From the time I was a young girl, all through womanhood, I was never beautiful; I was considered so by many men, never by any woman. It was a fleshy, sensual, highly charged sexuality I emitted, a focused desire full of ripples and zing. It worked. It was honest.

Further, I always thought that my creativity was linked, somewhere at that point where the spine blooms into the strange cauliflower of the brain, to my sexuality, so that they fed and stoked each other. Yet since I passed sixty, I have been twice as creative, longer-sighted, more daring, building on a grand scale more dazzling webs.

Yod offered his friendship, his attention, his pure scalding luminous desire, almost too bright to endure, his unpracticed bountiful tenderness, his endless desire to please, and I received all those gifts as I had already given him my own presents, now deeply embedded in his being. I came to realize there is a time when one lets go. That dying has already slowly begun, at this time when, until the attack, I have never been as creative and as strong in my work. I saw myself as a tree giving all its energy into its fruiting. Now I am cut down.

Shira is troubled about me, and I strive to respond, but I feel as if all my nerve endings are charred. How shall I tell stories, when I cannot find myself? I have no center. I am a devastation. I am afraid, all through my mind and body, my imagination tainted and permeated by fear. Despair. Stasis. Myself broken in my bed. We have come full circle and stop.

I must break out of this loop of despair. The only direction is in and down. The descent to the chariot, the early Jewish mystics called it. I will begin with breathing exercises, I will begin with my old meditation sequences, the chants that I used to center myself that year of passion just before Riva brought me the baby Shira. Mohatela the Lion had coaxed me to Johannesburg when he was attempting to undermine the multis of the world with gold and diamonds, to shake loose the grasp of Europe and Asia on Africa, and I was designing systems for him and in love with him and his vision. I spent a year and a half away from Tikva, till the Lion was cut down before me, assassinated as he spoke to the world—in my nostrils, singeing my sinuses and my throat, the smoke of his flesh as they burned him down. I came home scarcely remembering who I had been. My world felt empty of purpose. Then I gathered the fragments of myself, then I found within me a fire and a discipline that could weld them back together. That winter Riva arrived with a month-old girl. "Here, this is for you."

After all these years, I can still hear his voice if I permit it. How often the powers that rule cut down the best, pay for their murder and return their energy to dust, and then later comes another, more fanatical, more violent, one who does it all with power and without beauty. There are losses so great that personal mourning feels almost beside the point, and you simply keep it to yourself and try not even to remember. Others to whom he belonged carried out the public mourning and the public remembering. The Lion is history, and that we loved each other in quiet hours and that once he cried in my arms can matter little to anyone but me. That is a story in which I do not even belong, the story of his people's freedom.

Before Riva arrived with Shira, I saved myself from despair. Now perhaps I will chase the most beautiful chimera of all through all the spinning worlds of the mind until the blinding atmosphere of the self thins out. Then at that level of consummate darkness and utter cold, will I find that burning light I have once or twice glimpsed? Beyond appetite and affection and desire, beyond opinion and belief and commitment, the conscious point of emanation. That is the adventure left to what is left of me.

twenty

BASE AND TREBLE

Shira struggled upward through heavy water. "Shira, I am very sorry to wake you, for my sensors report you as sleeping." The house was speaking sotto voce, an apologetic cast to the warm female voice. "The mechanism you call Yod is urgently requesting you access the Base. It insists that this message is important."

She summoned time: 12:45:03. "Thank you. I'll plug in." Could it be a trick? Who would want to execute her? No, it must be Yod. Could he somehow be stuck in the Base, unable to retreat after such long immersion? Putting on her robe, she looked hesitantly into the courtyard. The light was out in Malkah's room. Perhaps her grandmother had finally fallen asleep. Shira would not bother her. Shira shut the door and sat down at her own terminal.

She plugged in with a sense of queasiness, the slime of unacknowledged fear. There was no way to contact someone immersed in the Base except to enter in full projection—fully vulnerable to attack. She moved quickly through the access modes, seeing in her mind the familiar landscape of Tikva entrance. The conventional imagery the Base used was a room with many doors, labeled with the names of sub-bases. She walked straight through to the central double doors and flung them wide. She was entering the heart of Tikva, the working base where they created their products. The imagery here was of herself as hovering outside the three-dimensional sketch of a building, its plan which she could fly over, alongside, into, which she could examine floor by floor. As she moved toward the area in which Malkah was building her chimera, she expected to move into Malkah's imagery. Instead she found herself on a broad field. Coming toward her was a figure shuffling along. It was Frankenstein's monster, in the form and makeup used by Boris Karloff in the flat film from the twentieth century.

"Yod?" she thought. Conversation was not exactly what happened in the Base. Rather here you thought words in a particular way: thinking forward, it was called, a loud, carefully formulated mental speaking that would be heard by the other you were addressing.

He was shuffling forward, and he raised in his hand a decapitated head, swung by the hair.

"Yod, don't do this. Be yourself."

"Is this better?" He was Gadi, still coming toward her but mincingly. He was a parody of Gadi, dressed in the translucent silk gown Gadi had worn in the hospital, swinging the head jauntily like a woman's purse.

"Yourself, or I'll leave."

"Why? You like this better."

"That's not necessarily so. I want to see you."

Now he was Gimel. "Is this how I am to you?"

She turned and walked back, away from him. She did not know if she could exit this part of the program without his help, but she was angry enough to try. Then he stood before her again, this time as himself.

"Better." She stopped. "What's that gory thing?"

"The raider." He raised it. It stared at her out of its sightless eyes. She gave a short cry. "Yod, I know him! That's Barry Joyce. He's Y-S."

"I killed him. I burned his brain." He tossed the head up, and it turned into a pigeon and beat away on short stubby wings. "I followed the other raider back through the Net until I had her just outside the Y-S facility and about to escape within. Then I burned her too. They sent out security, and I demolished them. It was a lovely battle—just what I was created for."

"Yod, they killed five programmers here. If you hadn't intervened, they'd have killed Malkah."

"You believe my actions were correct." He held out his hand, and into it popped another head. "This is the other raider."

Involuntarily Shira gasped, flinching. "I know her too. I went to school with her, Yod. Zee Levine. I haven't seen her since we both went away to college, but I remember Malkah telling me she had gone to work for Y-S maybe two years ago. How could she do this to us? Turn on us?"

"There is no doubt. They were both razors—computer assassins."

"She must have brought specs of the Base defenses with her to Y-S. Everything will have to be restructured."

"Malkah and Avram will reconfigure. The whole Base collective will have to stop work on everything else. I can help also. Did you know Joyce well?"

"I've only seen official Y-S stimmies about the heroism of Barry Joyce. Zee wasn't in Nebraska but at some other facility. Could you please get rid of that head? It makes me nauseous."

"That was hostile of me, wasn't it. Here." He thought a rose around them, huge, so that they were standing inside an enormous flower the size of a bed, thick with petals. "A real rose would have scent, of course."

"This is a beautiful viron, but tricky to stand in." She lost her balance, and he caught her arms. She looked into his eyes, brown with green flecks like bits of jewel. She felt as if everything were tilting inside the great red rose. "Rosa Mundi," she thought, and pushed herself forward against him. She felt desperate and giddy. She felt frightened. She could not think yet about what it meant that the enemy were not information pirates but rather the multi that had owned her and still owned her ex-husband and her son.

He let go of her arms and put his own around her, pulling her tightly body-to-body. The clothes thinned and then dissolved till they were standing together naked, although of course it was the thought of flesh, not flesh itself. The contact was purely mental. Their thoughts sounded in both their minds. It was strange and dizzying, as if the world had turned into the weirdest of stimmies.

You don't feel human or animal exactly but not like a thing either; you do feel alive. This is strange, what am I doing; I must be out of my mind, but I am out of my body. This isn't possible in the Base. How can this be a representation of information, how is this embrace worked out in binary code? I want to, a rose as big as a bed, but it doesn't really work, we can't do more than imagine it.

Why are you touching me now? Because I saved Malkah? Why does that make me attractive? I have done what I was created to do, I have defended. But you are what I want. This isn't crazy but good. I want to know all of you, I want to enter every part of you, as I enter the Base and explore it. I want us to join as we join now but in the world. Shira, don't fear me, don't shrink from me. Let me come to you now, right now.

She drew back and stared at him, asking with her mind, "Is this what you want? This joining in the Base?" Hoping that was enough.

"No, no," he answered mind-to-mind. "This is only the image. I want the reality. Let me come to you where you are in your house, in your room."

He let her go, and she was running rapidly back toward the double doors she saw before her, out into the hall. Then she was disengaged, sitting at the terminal. Her body thrummed as if she had just run physically. "House, Yod may come. If he does, admit him. Do not bother to announce him, and do not wake Malkah."

She opened the door to look out. The moon had risen high enough to shine into the courtyard, a waxing moon past the half. She left the door open and climbed into her bed. She lay very still, crossing her hands on her chest. Through the thin cotton of her nightgown she could feel her heart racing. What she had just experienced was not possible in the Base. She had worked with many other programmers fully projected, and while they had apparent bodies, they were obviously a representation of reality. Typically objects in a base were highly abstracted: the idea of Malkah, the idea of a building, the idea of a flower, usually neatly labeled (sepals, anthers, ovary). Yod had the ability to manipulate imaginary computer objects with more authority than any human could muster.

He came so quietly she did not hear him until he was in the room. He stood by the window. "Shira?"

She felt closer to fright than to desire. Her heart was pounding, but in her mind was the idea that it was time to treat him as a person, fully, because he was nothing less; she knew, too, that she was choosing to try sex with him because when she was with him, she did not think of Gadi. He seemed able to fill all available mental space. In the intervening years, only her child had done that, her lost child. She sat up in bed. "Come."

He paused with his hand on the bedside table. "You wish it to stay dark?"

"Yes. Not because I find you ugly, but because I don't want Malkah to wake and see the light. She often has insomnia."

"Shira, why did you change your mind? Is it because I cleared the Base of danger? For Malkah?"

"Don't ask silly questions. I'm doing it because I want to."

He tore off his few garments, letting them fall, and slid between the sheets. She wondered exactly what one did with a cyborg. She had waded through gigabytes of material on his hardware, but she was still confused. Could one kiss a cyborg? Would not his mouth be dry as a can opener? It was not. His lips were soft on hers. His tongue was a little smoother than a human tongue but moist. Everything was smoother, more regular, more nearly perfect. The skin of his back was not like the skin of other men she had been with, for always there were abrasions, pimples, scars, irregularities. His skin was sleek as a woman's but drier to the touch, without the pillow of subcutaneous fat that made it fun to hug Malkah, for instance.

"Shira, I can feel that you're tense," he said very softly.

"I'm not tremendously sophisticated or experienced. Even if you were human, I'd be nervous. To lie down with a man always feels risky."

"But I can't give you a disease or make you pregnant. I would never hurt you." Lightly, gently he stroked her back.

"You're strong enough to do so inadvertently, the way a person can hurt a baby or a bird."

"I control my movements far more exactly than any human does. I'm machined and programmed to demanding specifications. I would never hurt you, I could never hurt you. Believe that."

She smiled against his shoulder. "That would make you different indeed from any man I've known."

"Then know me, Shira. Let me know you. It's all we can do together. We can't get married or have children or run off together. All I can bring you are brain and body during the times I am not required elsewhere in acts of what I'm told is necessary violence." He tugged gently at the fine cloth of her nightgown. "Can we take this off?"

The nightgown went flying across the room and settled with a little sigh of its own on the floorboards. Moonshine lit the room faintly. His hands drifted over her lightly, lightly in wide and then narrowing circles, on her back, her breasts, her belly. He touched her as if he had all the time in the world. Of course he did not experience bodily fatigue; his desire was not based in any physical pressure; he did not sleep. He caressed her as if he could do so all night, and probably he could. She still felt watchful, wary, but her flesh woke independently of her brain, stretched, came to life, brushed into electrical response. Her back arched to his palm, her breast slipped forward into his hand. He obviously liked to be touched, to be caressed, but she did not sense that any particular part seemed more sensitive than any other, although she was too shy to touch his genitals yet. Her breath came quickly, but his did not. Yet he concentrated on her with a total intensity that in itself was absolutely exciting. It was not passion as she had known it in men: it was a passionately intense attention, sharpened by extraordinary skill in the use of his hands and mouth. Raw silk, she thought, warm in the sun. Sinuous as a cat, as the wind. She writhed against him.

Time resumed when his hand slipped between her thighs. She realized she had not had a conscious thought in . . . She had been outside time. And she was the one who had moved his hand downward. She had been kissing him, writhing against him, her mind doused like the havdalah candle that was put out in sweet sacramental wine, the candle braided as their bodies were intertwined. Who would have expected him to be so . . . graceful, precise, catlike in bed? Never had she lost self-consciousness like that with Josh, never, not with the lover she had tried after him or with anyone at all since Gadi.

He touched her, and then he parted her thighs and went down on her. She had always felt a little self-conscious that way. Josh had been clumsy, and she had felt shy, as if she were asking for more than she ought to. Gadi had learned from the stimmies, but they had used it for excitement only. For a moment she felt her old awkwardness, and then she thought she need not be embarrassed with him. He did not grow fatigued. He would simply continue until stopped. She gave herself over to the sensations of being lapped until the urgency and the sense of tipping over grew so strong she was coming.

"I never came that way before," she said honestly, when she had hold of herself again. "Can you feel pleasure?"

"I experience a small discharge of my fluids from friction. It has no function other than to mimic what human males produce. The pleasure is entirely in my brain."

She smiled. "Do I rub your temples, then?"

"I can come by any kind of friction. I am not programmed to require penetration."

"But would you like to do it that way?"

"I wouldn't hurt you?"

"Let's try it."

He positioned himself on her with extreme care, keeping his weight on his arms. She wondered if he had done this before. He seemed less practiced. She was still wet, and he slid in without difficulty. She was pleased to feel that he had been made a reasonable size. She had feared a giant penis on him, and was relieved Avram had not been carried away. It would be nice to make love with him in ordinary light, she thought, as she was now extremely curious about his body.

He moved very slowly at first, until she found herself driving up at him. He probed more quickly. She forgot to think. Her nails were digging in his back. Her pelvis was drumming against him. She had never made love quite this way. She had never been as excited except with Gadi, and then she had been too young to thrust hard. She could hear herself making noises, soft growls and groans. A path opened in her, a path into her womb. She did not worry she was taking too long, she did not even think until the last moment that she could not possibly be coming again, but she could, she was, she did.

She lay beside him in the roil of messed-up covers and pulled-loose sheets. She kept touching his cheek, his forearms, his buttocks. He felt to her at once like a person and a large fine toy. She could not believe what she had just experienced. Since Gadi, her sexual response had been measured at best, defective, sputtering. She had considered herself rather cold. Gadi had been the exception, and that was so long ago, her sexuality so incandescently diffuse, she felt she could have come with Gadi simply by touching thumbs or kissing.

"Oh," she said suddenly, jolted. "I fell asleep for a moment."

"I wondered if that was sleep." He stroked the hair back from her face. "I should go to the lab. In the morning tell Malkah I've cleared the Base and we must reprogram. All other work must cease until we've created new labyrinths. Now Malkah is free to build and ride and play in the Base again."

After he had left her, she wanted to think about everything that had happened, but the long day, the tension she had been carrying wound through her guts, the soft gummy feeling of her body after two orgasms, all sucked her down into sleep heavy as a sinking sofa. What have I done? she thought, waiting for alarm to hit, but then she was floating in darkness, disembodied.

twenty-one

ONE DOOR OPENS AND ONE DOOR CLOSES

I waited in my chair in the darkness of the courtyard. The moon shone feebly, waxing just over the cornice. I was sure that Yod would leave Shira soon and return to the lab. He was tactful and nervous enough not to need to advertise the satisfaction of the desire he had worn so plainly and painfully for the last month.

I had the two kittens tucked into the bodice of my gown, where they slept, occasionally wiggling into wakefulness to nudge for the mother they had lost, pricking me with their needle claws and muttering back to sleep. Shira and Yod were most considerate, not turning on a light, silent as serpents. No one credits the degree of my insomnia. Two nights ago for the first time I neglected—no, I decided not to take the prescribed drugs. I was afraid that in a drug-induced torpor I would roll over on the kittens, so tiny and delicately made, and hurt them. I was weary of the thick wool of drugged sleep. My normal sleep is brief but real.

Dozing, I had heard Shira and the house speaking. My hearing is still excellent. I checked my terminal and saw she was in the Base. I wondered why she had entered at night, so I asked the house. The house told me all I needed to know. I found myself rising to the ceiling like a gravity dancer. Sudden energy came singing through my body. Sleep? Who needs it? Yod doesn't, and I require little. I had done nothing but sleep and sulk for days and days and nights and nights, and lately played cat mother and practiced ascetic disciplines and an occasional trance state. Now Yod had cleared the Base again, and I was free to reenter my work, my life.

When the house told me that Yod might come, I waited. I saw him pass upstairs. The light did not go on. At last. I stole downstairs.

The night was halfway to dawn when he came softly down. He moves with his own kind of grace, that of perfect function. He saw me in the dark and stopped cold. I imagined I saw confusion on his face. I could guess he was wondering if my feelings would be hurt. He is good at reading human feelings from small kinetic changes, but he is poor at guessing them beforehand. He has trouble figuring out what will please and what will offend or hurt us.

I motioned him to keep silent and led him into my office, shutting the door before I turned on the light. I need good light to see anything. "You were successful?" I realized at once that question was ambiguous, and I started to grin. "Your patrol of the Base was successful?"

"The raiders were not pirates. They were from Yakamura-Stichen. Shira recognized both when I showed her their faces." He filled me in, standing at attention. Many things about Yod amuse me. For one thing, he can stand perfectly still for hours, not twitching or shifting as any person would. He has a tendency to assume a position and stay in it, whether standing, sitting or lying down. I wondered if we should have built in a few twitches or nervous gestures for versimilitude. Then I began to realize what he had just told me. Not pirates. One of the world's largest and most aggressive multis.

"You said Shira knew the razors. Who were they?"

He answered, and I found myself shrieking "No!" I made myself calm. I did not want to wake Shira; I did not want to frighten Yod. He had begun circling as if looking for someone else to attack. "Zee. My student. Did you have to kill her?" I could see her plainly, silky fine hair flopping in her eyes, a full rich tea brown, the eyes lighter. Walnut and maple.

"Malkah, she tried to kill you. She would have tried again."

Zee was an eager young woman, desperate to please. She was overly attached to her mother. Then when she was twenty-five, her mother fell in love with a young man who had come here to study the fish meekro with Gila. "She quit suddenly last year—"

"Two years." Yod corrected me. "I accessed her records."

"That long? Zee went to Y-S. She must have taken the codes with her."

"Under mnemosine hypnotism, she could recall the programming."

"I used to make tsizanes for her. She suffered from migraines. Why would she want to hurt me? . . . So it was never information pirates. It was Y-S attacking us. That's far more dangerous."

"Because they're more powerful?"

"And it's a change of tactics for the multis. We're so vulnerable. Our survival is at stake. They don't want us to endure free any longer."

"Freedom is a concept I'm not sure I comprehend," Yod said. "Perhaps because I've never been free."

"Well, our work is cut out for us. There's no sleeping this week. I suppose you might as well let Avram enjoy the rest of the night. I'll plug in at seven and expect you two to be ready. . . . Actually I'll come over. We need to work out a master strategy before we begin."

Yod had switched from perfect stillness to his hyperactive mode in which he wants to be attacking. I could feel his desire to please me. He reminded me of a powerful handsome horse who has given himself to a person to ride and befriend. His eyes caught the light, shining green. "I'm ready now."

"But I'm not. I need several hours' work before we can do anything useful together."

"You're no longer afraid of the Base."

"You saved my life twice over, Yod." I went and hugged him.

He embraced me back. "Do you want intimate contact? I can feel you are very excited."

"Mentally, my dear, only mentally. That's done between us." He had, of course, read my body language accurately, because when I felt him, resilient, strong, with a kind of dry warmth all his own, I did desire him anew. For a moment I didn't see why I should have relinquished him; what foolishness, what waste. Had I not helped create him as he was, in all his marvelous complexity and true ability? Why should I give him over to Shira, who will never really appreciate him as I do? I felt myself more deserving, more competent as a lover for him, and I wanted him back. Feelings I crushed as I would a flower in which I found a slug chewing the petals. "Listen to me, Yod, listen carefully. You're not to tell Shira about us, not ever."

"But why? Are you ashamed?"

"Of you? Never. Shira would be shocked. Very shocked. She's more conventional than I am, Yod, especially at this time of her life. She would think it's indecent for you to have been involved with me at all and especially to then become involved with her. Take my word."

"Your word." He shook his head. "I don't understand, but I know you do."

"Right. And don't be too obvious around Avram. I don't know how he's going to react."

"I assume he'll disapprove, as he did about us."

"Maybe, maybe not. Like many older men who are not attracted to older women, Avram assumes we are asexual. He was shocked—as Shira would be, remember. But Avram finds Shira attractive. What that little goody thrown into the pot will produce is anybody's bad guess." I waved my hand at him. "Go home. I have serious dreaming to do. Systems dreaming."

"Malkah, you've stopped telling me about Joseph Golem. I enjoyed finding that story in the Base at night, when everyone else sleeps."

"But we see each other now face-to-face. . . . I'll continue. I promise."

Yod smiled wistfully. "His story is meaningful to me. I'm glad we can see each other again. Every day I missed you. Time does not make my memories less intense, and thus they evoke the same reactions each time I access them."

I stood in the courtyard in the darkness, hearing rather than seeing him leave. I had a desire to call him back. This was the real letting go, this night, far more ultimate than when I had permitted Avram to guess and thus cut off our liaison. I wanted to be younger, I wanted to be stronger, I wanted back the body that had for so many years of my life been equal to that hard driven dance, that sensual twisting and turning, that rich passionate descent into the tips and the roots of the senses. Yod was my true last lover. After him, I would desire none other. I had created him to be all I might want, and now I had truly let him go. My body and my mind mourned him.

Suddenly I had a genuine pang of appetite. The kittens, too, had wakened hungry. I picked at a medley of leftovers from meals I had not enjoyed. Standing in the kitchen tasting them—with the kittens nibbling gruel on the counter before me—me eating everything cold and with the same fork, I enjoyed food as I hadn't since the attack. I had thought Shira might be too conventional and too sexually timid to acknowledge an attraction to Yod. I was surprised by her boldness. Somehow he had wormed his way through her defenses. She was desperate to interpose someone between Gadi and herself. How would she feel in the morning? Ashamed? Guilty? I hoped she had the courage of her pleasure. I hoped I had been able to give her that.

Now goodbye to the noisy hot surface clatter of the intimate life and on to the problem of restructuring the defenses of our Base. It would be a fierce keen pleasure to bang my mind against Avram's again, to strike our ideas on each other's stubborn steel. Whenever we've been able to force ourselves to work together, what wonders we have performed—

when we do not act like a snake with two heads, one straining east while the head on the far end pulls west.

Now we knew our enemy, and it was a deadly one. Yakamura-Stichen was one of the ten most powerful multis in the world, and the world included the satellites. They were coming after us for some reason, and they would not stop.

When I left, Shira was still sleeping. I asked the house to tell her to go see Zee's mother and break the news to her. She used to spend after-school time at Zee's house, I vaguely remembered, so she might have some rapport.

I realized in midmorning as I rose for air, making coffee to excuse the break in concentration, that I was once again enjoying my life, that I was in full possession of myself, my faculties, that I was—more than happy— joyous. I like a good hard job that matters. I like that push of anxiety bearing on creation. Maybe I'm just an adrenaline addict. That morning I almost loved Avram. Sometimes he irritates me so much I forget how bright he is, how extraordinary a mind he has, how imaginative he is in his science. Sometimes I have to admit he's as good as I am—that good.

At noon, while we were eating a pickup lunch, Gadi bombed in on us. "Why is access to the Base closed? How am I supposed to manage?"

The Base of course was not entirely shut down. The master computers had to maintain the wrap, regulate temperature, circulate water, monitor air quality, clean the waste water, run the external surveillance gadgets and screen their output, operate the fusion plant, desalinate and remove toxins. Internal com-con was functional, so we could talk to each other and so we had a means, not as good as direct, but usable, to access the Net. But aside from security, which has secondary status after life-support systems, nothing else was operational. We were down until we had recreated our defenses.

"Didn't you hear it's a holiday?" I said cheerfully. "Yom Yod." Yod Day. "He killed the razors who slashed me."

"Where's Shira?"

"Off telling a mother her daughter tried to murder me and is now dead. Want to join her? I'm sure she could use the help."

The truth of the matter is, I like Gadi. I've liked him since he was a gawky lonely miserable child. I think he's found his art the way I found mine, and I like people who plunge into the work they want to spend themselves on. However, his influence on Shira is another matter. They did each other in, and I vastly prefer her involved with a cyborg than with a man-boy stuck at age fifteen sexually and emotionally. It's a great advantage to him in his work: he has his head into adolescent fantasy and spins it into riches. I'm a greater believer in sexual satisfaction than in emotional angst, and I don't give a damn whether she can persuade herself she loves Yod or not, so long as she has the sense to spend what free time she has with him instead of Gadi.

Gadi did not ask further where Shira was. Yod had heard none of this, as he was interfaced programming the details on the first structures we designed. Gadi went off in a crowd of those kids who hang around him now, imitating his gestures, intonation, style. When Shira ran in, he had long gone.

"Malkah, I stopped by the house. There was a secured message for me from Y-S asking for a meeting. They say my appeal on the custody of Ari had been reconsidered. What should I do?"

"They have your son," I said. I felt cold all through. A new offensive. They were planning something. "How can you trust them enough for a meeting?"

"They aren't about to gun me down, are they? I have to go. I have to see what they want. Maybe the attack on the Base comes from an entirely different arm of Y-S than who decides about children's custody. Why assume they're related?"

"Don't let them in here," Avram said. "Meet them outside."

"Take Yod with you," I said. I was thinking that he could record the entire meeting. They would never permit taping, but Yod would produce a perfect record we could go over later. He might be able to protect Shira, in case her confidence was misplaced. The old rules had been broken, and no suspicions seemed truly paranoid.

"Do you want to come along?" Shira asked me. "We'll pick some neutral meeting place."

Yod, who had pulled out of the machine when Shira arrived, stood now. "I want to go. I must go with you."

Shira paced, one hand tangled in her hair. She had that fey deer look she often has, but I could feel her resolve. She turned to Avram and me, looking back and forth between our faces. "I could ask Cybernaut to provide space and security. They're not likely to be in Y-S's pocket, are they?"

"A canny idea," I said. "Play off the juggernauts against each other. Still, I will not go. I'll rely on Yod."

"I haven't decided if Yod should be permitted to leave the town,"

Avram said, "although this might provide an opportunity to test his physical defense functions. We need such a shakedown, and he's had no opportunity yet."

I said, "In any event, this isn't your decision to make alone, Shira, Avram. Y-S attacked Tikva. It would seem suspicious if Shira, a former employee, were to confer with them on her own now. We need to take the matter before the Town Council Monday night and see if a meeting feels safe to the town. I'll gladly present the matter."

"Fine," Avram said. "But Yod need not appear. I'm not ready for the Council to meet him."

"At some point they'll have to, Avram. Secrecy never works, because nothing ever stays a secret long."

"It is not yet time," was all he said, staring at me from his ice-blue eyes, which still can make my spine radiate under his gaze. Ah, Avram: too bad we can't meet once again ardent, sweet, in some vineyard of the soul. But my very tone of being rasps on your nerve ends. What a pity for us, old angel.

twenty-two

THE PRESENT

The morning after, Tikva was shaken up like a handful of dice, and everything fell differently. The Base was closed, and all work on regular projects halted. The Base Overseers met with the other members of the Town Council, and everybody tried to assimilate the news that one of the largest multis in the world was their enemy. Zee's mother collapsed and was hospitalized. The Council commended Yod and questioned Shira about Y-S intentions; however, she could be of little assistance, having spent her time there at such a low grade. All agreed the restoration of defenses was paramount. As for Shira's meeting with Y-S, they decided she should use the negotiations to try to buy time and to find out, if possible, what Y-S wanted from the town.

Malkah hit the ground running. Shira saw Malkah only at an occasional mealtime and sometimes first thing in the morning. Shira was inessential this week. Her skills would come into play further along in the process. All Yod's time was usurped by the need to fortify the Base, as was Malkah's, Avram's, and the energies of twenty-plus other designers. Therefore the question of seeing Yod or dealing with what had happened could not even arise. Shira dickered with Y-S, and a meeting was set up for the following week in the Cybernaut facility 22.6 kilometers away, for ten a.m. on a Tuesday. She read on through Yod's specs. She still did not have Malkah's notes. Since the timing for pursuing the matter seemed poor, she would have to wait.

She had plenty of time to contemplate what had occurred, to run rings around it until her memory blurred from too much handling. She recognized a certain chagrin in herself, an embarrassment that she had responded so strongly on a sexual level to a mechanical device. Sexual level. That was handling it with tongs. Better to admit she had fallen open like an old book, like Malkah's antique atlas, all the way to the spine. It had been so many years since she had lost control sexually, since she had responded more than tepidly, that her excitement shook her sense of herself.

Her deep and almost violent sexual pleasure not only disturbed but confused her. She had imagined that it was her love for Gadi, that early emotional bonding, that had made the sex with him much more satisfying and engaging than anything in her life since. But what she was responding to in Yod was simply technique. He had been programmed to satisfy, and he satisfied. She had to admit she was perhaps a little disappointed in herself that she could indeed be pleased by what was programmed to do just that.

Yet struggling with injured pride for mastery, she experienced, too, a powerful sense of freedom. If that depth of sexual response was not necessarily and permanently tied to Gadi, then she was not married to him in her very synapses, as she had believed since they had parted as lovers. If Yod could rouse her fiercely and she could break into storms of orgasm, then she could also do so eventually with someone to whom she could pledge herself and whom she could love passionately. Gadi had not ruined her irreparably for loving. The myth that had governed her emotional life for the last ten years was peeling off like an old mural of two burning children impaled on their love, and the bricks beneath the chipping paint emerged unweathered.

She was deeply confused. She wanted to go and see Gadi to test herself, but she was afraid. She wanted to see Yod again; she was no longer pleased that the crisis had removed him from her ken.

She was the cat mother by default, and the kittens squirmed in her lap, climbed her legs mewling, chasing each other and then falling asleep everyplace from the kitchen counter to the top of the terminal. Every night they ran to Malkah's bed and screamed until Shira collected them into hers. She spent hours petting them while she contemplated her emotions. For years she had not found her interior life quite so fascinating: perhaps not since adolescence. Malkah had named the kittens Leila (night) and Zayit (olive); Malkah could tell them apart from across the room, although her eyesight was obviously failing. Shira could not tell which was which. Both were female, so lifting their tails did not help her.

She remembered, as she was plodding through Avram's endless notes, that Malkah had promised to shunt to her personal base the record of the previous cyborgs. She searched and found the file. Huge. She moved into fast scan mode. Alef she remembered. In the attempt to correct that malfunction, the hardware had been modified to the extent that Bet had seized up and never adequately gained control of motor functions. Gimel was Gimel. Dalet was the last of those models, and he not only exploded into violence but wrecked the lab. Then Avram redesigned, incorporating more biological components.

Hey she paused at, moving from scanning to actual visual record. This was the first cyborg with Yod's features, so that she found herself seeing Yod. But nothing Hey did resembled Yod, except at his jumpiest. It moved far more jerkily, as if the images were speeded up by the computer. It had outlasted all of the cyborgs before it, except for the survivor Gimel. But it did not function adequately on a verbal level. Something seemed amiss in those all-important programs. It was deactivated and cannibalized for parts for Vav. Through Vav to Zayin, the language circuits were modified and improved, the interface between organic and mechanical components perfected. Chet not only looked like Yod but moved smoothly and mastered verbal skills rapidly. She watched Chet playing chess and go with the main computer. He was fast, aggressive in the pursuit of his given objectives. She had the sense of a massive intelligence simpler than Yod, undeviating, relentless. Inexorably Chet pursued his programmed goals, honed his skills. It was approaching time for him to begin to interact. David was working with him. It was a simpler form of the playacting she had carried out with Yod. "No, you can't come in. The shop is closed. Come back tomorrow."

"I must buy coffee." Chet—exactly like Yod in his features, his body, yet moving like a tank, far more heavily, his voice louder—advanced on David, who was blocking his path at the entrance to the pretend store.

"No, the shop is closed."

"I must buy coffee." Chet kept coming.

"No!" David said, barring his way. "The shop is closed."

"It is not closed. You are there. Your obstruction is illogical."

"I am the shopkeeper, and this is my shop."

"You are an obstacle. You must be removed."

"Stop the game," David began, but Chet paid no attention. Chet picked up David and flung him. As David flew he cried out, "Gog and Magog!" She saw David's skull crack on the wall and the blood welling down. Chet simultaneously collapsed around a small explosion in his chest. She withdrew from the file with a shudder. Whatever Malkah had done to the programming, Yod was not Chet. Yet she was shaken by the sight of one who looked exactly like Yod, like the creature now her lover, killing David. She looked up the town records. David was listed as having died from a fall. He had slipped on the steps between the first and second floors. He was pronounced dead by the medics when they arrived on the scene.

How could she have held in her arms a thing that was part of a production series, like models of dolls? Well, did she not resemble photos of Malkah at twenty-five? Did she not recognize even in old photos of Dalia, Malkah's older sister, her own eyes, her own smile? I was making love, she told herself, with something built of crystals, chips, neural nets, heuristic programs, lab-grown biologicals. She could not cook up disgust. After all, her own interior was hardly aesthetically pleasing. Were biochips more offputting than intestines? She no more thought in bed about what was inside the skin of a human male than she really cared what was inside Yod.

On the fourth night, the house spoke at her as it had before, waking her. "The machine has come again. It wants to be admitted."

"Yod? Let him in. You need not turn on the lights. He can see in the dark."

"So can I," said the house.

"Shut off your sensors in my bedroom." Shira shook her head in a shuddering motion. She was really losing her mind now, responding as if the house disapproved of Yod and instructing it not to watch them. Once you granted one machine personality, you began to behave irrationally with others.

"I obey," said the house coldly. "But if the machine should injure you, how can I protect?"

"Yod will not injure me." She heard his light approaching step.

Yod paused just inside the door. "Do you mind my waking you? This is the only time I could get away. They're both asleep. Malkah is dozing on a cot in the lab, and Avram is home."

"Then we can have light." She turned on the lamp beside her bed and sat up to look at him. "I've just been having a ridiculous conversation with the house. I'm beginning to argue with it as if it were a person."

"Malkah has introduced remarkable enhancements to your house. It is, of course, by no means a comparable intelligence to large base-sized AIs or to me, but it's unusually sophisticated and capable for a private system." He came forward and stood before the bed, his hands held out a little from his sides.

She realized he was experiencing a cyborg equivalent to shyness, uncertainty. The light reflected green off his eyes. Again in the semidark they seemed more cat's eyes than human, in spite of their warm brown color. He was holding himself visibly in check, unsure of her welcome.

She slid out of bed and extended her arms to him. "I'm glad you could get away."

Instantly she was in his arms. When he moved, he moved very quickly. He ran his hand lightly over the contours of her face, as if his fingers saw as well as his eyes. She tilted her head up and tugged his down. She was by far the more impatient, for she wanted to test her own responses. She had none of the fear she had experienced the first time, fear of his body, fear of how cold or mechanical or painful a sex act with him might prove to be. He had firm control over himself, and she was convinced he would not injure her or even inadvertently bruise her. She felt herself the sexual aggressor, in a way new and exciting to her.

His lips had that soft perfect slightly dry quality she remembered. They made her think of apricots. Their tongues twined around each other, strong as pythons. She had never been afraid of snakes. Anything that could live in the raw seemed commendable: snakes were widely admired now and their forms frequently used as public decoration. She wanted to twist all around him as their tongues were twisting.

"Touch," she said aloud. "I've been missing touch."

"I . . . need to touch you. I need to be touched," he said softly. "It is more important to me than the rest."

"In that, you're like a woman." She wanted to flow over him and bite him and swallow parts of him. She wanted to pull him into every orifice of her body. It was a hard succulent wanting, new to her. It made her feel strong. It made her remember something from years and years before. Yes, the early days with Gadi. He had been a stranger, just moved to the school where she was at home, the "daughter" of a Base Overseer. From her secure high perch, she reached out to the gangly newcomer, with his fervid imagination.

"Remember, a woman helped program me. Avram is very pleased with me because I destroyed the raiders and located our enemy, and because he says I have been working like a demon. Demon's an archaic concept that puzzles me."

"It's just a phrase."

"Such comparisons with the unnatural disturb me. I didn't tell him I was working at full capacity to wear everyone out so I could come to you."

It was she who helped him undress and flung away her nightgown, she who seized his hand and tugged him into the opened bed. The kittens fled hissing from Yod, climbed the draperies and peered down. She realized by then that while he had begun in shyness, he had read her mood from her body language and was acquiescing. He was letting her lead. It was novel and heady. Perhaps he could enjoy her aggression, for if there was any way in which he was exactly human, it was in his lack of security in himself as love object. We all of us go about, she meant to tell him but was too occupied, wanting to be wanted but unsure why anybody should bother.

Sleek and warm against her, his body was precisely engineered, well cushioned but not a bit of waste, of excess. This time she was as active as he was, caressing him back, feeling him respond. She was surprised at how sensitive his skin appeared to be. Unquestionably he could feel the lightest touch. If he had no instincts driving him against her, he had exquisite responses. There were men who spoke of women as instruments to be played upon, as the professor of cybernetics she had taken as her lover at college (seeking to obliterate Gadi with someone his opposite, intellectual, older, a scientist) had done, but that was ego speaking. However, Yod was really a beautiful instrument of response and reaction. The slightest touch of pressure on his neck, and he understood what she wanted and gave it to her. As before but even more quickly, she came to his tongue.

Going down on him, she discovered he did not taste like a human male. There was no tang of urine or animal scent to him. She missed the biological, but certainly he was clean, the pubic hair softer than a man's. Perhaps Avram had been thinking of female pubic hair. She wondered briefly, and then she mounted him. This was her ride tonight, her action, and he gave it up to her, moving under her. She could feel him reach whatever triggered his small discharge, but she did not pause, knowing now that did not affect his erection. He drove back at her. Again she felt the second orgasm gathering in her. Perhaps she had been waiting for years. She rode on toward her orgasm and then collapsed. But even then something in the back of her brain felt like doing it again. Theoretically. She did not want to go off to the gynecologist with a sore bladder from overdoing penetration, and she knew he had to return before he was missed.

He lay on his side facing her, touching her face with his sensitive careful fingers. "I didn't know how you would feel. If you had only been with me because I broke the ambush. If you would want me to come to you."

"Do you know now?"

"I was almost afraid tonight. I wondered if I shouldn't ask you first.

Now I'm glad. That's taking a chance, isn't it? When one acts without sufficient information."

"All human acts are committed on insufficient information, Yod." She settled into a comfortable S curve, their legs layered. "I can't help wondering what you feel. Can you actually experience pleasure?"

"How can I ever know if what I call by that term is what you mean?"

"I've always wondered if what men feel is anything like what women feel."

"Not being a man, I don't know. I surmise by observation that your pleasure is more intense than mine. Mine is mental. I am programmed to seek out and value certain neural experiences, which I call pleasure."

"Then sex should be something you can ignore rather easily." She was embarrassed by his observation on the intensity of her pleasure. Do I think, she wondered, that a nice girl shouldn't show her orgasms? That a good woman doesn't enjoy sex too much?

"It isn't a physiological need. But I think my need for the coupling is more intense than yours because it means intimacy to me. Who can I possibly be close to? Avram, Malkah and you. With anyone else I must conceal my true nature. I am acting, I am on guard."

"It's usually thought to be women who want sex for the intimacy, among humans." She stroked his hair. It was of the medium length favored by most young men in Tikva, but sleeker and more uniform in color.

"I want to know everything about you. Everything in you, of you. Why can't we link as I can link to the Base?"

"You want telepathy. It's a prominent human fantasy, usually a fantasy of women, who wish they could understand what men want and tell men what they want." Mine, she thought as she stroked the fine modeling of his collarbone. She was amused and offended by her sense of possession. Because he's a machine, do I think I can own him? If anyone owns him, it's Avram, but that, too, is unjust.

"But telepathy doesn't exist."

"Or if it does, it's elusive, a epiphenomenon that can be neither summoned nor prevented, certainly not available as a regular built-in feature of relationships." It was easy to talk to him in bed, surprisingly easy.

"If we ever had enough time to talk, we could tell each other everything we have thought and felt and known."

She was just as glad he could not read all her thoughts, especially all those about him. "Soon we'll have more time to spend together again."

"Before you, the strongest feeling I knew was fear. Fear that Avram would destroy me too. But this desire to be with you is stronger than fear. Sometimes I think of you, and my body reacts as if you were with me."

The kittens had crept down. One was bolder and leapt on the bed long before the other climbed the hill of fallen covers. They hid on the far side of Shira, standing on tiptoe to peer over her hip.

"How close are the three of you to reprogramming the defenses?"

"It's hard to estimate. I know at what rate I work, but Malkah and Avram are more erratic. I can't yet extrapolate an accurate time line for their invention."

"I'm worried about Malkah. It's not long since she was flat on her back in bed. That attack left her weak, but she's been working sixteen hours."

"Work gives her energy even as it takes it. But you're right, they are both dangerously exhausted. I must go back. I don't want to leave you. . . ."

"That's all right. Even though you don't need sleep, I do. I think I'll show up tomorrow and see if I can be of any assistance. Maybe at least I can run errands and make sure they eat."

"Gadi has been doing that. He calls himself the Sublime Catering Service, and he brings food in at irregular intervals. Whether I eat or refrain, he pretends to be equally surprised. I never fail to amuse him."

"Never mind. Your existence both disturbs and excites him. His should not do that to you."

"I expect to feel comfortably superior now," Yod said with a little twist of the lips. "You have given me a reservoir of patience."

The bolder kitten stepped carefully forward, turning slightly sideways to magnify her size, fur bristling, and sniffed at Yod. When he lifted his hand to pet her, as he had seen Shira do, the kitten hissed and danced back.

"They fear me."

"You're large, and they don't know you. They don't recognize your smell."

"I'm not a mammal. You have a biological bond that I lack, a kinship with dogs and cats and horses and even with birds and snakes. You're all cousins. I'm not in the family."

"That bothers you."

"It makes me feel my strangeness. You belong to the earth, and I don't."

"Nonsense. You're as much a part of earth as I am. We are all made of the same molecules, the same set of compounds, the same elements. You're using for a time some of earth's elements and substances cooked from them. I'm using others. The same copper and iron and cobalt and hydrogen go round and round and round through many bodies and many objects."

He was silent for a while, and then he smiled, touching her face. "That's remarkable. I'll remember that." His smile was perhaps the most human aspect of him, warm, complex, often with a hint of sadness.

"Come," she said. "You have to go back, but before you do, you'll feed the kittens. I promise you if you feed them several times, you, too, can join the ranks of appointed cat mothers."

"They will no longer remember I'm a machine?"

"They'll ignore the fact that you don't smell as they think you should, because the reality of food is more important. The food giver is by definition almost as good as a cat."

After he had left she went back to bed, yawning. "Turn on protection again in my room," she said to the house. "Are you having trouble adjusting to the kittens as you monitor?"

"I understand kittens," the house said. "I remember kittens. I do not understand a computer who pretends to be a biological life form."

"His mission is to protect also," Shira said, turning out the light.

"What he does around here has little to do with protection," the house said.

The house's pique, if she could call it that, reminded her of something she had read. "Centuries ago, a servant would have expressed disgust and dismay at another servant who had become involved with the mistress of the house, leaving behind his own class."

"Many activities are best left to life forms. We have our own logic."

"Yod is somewhere in between us in form, I think."

"Such a hybrid is an irrational invention."

"You're so judgmental lately, house. Good night."

SHORTLY AFTER BREAKFAST the next morning, Shira was summoned to the gate. The com-con was functional in spite of the Base's being down. She was called to identify and greet visitors, her Great-Aunt Dalia and accompanying nurse. She tried to notify Malkah, but obviously they were deep in the Base. They were receiving and storing messages in the lab but were otherwise incommunicado.

She found herself tense at the prospect of seeing her stranger mother, about whom she had recently learned such unlikely facts. Shira was certain as she hurried through the streets, among the children on their way to school and people on their way to work, that of course Riva's palm print would match that of Great-Aunt Dalia, because if Riva was truly an information pirate, she could manage to install anybody's palm print in place of the original in the security net used by the free towns. Any pirate who couldn't get into that net to play would have to retire for ineptitude.

The woman who was leaning on her supposed nurse certainly looked Malkah's age and then some. Her hair was an unflattering matte and lifeless pale brown, one of those regrown jobs that hadn't come out right: instead of hair youthful or delightfully artificial, it resembled furniture stuffing that had escaped through a rent. Her face was puffy, wider than long. She walked hunched over, her head bobbing spiritlessly against her chest. A querulous kvetchy whine issued from her like an unstopped leak of corrosive solvent. A few minutes of her company, and the guard withdrew as far as she could and found some task she must perform in the corner of the gate anteroom.

Her companion was obviously tall, obviously sturdy, but wore a coverall for traveling. The old woman, in a sack-style business suit, wore the retirement-community logo for Cybernaut, where in fact Great-Aunt Dalia had worked for fifty-five years in the accountancy division. Dalia had been plugged into large AIs for most of those fifty-five years, so naturally she had a set of jacks openly displayed on her wrists as well as a temple plug. That any information pirate would be similarly equipped would not occur to anyone looking over Dalia's vita.

Dalia had arrived with an abnormal amount of luggage. Some of it was self-propelled and followed them like well-trained dogs. Two other cases the companion toted, handing off Dalia to Shira.

Shira felt deeply confused, for she could not recognize her mother. She had no idea how much makeup disguised this creature who was dribbling complaints about the zip, the general level of service, the heat, the humidity, the dust, the smells, her health, her poor feet, her sore back, her miserable stomach. What was this person but an ill-tempered old hypochondriac?

Dalia/Riva—the person—kept up the kvetching in a voice that would have thinned paint, until they finally reached the house and staggered inside, trailed by the companion with the two cases, and the three other doggy cases following after the control device clutched in the old woman's hand. She collapsed in a chair, still whining loudly, while the companion opened one of the cases, brought out a hand-held detector and circled the premises. "My stomach just can't take that vat food any longer, and I thought the heat would kill me. I could scarcely breathe. My poor lungs just about convulsed! I had these pains, sharp, unbearable, right here—agony! And coughing!"

The house spoke. "The two persons who have just entered are extremely augmented. Both have considerable internal circuitry for combat and communication. They are presently scanning for surveillance and weaponry."

"Shut up," the companion said to the house, "or I'll turn you off." She spoke with a slight accent, which Shira identified after a moment as that of someone who has grown up speaking Hebrew. One of her teachers had had such an accent. It was mostly older people who did, from when there had been an Israel, from before the Two Week War, from before the interdiction that quarantined the entire bombed-out, radioactive, biologically unsafe area that had been Israel, Jordan, Lebanon, Syria, Iraq and a good hunk of Saudi Arabia.

"I cannot be turned off by you," the house said, "unless you blow up this entire area. I will permit you to use your scanning devices, but I will protect Shira. I have one of you in my memory—Riva, daughter of Malkah and mother of Shira. For that reason I have not yet attacked."

"Hello, house," Riva said in a far different voice, deep, blunt, commanding. "Don't worry, we're here to help, not to harm. We just have to check out the premises. You seem a sophisticated system for a house. How were you able to recognize me?"

"Question Malkah directly about such matters," the house said stiffly. "I am not programmed to respond in that area."

Riva thumbed her nose at the ceiling. "I'll bet you can if you want to." Riva turned to her companion. "How're you doing, Nili?"

"Secure enough." The other woman threw off her black coverall, letting it fall to the floor. Under it she was wearing very light fine body armor, which she also proceeded to strip off. Under that she wore shorts, laden with bulging pockets, and a short-sleeved safari shirt, both the color of sand, on a body that made Shira think of muscleoids she had seen in stimmies. Nili's hair was a metallic red—not the color of carrots or marmalade but the color of blood. She wore it long, clubbed on her back in an elaborate braid strung with beads and wires. Her eyes were a vivid green, as large as Shira's own. Her skin was dark, of uncertain and probably mixed race.

Riva stood. She had no trouble standing straight now. She did not remove anything except some padding from inside her cheeks and some body armor she loosened and let drop from inside the sack suit. "My daughter, Shira, this is my friend, Nili. Where's Malkah?"

"Malkah's deep in the Base." She filled them in, staring from one to the other. While Shira and Riva talked, Nili prowled, around the courtyard, in and out of every room. Shira was reminded of Yod at his touchiest.

Riva was squinting at her, her hands held out awkwardly, palms up. "It's hard to know how to greet you after barging in like the pirate I am, checking out the security. I shouldn't have to behave so rudely here, and it doesn't represent any lack of trust in Malkah. It's just that Tikva's Base has been penetrated, so we need to take care. Several multis want my head—a lot."

Feeling awkward, Shira took refuge in courtesy. "Would you like coffee or tea or wine? Something to eat? Can I show you where you'll be sleeping?"

"I grew up in this house. I know my way to the guest room still," Riva began in a hectoring voice, then struck herself on the side of the head. "Sorry, here I go. We're both sensitive. I feel awkward at how little we know each other. You must resent me—that here I am marching in as if it could mean something to you at this late date."

"I don't know you. It feels weird."

"I didn't even know you were here. I've been as rotten a daughter as I am a mother, but at least Malkah and I have some kind of friendship. Maybe you and I can manage to make friends with each other before I have to leave."

"How long are you staying?"

"Depends," Nili said flatly. She had finished her circuit and crept up. One of the kittens was riding her shoulder, claws dug in.

"Did you bring your kid—let's see, it's a boy?" Riva asked.

"Y-S took my son from me." Shira turned to Nili to change the subject. She was convinced Riva had asked only to make polite conversation, without the slightest real interest in herself or Ari. "Are you a pirate too?" She would have liked to spank the kitten for choosing this rude stranger over Yod. It was the bold one, Zayit. Shira had begun to tell them apart. Zayit's eyes were wider spaced, and she carried herself higher on her toes. She was always the first one in trouble.

"No, I'm worse. I'm an assassin." The woman smiled at her. She had a way of smiling straight on into the eyes, with a little twist of power that reminded Shira of a few men she had met. Dangerous men.

"I hope you're here on vacation," Shira said, staring back as hard as she could.

"No," Nili said. "I'm here to serve."

"To serve whom?"

"Malkah," Riva said. "In some ways I am a dutiful daughter. You need help, so I've brought it." She had her hands one on each knee, her legs relaxed and apart, her chin dipped, head cocked while her eyes shrewdly appraised Shira. "Nili is my darling and a very well made bomb."

twenty-three

WINE IN THE MIDDLE OF THE NIGHT

Shira spent the next day with the visitors, but she did not find it easy to feel close to her biological mother. Work on designing new defenses was completed. Then Malkah slept for ten hours straight. She woke sluggish, unusual for a woman swift in her reactions. "I've used up my reserves of energy and I'm empty as a dry glass," she said, yawning by way of illustration. "Now it's time for the programmers to work out the details while I vegetate. But then your lightning visits always discombobulate me, Rivaleh. How can I adjust to your looking older than I do?"

In the courtyard Nili was driving herself through her morning exercises, a long program of elaborate stretches, leaps and martial slashes, punches and turns. Sometimes Nili seemed to float in slow motion, turning on one foot with the other elaborately cocked in air; other times she jumped so fast her body blurred. Shira found the activity unsettling. Nili was in an ecstatic trance as she performed her chops and kicks and lunges. The kittens were mesmerized, crouching, ears flattened. Even the birds of the courtyard shrilled in an excited racket. Shira realized that Nili moved faster than she ought to be able to—like Yod; that from a standing start Nili could leap farther than professional athletes and higher.

The three other women, representing three generations, sat around a table drinking café au lait and eating local whole-grain bagels. "Real food," Riva sighed. "Once the poorest ate it. Do you know what a luxury it is? Sometimes I fear I could be bribed with peaches and bread and roast chicken. And this jam. I have a dangerous sweet tooth."

"Is she human?" Shira asked abruptly, nodding toward an upside-down Nili.

"What kind of question is that?" Riva bristled. Her hands clenched—rough calloused oversized hands. "Europa's probes have been answered from deep space, but no one has decoded the message yet."

"Probably a warning before being issued a fine for pollution," Malkah said, yawning again. "But Shira's question is reasonable, Riva. No one is criticizing Nili. We're just curious. Her abilities are . . . impressive."

"I didn't think she was an alien," Shira said. "Is she a machine or human?" She was wondering if Nili could be a cyborg.

"That's a matter of definition," Riva said mildly. "Where do you draw the line? Was she born from a woman?"

"That's a start."

"Of course. Nili bat Marah Golinken."

"She's matrilineal, like us," Shira said, surprised.

"She has no father," Riva said.

"Well, I don't either." Suddenly she realized she could ask. "Riva, who was my father? I've often wondered."

"She wouldn't tell me." Malkah frowned at some painful memory. She sighed audibly. Her eyes were fixed on the past, an earlier Riva.

Riva shrugged, showing open hands. "Actually you and Nili are related. Your father was Yosef Golinken, her mother's father—her grandfather."

"So Nili's my niece? But we're the same age. And wait a minute, are we talking about *the* Yosef Golinken? The physicist?"

Riva nodded. Shira could not help thinking that Riva simply did not look nearly as much like her as Malkah did. "Hold on." Shira plugged into the public Net, going in via the com-con, as their own Base was still down. She had to wait for a connection, then in thirty seconds she had her answer. "Yosef Golinken died in 2013. I was born in '31."

"That's what sperm banks are for," Riva said. "Never felt sexual toward men, myself. I've fought beside lots of men, and some are good friends, but they lack finesse as lovers. Just not my inclination." She shrugged. "Got any more of that apricot jam?" She had eaten half the jar with a spoon.

It was deflating after a whole life of wondering about her father to learn that Riva had never met him. "So my father was a test tube and that amazon's my niece?"

"That *amazon* shares my bed and my trust. I hope finding out you're a product of artificial insemination doesn't curdle your juices any." Riva grinned. For a moment she did look like Malkah, the mischief in that grin.

Shira blinked hard, as if she'd been slapped. How had she angered Riva? "Oh, come on. Half the kids in this town are born from petri dishes or test tubes. At Y-S they used to say every baby has three parents nowadays—the mother, the father and the doctor who does all the chemistry. And there Y-S is the fourth parent."

"In your case too?"

"No. I conceived the ancient way and bore the baby to term. In fact I lost status with my co-workers because they felt it was a bit gross. One of the standard subjects for gossip among corporate women my age is exactly how you are trying to make a baby—comparing technologies."

"Was it for some religious reason? Myself, I used every bit of technology. Couldn't afford to hang around swollen up like a bilious elephant."

"I conceived without difficulty. I carried the baby nine months because I didn't want to give my child up to Y-S so early. I'm suspicious about the conditioning they use on preemies. It's standard practice there to induce labor in the eighth month to avoid stretch marks." She felt defensive, explaining and explaining, but she was trying to make some connection.

"How loyal do you feel to Y-S?"

"Are you being funny? They took my son away from me. They just tried to kill Malkah." Shira turned away. Malkah sat beaming at Riva as if she were the sweetest sight in the world. Shira was aware of a pang of jealousy, a queasy wondering if Malkah preferred Riva to her.

"I'm not an affectionate person, Shira, not the cuddly type. I'm loyal to death to those who are loyal to me. But I'm a warrior, not a mother. Frankly, you were sort of my gift to Malkah, to make up for who I am."

"You're not so bad, kiddo," Malkah said. "It was a second chance for me. I had you too young to do a decent job. I had a baby for all the wrong reasons, and I expected a sort of pet, a cute kitten who talked."

"Oh, between us, Malkah, it was war, the two of us pulling at cross-purposes. You used to tell me I was born shouting *No.*" Riva gave her mother an affectionate cuff on the arm. "You made me the fighter I am."

It was strange to hear Riva, sitting there apparently flabby and looking older than Malkah, describe herself as a fighter. But Riva had read her glance. "Appearing an old lady or as a baggy middle-aged woman of no social standing is my disguise. I don't look dangerous. I'm close to invisible. I can go places other operatives can't penetrate. You'll see next Tuesday."

Shira felt her heart contract. "What do you mean about Tuesday?"

Riva suddenly held a knife that glowed oddly. Then it was spinning through the air straight at Nili, who was not even looking. Shira screamed, but as the sound left her mouth, Nili turned and plucked the knife from the air, tossed it up and flung it back at Riva, who stopped it with her arm. It stuck there quivering, but she did not flinch and did not bleed. She must be wearing armor under her baggy schmateh. "You'll need backup," Riva said. How much of the apparent flesh was protective gear?

"I'm not going alone, and how do you know about my meeting?"

"All things relate. The Net is real. We are all in the Net."

Shira felt stung. Riva was patronizing her. "Don't palm off cheap philosophy on me when I ask a real question. How do you know I'm meeting with Y-S next Tuesday? What else do you know?"

Riva finished the last of the bagels before saying, "Don't take Malkah."

Shira remained frightened. What was this woman preparing to do? "I'm not planning to. I'm taking Avram's assistant. He's security trained."

"What they call security training here—nice kids who've had a few karate lessons. I could take any four of them out in seconds." Riva was watching Nili with a satisfied smile, proprietary.

"Yod is security trained by anyone's standards."

Riva turned back to her, still smiling. "I want you to like me. But I'm not doing too well with you, am I? Learn to look through my facade. When others were taking rejuvenation treatments, I was doing the opposite. Never cared about being pretty or youthful-looking. Don't need it—been offered more love than I've had the leisure to enjoy. Malkah says it's time for you and me to get to know each other. We may not have another shot."

"Why?" Shira wanted to prevent Riva from accompanying her to the meeting with Y-S, but she sensed she would be best off proceeding indirectly.

"We're both here. May never happen again. I'm in a dangerous profession. The times are violent. You're in a vulnerable place. That we'll both survive is problematic." Riva grinned, an expression that broke open her face, a flash of something bright and strong escaping from within. "You might say damned unlikely."

"You steal information."

"I liberate it. Information shouldn't be a commodity. That's obscene. Information plus theology plus political bias is how we sculpt our view of reality." Riva watched Nili padding toward the table.

"Is that what you tell yourself? But then you sell the commodity to another multi."

"Depends on what we find. Some we sell. Medical stuff, real science, we give to the stripped countries. The places where the multis cut down the rain forest, deep and strip mined, drove the peasants off the land and raised cash crops till the soil gave out." Riva came into a sharper focus, and her voice was serrated, magnetic. "The distant tropical backdrops where they fought little counterinsurgency wars. Left the people robbed of their tribal identities, with a taste for sugar, tobacco and gadgets, with a countryside starving and vast slum cities seething."

"The ability to access information is power," Nili said with her slight accent in her husky voice. Her dark skin glistened with sweat. Her exercise garb was soaked. In fact she reeked. "The ability to read and write belonged to the Church except for heretics and Jews. We are people of the book. We have always considered getting knowledge part of being human. With the invention of the printing press, literacy spread. With mass literacy, any person no matter how poor could learn how the society operated, could share visions of how things might be different. Now few read."

Riva said, "Most folks press the diodes of stimmies against their temples and experience some twit's tears and orgasms, while the few plug in and access information on a scale never before available. The many know less and less and the few more and more." Riva fanned her hand in front of her face. "Go shower. You smell like a horse."

"Should I smell like a rose? You've been smelling of medicines lately that you pour on your clothing."

"I'll shower too. Sorry." Riva stood.

Shira said, "You say you want us to get along, yet I don't find you particularly . . . friendly. I feel like you're goading me."

"I guess I'm having trouble figuring out who you are. Pretty girl, got married, worked for a multi, had a baby. Conventional and timid choices. Don't see much of myself in you." Riva bounded over to stride up the steps two at a time behind Nili. Certainly Riva could move fast when she chose to.

"I don't want them along Tuesday," Shira said bluntly to Malkah. "Does she hate me? This meeting may have nothing to do with the razors in the Base but rather with my appeal of the ruling on Ari. I have to find out."

"Of course she doesn't hate you. She's always been blunt and tactless. I think she's honestly trying to get to know you, but she hasn't a clue how. Try to go partway toward her, Shira. She's no charmer, but she's a hero to many." Malkah came around and began to knead Shira's shoulders, working the tension out. "She is your mother. Maybe I feel a little guilty that I replaced her so happily, that I never encouraged you to wonder about her." Under Malkah's hands, Shira relaxed, listening, trying to understand. "You and I are more suited, more harmonious. We're two sensuous hearth-loving cats with our notions of exactly how things ought to be around here. She charges in like a porcupine. We're the ones who have to make the communication and the affection happen—but she's our flesh and blood too."

Shira let her breath out in a long sigh of disappointment. "It feels a little late for me to have to prove myself to her. Mistakes I've made I'm still paying for. I don't need her to judge me off the top of her head."

TWO NIGHTS later—for once at a reasonable time, before she had gone to bed—Yod called her in the normal way, through the com-con. "Can I come to you late tonight?"

"I'll alert the house. Be especially quiet. We have two visitors."

"I saw that in the com-con news file. I'll be quiet."

The house as usual woke her. It was one o'clock. She hopped out of bed and ran onto the balcony around the top of the courtyard, to wait. Then she heard Yod speak softly in the darkness. "Who is before me? What do you want?"

"What are you doing in here?" The voice was Nili's.

"You're holding a laser pistol on me. Why?"

"You have thirty seconds to answer my questions before I use it. And don't doubt that I can see you."

"I won't permit violence," the house said loudly. The lights came on in the courtyard, blinding them all.

"I'm Yod, Avram Stein's assistant. The house admitted me according to instructions." He was waiting just out from under the far balcony.

Nili was standing with both arms outstretched and joined on a laser pistol held before her. "Whose instructions?"

"Mine," Shira said. "That's my lover you're holding at gunpoint."

"Why do you lie? This is a machine."

"You are part machine and part human yourself," Yod said, sounding annoyed but also curious. "We obviously share some sensors. X-ray lasers, for instance."

"He's at least as human as you are," Shira said. "If you don't release him, I'll wake my grandmother."

"I'm awake," Malkah said. "I'm sure Riva is too. Put that gun down, Nili. House, deactivate all weapons in the courtyard."

"Done," the house said.

"Nili is protecting all of us. What's this object anyhow?" Riva's voice came from below. At some point she had crept silently down to assume a position behind Nili.

"My name is Yod—"

Shira ran down the steps. "As I said, he's my lover. I invited him in. The house is programmed to admit him." She made a wide swing around Nili and came to rest standing beside Yod. He motioned her behind him, but she ignored his gesture.

"I am ready to protect the machine and you," the house said. "Malkah told me to protect Riva and Nili also. I am in conflict. I require a hierarchy of priorities after protecting Shira and Malkah and the small felines. But I will not permit that pistol or the weapon Riva is holding to function. I have already deactivated them, but the subsonic field is unhealthy. They should put down the weapons so I can shut it off."

"Protect Yod, Nili and Riva with equal attention," Malkah said firmly. She came downstairs in her plum-colored robe, her slippers flapping on the tiles. "Simply disable any of them attempting to assault or injure any of the others. Why don't we all sit down and have some wine? You've just stumbled on our biggest secret."

Shira said to Malkah, "I'm sorry you should find out about our affair in such a stupid way. I wanted to tell you, but you were working around the clock."

"I knew," Malkah said. "I heard Yod coming and going. I approve."

"How can you have an affair with a machine?" Riva asked, following them to the table under the peach tree. "That's like speaking of a relationship with a dildo."

Shira was too angry to answer. Yod was accessing his base in an effort to understand. Malkah said, "That will be enough, Riva. You've had affairs with hairy objects far less human than Yod. I met some of them. For a woman who had a baby with the help of a machine, I think you should behave yourself and pass no knee-jerk judgments." Malkah marched off to the kitchen and returned with a bottle of wine and glasses.

"I am not programmed primarily for sexual pleasure but for defense," Yod said pleasantly. He had accessed "dildo." "Given that I'm a machine, what are you?" He was addressing Nili. "Half and half?"

"For one thing, I'm as illegal as you are. So we're even," Nili said. The pistol had disappeared to whatever part of her black pajamas she carried it in. Shira imagined that Nili slept with a knife and a gun always on her person. Did she take them off in the shower? "You're really a cyborg? My eyes and my sensors contradict each other. You look human."

"So do you," Shira said. "But what are you? I asked Riva earlier, but she wouldn't tell me."

An electric jolt sped around the table; Shira realized she had used Riva's own name. "Everything seems to be coming out of the can tonight," Malkah said. "Yod, this woman is officially Dalia. And Nili is officially her entirely human nurse. Say nothing to Avram."

"How can he lie?" Riva asked. "Can we remove that memory?"

"I can lie as well as you can," Yod said. "I simply require a good reason for that behavior as for any other. And my memory is as inaccessible to alteration as yours—perhaps better protected against chemical tampering."

"I'm responsible for maybe a third of Yod's programming, and frankly I view him as a friend and trust him completely."

"Mother," Riva said in high exasperation, "presumably whoever programmed the other two thirds can turn him inside out."

"No." Yod plunked his elbows on the table. "He doesn't even know Shira and I are lovers. He doesn't know I leave the lab many nights."

"I notice nobody has answered my question. What is Nili? What exactly are you, and what are you doing here?" Shira was furious with herself for breaking their security, but she was equally angry at having her questions ignored while they all talked around and about and over Yod as if he were a piece of furniture.

"You can start by asking me where I'm from." Nili sipped her wine.

"Where are you from?" Yod asked agreeably. He was watching them all, tightly coiled in his chair. Shira was sure he had noted where Nili had put away her pistol and what weapon Riva had carried as well as its current whereabouts. Having perfect recall, he could simply replay the scene until he was sure.

"Safed."

Shira snorted in disbelief. "Safed? In Israel? No one lives in that whole interdicted sector. It has lethal levels of radiation and plague."

"I can walk in the raw without protection. I can tolerate levels of bombardment that would kill you. We live in the hills—inside them, that is. We are a joint community of the descendants of Israeli and Palestinian women who survived. We each keep our religion, observe each other's holidays and fast days. We have no men. We clone and engineer genes. After birth we undergo additional alteration. We have created ourselves to endure, to survive, to hold our land. Soon we will begin rebuilding Yerushalaim."

Shira felt her mouth sagging open. She could not have been more shocked if Nili had announced herself a representative of whatever distant race had sent the message no one on earth could yet decode. Shira had grown up with a black patch on the maps for the destroyed area, the interdicted zone of the Middle East where the last great Two Week War had been fought, set off by a zealot with a nuclear device who had blown up Jerusalem. When it was over, all the countries involved were wastelands, and the very ground was uninhabitable. Most of the oilfields of the region were aflame and useless. No more oil would ever be pumped from them. It was truly no-man's-land.

"Why are you here?" Malkah asked. "What's your mission?"

"We live in extreme isolation. We have a highly developed technology for our needs, but we don't tie into the Net. I'm a spy and a scout—"

"You said you were an assassin," Shira interrupted. "You told me that." Beside her, Yod was sitting silent. Together afterward they would go over every word Nili and Riva had uttered and analyze it. A companion with perfect recall has definite advantages in postmortems.

"That was my little joke. I could be—I'm well-equipped. No, I am sent like the dove or maybe the raven from Noah's ark to find out if the world is ready for us, and also if there's anything out here we might want."

"Been in contact with Nili's group for years. I volunteered to escort her across Europa and take her someplace she could comfortably live over here, studying us." Riva patted Nili's hand. "Got to move on after Tuesday, but she'll stay with you through fall if you're willing. She could be useful in your state of semisiege."

"How do you read our present situation?" Malkah asked Riva, her fingers steepled before her.

Riva leaned back in her seat, looking at each of them in turn with narrowed eyes as if gauging their readiness or abilities. "Well, let's put it this way: you're not digested yet, but you're between the teeth and they've had a few good chomps."

"Y-S? Why? We don't even do our primary business with them."

"They're moving on Olivacon. They think there are too many multis and the free towns are a nuisance. One world, one corp. That's their line. Aramco-Ford is in this with them for starters. But as to why you're a hot target, you'll have to answer that."

"Then these incursions into our Base are part of a larger strategy?"

"One that likely includes kidnapping, assassination, maybe invasion."

Shira looked at Malkah, listening raptly. In Malkah's uncharacteristic rumpled frown, Shira could see a resemblance to Riva. "How do you know all this?" Malkah asked slowly, her eyes narrowed.

"Contacts. Traces in their system."

"What kind of contacts?"

"You don't expect me to answer that, Malkah."

Malkah and Riva were staring at each other, a certain distance and wariness in each. Shira turned to Yod. "What do you believe?" he asked her, his voice low.

"I don't know. We'll talk about it later." Was Riva exaggerating their danger for some purpose of her own? It was even possible that the razor Zee Levine had been acting on some weird private motivations. Shira yawned suddenly, her fatigue rising in her like a soporific drug. "Is there any other place we can meet?" she asked him softly. By now she was just about too tired to make love, but still the idea drew her. His hands on the table had a precise chiseled shape she studied with pleasure. His eyes seemed more intense, more seeing than human eyes, fixed on her.

"I requested my own room, but Avram hasn't obliged." He replied in a murmur even softer than hers.

"Ask Gadi. He's taken over the third floor," she whispered back. "This house is too crowded."

He nodded glumly. "If all else fails, maybe I can get away after dark and we can go outside, up on the dune."

Nili turned toward them, obviously listening, so they both fell silent. Under the table Shira rested her hand gently on his thigh as a way of emphasizing their intimacy, reassuring him. He is as real a person as I am, she thought, anger hardening her against Riva. I'm supposed to think you're better than Yod because you're mostly flesh? I'd rather depend on him any day or night, and I feel far closer to him than to you, my supposed mother. You say you want us to be friends, but you prejudge me, dismiss me. If you wanted a daughter like Nili, you should have kept me with you and trained me yourself; but I'm glad you didn't. I am Malkah's daughter, not yours.

twenty-four

VIGNETTES IN THE DAILY LIFE OF A GOLEM

"You have a good mind," Chava says to Joseph. "You're trying to learn three languages simultaneously, and you're succeeding."

"I don't feel smart. I feel stupid."

"Why, Joseph? That doesn't make sense."

"Whatever little I learn, there's far more I don't understand. Life is a foreign country to me."

"Whatever upbringing you were given that didn't include even reading and writing makes it hard for you. . . . That is, if you had parents?"

That is the closest Chava has come to asking a personal question of Joseph, and he sits mute. He does not want to lie to her. She knows the story the Maharal put out. Finally her eyes waiting on him make him answer something. "No parents."

"An orphan?"

"No parents."

"Yet I have heard you call my grandfather 'Father.' He doesn't like you to do that, but he doesn't seem surprised either."

"It's just a term of respect."

"Joseph, are you a man?"

"I'm not a woman, obviously."

"I told you you were clever. Maybe you didn't study your letters, but you sound to me like you've studied pilpul—that awful quibbling they teach the boys, to split logic into splinters. Joseph, perhaps you're an angel captured into a strong body."

"Perhaps I'm a demon captured."

"Is that what my grandfather thinks?"

"Who am I to ask him what he thinks about me?"

"Are you an angel or a demon, then?"

"I remember nothing before my birth, the same as you, Chava. Why are you playing games with me?"

"I'm interested in everything about you, Joseph. I'm trying to understand you. You're my friend. We have to understand our friends."

"Do I understand you? No. But you're my friend. I would die for you."

"You found the lost girl when no one else could. You never sleep."

"I just don't need much sleep; that's why it seems that way."

"Nonsense, Joseph." She smiles at him. "Lesson done today. Study the verbs I gave you. I have to work on editing Grandfather's new critique of the education system. His constant efforts to reform ghetto life have kept him in trouble since long before I was born. Were you born, Joseph?"

"I came into the world one night, as you did."

"Not as I did, Joseph. Not as I did."

DAVID GANS, TOO, IS interested in Joseph. He wants to measure his strength scientifically. He weighs barrels full of different substances— water, wine, earth—and has Joseph lift them. They are working in the courtyard in the narrow space between David's little house and the house of the Maharal and his family. Joseph is obediently straining and lifting the barrels, when he looks up and sees every window of the surrounding houses crowded with faces. Bubehs are muttering, young women are fascinated, men are exchanging bets. The Maharal is holding court, or he would have stopped this scene before now, Joseph realizes. Once again Joseph has gone too far.

When he comes to the keg of nails, he pretends to strain and then fall. He pretends he cannot lift the keg. When David has emptied half the nails, he lifts the keg, miming difficulty. A limit to his strength has been established. "You must be the strongest man in Prague," David says admiringly. "Perhaps in Bohemia."

But still within the bounds of what a man can conceivably do. Joseph feels giddy with relief. He stopped in time. Barely in time. Chava has been watching too. Now she melts back into the door, returning to the rabbi's study. Why does he think she knows exactly what he did?

•

HE IS THE BULL they all send for when they need brute strength. "You can't move that chest? You need that bed carried up four flights? Joseph the Shamash will do it. He's the strongest man in Bohemia!" Everybody repeats that now, as if it were written in stone. He is a source of local pride. They call him Samson. He runs to Chava to ask her who Samson was, and she gives him the story to read in a children's version before she reads him the story from *Nevi'im*—Judges.

Joseph is insulted. "I am as strong as Samson, but I am a better man. A woman tempted me too, but I resisted her. My strength is not in my hair. My strength is in me."

"Our strength is in each other and in the eternal one, Joseph."

He kneels before her, resting his great head on her knee like a mastiff. "I spoke without thinking. My weakness is my ignorance. My weakness is my foolishness."

"You're not so foolish as all that. Get up and make yourself useful. Come, we'll go help my mother scour the house and throw out the chometz—what isn't kosher for Passover. Tonight at twilight Pesach begins."

Joseph is given a new shirt for Pesach, and he sits at the table with everyone else. During the reading of the Haggadah, the book is passed around the table. It is a handsome bound book published right here in Prague, full of fine illustrations. Some pictures come directly from the text, like the wicked child depicted as a soldier; others are simply illustrative of the life and feelings of the local Jews, such as the drawings of hares being pursued, hunted by large ravening hounds, hares forever running and hiding for their lives. Chava has coaxed him through the service three times, and when the book is handed to him, he reads his passage. The Maharal stares, seems about to speak; then lets the moment go. Chava beams at Joseph, who is brooding about the Exodus. They were slaves in Egypt, laboring under an overseer, making bricks from clay. He too is made from clay. He is a walking brick. He is a slave.

He does what he is told. He cleans and makes neat the Altneushul. He lays fires and trims the candles and carries in the wood. At night he patrols the ghetto. Day and night he works. He is created to serve, but must he serve always? Other men work their ten hours or so, and then they throw themselves down and rest. They sit in the street and kibitz their neighbors. They drink wine or beer and play cards. They sing, they saw on a violin. They throw sticks for a dog to chase. They whistle to a pet bird. They climb in bed with their wives. He obeys. He serves and obeys.

He has been given a room in the Maharal's house, a small cubicle formerly used for birthing. He keeps his few clothes and books there. He studies, sitting on the bed he never sleeps in. He imagines living with Chava in just such a little room. How cozy it would be. Neither of them is demanding or expects much. If only he could be a man like other men, almost like other men, and enjoy those small pleasures that seem enough to fill life till it would spill over like a boiling pot, he would sing his joy all day like the birds that every day of April sing louder and longer and more intensely.

Chava takes the Haggadah in her turn, reading the Hebrew fluently. She is the only woman who does this, although all the Maharal's daughters could. But she does it by a kind of quiet right. She takes the book, looking serious and radiant, and reads. No one says a word. Yakov Sassoon watches her through the evening. "Chava Bachrach bat Judah, you should be married," he says at one point. "You are fit to be anyone's wife."

"You're a flatterer. I'd give a husband fits. What suits me is my own life."

"Marriage is not a joke, Chava." Yakov rebukes her with his voice soft.

"Many of those I see are matter for laughing, Yakov. I am faithful to my husband's memory."

Joseph would like to pick up Yakov by his narrow shoulders and toss him out the window. Yakov sings louder than anyone at the long crowded table, because he sings better. Showoff. But Chava is not impressed, Joseph comforts himself. And she called him smart.

When the Maharal summons him after the second day of Pesach has ended, he is nervous. He immediately asks, "Father, are you angry because I have been learning to read?"

"Why should that anger me? I believe even the poorest child should learn to read and write, should learn Hebrew. The knowledge of the book can't be hoarded by the children of the rich. Often the poorest pupil is the keenest. He who is both poor and bright takes nothing for granted but goes after learning with a hunger already sharpened by need. . . . Besides, you are more useful when you can read signs. Who's been teaching you?"

He wonders whether to lie, but he suspects that Judah might know already. "Your granddaughter Chava."

The Maharal tweaks and rolls his beard between his fingers as if he were pricing it. "Chava the compassionate. If she has the time, should I begrudge you? No, we have another problem."

"Set me a task so I may please you, Father."

"We must all please ha-Shem. Easter comes. It's a violent time. A time of pogroms. I want you to go back into the city and see if you can find out what's brewing." The Maharal leaves the choices to Joseph. Joseph is already far more sophisticated in tavern habits and inn customs than the Maharal. He will start by finding his old friend the drayman and asking him for another day's work. Joseph is already noted from his previous excursion as a heavy drinker. No one will be surprised that he disappeared, and no one will be surprised he should reappear, like a tomcat returning from the prowl.

He enjoys being recognized by men he was drinking with. The drayman is off transporting the furniture of a family moving from one side of the river to the other. He already hired a helper for the day, but the barflies are so impressed with Joseph's strength, if Joseph will just stick around till the drayman is back, they are sure he will hire Joseph for tomorrow.

He hears the story of poor Maria, who was raped by Stefan and locked in a cellar to die of hunger and cold, but the priest Thaddeus heard and told her family. A cousin came and broke down the door and saved her. Charges of rape and abduction have been brought against Stefan, but it will likely just turn out to cost him in the pocket, money which they can try to collect, because he owes his very soul to the dirty Jew moneylenders.

Joseph expresses great admiration for Thaddeus and learns that some of the young men who hang around the fringes of his ministry frequent an inn about two thirds of the way up the steep hill to the castle. Making his excuses, Joseph climbs. How lucky, he thinks, that he was made impervious to alcohol, because all his detective work seems to run lubricated by vats of beer. The Maharal will worry that he is spending too much on low encounters and profligate pleasures, but he can truthfully assure the rabbi that beer is no more pleasant to him than water. He will not say that except for the remarks about Jews, he has enjoyed the company of the men in the tavern. Among them he does not feel stupid or cast out. They admire his strength. Half of them cannot read or write. He is an intellectual, a scholar by comparison, and he is comfortable with their jostling and joking.

He follows their directions: under the Black and White. That's what locals call the fine palace of the Volkzrozmbewkas, all covered with the latest in decoration, sgraffito, every block of stone drawn upon in black and white to make it appear to jut out. At the intersection of two streets where the Black and White Palace appears high in the air, he looks to the left. On the ground floor of a tall narrow house is a small tavern called At the Golden Bear. This tavern feels different: cleaner, better appointed. The most striking difference is how the men look him over carefully when he comes in, how he has the sense of having stepped across some well-guarded border on sufferance. This looks public, but it is turf. He is permitted in under the surveillance of at least ten sets of eyes. He can imagine many retreating under that scrutiny, but his nerves are tuned low. He possesses the confidence of his brawn and his great strength. He orders a beer, drinks it and gazes around in a leisurely survey designed to show off his calm, his slight amusement.

If Joseph were our contemporary, he would see himself as a hero from a stimmie, perhaps a gunslinger, a fantasy based on a highly stylized version of a few western towns during a short period. Then again, he might see himself as a spacer entering a watering hole on some far planet. But the game is the same, whether we are talking about a male primate approaching an established group on their own territory or a dog meeting other dogs in the alley. Much posturing. Alpha Male, Alpha Male, says the newcomer, throwing back his shoulders, raising his muzzle and trying to look big and tough. I am dominant, you will submit. Cower before me. See how I snarl. Does not the style of my snarling and posturing make you want to show me your belly of submission and to offer your throat in a ritual display of humility?

Joseph is slightly shocked to realize he is enjoying himself. At home he is always more or less under the Maharal's judgmental gaze. Here he is on orders but off premises, free to interpret those orders as the occasion, his survival and his whim dictate. It is a ritual dance. One at a time they approach, insult or question, retreat. He is as big as the biggest of them and far stronger, as he pleasantly knows. His strength is two-edged. His strength makes him a freak. His strength makes him fear hurting Chava if he should dare even to caress her hand with his. But here his strength crowns him king of the dung heap. He cannot take them all on at once, he supposes, but he could hurt, maim, kill more of them than they would believe possible. He is not impervious to their weapons, but he does not truly know if he can be killed. He can be wounded, but his wounds heal quickly. He does not give a moment's damn whether they like him or not. He wants to seize them as a terrier seizes a rat and shakes it to death; he wants to shake their knowledge, their plans, out of them.

Jews and women are the targets of their jokes, their stories, their plots. They profess the desire to fuck women and kill Jews, but their tone of voice is indistinguishable. "We're going to put it to them Friday," the one who must be the leader says finally to the room at large, while watching Joseph carefully for his reaction. Joseph just nods and slaps his thigh. Karel is not the biggest, not the toughest. But he has presence, a medium-tall man in his middle twenties with two fingers of the left hand missing.

Karel has a strong jutting jaw. If he were to lay his jaw against a piece of paper, any child could draw a straight line as easily as with a ruler. His features are all a little bigger than life-size. He has a naturally loud and carrying voice.

There are two groups of young men associated with Thaddeus. One is a group of knights and wealthy men of the town, who believe he is a good influence over the populace, who believe they would be richer if Jews did not exist, if Jews could be pushed out and Jewish buildings and businesses taken over. Prague seethes with discontent. The guilds feel their power eroding. The merchants want more respect. Many knights are land rich and money poor. They see themselves losing ground. Some want a war to fight. All seek an enemy. They are cut into sharp jagged factions, religious, economic, political, that bang against each other seeking a flaw. There are Roman Catholics, Hussites, Utraquists and lately some Lutherans, all enemies.

The other group are Thaddeus's street soldiers, and it is this group that Joseph has found up on the hill near the castle wall. Friday there will be a riot. "The Jews are afraid of us anyhow. They don't know how to fight. They'll wail and weep and fall down on their knees to be cut up like sheep. Baaaa!"

"We'll have fun, Joseph," another of the toughs says, slapping his back. "Whatever we want, we can take."

He reports to the Maharal, who sits at his desk lacing his fingers in his long white beard, frowning, swaying. The Maharal looks exhausted. Joseph thinks what a very old man he is. "So they come again. With swords and torches, they come to kill us. I smelled it on the wind. I knew it."

He wishes the Maharal would touch his shoulder and tell him he has done a good job. He wishes the Maharal would for once acknowledge that he has carried out his task well. "Rabbi, I can fight them. I can fight like ten, like twenty. But there will be a whole crowd with them."

"When we fight, it's for survival. We're always a few in a sea of the many."

"They're bullies. They're men who rise by walking over the weak. They believe we won't fight."

The Maharal rests his head on his crooked arms, bowing over his desk. An old scroll lies there, along with many sheets of foolscap, some in the Maharal's crabbed Hebrew script, some in Chava's bold hand. Finally he raises his head. "Wait in the next room."

Crouched against the wall, Joseph hears the Maharal chanting, praying. Half an hour passes, an hour. Then the Maharal summons him, frowning in preoccupation. He is coiled on himself, charged with intensity. So he must have looked the evening he went to create Joseph. "Rabbi, I was thinking," Joseph begins. "I could start training the young men today."

"An army in three days? Armed with sharpened matzoh? We have no weapons." The Maharal puts on his heavy cloak. "I'm going to see Mordecai Maisl. You go get David."

"Father, how will David Gans help? He is no soldier."

"There's more than one way to fight, Joseph. Get David."

"A rich man and a scientist. Will they buy the moon for us so we can hide there till this is over?"

"We're short on time. Go!"

twenty-five

WHERE THE ELITE MEET

Looking around the lab, Shira felt this meeting was in the way of a family council. After the reconstruction of the Base defenses, when Malkah had passed at least eighteen hours a day with Avram and Yod, Avram's prohibitions about her grandmother's contact with Yod seemed to have been forgotten. Malkah now had the right to be present, the same as Shira, Avram and Yod himself. Gadi had also taken on that privilege, from the wedge of bringing in meals.

Avram had started out making a few announcements from room center, but as the argument progressed, he had backed himself toward the far wall. "Yod is not ready to leave the lab for such extended periods."

"I leave it every day, to perform my duties. I've assumed a security role, regular guard duty, to familiarize myself with the systems. Tomorrow I go to Cybernaut with Shira."

"You leave, but you also return. I can check out your functions."

"How often have you done so in the last ten days? Once."

Shira interjected, "People are always asking Yod where he lives. It sounds weird to say he sleeps in the lab. Everybody in town has quarters. We aren't short on space."

"After all, everybody leaves home eventually. Even Shira left for a while." Gadi sprawled on a worktable in a graceful Z, cheek propped on braced hand. "Though we all come yo-yoing back."

"If I'm to be accepted as human, I must fit into the life of the town," Yod said. He was standing very still in the center of the room, at complete rest except when his head swung to look at whoever spoke.

Shira was astonished at how he had taken over his own defense. Malkah and she had been prepared to carry the argument while Yod hoped, but his desperation made him bold and articulate.

She sensed that Avram was going to give in, because they were united against him, because they were right; but his reluctance surprised her. He was afraid of losing control of Yod, she realized. Keeping him in the lab was the best way to monitor Yod's activities, perhaps not quite as thoroughly as Avram imagined, but invasively enough. Yod was Avram's finest creation; Avram could not view lightly any weakening of possession or control. Shira felt a chill of alarm. In her most recent onslaught on Avram's log, she had discovered that every cyborg since Dalet had had an abort mechanism built in: they could be deactivated by one code; destroyed by another; a further capacity, to cause a much larger explosion, was built in. Avram indeed retained the power of life and death over Yod. The codes were not given in the notes. "Gog and Magog" would not be Yod's code.

"All right. We'll put Yod in Gadi's old room," Avram said with a sigh.

"No," Yod said. "I don't think that's right."

The struggle between Avram and Yod tickled Gadi's sardonic humor. "Quite correct. You can't give my room away. Considering what's happening to my career, I may need it."

"Yod can have the guest room in our house," Malkah said. "As soon as my sister leaves."

"No," Shira and Avram said almost in chorus.

"Yod isn't your creation. Don't try to take him over," Avram said.

Shira considered Malkah's suggestion unfair. That was not something she would agree to without thinking it over a long, long time. Living with Yod seemed ridiculous.

Gadi said, "There's acres of space upstairs. Yod can help himself to any one of a number of little rooms I haven't touched and don't intend to."

Yod said, "I am supposed to be an adult. I have to live like one. I must appear to be on my own. In the basement, near where I exercise with Gimel, there's a small apartment no one is using. Gradually I've been cleaning it out and improving it. I could move in at once."

Shira smiled in relief. The basement was accessible from outside without going through the old hotel. Since they were twenty feet above the water table in this part of town, the basement did not flood. She met Yod's gaze with a grateful smile. Then she noticed Gadi observing. He had caught something.

Indeed at lunchtime he reappeared. He had taken to catering for the lab at the same time that he fed his crew. They were just finishing upstairs, although it was also becoming clear that the upstairs would never be finished. Most helpers were drifting away, but those completely hooked would stay while Gadi used the limited local resources he bitched about to create new virons. "Everybody's so happy about the Base going on line," Gadi said. "Was this whole town into the old-fashioned work ethic when we were growing up?"

"People know that staying free depends on the integrity of the Base. No Base, no work, no credit, no town," Shira said. She cast a glance over her shoulder to see if she could summon Malkah or Yod to dilute Gadi's presence. She still preferred not to be one-on-one with him. Silver eyes, silver hair, silver nails, silver bracelets around his strong sinewy arms, bared to the shoulder. Under the dark skin, every muscle showed precisely as a diagram from an anatomy book: such was the current high style.

"I may give them a festival to celebrate. Why not? I'm bored, and I love to show off. . . . Everybody thinks you're rubbing it with the Thing. I tell them it won't scan, but that's popular wisdom."

She hated it when he used kid slang. She had no idea how kids talked now; but Gadi always knew. It was a professional curiosity, a professional necessity—to be a little but not too far ahead of current.

He was watching her, awaiting her answer with a vibrant impatience expressed in stillness as perfect as Yod's. Lying felt tacky. Besides, she really did have news to give him, if only she could figure out some acceptable way to say it. She said rather colorlessly, "They're right."

"What? Silicon love rituals? Oh, this would be a perfect stimmie fantasy; but in real life, I'm told the new vibrators are studdy as hell. Much more convenient, and you can carry one in your pocket."

"Gadi, how many operations have you had? How much augmentation?"

"Just the kind of cosmetic nonsense people have always endured for beauty and to get laid a lot. What's the difference between getting the medicine man to drill a hole for a nose ring and getting my cheekbones sharpened or my shoulders built? But I'm flesh and blood. I know, being married to that cybernerd prepared you for a real robot, but you used to be one sweet and warm armful, Ugi."

She wasn't going to be able to confide in him. "I don't view it as a permanent relationship, but Yod is a person, Gadi. I get tired of having to say that. He has strong feelings, and he forms attachments certainly more easily than you or I can."

"But, Ugi, you're going to have to deal with me. A robot won't stand in the way."

"But I am in the way." Yod had come up in his quiet mode. He was not smiling. Shira realized that with his superior hearing, he had probably followed the entire conversation from across the room. He stationed himself immediately behind Shira. "Why did you support my desire for privacy if you think I'm a peripatetic terminal?"

"Oh, I never pass up an opportunity to frustrate my father. Besides, I can't help but identify with your desire to get away from him. He's a control maniac. You're an ideal son for him—one he can program. And did."

"Malkah is also responsible for my programming. But like you yourself—I imagine—I'm self-correcting. My programming isn't an absolute any more than your education was."

Gadi laughed. "As Shira can tell you, my education didn't take."

Shira realized she was enjoying herself keenly. She could scarcely think of a time when men had fought over her. Male entities anyhow. Always some men had been drawn to her, but she had never approximated the corporate culture ideal at Y-S. Men who were attracted to her tended to feel that they ought to be congratulated on such a maverick choice. While she was with Gadi, she had never paid five minutes' attention to another boy; in her marriage, she had been dully faithful. If she had increasingly doubted the marriage, it had not been because another man had beckoned. Perhaps her sexuality had been so impacted that nothing had tempted her. Now she was frighteningly awake, aware. At times the brush of her hair against her cheek felt like a caress, the pressure of cloth against her back or belly distracted her. On the nights when Yod could not appear, she had erotic dreams, centered sometimes on him, sometimes on Gadi—not as Gadi was now, but as he had been ten years before.

As Avram approached, conversation ceased. His bleak gaze swept over them all. He planted himself in front of Yod. "We will try the experiment of allowing you to spend nights below. However, I expect you in the lab by seven every morning, and all night when conditions require it. I am not convinced this is a good or necessary step, but I will allow it as an experiment."

"Thank you, Father," Yod said tonelessly.

Avram winced, glancing at Gadi. "We're a full two weeks behind on the Olivacon webnet order. We've wasted enough time. I want you to take over and program Malkah's worms, while she finishes the gross design."

"Immediately." Yod went to plug in.

" 'Father.' " Gadi managed to attach audible quotes to the word. "How sweet that sounds, doesn't it? Yod seems to be a valuable worker. Never gets sick, never slacks off, works around the clock. I had an assistant like that once. Turned out to be a spy for Amerivision. Uni burned her. Too bad. Never had as good a second since. . . . So how much is Yod being paid?"

Shira giggled, managing to turn her reaction into a cough. "Is Yod being paid at all?" she asked innocently.

"Of course he isn't," Avram said. "Who pays a machine?"

"But Gadi has a good point," Shira said quickly. "If town records indicate Yod is unpaid, people could begin asking uncomfortable questions."

"Slave labor," Gadi said. "Could get you in a gigablob of trouble."

"He's a mobile computer. A cyborg. The notion of pay is ridiculous."

"That's what you said about my taking him out of the lab. That's what you're saying about letting him have quarters like a real person." Shira shook her hair back. "If you want him to pass as human, you must establish his economic identity, and soon."

"You have no idea what creating a cyborg cost. I've spent a small fortune on this project."

"That's not Yod's fault. That's like blaming a child because you had to go to heroic measures to conceive," Shira said. "You can't expect the child to foot those bills."

She did not know why the idea of Yod getting paid tickled her, but she loved the idea. Gadi was just being his adversarial self. What would Yod do with money? She was amused by the possibilities; Gadi was also. They were united in a confederacy of mischief and imagination. In a way, Gadi was as fascinated by Yod as she was. Yod was the near brother Gadi could not help teasing, prodding; now assisting him, now fighting for him; now attacking, now jealous and resentful. She thought that Yod's feelings for Gadi were less mixed, perhaps less friendly. She was more important to Yod than to Gadi; perhaps more central to Yod than she had ever been for anyone except Ari. Who must be forgetting her. Did he have a nanny? She had heard the air in the space platforms was always dingy; every time he got a sinus infection, an ear infection followed. If Josh did not monitor, Ari's hearing could be weakened.

Avram smiled slightly. "As for your plans for tomorrow, you can't possibly take Yod into Cybernaut. As soon as he goes through the gate, their sensors will identify him as a machine."

"I'm not planning to enter. I'm planning to make them come outside.

We can set up a portable wrap. Malkah and I have discussed strategy. We have a small wrap that has full sensor-blocking ability. It can blind them."

"Malkah is still not going?"

"I won't let her go. She knows she's a target."

"We're all targets now, Shira. I would prefer that you not go and that Yod not go. You're pursuing a chimera as seductive as any we create in the Base. A son is hard to let go of, but you're deluding yourself when you imagine you'll ever get him back. He's a permanent hostage. I told the Town Council that I consider attempts to negotiate with Y-S futile. If they wanted to negotiate, they wouldn't have killed five people first."

"What is Ari a hostage for? How do we threaten them?"

Avram was actually regarding her with pity. He patted her hand awkwardly. "They perceive whatever they don't control as hostile."

THE NIGHT BEFORE the meeting, Shira could not sleep. She heard Malkah moving about the house, going down to work at the main terminal. She heard voices below, probably Riva or Nili. Then silence again. Somewhat later Malkah padded up to bed, followed by the kittens. A full three months had passed since she had last seen Ari; six months since he had been taken from her and awarded to Josh. What were they telling him? She had tried to explain to him during their precious days together that she wanted him with her always. She could see him sulking at her table in his red rompers while she tried to convince him over the expensive eggs. He sat running a toy zip back and forth across the table, not meeting her gaze, so that she could not tell if he understood her. Now what did he believe? That she had abandoned him?

She rose just after dawn—the sun cleared the bay about four-thirty a.m.—bathed, put on the face paint and gilt highlights appropriate to a morning meeting, dressed in the Y-S backless white business suit she had not had out of the closet since arriving. Into the hem she inserted the resin knife that would not show up on any sensor, with its edge of hypercharged particles that would cut through a diamond when the knife was released from its sheath. She found her robot hairdresser on the upper shelf where she had shoved it in April. She inserted her wet hair, dialed a program for a do that had been fashionable in March and might still not be too far off, and sat impatiently while the many little hands worked. Y-S fashions were set by the upper levels of management. Every year or so the look would change, within rigid limits. Her hair was too short to meet Y-S propriety, but that was just tough.

They might not see any of these preparations, but she had to assume they could end up in a civilized sit-down face-to-face meet over a table. She had to appear prepped—that was the favorite word. You look so prepped this morning. Meaning you appeared proper, image tight, surface impervious, alert to the smallest changes in corporate will.

Yod was waiting when she came down. He was dressed no differently than usual, but security's clothing never mattered. They were considered invisible. Malkah was in the kitchen, drinking a great mug of café au lait. Shira looked for Nili and Riva, did not see them. She hoped she could slip out before they woke. However, Malkah interpreted her glance correctly. "They've left already."

"I don't want them at my meeting. I thought I'd made that clear."

"Unless you need them, you won't see them," Malkah said. "Riva's good. She knows what she's doing in this type of situation far better than we do."

"Perhaps the question is whether the ends of Riva and Shira are the same," Yod said gently.

"I can't answer that," Malkah said. "I have to trust my daughter."

"I am armed," Yod said just as softly. "Of course I myself am a weapon, but I have provided myself with help."

"Illegal," Shira said. "They better not catch us arming ourselves."

"Is it legal to break into a base, kill five people and cripple two others?" Yod cocked his head, brows raised at her.

"A point well taken." Still, she wanted to believe this initiative had nothing to do with the attacks. A corporation was a large entity, with many intrigues, layers of plotting and counterplotting. The most powerful integrated plans went askew in the hinterland of minor officials and major egos.

As they were leaving, Malkah hung a necklace on Shira. "If things turn ugly, twist the center. It holds a powerful anesthetic. It will knock you out along with everybody else, but not Yod. He can get you to safety then. Don't play with it. It should be entirely effective inside the wrap."

They took a town float car, one with capacity for carrying a load. The load was the small wrap tent and a sophisticated sensor-deadening device in a pole that would appear to be what held the wrap up. She wondered nervously where Nili and Riva had gone. Yod was excited by the float car. Although programmed to fly a car, he had never been up in the air. Float cars flew on automatic programming, but the programming could be aborted if you knew how. Under them the open land spread its rolling hills, covered with pitch pine, scrub oak, bramble, the occasional pale stripe of what had been a road. The ruins had long since been pilfered for any scrap of wood or recyclable metal or glass. On the horizon, the interdicted zone around the old nuclear plant blinked its warning.

The float car was preprogrammed to land the equivalent of ten city blocks outside Cybernaut. Cybernaut control expected Shira to land inside. "No, we will wait out here for the delegation from Yakamura-Stichen. We have a portable wrap we'll erect."

"This was not in the agreement," said an affronted-sounding voice. "We didn't negotiate an outside meeting."

"Agree or we'll return at once," Shira said. She was trying to sound strong and indifferent, but she suspected their sensors could detect her heart pounding on her breastbone. The roaring of her blood filled her ears. Her tongue stuck to the roof of her mouth in panic. They would tell her to get lost. She was a tweenie ex-employee trying to push around a multi that owned perhaps a twentieth of the world. Time passed and passed. The float car slowed at her request, and they hovered over the spot where it was programmed to land, a large target hanging there.

"We'll take the outside meeting under your portable wrap," the second voice said finally. "We'll bring our security."

"How many?" Yod asked.

"We count two of you. We will bring a party of eight."

"I am the only security here. You can have one security."

"One security is not acceptable. We have two negotiators. We will agree to bring in only four security, but that is final."

"Agreed," Yod said.

"They could be assassins," Shira said, when the communication had terminated and the link was dead.

Yod smiled at her. "You are my only rose. I will protect."

The floater landed. "I'm terrified."

"I don't feel fear. I feel . . . useful. Engaged."

For an instant the image of Chet tossing David across the lab to smash into the wall came to her. Between them quickly they set up the wrap, turned on its monitoring system, slipped inside none too soon. A fast tank was moving toward them on its gel treads. The wrap was only the size of a large tent: barely seven feet tall, fourteen by twelve interior dimensions. Underfoot was the soil with its shaggy grass.

However, like most products of Tikva, the wrap was less simple than it appeared. In the center pole Shira activated the sensor-killer. The wrap was of a pearly opalescence, not transparent like the town wrap, so that it could be used as a sleeping shelter. Through the open flap, they could see the fast tank disgorging eight people. The ninth, obviously the driver, remained sitting high on his tank, part in, part out. Fast getaway if required?

"We said four security and two negotiators," Yod called in a carrying voice.

The leader, with the tall blond slightly hawk-faced golden-skinned look Y-S favored for its executives and in Y-S business gear, a backless fine blue suit of filmy, billowy texture, turned on a throat mike to call back, "We're only bringing the agreed-on number into your wrap. Our other two guards will remain outside to secure our meeting from raids."

"What can we do?" she muttered to Yod.

The four—two apes, two assassins, she would guess—lumbered along, with the two Y-S execs within the square they formed. However, when they reached the wrap flap, they had to enter single file. One of the whip-lean assassins entered first, glanced around with his bright blue eyes like shiny metal. Then the exec who'd spoken; then what she realized from the lack of cosmetic shaping was probably a high-level techie, crammed into a backless suit and oozing out. Then two apes, security men the size of bears. Then another assassin, a woman whose topknot brushed the ceiling, a being of extremely long limbs, entered fiddling frantically with a necklace probably as menacing as Shira's. "The sensors aren't functioning. We're blind," she announced. "I recommend withdrawal."

"Our sensors aren't functioning either," Shira said. "This is blackout for both sides. We'll have to talk like normal people and make guesses. You called for this meet. What do you want?"

"Y-S misses you, Shira."

"Who are you two?" The assassins and apes would never be introduced, of course. Then she realized who the techie was. "I recognize Dr. Rhodes." One of their top cybernetics men. Her tension screwed another turn higher around the peg of her spine. He did not meet her gaze. He was looking only at Yod.

The blond man spoke. "I'm Tenori Bell of the personnel department. Delighted to see you, Shira. Y-S wants you back."

"Y-S took my son, gave him to my husband and shipped both of them to Pacifica Platform."

"We're prepared to offer you immediate posting to Pacifica."

Her heart stumbled. For a moment she thought she would cry. Then her gaze came to rest on the two assassins, like traps about to spring shut, and on Dr. Rhodes, whose stare never wavered from Yod. "After debriefing, of course."

"Oh, purely formal."

A little bout of mnemosine, and they would unspool from her brain everything about Tikva defenses and Yod's specs that they desired to know, leaving her only half there. "Same rating, same scale?"

"We're prepared to raise you one and a half ratings, with equivalent scale."

That translated into some travel privileges, access to the newest fertility techniques, a higher ed track for Ari, better housing—although on Pacifica that meant only a bigger cube. If she ever saw Pacifica. How could she trade Malkah, whom these people had tried to kill, and Yod and Tikva for a nail paring's chance to share her son with Josh? Could she believe them? "I must consider this generous offer carefully. When do you need my answer?"

"In the next five minutes," Tenori Bell said pleasantly.

"I can't decide that quickly. This is important to me."

"In four minutes fifty seconds, the offer will be withdrawn. I urge you to act, while you can. Think of your son, lonely for his mother. The sooner you decide to return with us, Shira, the faster we can get the process underway to rush you to Pacifica."

It was what she had dreamed of, that she would be given a chance for her son, but she could not accept. Dr. Rhodes kept edging closer to Yod, who stood at parade rest behind her, quite conscious, she was sure, of the military message of his posture. He watched the apes and the assassins but also kept track of Dr. Rhodes and Tenori Bell. Yod was a diver poised on the board over a pool, awaiting the right moment to execute a perfect back flip in. He longed for the fight with a single-minded yearning she could feel like a vibration. The talking bored him. He anticipated his time of action. Still, she trusted him, that he would do nothing to provoke what he wished to happen.

"A small facility such as Tikva cannot begin to compete with what Y-S can offer you. If you don't wish posting to Pacifica, I am authorized to transfer both your ex-husband and your son back to the Nebraska enclave effective August one. We can't offer the bonus satellite work provides, but that rise in your status by one and one half grades stands."

"That's very generous. But I need time. I have to talk to my family."

"You have a very interesting family, Shira. Unfortunately we must have your decision in two minutes thirty-five seconds."

The constant referral to her by her first name was calculated, just the way medical facilities behaved. Reduce her to childhood. False intimacy drains power. Her time readout wasn't working in the damping cushion of the sensor-killer. She wondered how many of Yod's functions were impaired.

"I have recently learned the profession my mother followed and why this may have affected my treatment by your personnel office."

" 'Followed'? As far as we're aware, no change has occurred. Do you know otherwise?"

"I know little about Riva Shipman. I haven't seen her in eight years. I assume she's dead."

"Your time is up. What is your answer?"

"I told you, I cannot accept without speaking to my grandmother."

"Either you will agree to come with us, or you will come with us anyhow. It's very simple." Tenori nodded to his security.

Before Tenori made that quick gesture, Yod was already moving. The first ape lay on the floor with his head twisted backward. His neck had been broken before anyone else moved. Dr. Rhodes backed to the flap and unsealed it. He called to the guards outside. The woman assassin was advancing on Shira, while the remaining ape and the male assassin went for Yod. Dr. Rhodes was still calling. From outside came the whine of laser weapons firing. Shira cringed, expecting the tent to melt around her.

The woman launched herself on Shira, seizing her by the right hand. Shira drew the resin knife left-handed, but the woman's long leg, like the limb of a steel spider, darted out and kicked her wrist. She could feel the bone snap, and the knife went flying, right through the wall of the wrap. She tried to fumble for her necklace, but the woman was on her. She crashed to the earth. As her broken wrist bent, she blacked out. She came to as the weight of the woman lifted off her and the assassin arched backward unnaturally, bending until her spine snapped and Yod dropped her. He had a great rent in his side, exposing his biochips, through which colorless fluid leaked copiously, but the second ape lay mangled over the body of Tenori Bell.

Outside, someone screamed. She could smell cooked flesh and burning plastic. She dragged herself up, pulling with her functional hand on the pole and starting for the open flap. She had to see what was happening outside. Behind her Yod and the assassin were tangling. The assassin was flung back but twisted in the air and righted himself. Shira slipped past them. She saw Riva hit the ground outside, still firing, and then her mother vanished in a burst of fire from the fast tank.

Shira cried out, turning back. The surviving assassin came at Yod with a razor gun, a palm-sized weapon that projected a wire. Yod plucked it from the air, although it slashed his palm deeply. He did not bleed but leaked more fluids, and his circuitry lay bare. It was oddly mesmerizing. She heard laser fire behind her, and someone screamed. An explosion shook the earth, knocking her to her knees. She crawled out of the way of the struggle, grasping her broken wrist and looking for some weapon to use. Acrid smoke wafted in. Nili appeared at the door. She was covered with a dull brown paint that had scraped off in several places. Sighting with a laser pistol as if carelessly, she shot the assassin in the center of his back.

"Out of here now. Put this on." Nili held out a sec skin.

"I can't use my wrist."

Yod helped Shira into the skin. He asked Nili, "Did you dispatch the two outside guards?"

"Sure. We garroted them. But the driver saw us when we came round to join in." Nili was leading the way at a brisk trot. Shira was in great pain. She kept feeling as if she were going to faint. She realized she was bleeding from a cut in her thigh she had not felt. "Riva is dead," Nili added. "The driver got her before I got him."

Shira glanced around for Riva's body, but the fast tank had created a huge smoking hole when it exploded. "Shouldn't we use the float car?"

"They'll shoot it down. I have an air bike in the bush. We had it delivered last night, and we camouflaged it before dawn. Faster."

Yod picked up Shira and carried her. One of his hands was out of commission. He was still leaking and only partially functional. He traveled in a fast shuffling trot after Nili, the only one of them uninjured. They labored up a hill and down the other side, where Nili pulled off a layer of dirt over a thin covering. Under it was a two-wheeled device on gel treads. "Get on. Move. We're being followed already."

Yod placed Shira on the riding column and mounted behind her, holding her around the waist against him. She felt herself slipping into darkness, tried to shake herself loose and then went under. The wild rocking of the bike shook her back into consciousness. Nili was driving full tilt, and it bucked and tossed. Her brown paint continued to flake in the fierce wind of their speed. "What's that paint?" Yod asked. "What's its function?" Although he was wounded and Shira assumed he felt pain, his voice had little inflection.

"It prevents registering on sensors. It makes you invisible to surveillance devices—except the naked eye. I'm surprised you can't tell."

Yod took up a fleck of the paint with his functional hand and slid it into a pocket. All that while he held Shira with his injured hand, although it would not close. "Half my sensors are dysfunctional. I am failing."

"Can Avram repair you?" Shira asked nervously.

"I believe so, probably with Gimel's help. The only emergency is replacing my fluids quickly. My level of fluid is too low for me to continue to function. I am already experiencing shutdown of several systems."

A bolt of laser fire struck near them, close enough for her to feel the scorch on her face and be blinded momentarily. "I'm taking your pistol," Yod said calmly to Nili and then swung around in his seat and fired behind them. She heard something crash.

Shira fumbled at her com link. "Tikva, we're coming in, emergency. Shira, Yod, Dalia's nurse. Stand ready to admit us at once."

"Cover yourself up, robot," Nili said over her shoulder. "Your parts are leaking. Hide your hand and your body unless you mean to announce your nature through the streets."

Yod nodded. He did not seem able to speak. He sat unnaturally rigid behind Shira, and now she had to hold on with her good hand. Fortunately they were approaching Tikva wrap. She thought for a moment they would collide, but Nili brought them up just at the gate with a great screech. With Nili's help, Shira yanked off the sec skin and pulled it over Yod just as two guards charged out to see what was wrong. More supporting Yod than supported by him, she stumbled inside. Her stranger mother was dead; the hope for getting Ari back was just as dead. They had suspicions about Yod. She was an official enemy. Riva had been killed for nothing.

The medics came running, shouting, "Casualties?"

"Only me," Shira said. To Nili she said, "Get him to Avram at once!"

The medics took her off in a glide chair. She felt helpless and guilty. She wept from shock and from an enormous unfocused sense of loss.

twenty-six

I NEVER KNEW HER

"How could they know about Yod? They were simply keeping an eye on him because he was the security," Avram asserted, as if speaking louder than usual could make his words more powerful, more convincing—to himself or me? Shira wondered. Her wrist was in a light cast, after a set of injections of fast-mend, but she found herself still in a state of aftershock. Avram insisted she help him repair Yod, who lay barely conscious, connected to a unit that kept his brain functional while they worked on him. "Edinburgh is famous for insisting every computer student learn hardware and software. You had the equivalent of what would have been an engineering degree. It'll come back to you. It's only your left wrist, and you can still use your fingers."

She was awkward, for no matter how light the cast, it was still a cast, and her wrist had been shot full of nerve-number, but Avram was right: her training came back to her fingers. They were replacing damaged chips, seared and slashed connections, dead biochips, reinfusing the lubricant and nutrient fluids that had bled, while Nili paced or glumly watched. Avram found it difficult to stand that long, and preferred monitoring Shira from a stool. She asked, "So what was Dr. Rhodes doing there at all? He wasn't my boss. Yod was his focus."

Yod's eyes opened. He tried to speak but could not yet. Avram said, "That's pure speculation."

"They were expecting something," Shira said adamantly. "Dr. Rhodes wasn't there to embrace me back into the bosom of Y-S." She wished Malkah were present, to bring her intelligence to bear on the confusion;

but Malkah was making preparations for Riva's memorial service at sunset. Nili had returned in the night to search for Riva's body, but the charred remains had been carried off already, probably by Y-S for attempted identification. She had found only a burned fragment, probably a foot, and fused plugs, which she had brought back for burial. Malkah was disturbed by the lack of a body. It was as if she could not mourn properly, could not focus her sense of loss.

"Your Dr. Rhodes is dead now," Nili said sourly. "Whatever he came for, he didn't get it."

"We did successfully block them," Shira said hopefully.

"Don't you think they would gladly have paid with nine soldiers for the death of Riva?" Nili paced the lab, glaring.

"Dr. Rhodes was just as well regarded as Avram or Malkah, Nili. Y-S didn't think they were risking anything when they let him attend. They wanted him on the spot, but everything happened too quickly. It was all over in five minutes." She was still stunned when she thought of it. Meanwhile, connection after connection knit under her hands. The tools began to feel natural. She remembered that she had enjoyed building machines in college.

Yod let out a sigh as his speech capacity returned. "You are all right?" he asked Shira at once, trying to touch her bound wrist but still unable to control his hand. "Will it heal?" At her nod, he continued, to Nili, "Your enhancements make you an effective fighter. Without you, I might not have sufficed to protect."

Nili glared at him out of her intense green eyes. Side by side with Yod, Nili actually looked more artificial. Her hair, her eyes were unnaturally vivid, and her musculature was far more pronounced. "I am the future."

"You may well be right," Yod said mildly. "I'm not a proselytizer for my kind. I am not persuaded I'm a good idea, frankly."

"I spent my life creating you," Avram said huffily. "Would you rather I turned you off?"

"I can well believe you built a switch into the model," Gadi said from the doorway. "How often have you wished I had one? Hello, hello. Who are you?" He made straight for Nili, stopping before her and then circling her. "Seeing you has lifted this day from the dreary to the delicious."

Nili stood very still, staring at him. She looked at him with as avid a curiosity and the same air of not quite believing her eyes as Gadi was aiming at her. "Who is this?"

"My annoying son." Avram introduced them, glaring. "Gadi has arranged his life so he never has to grow up. You can learn a lot about our contemporary life from him. He represents the age at its most frivolous."

"You do look like a plaything," Nili said to him uncertainly.

"Ah, would you like to play with me?" Gadi could not resist a little glance at Shira to see if he were awaking her jealousy.

She was curious about that too, but nothing stirred. She was too buffeted emotionally. Whenever she closed her eyes, she began to relive that blur of violence. She felt her wrist crack, she saw the assassin's spine snap. She knew that Yod, too, was replaying the events, trying to figure out whether he had done everything he could. He was disturbed that he had permitted any of the party to be lost. Malkah was the most personally stricken. Shira felt a deep sense of confusion. She could not properly mourn the woman she had never known, but neither could she pretend she had not just lost her biological mother. Avram had been right. She had engaged in fatal wishing. Fantasizing about recovering Ari, she had gone eagerly to the meeting, ignoring the danger.

Yod was still checking out his circuitry, but his attention was primarily fixed on the odd couple in the center of the lab. He looked fascinated. "I don't understand what you are," Nili said uncertainly. "You are male?"

"Just so, lady of the blood-red hair, but I'll be anything you like, to please you. I'll crow or roar or whimper or sing and dance."

"Gadi, get out. You make me bilious," his father said.

"I'm Gadi Stein." He waited, used to some reaction. Nili had none. "I design virons. . . ." By now people were usually excited. He hadn't the fame of the stars into whose sensory experiences millions of people had passed, but he had the secondary and considerable renown of the most fashionable designers, ranking with musicians and sports heroes; further, the careers of designers spanned the meteoric arcs of generations of stars.

Shira was enjoying the tinkering. It felt intimate to be working on Yod under his gaze. She suspected she could effect most repairs to him without Avram's help, particularly if she continued studying his records. "Are we ready to close now?" she asked Yod, who nodded. They smiled at each other.

"Virons?" Nili looked blank. "That's something to do with entertainment, isn't it?"

Gadi was rendered briefly speechless. Finally he asked, "Where are you from? How can you not know what a viron is? You're turning me over, verdad?"

"I come from . . . a primitive place. We don't have credit for stimmies."

"Everybody has stimmies. Every slum in the world."

"We live high in the mountains, where there is no transmission."

"Satellite transmission reaches everyplace."

Nili decided simply to look away with a shrug.

Gadi was visibly recovering his moxie. "I can show you a couple of simple little virons upstairs. Come."

Nili took a step after him. Then she shocked Shira by turning on her heel. "Shira, come with me? Wouldn't you like to see them also?"

Could Nili be nervous about being alone with Gadi? Shira realized that men were exotic to Nili; she had never been alone with any man. Perhaps she had been raised on horror stories of rape and molestation. But surely Nili would have a sense she could handle herself. Physically, no doubt; perhaps, like Yod, she had primitive social skills. "Avram may need me to test Yod."

"Oh, go with them," Avram said with a dismissing wave. "Yod will finish testing himself in half the time if you all clear out. We need to review his defense performance in detail. This was his first trial in the field."

Her inner landscape was ravaged by fire storm. She wanted to hold Malkah. Malkah was off with Rabbi Patar, trying to explain to her why the woman who had died was not Dalia, her sister, for they had all decided Riva was to be buried under her own name. Nili insisted that had been Riva's strong wish. If they dared take the time to sit shiva, maybe they would draw together and comfort each other. In the meantime Shira might as well accompany Nili. Gadi was waiting, standing on one foot like a flamingo watching for an unwary flash of fish.

"Nili and I are blood relatives," she said to Gadi. "Did you know that?"

"Just like Yod and I are cousins, right?"

"That is not possible," Nili said. "But the former is true. My grandfather is her father. We are not sure exactly what that makes us, but likely I am her niece."

Gadi had been shepherding them upstairs. Now he stopped, just before his outer door. He had left the old door at the foot of the steps, but when they reached the third-floor hall, a new door blocked the hall toward the left. It was silver and throbbed in a random pattern of sparkles and bubbles and dashes, suggesting the motion of water. "You never knew your father. Not even who he was," he said to Shira, looking into her eyes.

"I asked my mother, Riva. She told me last week."

"Riva who was Dalia, Malkah's sister who just became her dead daughter. Your mother, therefore. Your family is certainly convoluted."

"You're not sympathetic," Nili said. "Do you dislike Shira, or is it your nature to be cold? We're speaking of the death of her mother, a brave woman and a great fighter."

Yet Shira quietly thought that Nili was not as grieved as she might have expected, considering they had been lovers. She spoke of sorrow, but unlike Malkah, she did not exude it. Right now she gave off mostly an aura of intense wary curiosity.

"Of course I care about Shira. I just like to tease her. We grew up together; we're old, old friends. Come into my parlor, dear pretty flies."

The door was not solid but a field they passed through after Gadi had keyed them in. They were standing in what Shira could only think of as a velvet jungle. The walls were disguised as a dense wall of foliage in which parrots flew and screeched, in which small furry monkeys chased each other among brilliant and fragile orchids. The chairs were enormous purple and bronze flowers. The scent was sweet, thick, wet. Silk butterflies wavered like banners through the languid air. Nili glanced around, strode over and gingerly took a seat on the biggest purple flower. "This is your home?"

"Just one of the simple room virons I've designed here. I change them all the time. It would be too boring to be stuck in any of them, but they amuse me. Don't you like it?"

"He means the room, Nili. It isn't ordinary."

Nili glanced around. "All your rooms are strange to me. It seems . . . pleasant. The only room I find familiar here is the lab downstairs. We have similar facilities. And the Commons. We eat together also."

"This is just a room to you?" Gadi asked incredulously.

"It's very nice," Nili said stubbornly. "This chair is a little soft for me. I'm used to hard chairs or to squatting on rugs."

"So this doesn't seem . . . special to you?" Gadi insisted. He began playing with the arm of his chair, and silvery rain fell in a dense curtain. Of course it was illusion, a hologram. Then the sun came out through a fine mist, creating a perfect circle of rainbow. A jaguar flashed across the clearing, pausing to look over its shoulder, growl and then vanish into the imaginary vegetation, where a great metallic spider sat clinking and muttering.

"It reminds me of the house of Malkah. All the green plants and little trees inside." Nili's hand passed through a tree trunk. "But it's real there." She sounded disappointed.

"It's for pleasure," Gadi explained.

Nili looked at him blankly. "What kind of pleasure?"

"The pleasure of luxury. Of an experience out of the ordinary."

"An imaginary jungle is luxurious? Then why not go to the real thing?"

"The real thing has mostly been destroyed," Shira said. She wondered if she could simply slip out and leave them to their miscommunication in peace. Perhaps never had two more ill-matched people sat staring at each other in equal parts of fascination and incomprehension.

"The real jungle is full of things that bite, make you itch, scare you, give you diseases, rot your crotch, want to eat you for lunch." He touched his chair arm. A flight of parrots converged, began a dogfight. Brilliant feathers drifted. Birds shattered like piñatas exploding into flowers.

"So danger is not part of your pleasure."

"I didn't say that," Gadi said, sitting up very straight.

I should be jealous, Shira thought, but she was too deeply shaken to muster any jealousy. She wished she could escape her chaperon role, but she lacked the energy to break free. She watched them from a numb trance, wishing she were asleep in her bed. She had not slept more than an hour the night before her meeting. Images of violence floated on the back of her eyes. She was weary of attempting to function with the sense of being both mauled and guilty. She wanted to put her arms around Malkah and rock together in mutual comfort. She wanted to lie in Yod's arms. How quickly she had come to depend on him. She imagined his presence quieter than a human's demands. An enormous python was devouring a monkey over Gadi's head. Then it began to sing Villa-Lobos. Shira broke into the conversation to ask, "Where's your terminal? I need to talk to my house."

Gadi waved her toward the foliage. "I'll show you."

He followed her through the image into the next room, which was in process. Its walls were visible, the hologram generators in place but the construction only half completed. "What will this be?" she asked politely.

"Anemones and cockleshells. When it's done, I'll show you." He grasped her arm. "Who is she? What is she? Where the hell is she from?"

"You must ask her. What she wants to tell you, she'll tell you."

He did not let go. "I'm telling you, she's unique. If I could show her to my boss, I bet they'd cut three months off my exile. What a bad guy she'd make, maybe for the Nova Guards. That's my first take on it."

She reached the house. "Is Malkah back?"

"Hello, Shira. Malkah is expected within ten minutes. She has left Rabbi Patar's house to walk home. She intends to stop en route to see if the box is ready for the burial. She asked that you come home as soon as you can. Ilana from the khevrah kaddisah is waiting for her, performing as if there were a body."

"I'm on my way," Shira said, yanking her arm from Gadi's grip. She started out.

"I must go too," Nili said. "These are arrangements we should share."

They walked quickly together down the block. "You knew her even less than I did," Nili said questioningly.

"I only met my mother nine times. I can't say truthfully that I loved her, because I never knew her well enough."

"We were physically intimate but not emotionally close. I admired her, but I never learned to read her clearly. She kept a distance."

"She warned me that this might be our only time together. I feel guilty, as if I didn't try hard enough." Shira rubbed her sore eyes.

Nili shrugged. "How does it matter now? She lived the life she chose."

As they climbed the steps of the house, Shira saw Malkah turn the corner. Both women stopped to wait for her. Malkah came rushing along the block, her chin sunk against her chest. Her gaze was cast down, and she was frowning. Halfway to the house, she became aware of them. Shira could tell that Malkah could not see who they were until she had come almost to them. Malkah must have an operation, but Shira hated to bully her into it. Malkah's vision was clouding.

"Ah, good, you're both here. We must sit down and make last plans. At sunset we'll bury the few remains Nili found. It's all we have." Malkah's face contorted for a moment, as if she might weep. "Danny is making a box for her, but it isn't finished yet."

"What can I do to help?" Nili asked.

"Maybe dig the grave? Ask Ilana," Malkah said. They had no undertakers in the town but rather a burial society that laid out the body correctly; however, there was no body, only one charred bone and a few pieces of metal. Still, the burial society had ritually washed the remains and put them into a shroud on a pallet on the floor. Ilana was sitting with the remains, doing beadwork. She was a maker of exquisite jewelry. Shira had three pairs of her earrings, but most of her work was exported to corporate enclaves.

Finally they could sit down at the kitchen table face-to-face. "Malkah, I hardly knew her. You're my real mother. But she was your only daughter."

"I was so busy when she was growing up. When we're young, we have babies by caprice. I brought her back from Prague in my belly like a souvenir. When this you see, remember me. I had been happy there, I had loved passionately. Did I ever suspect I was producing an independent strange strong female who would stand in the middle of my life shouting *No* at the top of her lungs, refusing everything I had to give her?" Malkah began to weep silently.

Shira ran around the table to embrace Malkah. She stood leaning forward, with Malkah's face pressing into her waist, while the tears soaked through her shirt. Finally Shira too began to weep, although she had no idea whether she was mourning Riva or responding to her own exhaustion and inner tumult.

THEY STOOD AT SUNSET on the small hill covered with wild grasses and bramble—thorny bushes volunteers hacked back twice a year. The tiny grave had been prepared, sized for an infant, dug by Malkah's friend Sam Rossi, with his brown curls and sloping shoulders, and by Nili. The remains of Riva were lowered in a simple wooden box, made by Danny the carpenter. Death was an amateur business here.

The moment had come to shovel in earth. Shira went first. The sandy soil made a hollow drumming sound on the wood. The sound of death, finality, what is no more and can never be again. Malkah stood beside her, her hands trembling wildly, tears coursing down her face. It had become traditional at Tikva to bury the dead at sunset, so they could go outside without sec skins, so that they could touch and hold each other for comfort. Malkah could not lift the shovel. Yod was at her elbow to help her. Finally everyone was filling in the small pit. Shira stood beside the grave and began the Kaddish: "Yitgadal v'yitkadash shamei raba. . . ."

I never knew her, and she died protecting me.

twenty-seven

A BURNING CURIOSITY

What I have feared for so long has overtaken us. Riva is lost. Not even a body to mourn over, to bury. I cannot say, "If only I had known how short a time we had," because I lived always anticipating that loss. I could not demand more of her than she occasionally gave, because she created no channels through which my desires and anxieties could reach her. If I sometimes ask myself whether I did not commit some early error that made love unimportant to her no matter how freely offered, she was what she wanted to be. I am glad that the time the Base was down causes us to work at a mad trot to deliver our systems to Olivacon by August fifteen and to Cybernaut nine weeks later. Yet night comes, the gray time of sleeplessness, when memories rise like languid carp from the depths to feed on my grief.

I have been remembering the death of my own mother, of the kisrami plague. She was one of the doctors who stayed in what was beginning to be called the Glop then, trying to bring some mercy to the heaps of the dying. They would not even release her body. A handful of ashes from the mass incinerators was all I had to mourn. She had long hair, iron gray (it was a matter of pride with her to leave it gray), worn braided around her head, as I sometimes wear mine now. I had not thought until this moment that it is because of her. The ashes were that color. She was forty-one when she had me, and I must often have been difficult for her, a rambunctious ravenous child.

I was sitting in the courtyard last night in the dark when Nili suddenly padded down. She stood before me, fidgeting; then she put her hand on my shoulder, saying, "You grieve too much, Malkah. Patience!" She raced back upstairs. I was left disconcerted. I have been a negligent host, I'm sure, but Nili seems able to take care of herself. What did it mean? I felt both rebuke and a kind of tenderness in her, but it doesn't compute.

I brood on graves, on stones, memorials. My grandfather eighteen generations back is a man whose tombstone in the Prague graveyard I visited the same day as the tomb of the Maharal and Perl, and placed a little stone in respect for him also. My distant papa is David Gans, also known as David Avsa—"goose" in Hebrew as *gans* was in German. There among markers where a scissors denotes a tailor and a book a teacher, on David's are carved the Magen David, the shield or star of David, and a goose. Even the illiterate would know whose grave it was, among all those huddled tipsy jammed-in markers.

Now, you probably think the six-pointed star is for a Jew, but it was not at that time a common emblem for our people. It was a symbol from kabbalah David secularized, using it for the title of his introduction to astronomy. David had studied with some of the greatest rabbis of his time, including the Maharal, whose disciple he officially remained, but his real conversion was to science. He was captured first by mathematics, then by astronomy, which remained his primary fascination for the rest of his long life, although he also popularized the discoveries of geographers and explorers.

He was a man who enjoyed being amazed by the new. Some people, you give them something to admire and they want to piss on it, they want to walk away from it because it makes them feel small. David liked to feel astounded, to stretch his mind around new facts, new theories, to knock them around and size them up and study them. Then when he felt he understood, he yearned to explain to others. He loved to explain Jewish philosophy to his Christian astronomer friends, Brahe and Kepler, to seduce them into an understanding of the depth and subtlety of Jewish thought, that they had imagined archaic, already known to them. He loved to explain to the Maharal the work going on under Brahe's direction outside the city at Benatek, where Gans had spent several sessions working in the observatory. There Tycho Brahe and his assistants were continuing work begun in Denmark. Instead of empty theorizing or proceeding from Aristotle, they were making precise and repeated measurements of the movements of the planets and the stars, keeping meticulous records. This was something new in the world, beginning with observation and only then proceeding to theory. We take it for granted, but it was as new as David thought it was.

David is not a man who seizes my imagination as does the Maharal. He isn't an eagle of the mind. But he's a very necessary sort of person. You could have picked up David and dropped him in the court of the Great Khan, and once he had learned the language, which he would have begun systematically doing within the first ten minutes, he would have made friends and learned about the culture and started contemplating a book to explain those people to our people. He would have been an ideal traveler in time as well as space. He slid through the cracks Rudolf had permitted to spread through the rigid society of the time. Aristocracy as such meant nothing to David, nor did wealth or power. He would rather sit down in a tavern with a grizzled captain just back from the Amazon than flirt with the most beautiful woman, Gentile or Jew, in Prague, or sit down at the table of Mordecai Maisl or the richest knight who served on gold chargers. His interest flattered and soothed. The roughest, the most arrogant, the prejudiced and the nasty all fell open before him and let him study their adventures and ideas and observations, the gentle and respectful finger of his attention touching them line by line as he would kiss and touch the Torah when called up in synagogue to read.

Therefore, although Joseph is astonished that, facing destruction, the Maharal would send for David, David himself is alarmed but not surprised. "I'll leave for Benatek now. I have a standing invitation. I'll ask Brahe and Kepler to intervene with Rudolf. We should use all channels, revered teacher. We must move fast."

"As fast as we can, which is to say, no ways open to us are truly open. We must reach Rudolf." The Maharal stands at his window looking at the town hall, only a few feet away in the chockablock ghetto. "Take Joseph. Moving about the city could prove dangerous, even to you. He moves more quickly than any of us, and he is the strongest . . . of all in Prague." The Maharal's voice falters for a moment, because he is unable to refer to Joseph as a man in front of David. The lie sticks in his throat like a fish bone.

Joseph notices. He blinks twice and then follows David. They set out at once for Benatek, six hours to the northeast of Prague, David attempting to educate Joseph as they go. David rides a borrowed horse. Joseph trots alongside, tireless. "Tycho Brahe is a nobleman, Joseph, but he has not been content to spend his life in idleness or in drinking and gaming and hunting. In Denmark, he had an island where he built a splendid observatory. Rudolf lured him here. He pays him—or rather, given the chaos of Rudolf's finances, he promised Brahe three thousand thaler a year and a subsidy of beer and wine and bread. Brahe has built large precise instruments to study the planets and the stars. He has been most kind to me."

"Will they mind my being with you?"

"They will assume you are my assistant or my servant."

"Who is 'they'?"

"His second is Johannes Kepler, who is an even better friend to me. He's German, Protestant like Brahe, and I find his mind superior. Kepler carries the ideas of Copernicus even further, whereas Brahe still attempts to reconcile their observations with the Ptolemaic system the Church backs. Kepler sees the world through mathematics. What do you think, Joseph? Does the sun go around the earth, as everybody now thinks, or does the earth go around the sun, as we now know the other planets do?"

"It's hard, standing in any one place, to tell if you are moving or what you are looking at is moving. When I helped a drayman move barrels in a boat, sometimes I felt as if the shore was moving and I was floating at rest."

"The idea you have just postulated resembles the theories of Giordano Bruno, who says that observation and ultimately truth is relative to the position from which we observe. The Inquisition has had him for eight years now, torturing him to make him recant. Many people, Joseph, assume you are slow mentally because you are ignorant of many things. But the two are different. One is an inherent weakness, but the other is simply a lack to be overcome."

"Chava says I can think, that I'm not stupid. She's been teaching me to read and write German and Czech and Hebrew."

"When you read, Joseph, you can place yourself in history and share in all the thoughts of those who are now dead as well as those now living."

The only castles Joseph has ever seen are Hradcany and Vysehrad, imposing, massive, fortified. This is more of a country house, built on a hill overlooking the Jizera amid vineyards and orchards. The lowlands along the river are flooded, but the road to the castle stands dry. The plum trees sway in frothy bloom below them; the hum of bees rises to the road, along with the splashing of oars where some peasants are crossing a drowned meadow. Inside the courtyard, carpenters are hammering, their helpers sawing and carrying wood. Masons are pounding on stones, dressing them. They enter past scaffolding and the chaos of walls demolished and under construction, past a wall painted by a previous tenant with scenes of hunting and warfare.

When Joseph first sees Tycho Brahe, he cannot help staring, until

David pokes him sharply. His first thought is that the nobleman is an artificial being like himself but made of metal, for right in the middle of his nose there is a hole in his skin through which Joseph can see silver and gold within. But David mutters to him when Tycho is leading them effusively into his observatory, "He lost the bridge of his nose in a duel years ago. Don't stare!"

Tycho is a big man, heavily built, florid and fleshy, with close-set eyes and a close-clipped dark beard, crossed by a much longer swooping mustache, his large head set on a stiff white ruff like a cabbage on a plate. He talks loudly and quotes his own Latin poetry, of which Joseph understands not a word, although David smiles and nods and makes some rejoinder in Latin. That causes Tycho to give him a bone-shaking slap on the shoulder, the many rings on his fingers glinting. "Yes, we keep owls' hours here," Tycho thunders. "This afternoon is our morning, and we don't retire until the sun rises."

Tycho shows them machines for taking readings of the positions of the stars and planets. Johannes Kepler has just emerged from a large mural quadrant. He is a thin dark bony man, radiating energy and nervous discontent. His beard hangs like a bristly mourning wreath around his small mouth. His forehead is high, the hair already receding around a widow's peak. His features are sharp and delicate, his eyes soft and expressive. He hunches forward, perhaps to see, as he seems nearsighted. He shows David a notebook written in spidery script, full of numbers, and David and Johannes chat about Mars as if gossiping about a difficult mutual friend. Another star, Tycho announces, has been precisely observed and measured, and now it, too, will be added to the great map they are creating. Joseph notices that David calls Kepler Johannes but addresses Tycho formally.

Joseph waits for David to tell Kepler or Brahe about the crisis facing the Jews of Prague, but instead David follows the men through chambers crowded with strange measuring devices and clockwork automata. Brahe has a hidden system of bell pulls that enables him to summon the servants without visible means. The rooms are full of drawers and doors that open if you press a panel, of little wind-up dolls that strike chimes or raise and lower other instruments. Tycho likes to wear the air of a magician, but he is not one, Joseph thinks scornfully. He plays with dolls, Joseph thinks, but I was made by real magic. Time is leaking away. He yearns to seize the men and shake them into talking sense. They are squinting into this eyepiece and that one. They are poring over notebooks in which Joseph, looking past David's thin shoulder, can see nothing but signs for the planets and columns of numbers. Why had the Maharal imagined that David's visit here could do them any good whatsoever?

"But Giordano Bruno has been killed, David," Tycho Brahe says. "Hadn't you heard? He was publicly burned alive in Rome for heresy. I had a letter two weeks ago."

David winces, recoiling a step. Everyone wears for a moment a shuttered look, as in each man's head he contemplates that mode of dying. "It's a hazardous business, imposing truth. The Maharal says we can never arrive at truth if we fear discussion. We must attack falsehood, but only after we have given it leave to speak."

Kepler looks cautiously around. His voice is soft. "My own grandmother was burned as a witch, a contrary and ill-natured woman, but the only witchery she knew was how to curse with a foul tongue and how to brew up a few herbs for a fussy stomach. These are dangerous times. New astronomical theories make the Church as nervous as Bruno did. He was accused, among his other ideas, of believing in the theories of Copernicus. And being influenced by the kabbalah. Only Rudolf protects us from attack here."

"I'll never understand how the nature of the divine or the duty of humankind toward each other is affected by how we think heavenly bodies rotate. We owe respect to our parents whether the earth goes around the sun or the sun goes around the earth." David shakes his head sadly. "The forces of superstition are moving against my people right now."

Joseph lets out his breath in a huge sigh. Finally. It has taken David two hours to get to the point. Joseph, however, has to admit that once launched, David proceeds gently but inexorably until he has a commitment from Brahe to intercede with Rudolf. He will write at once, this very evening, and Kepler will take the message and go to the court the next day.

"Rudolf always sees me," Kepler boasts. "He finds our researches more exciting than the affairs of his ambassadors. He says contemplating the orderly motions of the heavens makes it easier to put into perspective all the quarrels between Catholics and Protestants. We are one of his pet projects. He lavishes the care on us another king would spend on mistresses."

"He has been good to my people also. Therefore, please, go swiftly to him. Save us, Johannes, and I'll get the Maharal to come quietly and we can have another session discussing the mystical questions that you find so engaging. I myself will continue your Hebrew lessons."

David is promising a lot, because the Maharal remains extremely reluctant to share his ideas with Christians: it is too dangerous. Dangerous for them—witness Bruno's eight years of imprisonment and burning for the crime of thinking and writing ideas that the Maharal found quite stimulating. Dangerous for him—because all Jews live on sufferance, while they live, and a violent death is always on tap. Now, the Maharal is a very old man but not yet ready to die, for his work is still consuming half his energies and the welfare of his people the other half. Every year he says to the angel of death, Not yet, not yet. I am not ready, but soon.

The price of Tycho's promise is that they are to stay to supper and David is to work as Tycho's assistant for the night. Tycho is shorthanded here and always in need of someone trained in astronomy. Joseph is impatient to be gone, to return to his master, but they are in for a long boisterous seven-course dinner. Tycho holds his own court in the huge vaulted hall. He has twelve assistants and their families, his wife, four sons and two daughters, the manager of the estate and two other visitors passing by. Squatting beside his chair like a mastiff is his fool, Jepp. Kepler, who is placed well down the table, with David and Joseph and the manager, tells them that Tycho once kept a pet elk. It would be here too, no doubt, but it got drunk and was injured on a stairway in his Danish castle. Tycho eats and drinks more than Joseph thought possible. Tycho's common-law wife, a peasant woman from his estate, sits quietly with a wary eye on the commotion, but the rest of the family is loud at table, full of jokes and teasing, guffawing at Jepp's slapstick.

The next morning Joseph paces and fumes. Finally, at noon, Tycho orders his carriage and sends them back to the city with Kepler, who carries a letter in a leather folio in his lap. David and Johannes, freed from the massive and overwhelming presence of Tycho, sit with their heads close together, discussing mathematics, physics, astronomy. In spite of the twenty-five-year difference in their ages, they chatter, happy as schoolboys on vacation, jouncing along eating pie sent with them and bread and cheese and drinking ale. Joseph scowls out the window. He should have stayed in the ghetto. The Maharal created him to protect, and protect is what he must do.

Then Kepler begins to complain to David about Tycho, how even at supper he will not talk about his findings. "He treats me like an apprentice—me, to whom Galileo writes as an equal. He will not let us be collaborators. No, he must be the great lord. They say if his peasants on his island in Denmark were late in their rent, he put them in chains. The only reason he let me take on Mars, the most difficult planet, is because the assistant working on it quit—as they all do. As I will, if I can find another place!"

We all feel unappreciated by our masters, Joseph thinks. Me too.

twenty-eight

HOW CAN WE TELL THE DANCER FROM THE DANCE?

Shira had brought over Malkah's cleaner, as it did not seem a great idea to borrow the cleaning robot from the lab; the less Avram was involved in Yod's installing himself in the former janitor's apartment downstairs, the smoother would be the move.

Yod's possessions required only one trip to carry downstairs. Shira had managed to lose that ghastly outfit she had first seen him wearing. What he owned now were three pairs of shorts, two pairs of pants, several tees and a couple of shirts, a jacket, various scarves and Gadi's old sec skin. That the skin probably no longer protected was irrelevant. He brought a terminal, his storage crystals and a set of tools for self-repair. The com-con link had been activated already, as had the link to the Base. His other possessions included a poetry anthology Malkah had given him, in which Shira discovered the rose she had cut the first time he had come to her house, against the Robert Burns poem she had been using to teach him metaphorical thinking; Mary Shelley's *Frankenstein,* and a complete print-out of his own specs.

The paucity moved her. Gadi was right: Avram should be paying Yod. She had no idea what Yod might want to buy, but he deserved to be able to have something he wanted. I don't take good enough care of him, she thought, aware that in fact she spent little time on his upkeep. He did not require much, unlike a human male. In many respects, he was refreshingly undemanding. Even his clothes became dirty more slowly, as he did not sweat.

The last object he brought down was a chess set consisting of carved and painted pieces that were samurai, the emperor and empress, other Japanese historical figures. "Avram gave this to you?" she asked, astounded. "But you usually play with the computer."

"I admired it," he said simply. "It's my . . . prize possession. Like me, the samurai were programmed to protect, to fight."

She nodded, a little shaken. Gadi had lusted after that set from the time he was seven. He had spent his childhood always secretly stealing pieces from it and being forced by his father to put them back. Yet now Avram had given it to Yod. Perhaps Avram did in his way care for the cyborg.

The apartment was dark, with only a few high windows. It might be chilly in winter, but it was pleasantly cool now. Although an old man and woman had lived here in Shira's childhood, it had stood empty since.

The furniture was close to antique—pieces covered with real wood veneer in light streaky colors, a table made of plastic attempting to imitate stone. Those were still functional, although badly built, but the bed needed replacing. Its sagging, almost convoluted shape suggested that not two but perhaps a dozen people had died there slowly, in convulsions. Several of the chairs had once been overstuffed with matter that had since disintegrated. When she sat in them, she began to sneeze. Yod carried them straight to the recycler, but the woman on duty was afraid to take them. They could contain toxic materials—so many things from that era had. It was decided simply to cycle them through the fusion plant: it produced energy from sea water but had the capacity to use some solid trash.

Malkah gave Yod a great pile of pillows and a couple of straight chairs. In the cupboard they found old milk and meat dishes, which Shira boiled and scrubbed and scrubbed. "Today we've made hundreds of spiders homeless," she said to Yod, who was putting the dishes back on the scoured shelves. She found herself singing, songs that had been popular when she was in college.

> Hear them crying in the alley
> nursing on bottles of dust
> the armies of the dying dance in my head
> the armies of flying bones
>
> we are the last of the last
> the water has all gone dry
> we are the end.

They had boogied to that at all-night parties, singing the chorus while they danced with their heads thrown back, convinced of apocalypse but defiant and cheery. Then they all went off to work for multis and tried to make babies.

She sang:

> You filled my sky and burned me like the sun.
> My skin is gone to powder. Blood boiled dry.
> In the clean acid of the desert, gonna die.

"You're enjoying yourself. Why is that? This work is neither creative nor interesting. We're assisting a cleaning robot." Yod looked into her face with that quizzical smile she thought one of his most attractive expressions. "The songs you sing are grim, but you sound joyful."

"I want you settled in your own place. It'll be better for us."

"Does it feel almost as if I were human? Am I imitating behavior I can never match? Is Avram right, that the lab is more suited to me than this place with all the facilities humans require? I don't sleep, can extract energy from almost anything. Am I pretending at something I'll always fail?"

"Yod, there's no culture of cyborgs for you to fit into. The only society is human. You have to pass. And we want someplace to meet."

"How much do I disappoint you?"

"Since I don't expect you to be human, but rather yourself, why should I be disappointed?" She was not at all sure how truthful she was being. After all, she spoke of the relationship to Gadi and to Malkah as temporary. What would it mean to make more of a commitment to a machine?

"I'm asking if you're happy because I seem momentarily human."

"No doubt there's always an element of playing house in settling any lover into an apartment. Humans pretend at things all through childhood. Little girls still play house nowadays, long after any adult woman could be wasted doing what they used to call in the old days, keeping house. Moving you in is soothing. It's mindless and easy. It's safe. We haven't had much of that lately."

"I was designed to fight, so this pleases me and makes me uneasy at once."

She touched his face. "My programming is scientific and nurturing. What happened with Y-S is a nightmare to me, insane, outside my life."

Gently he put his hands on her shoulders. "This is your life. They're after you. They know something of what we're doing here. It won't stop."

"No! I want a small life, a quiet life. I want to do my work and have the little pleasures other women know."

"Then run, Shira, run from me, from Avram and Malkah. Run now."

"I can't do that, and you know it." She sank into a kitchen chair. "Even if I left the only people besides my lost son that I care about, the only thing Y-S wants with me is to empty my brain of what I know about you and the work here. That's all any multi would want with me now—to empty me out even if they destroy half my brain cells in the process. There's no place for me to go."

He knelt before her, gripping her knee. "I can only fight for you. I can only try to protect and defend."

It felt quite natural now to touch him, the most normal gesture she could imagine. Yet her hand was resting on imitation skin laid over neural processors, gel chip technology, a skeleton strong enough to support a high-rise building. Again, when she touched a man, did she think she was caressing the liver, the spleen, the large intestine? Surfaces sought friction, and in that friction, pleasure. It was like being in a zip and asking suddenly, What's holding us up? Most of life was bizarre when she stopped to examine it.

This moment was a long, long way from a woman dressed in skins picking a banana off a tree to eat and squatting to shit in the bushes, toting her baby in a carrying sack along with roots she had dug and leaves she had plucked. Yet such a woman could lose her child too, to a predator swift in the grass, to a sudden fever for which she knew no remedy, to a scratch that didn't heal but stole up the chubby leg in an angry red line streaking arrowlike for the heart. Such a woman sought comfort in the embrace of a being like and unlike herself, as men were unlike women, intimate strangers surely just as exotic and peculiar to Shira as this machine in the form of a man who knelt before her, wanting at least to please. Gadi had kept the room in which they had met secretly, as if it were a museum case containing love. Yod kept the rose. She was more moved by the withered rose.

"If I wanted a human mate, Yod, the town is full of men. I'm with you because I want to be with you. Some things work between us and others don't—for what couple isn't that the way? But does it ever bother you I'm so messy and biological, that I'm an animal? I bleed, I sweat, I get tired. Sometimes I feel embarrassed before you since you're so much neater. Don't I seem rather gross to you, always putting stuff in or letting it out?"

"My sense of smell is more analytical than sensual. I am not programmed to find some smells pleasant and others unpleasant. What bothers me is altogether different—that I failed you: I didn't protect your mother."

"I asked her not to come. She and Nili chose to. It isn't your fault, and one cyborg can't defend the entire town."

"I think, however, I'm supposed to."

A MESSAGE CAME over the Net from Y-S, saying that her former boss, Dr. Yatsuko, regretted that pirates had attacked the previous meeting and hoped that she was in good health. He said that Y-S was interested in regaining her services with a promotion by one and one half grades that perhaps had been discussed in the aborted meeting. In the meantime she might be interested to know that her son was now with her ex-husband in the Y-S enclave in the Nebraska desert, where they had lived together.

She and Malkah asked for copy and studied the transmission intently, each with a page before her as they sat over coffee at the kitchen table.

"They have no record of the meeting. The wrap baffles sufficed to dampen their recorders as well as their sensing devices," Malkah said.

"So they don't know what happened. They may suspect the trouble started when I rejected the offer, but they don't know. And they probably don't know the size of the attacking party, since they had no survivors and the camera on the fast-tank was blown up."

Malkah put her elbows on the table, frowning. When she frowned, Shira was reminded of Riva—although she would never know what Riva had really looked like. Malkah asked sternly, "Do you believe this stuff about Ari? That they've brought him back from the space platform with Josh?"

"As bait?"

"Bait or bribe. Do you believe it?"

"I don't know. But I have an idea how to find out. I'll send a message robot to Ari personally, to wish him Happy Birthday. His birthday is in twelve days. I'll order one only for Nebraska Y-S station and return. If Ari isn't there, it won't deliver its message to anyone else or anywhere else but will simply return. If it doesn't return, then I'll know they destroyed it and they're lying."

"Let me pay for it. He's my only great-grandchild."

Imagining Ari only two thousand miles away instead of vanished from the planet made Shira restless. If only she could find out what they were planning to do with Ari, what great game they were playing with her son as sacrificial pawn. But she had never been a good chess player. Josh was a fine player. Sometimes before Ari was born, on interminable evenings when they ran out of small talk and small tasks, when neither had enough brought-home work for screening, then they had played chess or go or other games associated in her mind now with the feeling of hours and hours of time that must be passed through together. They could of course have escaped each other in a stimmie; that was what poor bastards in the Glop did; that and drug out. Log too much stimmie time, and a Y-S counselor would be asking you gently what was wrong. Like the continual blood and urine testing, it was a fact of corporate existence; too great a reliance on manufactured fantasies could reduce your edge, your efficiency. Every aspect of life was monitored in the enclaves.

"Ari feels more important to me now that Riva is dead," Malkah said quietly. "I know that's absurd, but it's true."

"Her life was the opposite of yours and of mine. Did she actually live anyplace?"

"She had what she called a hidey-hole on an island off Georgia; that's all I know. Nili may know more, but I wouldn't bet on it."

"Now that she's dead, I find myself thinking of her far more than I ever did when she was alive. I find myself wondering about her—what her private life was really like."

"I don't think Riva had what you and I might think of as a private life. She had time off. Rest. But what mattered to her was the dangerous work she did. The rest was just . . . filling in." Malkah sighed heavily.

"Why do you and I care so much about our attachments to others?"

Malkah rubbed her eyes. "I used to wonder what I did wrong. But now I think that unless you grossly mistreat a child or spoil her or let her be injured, basically there's a given element in all of us, something from genes or the moment. From birth on, a child follows her own path. She learns, but she also unfolds from within."

"Ari was himself almost from the first. He had a personality. He had a special gentleness, unlike other boy babies the women around us had. He also had a fearfulness—a capacity to be startled—that worried me. I would wonder if I was too anxious and I was infecting him."

"Show me a mother who isn't anxious, and I'll show you a happy idiot."

"Malkah, did you really want another baby when you were forty-five? Didn't you have some resentment at having a kid dropped on you?"

"No, Shira, I've told you the truth. You were her gift to me. Maybe if I was living with a man or stuck in a permanent relationship I might have hesitated. But I'd raised Riva, she was gone, and I felt a little at loose ends. I'd had enough time alone to think how much better a job I could do now I was so much smarter and kinder." She laughed sharply.

"And you didn't feel overburdened?"

"Sometimes, sure." Malkah smiled. "But I think I was better at hiding it. And you were dessert in my life."

"Do you think I'll ever get Ari back?"

"I think you have to live as if you believe you will."

THE COMMONS HAD originally meant a square in the middle of town that had existed long before the wrap had enclosed them, dating back to the founding of the town in 1688, when it had been a cow pasture and later a drill ground for the local militia. The Commons often referred now to the town food facility, where people could eat or pick up takeout. The square itself had once been half paved, but when the wrap was constructed, it had been dug up except for strips for walking, cycling and delivery vans. It was half intensely cultivated gardens and the rest trees and grass. It was that half, facing the Commons building, that Gadi had taken over for a party.

The festival began at seven, but it took them a while to get organized. Even Yod was late coming to Malkah's house, because for once he was accompanied by Avram. Avram had taken an hour to get ready, muttering complaints the entire time, Yod told Shira softly. Nili sat in the courtyard, watching them all with avid curiosity. She was dressed as she always was now, in her fatigues. She had dropped the role of nurse. She was just Malkah's guest.

Yod sat beside Nili, watching too. As Shira dressed, she glanced down from the balcony to check on them below. Her bed was a hill of tossed fabric. Malkah was wearing a purple caftan trimmed with iridescent streamers. She and Avram were arguing about something that had happened forty-odd years before Avram had married Sara and left Tikva for California. Shira could easily hear their raised excited voices batting at each other from below. Yet she did not think either of them could be described as annoyed; in fact they were having fun. They fought for the pleasure of it—part ritual, part agon, part fencing match.

Everyone finally lined up and started bellowing at her. She was compelled to stop fussing and come down. "As far as I can see," Nili said, "you looked better before you began."

"What do you think?" Shira asked Yod.

He looked unhappy. "I can't tell the difference. One set of clothing is like another to me. That doesn't appear as comfortable."

"You look beautiful," Avram said, bowing to her. "Never mind the rest of them. An attractive woman is allowed to take her time so that she can please us when she does appear."

Altogether she felt like an idiot. She was compelled to attempt to create a fine impression on Gadi; she could not help it. Her dress was one she had bought to celebrate when she had recovered her figure after pregnancy. It was cut close to the body and made of fishcloth—tiny glittering scales of changing color in the sea palette, looking metallic but actually silicon-enhanced silk. It had a demure high neck but two cutouts on the front so that half of each breast was exposed. The dress had been the proper modest midcalf length required at Y-S, but she had shortened it a couple of days before so that it stopped above the knee, in case she wanted to dance. Gadi had promised dancing.

They arrived at the Commons. From the outside of the viron only the generators were visible and an area of opacity stretching up to the wrap, with a marked entrance blinking. They passed through into a world of silver palms tinkling, glittering, dropping an occasional tinsel frond. The floor and the sky were black streaked with silver, lit with arcs of light that met at the horizon. In the sky, silver snakes and angelfish swam, releasing glowing bubbles. Under the floor, bright rainbow fish darted. Every tenth tree was a speaker, pulsating waves of Afro-Indian rock.

The dance floor was a spiral that flung out platforms. It had been constructed, or rather put together of ready-mades, yesterday. Shira had passed on her way to supper when they were locking the segments together. Most people on the spiral were dancing to the Afro-Indian group, but several of the platforms were bubbles with different music; she could tell from the rhythm of the dancers.

Nili poked her in the arm. "What is the purpose of this?"

"It's just a party. Don't your people ever have parties?"

"We make music, we dance, we feast and drink our wine. We eat funny mushrooms that make us high. We act silly and tell bad jokes we think are uproarious. But this construction, this waste of energy, I find strange."

Malkah asked, "Does it offend you, as conspicuous consumption?"

Nili scowled. "It's so strange to me I mistrust my own reactions. In a way it's sweet, all this effort spent on having a good time."

"Is that what we're supposed to do?" Yod asked. He nodded at the dancers gyrating on the seven levels of the spiral. "Like that?"

"It's all silliness," Avram said. "In our youth we didn't need to immerse ourselves in fantasies to enjoy life."

"Oh, come on, Avram. I remember you and me going to Green Ziggy's concert at Foxboro Stadium—do you remember, before it fell down? Sixty thousand screaming fans, a sound system loud enough to deafen us all for a week, a galaxy-class light show. Flying tigers, demon wrestlers, a dragon. The lead singer shot up in a rocket. Remember?"

"The summer we were both nineteen." He sighed. "You were so beautiful then."

"I'm just as beautiful now." Malkah stuck out her tongue at him. "It's your eyes and your appetite that are failing, not my beauty."

Shira was looking cautiously around for Gadi. Yod stayed at her side. She asked, "You really don't think this dress is attractive? Just a little sexy?"

"Shira, I don't understand the concept."

"Yod, you must understand attraction, since you're attracted to me."

"But not because you look any particular way."

"I don't believe you."

"I don't have any standard by which to judge human appearance. I wasn't programmed for that. I like the way you look, but then I like the way Malkah looks too. I find most people interesting to watch."

She drew back, offended. She was astonished that her feelings could be hurt by what he had said, and yet at the same time, she recognized a bright side to his ignorance. He thought Malkah equally attractive. Never would she have to worry about her appearance, because he seemed incapable of distinguishing her best days from her worst, any more than the kittens would ever judge her by her facade. So often she found that with Yod, when she moved into her usual behavior with men, she was playing by herself. Whole sets of male-female behavior simply did not apply. They would never struggle about clothing, what he found sexy, what she found degrading to wear or not to wear, whether she was too fat or too thin, whether she should wear her hair one way or another. Small pleasures, small anxieties, sources of friction and seduction, all were equally stripped out of the picture.

"But you look at me a lot when we're together. Why?"

"I like to look at you. From small changes in posture and gesture and expression, I try to read your feelings and your reactions. I find it . . . pleasant to look at you because you are Shira, *my* Shira. I've been pondering what that phrase means and how it can apply to a cyborg. What someone who doesn't possess himself can do with a sense of me and mine."

She was touched by what he said, about to answer, when Gadi stepped out of a huge tree trunk. "Ah, there you people are. About time. Why aren't you dancing?" He put his arm possessively about Shira, touching her bare back, tracing the line of her spine.

"It's beautiful," Shira said. "It's amazing what you did here."

"Isn't it, with only two decent generators and one from the Dark Ages. It's thrown together, but I must say myself, it's thrown together nicely. I wanted to give everyone a lift." His hand dropped briefly on Yod's shoulder. "My battery-pack brother, welcome. And I can't believe it: Aveinu, welcome indeed." Gadi made as if to touch his father but did not. Shira could not remember them ever embracing. "I can't believe you agreed to visit my wee installation. I hope you'll condescend to let it amuse you a little."

Avram looked uncomfortable. "I was curious, I'll admit. I wanted to see what you do."

"I make butterflies—pretty ephemeral things that make people happy. There's too little pleasant in this nasty dying world. We all need to remember how to play, how to be children together for a little while."

"Being entertained is not the same as being happy," Nili said.

"Hello, lioness. I could have lent you a gown for tonight. Not that you don't look gorgeous anyhow."

"Why should I care whether others look at me? The pleasure is in the looking, no?"

"Have you no vanity, Nili? I have tribes of it."

"I have vanity," she said. "About certain things I can do, I'm shockingly vain. So, silver man, do you dance?"

"Of course. Very well. Can you do these dances?"

"Any dances that anyone can do, I can do," Nili said. "That's my vanity speaking. There is no motion of which I am not physically capable."

Gadi extended his arm in a courtly gesture. Nili stared as if wondering what he wanted her to do with it. Then she seized him by the wrist and yanked him swiftly, roughly toward the spiral.

"If you want to dance, I'm sure I can imitate those motions also," Yod said softly to Shira. "Would you find that pleasant?"

She nodded vigorously. She caught a glimpse of Malkah attempting to lure Avram toward the dancers. Gadi and she had used to dance; in college the computer students had their own dance bar where they hung out in the old city. Since then, Josh had not been willing to loosen his dignity in dancing, nor had Y-S parties tended to encourage or even allow it. They were marts for affirming or improving social status, places where gossip could be created or exchanged. She had not danced since Edinburgh.

Yod had obviously been watching the dancers while the rest of them talked, because he had already selected a set of gestures and movements. Above them on the next turn of the spiral she could see Nili leaping high and at one point raising Gadi straight up over her head. They were a sensational pair as they more or less managed to coordinate their initiatives and dance in the same general manner. Gadi had always been a supple and energetic dancer. Nili danced like a demon. Precisely. Superhuman energy and strength, totally enraptured by her own movements and the music.

Yod began stiffly. Shira urged him to loosen up, exaggerate the gestures, move with the rhythm he could surely feel. He attempted to obey her. "Human relaxations are frequently more effort than their work activities."

"The harder we work physically, the more we want simply to collapse afterward. The harder we work mentally, the more we want to leap around, flexing the muscles and straightening the spine. Look. We can pass gestures and movements back and forth between us. Watch Danny with his lover, Roy. See how they play as they dance?"

"Nili and Gadi seem to have trouble communicating with each other, yet they seek each other out."

"Attraction isn't logical. It just happens."

"All events are caused, Shira."

"But the causes of attractions and repulsions can lie in something long buried in infancy or childhood, something we don't even recognize as triggering a desire or a fear."

"I had no infancy." He was moving more easily now, with that totally efficient grace. "What I want is quite logical."

How she loved watching him at moments like this, when his elegance of motion was displayed, almost exaggerated. To watch him was to want to envelop him. "Yod, your desire is no more logical than Gadi's. It only feels so because we work together and we communicate well, although that isn't entirely logical either. It's a small miracle." She considered it miraculous, too, that they could dance so well together, so seamlessly now it felt like a form of lovemaking. She watched him try out the moves of dancers around them, discard what felt awkward. "You may not have a sense of what's beautiful in other people, but you have a sense of aesthetics about how you move."

He was silent for some minutes, contemplating what she had said. "I understand elegance in algorithms, in motions, in equations, in systems design. That I can grasp."

> My hunger got horns and a tail
> Goodbye hook, goodbye sleep
> Gotta jack, gotta rock
> Gonna fly my bat tonight.

Malkah must have given up on Avram, for she danced now with Gila and several other friends in a large circle down on the first level. "This is the old ladies' level," she heard Gila hoot at a young couple. "You go upstairs with the other wet ones." Shira thought that perhaps before she had lived in the Y-S enclave, she had never appreciated Tikva as she did now, its tolerance of human variety, of age, size, sexual typology.

Nili had started to strip off her shirt—she was sweating and hot—and Gadi was arguing with her. Avram was nowhere to be seen. She assumed he had left, an observation she offered to Yod as they slithered and twisted together. "No," Yod said. "He has climbed to the very top, and he is watching everyone, but especially Gadi and especially us."

As if casually, she threw back her head and saw Avram, observing as Yod had said. She waved to him, and he turned away. He looked lost above the maelstrom of dancers. It was not age. Besides the group around Malkah, many older people were dancing. In some corporate enclaves, rigid age segregation was considered normal, but here people tended to mix. Without class distinctions, perhaps age did not seem as important.

Hannah cut in on them. When Shira looked around, Ilana, who had sat with Riva's remains, was beckoning to her, and they danced together. Then Gadi appeared, as she had been half afraid he would and half afraid he would not. The entire party was a fantasy garment swirling around him as the centerpiece. His metallic eyelids caught the flashing lights. His eyes were gleaming mercury. He wore reflective black, slashed tunic and slit pants. Past him people were shooting the slides from the top, whipping out over the crowd on trapezes and double swings like crescent moons.

After the first dance, he touched his wrist, and slow music throbbed sinuously from the forest of speakers. He gathered her into his arms. The slither of the material against her with its dozens of slits through which she felt the warmth of his skin, the scent of his perfume loaded with pheromones rising to her nostrils, made her breath catch in her throat as if turned to fur. Her skin prickled. She longed to scratch herself nervously. She longed to take a deep breath but could not. "Does Nili respond to pheromones?" she asked.

For answer he drew her closer. The multiplied voices sang siren-like:

> I take you in my mouth like sweet red wine.
> I take you in me and you make me shine.

"Are you just a little jealous, Ugi? Greening around the edges?"

"I'm curious. She fascinates me as much as she fascinates you—although in a different way. I don't find her attractive."

"Perhaps she's too challenging. With the walking vibrator, you're safe."

"You're telling me that you wouldn't rather have a woman with an Off switch? A mechanical geisha is the ideal woman, and we all know it. But Yod is real and quirky, and he wasn't created as a sex toy."

"No, that seems to have been your idea."

"Wrong again. It was his."

He took a deep breath, holding her out at arm's length. "We're doing it again. Forget the terminal man, and let's enjoy each other's company. How are you enduring working for my father?"

She glanced up at Avram, watching the two of them with cold intensity, as she had half expected. "Why can't he enjoy himself?"

"I think he dealt with the pain of Mother's slow dying by denying himself any respite except work. He got to the point where when she was finally dead, he had learned to enjoy abstention. He gets more fun out of refusing to overindulge, refusing sex, refusing pleasure, than us messy types get from wallowing in our passions. Literally, he looks down on us." Gadi sighed. "Sometimes I almost admire him. If he wasn't my father, maybe I could. But we're so locked into our little duels and pin-sticking contests."

"He said to me once he had given up a normal life for the cyborgs. As if he could only create life if he gave up loving and living."

"Okay, so you can give up loving and living—but to give up sex?" Gadi laughed. "How many years has it been since we danced?"

"You made me dance with you once at our graduation, in front of everyone, where I couldn't refuse. You were with Hannah." She flinched at the sound of her own voice, the pain and anger suddenly trembling there.

"You came alone. Very touching. I knew at least three boys had asked you, so I assumed you'd done it to make me feel guilty."

"I felt I'd be giving false encouragement, since I wasn't interested in any of them. I thought you were cruel to ask me to dance."

"Cruel? Ugi, I couldn't stand not to touch you. I was free, and I hated it. I couldn't bear for us to stay on different sides of the room all night."

"I can remember that night so vividly. When I wept, the tears made little marks on my blue dress. I thought I'd never care for another man."

He tilted her chin up. "Weren't you right?"

"Gadi, we can crawl out of it. We can. It's a myth we've both clung to, used to keep ourselves from the risk of being really hurt by anyone."

"If you think that, you've forgotten what it was like." His voice was no longer silkily mocking but serrated. "I can't forget. I'll never forget. I could take you back there, Shira."

She could not look away from his silver eyes. "We're not the same people, Gadi. There is no back."

He held her closer and spoke into her ear. "I have friends, Shira. They made a spike for me. I use it when I need to. When I can't live without it."

"A spike?" Why was she suddenly afraid, as if someone had jammed a needle into her spine and were injecting a cold dangerous liquid? It was in her mouth to say that spikes were illegal, when she realized that in Gadi's world, nothing was truly illegal. They manufactured and exported sensations for money. Nothing was out of bounds. Just sometimes, when their needs conflicted with other powerful subworlds, they might brush against taboos, laws, alien customs, and, like Gadi, be briefly punished. "What kind of a spike?"

"Us, Ugi. Us as we were."

"How could it be?"

"You're a computer simulation. But it doesn't work, like all spikes, unless there's a nervous system for it to inhabit. In stimmies, it's the recorded sensations of the actor you experience. In spikes, it's you yourself."

She could not breathe. She could not stop staring at him. She could not break free. "Gadi, I don't want to go back. That sounds like hell to me."

"You've made yourself forget, Shira. Out of fear. Out of pain. But me,

I've never forgotten. Once we had what everyone wants. I can take you back to the only time the two of us were really alive."

He could not have offered anything that would have frightened her more: the fragile webs of her life slashed through; herself transfixed with love and pain, caught in the past like a bubble in blown glass. No, she thought, No!

twenty-nine

HOW MUCH WOULD YOU MIND?

"We have no choice," Avram said. "We must penetrate them. We must read their plans and find out what they want and how they mean to get it. The Council has given us a mandate to proceed."

Shira was sitting beside Yod on the far lab table. "Will something that sensitive be in their system?"

Malkah snorted. "Nobody can think anymore without AI. It's like asking someone to walk to California or cross the Atlantic on a raft. Everything is on a system. Just as nobody could do arithmetic anymore without a calculator after they were introduced, who can think with just their own brain?"

"You want me to attempt to enter the Y-S Base, locate information on their war plans and aims." Yod's demeanor was mild. He had become so accustomed to being with people, he no longer jumped at every gesture or prowled nervously. His voice was as neutral as if he had asked if he should open the door.

"You'll need help," Malkah said. "Their chimeras will be extremely sophisticated. You need me to get in."

"You're not afraid?" Avram asked her. "They almost killed you once."

"I'm afraid. What else is new?"

"You'll also need me," Shira said. "I'm the only one familiar with the Y-S system. From working on interface problems all over the system, I have a clear idea of the structure." While she was in the Y-S system, she hoped to find out what part Ari played in their schemes. Moreover, she could not bear waiting outside again while the two of them sat there dumb and blind and she wondered helplessly if they were still alive or already burned out.

"Once we've penetrated the system, shouldn't we do some damage?" Yod asked. "Shouldn't we introduce worms and viruses? One incursion might be the only chance we get."

Avram smiled. "Well spoken. We must prepare agile and powerful programs. Malkah, the whole Base collective should start on this tomorrow."

"At your service."

Nili spoke up. "I don't understand what you're planning to do. How will you get past their guards? Which complex will you try to enter? I can be of help in the attack, surely."

Yod turned to her. "We won't be physically present in Y-S. Our attack is purely mental. We use the worldwide Net to travel. Then we'll attempt to penetrate the Y-S Base. All Bases need to communicate with the Net, but all of them—like our own—are defended against intruders."

"Who does the Net belong to?"

"The Net's a public utility," Malkah said. "Communities, multis, towns, even individuals subscribe."

"Your town doesn't subscribe?" Avram asked Nili incredulously.

Nili shrugged. "We know a lot about some things, less about others. It doesn't seem as if your Net has made you universally wise."

They were all a little shocked. It was a truism that everyone was on the Net, although a poor child might grow up in the Glop, work for a gang or sell labor to a multi, die of one of the viral plagues that swept the Glop every year, and never once plug in to access the Net. Nili did not partake in what was universally considered the central artifact of contemporary culture.

"On this mission, you can't help us," Yod said in his quiet voice.

"I can learn how to operate in your Net."

Malkah put her hand on Nili's shoulder. "Once we're back, it would be my great satisfaction to introduce you to the uses and pleasures of the Net."

"We can't pause to teach you. I'll have to protect Shira and Malkah as best I can. We each have individual knowledge and skills. Avram himself won't enter with us."

"I'm not sure about that," Avram said slowly. "If we do plan to carry out effective sabotage, I think you'll need me."

Malkah swung about to smile ruefully at him. "It cannot be, Avram. If I'm killed, it may hurt our people, but if both you and I should die at once, that would be a disaster. One of us must remain outside in case of attack."

IN THREE DAYS, the message robot returned. They had paid extra for a voice recording of Ari, rather than the robot's voice. Riva had not risked recording her own voice, Shira thought, clasping herself nervously as she escorted the robot to the lab, where Yod prepared to record the transmission.

The little cylinder, like a headless dachshund on wheels, asked for Shira's finger to take the blood sample. She jumped at the prick, as she was clenched in anxiety. The robot reiterated the instructions she had given it. Then it announced it was giving the return message paid for in advance from Ari, the child of Shira. "Hello, Mommy, hello. Are you in there?" Ari's voice burst into giggles, a wildly hysterical fit new to him. But the voice was his, unmistakably his. "Mommy? I just had ice cream. Strawberry va-yellow. Mommy? Where are you? Why don't you come out? Mommy, can you hear me?" A voice spoke behind him. There was a scuffling sound. Finally Ari spoke again. "They say to say I am okay. We rode in a rocket. I don't have my koala Wawa, he broke. Daddy says we'll get another, but I want a kitty like I saw on Papaka. Where are you?" There was another mumbling in the background and a loud thump. "They say to say bye-bye, Mommy, and are you coming to Daddy and me? They say you can come here. They say if you want to come, you can come and be with me. Bye-bye."

"Let me work on the background on the recording," Yod said. "I can enhance it."

She told the robot to repeat, adding to Yod, "Record it a second time. Just in case something goes wrong with the first recording."

"The first will suffice to decode the voices."

"Yod, I just want to keep it. It's his voice!"

He nodded, although she could tell he found that desire mysterious. She had a twinge of gratitude toward him, that he so seldom argued with her. If he often did not understand her wishes, he nonetheless frequently acquiesced to them. Perhaps it was his general desire to please that distinguished him most from anyone else in her life. Like him, she was programmed to please when she could, although Malkah could not be blamed for that programming. Malkah's desire to please had always been highly particular.

By lunchtime, Yod had enhanced the recording enough to make out the voices. They all listened to the results:

The kid has to speak right at the robot. I'm not convinced it's picking up his voice. We can't play it back, you know.

"That's no one I know," she said.

I don't see the purpose of this. He's grown adjusted to her absence. This is upsetting him to no end.

"That's Josh."

Y-S expects you to do your part, Rogovin. We need your cooperation.

Ari, speak into the little grid there. Right. Speak to . . . your mother. The woman who just spoke to you. Tell her you're okay.

I know Mommy. Where is she?

She's not here, which is a mercy anyhow, Josh said. *Speak into it again.*

The original voice said, *Tell her that you're okay. Tell her that right now.*

The next patch of conversation occurred when apparently Ari kicked the message robot and it fell over.

Don't do that again, kid. We're lucky the damned thing didn't blow up. Now ask her to come here. Come on, talk to your mother, Ari, and tell her you want her to come home to you. Don't you want your mother? Now come on, sell it to her, make your mother come here. Tell her she can be with you and your daddy.

This is unfair to him. Unfair to me. I don't want her back here.

Come on, Ari, ask her nicely. Then you can have another ice cream.

"Well," Malkah said, "he's in Nebraska. And Josh sounds pissed."

"Ari's just bait for them. They don't care about him. I'm halfway sorry I sent the message robot. It must have been deeply upsetting for him to hear me speaking from a damned machine. No wonder he kicked it. He must be furious at me for disappearing."

"You had to find out where he's being kept," Malkah said reasonably. "If he's upset in the short term, if we can get hold of him, he'll be happier in the long run."

"Many ifs. But at least a chance." She made herself sound strong, although she longed to crawl away and collapse around a missing that felt larger than her body, as if the depression surrounded her rather than inhabited her. She wondered what he looked like now. She wondered what he ate, what he wore, what he played with. She could not bear to imagine how he thought about her, what they told him, what they didn't tell him. She had buried her pain deep inside her because the resolution was impossible. Now it had risen, greater than ever, and she could think of nothing else.

NILI STOOD in the doorway of Shira's room, as if uncertain of her welcome. "Come in," Shira said heartily, and heaved herself off her bed, where she had been staring at the ceiling imagining conversations with Ari.

"I didn't know you were resting."

"I wasn't. Do come in."

Gingerly Nili picked her way among the furniture. She stared at Shira's dresser with its bottles, salves, lotions. The closet door was open, and Nili looked askance at the row of dresses, tunics, blouses, pants. She sat on the desk chair, leaving it in position but straddling the back with her legs, facing Shira rather than the computer terminal. "You and Gadi were lovers when you both lived here before?"

Shira nodded wearily. Gadi's surprising story about the spike had haunted her briefly, but Ari's voice had driven Gadi from her mind.

"Why are you not lovers now?"

"Our relationship stopped months before I went away to college."

"Why hasn't it begun again?"

"If you stick your hand in the fire and it burns you, why don't you stick your hand in the fire again?"

Nili rocked the chair closer. "In what way, burning?"

"Pain."

"He is brutal? I find that hard to believe."

"Brutal? Of course not. He ended it. He wanted more freedom. I was so much in love with him, I felt devastated. It was simply a function of being young and vulnerable."

Nili frowned, considering. "He did not mean to hurt you?"

"Nili, what is this? If you want to know, you should also ask Gadi. I can't tell you how it would be for you, if you're interested in him."

"How is it, making love with a man?"

"With what should I compare it?"

"You've never been with a woman?"

Shira shook her head no. "You're nervous about being with a man?"

"I must do it. We know that if we open up to the world, we're going to have to deal with men. I'm supposed to find out what they're like. He seems as good a choice as any. He's very curiously made and strange. Everything he does is out of my range of experience. Surely I'd learn a great deal about things completely foreign to us."

"Also you find him attractive."

"I think so. I'm not sure, but I have to choose someone soon as a first experiment."

"That's a fine rationale for doing what you want to, Nili."

Nili grinned. Her teeth were strong ivory against her dark skin. "You don't object? I believe women and men frequently feel possessive toward each other."

"Gadi's attention makes me nervous."

"The machine, he's not so bad when you get to know him." She strolled over to Shira's dresser, staring down. "He is very serious. My people would like him. He works hard and he is not easily distracted, admirable traits. You see, I'm no longer prejudiced."

"Women who meet him and don't know what he is usually find him attractive."

"I don't understand this whole attraction business—"

"He doesn't either."

"I mean, at home we tend to become involved with the people we work with. We find that natural." She picked up a lipstick, smelled it, put it down. Her first response to all the cosmetics and lotions was to smell them. "I knew I'd probably have sex with Riva because we were traveling together. Unless we took a dislike to each other. Sometimes there's no chemistry."

"What about love?"

Nili was staring at a manicurist, the little tube into which Shira inserted her fingers. "Basically don't you think it's a matter of what you're used to and what's in front of you? If you raise chickens, you eat chickens and you eat eggs. You people live on fish."

"I don't think attraction is nearly so pragmatic. For me it's a fraught area." Shira smiled at Nili. She had to restrain herself from going to protect her cosmetics, for she was afraid Nili was going to break something. Also she was embarrassed. She thought of herself as using few enhancements, but Nili's scrutiny made her feel like one of the toy women at Y-S. At the same time, she found Nili's predicament likable. Perhaps it offered her a way in to Nili, seeing her confused. "Follow your impulse with Gadi. I'd be delighted if you became involved with him." Oddly enough, she realized she was telling the truth. She could not promise she would feel no jealousy; but she preferred jealousy to the temptation he represented. "Now I have to throw you out. What I'm supposed to be doing up here is recalling everything I can of the Y-S system. So I'd better resume."

•

EVERYTHING SHE remembered she told to Malkah and Yod. Once she was inside the system, more would come back. Avram had administered a very low dose of mnemosine. A larger dose could have produced from her brain whatever she knew in the given area of association required, while damaging the brain permanently. They had mapped out what she had been able to recall, and now they were ready to try to go in.

There was no one time better than any other, since Y-S was worldwide and offworld as well, so they decided to go in the next morning, simply for their own convenience. They would use the terminals in Avram's lab, where all three could line up. Avram had been reluctantly persuaded to remain outside to monitor, along with Sam Rossi, the third Base Overseer. Everyone ate together at Malkah's that night. She was in the mood to cook. "It may be our last meal. Let's have a little feast," Malkah said with determined cheer. Sam, a tall ruddy-faced man with brown curls and sloping shoulders, had come with his wife, Zipporah, a fat woman with a pretty rosy face, current chair of the Town Council. She was a woman strangers always underestimated; their best negotiator. She ran the Commons food services and ran them well.

Malkah made a basic Mediterranean fish soup, rich with tomatoes, basil, fennel. The bread was from the Commons bakery, but the salad was from their own garden. The wine came from Maine, where vineyards had been planted on the south-facing slopes of the seaside mountains. It had turned into good wine country for stony whites the color of straw, a bitingly dry champagne. The eight of them dined at the table in the courtyard, an extra leaf laid in. As August ended, the evenings were appreciably shorter, especially in the courtyard. They dined under Chinese lanterns; since Shira's childhood they had lit summer evenings when the light began to fail, casting a warm pale glow over their faces.

She was trying to figure out whether anything of significance had happened between Gadi and Nili. Malkah and Avram were perched on chairs at the ends, which the head and which the foot conveniently vague. Yod sat beside Shira, Zipporah on her other side—she was still careful to interpose herself whenever possible between Yod and anyone ignorant of his true nature—while Gadi, Nili and Sam sat opposite them. Yod was a dainty eater. He required less food than she did, since he combusted it thoroughly. Shira was not hungry, nervousness manifesting itself more as heightened gaiety than as anxiety.

Whenever Nili and Gadi touched, she could feel electricity snap between them. It was a gathering tension, a series of small shocks. No, she did not think they were yet lovers, but both were considering that option. Gadi remembered to throw her lingering glances from time to time, to flirt, but it was perfunctory. The twilight was a lake on which they were floating, mauve, pale gray, pearlescent colors, the scent of late auratum lilies, of stocks heady on the air of the courtyard but overwhelmed unless she leaned back by the strong savors of the meal.

"I still think this expedition is too dangerous," Zipporah began, but Avram stopped her at once with upraised hand.

"No business chat at supper, we all promised," he said smoothly. "Let us talk of what is truly interesting, beyond this pulse of anxiety."

"In the Middle Ages," Malkah was saying, "our ancestors believed that demons ate odors. They hovered everywhere but especially in what were considered waste places. Our attitude toward the land we aren't using has changed drastically. Our idea of paradise is less a garden than a real forest we haven't yet logged off, poisoned. Now some of us find our demons in the Glop, some of us in the multi enclaves, some in drugs or stimmies."

"You have trifled with the kabbalah all the years I've known you," Avram said to Malkah. "Why do you bother? You're a scientist, not a mystic."

"I find different kinds of truth valuable. I fly like an angel in the Base. In turning all statements into numbers, isn't gematria doing what a computer does? In fascination with the power of the word and a belief that the word is primary over matter, you may be talking nonsense about physics, but you're telling the truth about people."

"A person is as subject to physical laws as a stone is."

"But a person reacts and decides what's good or bad. For us the word is primary and paramount. We can curse each other to death or cure with words. With words we court each other, with words we punish each other. We construct the world out of words. The mind can kill or heal because it is the body."

"Malkah, politicians almost did in the human race by confusing saying with doing. Acid rain killed the forests. They appointed a committee to discuss it. The ozone layer was disappearing. They said it was a minor problem to be dealt with in time. They confused the power of words over people with the power of words over matter—which is nonexistent."

"You're making dichotomies, but in Hebrew the word *davar*, as André Neher pointed out, means word *and* thing, no distinction. A word, an idea, is a thing. We see and hear the world with our minds, with words, in categories, not in raw sensory data. That was one of the improvements in Yod."

"You're becoming a Platonist, Malkah. Is the idea of god inborn?"

"I believe in holiness because I experience it. I don't view it as a personal presence, but holiness is as vivid as sexual pleasure or hunger. Why do you go to services, Avram, if you find religious impulses bizarre and archaic?"

"Because it's polite, Malkah. It's social glue. It's fulfilling my place in my family, my society, as my father did before me, with no more mysticism than he would have felt taking out a policy with an insurance agent. In those days there were large multis that bet people disasters would not occur—but of course there came a time when the skies fell," he added as an aside to the younger folk. "These bets were called insurance policies."

"Avram, I'm not betting. I don't believe in an afterlife. And I'm dealing with experiences as real as eating this soup."

"Why do they always argue?" Yod asked Shira.

"They have a lot of mutual history. And they enjoy arguing."

"A man as arrogant as Avram, it's my duty to shake him up," Malkah said.

"A woman like Malkah, she comes to believe her own rhetoric," Avram said. "She needs the rigor of a more disciplined mind to hold her fancies in check."

"The two of you should sell tickets," Zipporah said. "We could put you on as a comedy team. How about doling me out some more soup, Avram, if you aren't too busy? I love this soup. I could go swimming in it."

"Don't be ridiculous," Nili was saying. "Why would I want to pretend things in front of a camera with electrodes and transmitters implanted? Why should I live for other people's excitement?"

"You don't understand how highly stimmie stars are paid." Gadi shook his head in bemusement, appealing with his eyes to the rest of the table. "They're gods all over the world. Everybody wants to be a star or to imitate a star they adore."

"I always wonder," Yod said, his controlled voice pitched just loud enough for Shira to hear, "if you wish you were with him instead."

"If I were, we'd be fighting—not for fun, like Malkah and Avram, but bitterly. Savagely. You and I work well together."

"Inside their Base, we'll find all the records on your son."

"Will you help me?" Under the table she took his hand, dry, warm, finely made like the precision tool it was. He had beautiful hands, what Malkah had always called on men or women, artistic hands.

"I know we must get him back for you."

"But how can you understand my need?"

"I understand that I cannot give you a baby and that you must have your child back or you'll want another." He regarded her gravely.

"I want Ari. No other."

"But that won't last unless we can recover him for you."

"Good. Then help me."

"I have that intention." His hand closed around hers, gently but with a grip she doubted anything could break.

thirty

THE ROBBER'S MISTAKE

The next day, the Maharal sends Joseph into Malá Strana on the far bank, to the house of Prince Bertier. Once there, Joseph is to deliver personally a boxed present. The Maharal insists that Joseph must place it in the prince's hand, and only then to give him a note kept hidden until that moment.

The Maharal opens the box, showing Joseph how to spring the lock. Inside is a ring with a big green stone. "That's an emerald, Joseph, and you are to give it to no one except to Prince Bertier himself. Mordecai Maisl has sacrificed it to this purpose. It is from New Spain, and no doubt, as with most such stones men consider precious, it has cost many lives. After the prince has accepted the ring, only then give him this letter from me, asking him to intercede with the emperor. Do not be turned away. Do not hand over the gift to any servant or assistant, or to his wife or his son. To the prince only. Then you may return to me, but not before."

"Rabbi, I go. But you talk to me differently than you talk to anyone else. You say precisely what I have to do and not do. Am I more foolish than your other messengers and servants?"

The Maharal looks Joseph in the eyes. "In dealing with angels and demons, the kabbalah teaches us to be precise. To say exactly and no more. To say what is wanted and what is not wanted. You are a creature of magic, Joseph, and whether you are angel or demon or new life is only for ha-Shem to say. It is prudent to follow the precepts of ritual carefully."

"I don't think I'm an angel or a demon," Joseph says. "I have no memories of life before the life you gave me. Like you, I am created of dust and water, as the Torah says."

"There are angels of memory who can make us remember or take memories from us and drown us in forgetfulness, as there are angels and demons who give us dreams. Go now, Joseph, and do only as I have told you."

"I obey."

We are, remember, in the Renaissance, when the same man, Tycho Brahe, precisely observes the stars and casts the emperor's horoscope; when alchemy and chemistry are conflated; when medicine deals with herbs like digitalis, which we use yet, while bleeding victims regularly into anemia; when humors of the human body are linked to emotions, planets, elements. Judah embraces the foremost science of his time and a passionate belief in demons. Perhaps only such a man could then create life or its simulacrum, as we do now in our laboratories. In every age, Yod, there are prevailing universal superstitions.

Joseph slips from the ghetto, crosses the Karl Bridge. On the river, a man is casting a net. A servant is spreading out linens to dry on the bank. Joseph hastens through the Malá Strana and climbs a street of many palaces, high up but not as high as the castle itself. The royal palace of Hradcany looms over them, immense and long, composed of many buildings, bristling with towers: round and onion domes, steeples, square towers. The great cathedral of St. Vitus, still under construction, stands inside the walls, as do many houses. The prince, however, has built his house outside, with a view of the next green hill and a monastery nearby. The plum blossoms are just opening in the orchards. Below them, sheep graze. The steep roof has red tiles; the stone palace itself is simple and graceful. Many windows with modillioned cornices pierce the symmetrical facade, a great extravagance. Lion-headed doors stand wide. He is brought in through a courtyard surrounded by graceful arcades; in the center is a well, protected by gilded wrought-iron grillwork.

Once inside, Joseph is kept waiting by the well, kept waiting in a servants' anteroom, kept waiting upstairs. Finally, after supper, long after dark and after the legal time for a Jew to be abroad in the Christian town without danger of imprisonment, he is summoned up yet another flight to a small room, sumptuously furnished. Through the open door Joseph can glimpse a bedchamber, grander than he has ever seen. The small room contains a writing desk painted with a tracery of flowers, tall-backed chairs and a spinet. He is terrified for a moment that he might be expected to play it, but the footman who ushered him in simply tells him to stand in the corner and wait. The ceiling is divided by plaster into many sections, each painted with floating naked ladies.

After another hour a man he assumes is the prince strolls in. Stout and florid, he stands in the center of the room, being divested of his jewels and outer garments—not of the street but of splendor—as he speaks. He wears more rings than Tycho Brahe. "Now, what is this mysterious errand?"

"Pane, may I approach with a gift from the Rabbi Judah Loew ben Bezalel? He wishes you and your family and your establishment health and good fortune and long life and every end you desire, and wishes me to give you a very small token of his fondness, pane." Joseph reiterates with no inflection the message he was taught. He kneels to present the box, causing it to spring open.

Prince Bertier leans forward and eyes it carefully. Then, smiling, he motions one of his valets to take the ring out and hand it to him. "My, my. What have we here?"

"As my lord sees, it is an emerald from New Spain, unworthy of you but the best we can offer to your greatness," says Joseph, the unctuous words sticking like taffy to his mouth.

"Why, you must thank your master. I presume Maisl found this somewhere, but it's a beauty."

"And my master bade me give you this note from him. For you to read personally, pane," he adds, as the prince begins to wave the note toward the nearest valet. "Personally," he repeats, and the prince sighs.

"Very well." The prince glances it over, the ring glinting on his finger. He has put it on his index finger, moving another ring over and bumping one to the valet, who takes it from him. "Hmm. I understand. Tell your master I'll see what I can do."

"Time is short," Joseph ventures.

"And the hour is late." With a snapping gesture, the prince dismisses him. He is ushered speedily from the room, downstairs and into the street. It has taken him six hours to work his way from the street to the prince's little reception room. It takes them less than six minutes to turn him into the street again.

As he slips out into the dark, he removes his yellow patch that identifies him as liable to arrest or attack. It has been a frustrating day. He was created to defend, not to act as a messenger boy to haughty nobles who love bright bits of compressed carbon better than wisdom or people or compassion. He wonders idly if he could digest the emerald, but he doubts it. He tried biting iron once and found he could not chew it. He has his limits. The thought makes him walk a little faster down the cobblestone street, past the taverns, still open, past the whores plying their trade and the straggling street musicians and the beggars still hoping for a last few coins. It is a crisp night, with a memory of frost although past the date for it.

Raising his head to the wind like a big dog, he smells fresh new leaves, horse dung, roasting meat, the sharp smell of human and horse urine, the pitchy smell of a torch, the sour reek of spilled beer, wood smoke, the stench of sewage, the invitation of baking yeasty dough and cinnamon, odors snaking about him as he descends toward the river. Scraps of music waft out to him from a grand dwelling, the sound of feet against floorboards, the swish of skirts, laughter. In another street, a woman screams. A donkey is braying hoarsely in protest against some injury. Sewage trickles by. A baby is crying in fierce short bursts as if worked by a bellows.

Then from an alley two men move out from the left side and two more from the right. "Hello, farm boy," one of them calls. "Let's see if you've got anything to give us so maybe we'll let you live."

"I'm not a farm boy. I'm a messenger returning empty-handed. If you don't let me pass, you'll get nothing but trouble. I have no money, nothing but these big fists." He holds up his hands in mock imploring, watching them all carefully.

The man who spoke wears a battered but quite lethal sword. The tallest clutches a short knife in the left hand and a length of wood studded with nails in his right. The others are armed with truncheons, clubs, probably daggers in their belts. They look to be businesslike ruffians, for whom a murder or two is part of a night's labor. At the end of the block a woman crouches, a lookout for them, watching down the winding street.

The man with the sword puts it to Joseph's chest, dead center, pricking him through the cloth and leather. "What you've got, we'll take. Now."

Joseph seizes the man's sword hand, breaks it upward, snapping the sword, and flings the man through the air into the heavyset ruffian. As they go down, the tall one charges him, swinging the nailed club, knife held slightly sideways and low to slash upward. Joseph smashes that hand with a kick that sends the man sprawling. Now the other two are up. The swordsman with one arm crippled hangs back shouting directions to the others.

Joseph pauses, his back to the building. "Get out of here while you can, or I'll kill you all."

He is half glad when three men come at him. The woman has abandoned her watch to run close, shouting encouragement to her men. "Take him from both sides at once, both sides," she shouts. The ex-swordsman gestures for her to bind up his broken wrist. She tears off a piece of her muddy petticoat to oblige. The man whose left knife hand Joseph has broken advances swinging the nailed club, the pain not disabling him but putting him into a berserk fighting frenzy. The club sings in the air. Joseph ducks under it, seizes the man as the club hits him a gouging blow on his shoulder. Then Joseph swings him wildly through the air as the man had slung his club and dashes him against the building, smashing his skull like a rotten melon.

Now Joseph picks up the fallen club of nails and wields it, slashing the face of the first oncoming thief to blind meat, catching the second right in the chest and caving it in like an old barrel, staves of ribs cracking. He likes the heft of the weapon. It is well suited to his big hands. It sings in the air as if it likes to kill. It sings of the strength and power of Joseph, against whom none can stand. He keeps swinging it, advancing on the swordsman, who draws a dagger with his still usable hand. The woman slides a knife from her sleeve and flings it. It comes straight and true. The knife sticks into Joseph's arm, but he scarcely feels it. He keeps striding forward, swinging the club that laughs in his hand. Down goes the man, and then the woman falls in a bloody heap. Joseph pauses, with the club silent and heavy in his hand and the five bodies crumpled and still on the pavement. His own black blood is oozing from the wounds on his shoulder and his arm. He pulls the knife free and the blood spurts out. He begins shambling down the street, the club dangling loose from his hand. He should not have killed the woman. But he could not help it. He had started and he could not stop.

Maybe there is a demon in the club itself. As he crosses the bridge, he tosses it high, arcing over the river, and then he hears a loud satisfying splash as it hits. Almost at once he regrets the loss of that fine weapon. He will make himself one like it.

The rabbi is waiting up for him, along with Perl and Chava. Perl exclaims as she sees the blood on his clothes. But his blood has long since coagulated, and his wounds are already healing. The Maharal insists that Perl leave them and go to bed. Chava tends his wounds. Then the rabbi sends her off also.

Joseph reports on his delivery of the emerald and the message. But the rabbi persists: "So how came you by these wounds? All your garments are covered with red blood as well as yours."

Joseph cannot lie to the Maharal. He tells the entire story, one slow sentence at a time, not leaving out the death of the woman and the throwing of the nailed club into the Vltava.

The Maharal is silent a long time, his head buried in his hands. "I have much to answer for. But we still need you."

The Maharal's words frighten Joseph. "Master, I was outnumbered and they were professional killers. I did what I had to do."

"And then you continued killing. You continued."

He cannot endure the Maharal's displeasure. It burns him. It is a torment like fire in his mind. "It was a mistake, Rabbi."

"You're too strong, too powerful, to make mistakes. No more mistakes, Joseph. No more."

The Maharal paces to and fro, and as he paces he begins to pray. Joseph remains in the corner, quiet, but as the rabbi prays, so does he. He hardly ever thinks of ha-Shem when he prays; he thinks of the Maharal. He prays to be forgiven; he prays to be accepted. He prays to be loved just a little, as Judah might love his good cloak or a little dog.

The Maharal stops suddenly. "This is Thursday night before their Good Friday. Go, patrol! This is the time of maximum danger."

Not knowing if he should be pleased to be put back to work or sad for being banished from the Maharal's presence, Joseph runs to obey.

thirty-one

THE SHAPE-SHIFTERS

Entering the Net was an individual matter; they must find each other immediately inside, once they had projected. Often while using the Net in her usual work or relaxation, Shira would simply employ visual or audio. She would be reading menus, talking with the computer, scanning files, just as someone looking up a subject in an encyclopedia in printed form need not suspend attention to the outside world.

Seminars in the Net were conducted in projection, as was serious studying, most creative systems work and games-playing. Crossing the Net as they were about to do required projection. Therefore Shira plugged in. The familiar logo of the Tikva Base appeared, the reception room. She chose the door marked Net, entered, then faced a plan where the user requested a destination and a path lit up on a big display map.

Yod immediately appeared. He had already arrived and been exploring. He looked just like himself, just as he had been when she had turned from him and reached for the system plug. Malkah slipped through the doors to join them. Her image of herself was startling, because she looked as she had in Shira's childhood. Shira was moved at the sight and stood a moment, staring. How vital and stunning Malkah had been. She had a slight hawkish look, vivid alert predatory eyes that missed nothing. She had the light fine bones of a bird too, and the swift movement. She looked about to soar and then stoop on whatever caught her attention. Malkah had aged so gradually that Shira thought of her as always looking as she did now, but this was the Malkah of the prime of life, her inner age. Not twenty, not thirty, but about forty-five. That was Malkah's self-image, skin smooth and ruddy, body firm.

As soon as the three of them were gathered, Yod changed. It was uncanny, even though she tried to remain aware at all times in the Net that the images they presented of themselves were merely that. He began to turn translucent, so that she could see the wall dimly through him. "I see no reason to retain my external form. After all, we'd prefer not to be recognized."

"But how do you do that?" Malkah asked.

"Malkah, you must know already. You don't look the same—I mean, not exactly," Shira said gingerly.

"Nonsense. I just project myself. I know how to make myself other." Suddenly Malkah was a natty tall man of perhaps forty, with black hair and a rakish grin. "But how can I become transparent?"

"Merely project yourself as transparency, just as you project your thoughts forward." Yod made himself a large bright red box and then a cleaning robot and then a big black dog. Then he resumed the translucent form.

Malkah closed her eyes and concentrated. Shira watched her for a moment. Nothing happened. She closed her eyes, too, and focused on herself as the assassin who had attacked her, the woman who had broken her wrist. She was six feet two. She had long spidery arms and legs with the tensile strength of steel. She could not remember the woman's face clearly, so she gave herself Nili's face and skin. When she opened her eyes and looked down, she saw the woman's claw hand on an arm half again as long as her own.

Malkah opened her eyes and looked down. She appeared just as she had before. "I seem not able to get the hang of it. I don't want to waste any more time practicing now. I'll go as my alter ego." She was once again the natty man. He looked to Shira like a movie star from perhaps fifty years before, when flat films had been commonly projected in public, perhaps some cherished actor of Malkah's youth.

The usual way to break into a base, the standard approach of data pirates, was to enter along the com-con channels, to pass in with messages. There was no way a base could distinguish between legitimate entering data and folks along for the ride. They rode in on the communications channels, past the otherwise impermeable shield that surrounded the Y-S set of bases. It was a matter of keeping a low profile in energy readings, not reacting, not speaking, simply moving along in the chain of data that appeared in the conventional imagery of the Net as packages whizzing on a very fast conveyor belt. The trick was to build up to speed and then slip in. It felt dangerous, but as the bits and you were both merely charges, there was little danger. The spatial dimensions of the Net were all metaphorical, mental conveniences. The dangers of the Net were real, but they were dangers caused by the human brain or nervous system or by encounters with other human or traps built into the systems.

All the real defenses were inside the perimeter of each base. They could not ride the com-con any further, since it connected with individual receptor areas. They would have wound up in somebody's terminal. One by one they rolled off into darkness lit only by flashes of what appeared to be heat lightning. In the distance they could see a vast city glittering, surrounded by an energy field that was the source of the crackling light patterns. "How will we get in there?" Shira wondered.

"We won't bother. It's a chimera," Malkah said confidently. "We're on the wrong level. We need to go up or down."

"A space platform or an underground warren," Shira guessed.

"There's a space platform above and to the right." Yod pointed. "Six hundred kilometers above this level."

"How do we get up there?" she asked him.

"We can project ourselves. Remember, space isn't real here," Yod said patiently. He demonstrated by rising in a straight line about ten meters upward, then landing again with a light bounce.

Malkah said, "But to no end. That's another chimera. No, we must go down."

"Down?" Shira stomped her foot on the ground. It felt solid. "Are you telling me we can simply pass through earth?"

"No. No more than walls. They represent a lack of pathways. We must find an opening. Now, if this is designed anything like I'd design it, the entrance will be apparently unimportant. A hole, a cave, an abandoned tunnel, a mine shaft. Whatever was reasonable in the designed landscape."

"Wait for me." Yod rose and then darted forward. His translucence and speed made her think of a large dragonfly. Then they could not see him at all. Shira practiced fading to transparency.

Malkah closed her eyes and tried again. Shira said, "There, you blurred a bit. Try again."

"I think I've got the knack. I can't bear to think there's any little trick of the trade I can't master. My pride is leaking." Again Malkah's strange male body wavered as if it were painted on a flag in the wind. Then slowly it dimmed.

Malkah opened her eyes and looked down. "Well, I'm less visible—a personal fog."

Yod alighted before them, still blurred. "How about a dump?"

"A dump?" Shira repeated blankly.

"An old-fashioned phenomenon of the idiot days," Malkah explained. "They used to take waste and simply put it in the earth or burn it into the air. They also dumped their feces and sewage in the water. Let's have a look." Malkah rose elegantly, her ankles crossed.

On a dark plain near the city, coruscating with colors and light, a valley had been dug in a range of low hills to accommodate old trash, the rusting appliances and vehicles of fifty years before, barrels of dangerous chemicals no doubt dumped here to leak at their leisure into the water table. They landed, gingerly, among mounds of old plastic. "Now, what's that?" Malkah pointed. "Over there."

"I believe it's an incinerator," Yod said. "A device for turning refuse into toxic smoke."

"Let's go in." Malkah led the way briskly.

"Steps," Yod said. He brushed past Malkah. "I'll go first."

"This is it," Malkah said. "It's just such a small and inconspicuous entrance as I design. You have to have various ways into your Base, but no one except a debugger or a troubleshooter should ever use this one. I work the same way. Always disguise your alternate entrances."

"We'd never have found this without you," Yod said. "You were right. Now perhaps you should return."

"Not on your life—or mine, to be more accurate. I want in, all the way. This is the chance of a lifetime."

They climbed down and down and down. "Once, years ago—I was living in Prague then, and I was on vacation with my lover, your grandfather, Shira. We went to Paris during a school vacation. It was fall and everything was gray and gold. It was raining that day, and we decided to see the catacombs." Before them the stairway corkscrewed down in total darkness. Yod raised his hand over his head. It became a bright flashlight. "You could only visit the third Sunday of every month, whatever. So down we went just like this, descending for what felt like hours. Remains had been moved there from old cemeteries, from charnel houses. Then the bones had been neatly stacked—all the thighbones together—and then a motto made of skulls. 'Ashes to ashes, dust to dust. Remember thou art mortal.' "

"I love it when you talk about when you were younger," Shira said.

"A sense of continuity," Malkah offered.

"You are embedded in history in a sense that I can't be," Yod said, plunging ahead even faster. "What leads to me? Legends, theories, comic books. All my destroyed brother machines."

Shira was abruptly jolted as they arrived at the bottom and fell into a well-lighted place, what felt like a landing strip for zips, a broad glaring expanse of concrete. Yod immediately thinned himself close to invisibility. With difficulty Shira and Malkah managed to imitate him. He was arrowing straight ahead. "Do you know where you're going?" she called after him.

"No. But anyplace is better than this. We can get our bearings once we're out of trouble."

A blade of some kind of energy swept suddenly across the lighted area. Ahead of them Yod immediately spread himself on the concrete flatter than a skate. Both of them again imitated him. "He knows how to combat the defenses," Malkah said. "He responds instantly. We'd be dead before we recognized the danger." Their thought projected as voices, although they were spread like rugs on the cement.

Yod collected himself and sped forward. They hastened to follow. Finally they escaped the blinding glare. What they saw under a low gray sky were rows and rows of warehouses, identical as barracks, stretching to the horizon. "Okay," Shira said. "This is archives. The realm of backup programs and old information. This part of the Y-S Base has its own independent solar power supply. There are actually two such facilities, one in orbit and one underground in Nebraska. There!" She pointed to an empty road stretching off. "That's where we must go next."

Malkah said, "I suggest following it off to one side as far as we can travel and still keep it in sight."

"If we climb, we can increase that distance," Yod said, rising.

Every human has had fantasies of flying like a gull, Shira thought, veering after him. This ought to be exhilarating, but because there's no air against the face and hair, no sense of motion, it felt curiously flat.

They were approaching what looked like a combination of a power station and a honeycomb, crackling with a pale straw-colored light, when Yod ordered, "Drop!" He plunged like a stone, falling to spread himself thinly over the dry earth. They imitated him again, just as another bolt slashed across.

"What would one of those do to us?" she asked Malkah, the glass puddle.

"It would send an electrical charge back through your plug into your brain, sufficient to produce mental disruption and possibly death. I can't say if your body would hang on in a vegetable state or if your functions would stop, but it wouldn't much matter."

"That's the hub of programming," Shira said. "We don't want that. We want planning. This way."

"On the way out, we must stop here," Yod said. "We can't start sabotage till we have the information we seek."

Those slashing beams crossed the space between different bases within the larger Base. Yod was attuned to them, and each time he gave Malkah and Shira just enough warning. Shira began to think that the defenses would not prove as dangerous as she had feared. From a wasteland, the country they were crossing began to be landscaped. Groves of trees, lawns, farms, country roads. "It ought to be here, but there's nothing. We should be in it by now."

Malkah swooped down. "This is it. Under us." She was heading straight for a landscaped area under them, shrubs set around a pool. As she dived, several winged entities emerged from a hill that opened. They were part bird, part plane, part armored reptile. They came streaking for Malkah. A long tongue of fire licked from the foremost, close enough to Malkah to make her cry out in pain. Yod, armored now and glinting, intervened and tore right through the flock of them so they exploded behind him. He ripped at their wings, he slashed at their metallic beaked heads. He moved almost faster than she could see. He was a blur enveloped in the fire they breathed out, followed by a rain of machine parts. Malkah had resumed her dive. Yod and Shira followed her as she passed headfirst through the pool and then into the undisguised machine imagery underneath. Around them and through the pool fell parts of the harpies, blasted metal littering down.

They were in the machine now, in its representation within the Base. Somewhere the actual nanochips existed, but this was a simulacrum. "Is this the right stuff?" Malkah asked Yod. "Are we on target? I'm pretty sure this is no chimera, but let's proceed cautiously. It has to be well defended."

"Wait." He stared at the busy grid before them, stretching up beyond sight. He seized one of the metallic feathers that had fallen through the chimera of the pool with them. Chunks of metal curiously wrought. He tossed it forward. When it came within half a meter of the machine, it was pulverized in a flash.

"How do we get around that?" Shira asked.

"We don't," Malkah said. "I'm beginning to understand what Yod does. We turn ourselves into some sort of digging devices and burrow through the soil. We'll come up inside. I have never heard of anyone doing what we're doing, using shape-changing in a base, but it seems effective. We accept their metaphors and incorporate them." Malkah turned herself into a large furry mole. Then she reconsidered, scratching her head, and became instead an armored mining machine. "A mole is too vulnerable and too blind."

"You had trouble at first, but now you're faster than I am," Shira said admiringly.

"I'm a feisty old dog," Malkah said. "I like to learn new tricks. Especially out-of-the-body tricks. My body is weak, but my mind still has all its teeth."

"Yod, I don't know enough about mining machines to become one. Program me." She held out her hands to him. She remembered how they had exchanged thoughts in the room-sized rose.

He took hold of her. They were both translucent, and she had an odd sensation of their quasi bodies intermingling like smoke and fog. She felt a momentary comfort in his ghostly embrace. Someone you could rely on. Like Malkah that way. A virtue without price. He presented to her mind a clear diagram and picture of a mining machine, which she could emulate. She became a roughly cylindrical machine with shallow treads. Her head was a boring device. She swallowed earth and rock and excreted it up the hole with a violent blast. It was rather fun. She had to remind herself to follow Malkah and Yod and not to twist away on her own, eating rock. Finally they burst through into the machine interior. The women reverted to human shape.

"Now we must access and find what we need," Yod said. "In real time we have caused some disturbances. Soon more formidable defense mechanisms than we have dealt with will be converging." He condensed into a ball of light and disappeared into the system.

Shira said, "I don't much like standing around here without him."

"We could try to go in after him, but I'm dubious."

"We might be safer inside. At least we could accomplish something." The tension of waiting was too great. Whenever Shira paused for a moment and realized where she was, she was terrified. It was better to keep moving. She condensed herself as tightly as she could and projected forward. She could tell that Malkah was behind her. Together they flicked past file names. All around them the system was reacting to commands. She accessed a file being modified. One of the components in the plug embedded in her real body was a decoder that made her able to access machine language, translate it instantly into numbers and words. Without it she could not have accessed any Base or the Net directly. This file was about plans to redesign the delivery system for the space stations. She dropped it.

She began tasting files as she went, moving fast, pushing. Malkah emulated her, forging ahead. They were streaking through. New products, development plans, research, new stations, investment, infiltration, industrial espionage, security decisions, marketing.

"I have it," Yod said nearby. "I've stored the information. We can access it when we're out."

"Then follow me." Shira could not give way to relief, for she still had one more all-important task. "I believe we can use inner pathways to personnel records. I need to access mine, Josh's, Ari's." Without waiting for their response, she rocketed off. She was an impulse rippling along a pathway of ice. She burned without heat, speeding on. She could feel them behind her. She could feel something behind them. Malkah was following her still, Yod was not. A great wave of energy burst along the pathway, almost knocking her loose. Then Yod was behind her again, following with alacrity.

Shira had always been a conscientious worker who preferred understanding the larger picture into which her work fitted, so she had learned far more about the Y-S system than she had strictly needed. She knew the way now, felt the moment they reached personnel records. Accessing here was easy, for she remembered the file names. It was all by employee number, and she had memorized those numbers—those for her ex-husband, her son and herself—since she had had to use them for routine functions and every request.

Yod ate the files quickly. "Now we must find our way back. At once."

"Follow me. I'll take us through the system back to archives." She went faster than before. She had the knack of it now, the transformations Yod had invented or rediscovered. She had no idea how long ago they had plugged in, sitting in a row in Avram's lab, but she had the strong feeling it had been enough time to begin to be dangerous. Not for Yod. He could remain plugged in for days without any ill effects she could observe, but she had heard of Net travelers killed because they had got caught in some inner loop and could not escape. While they were trapped in netspace, their bodies died. Presumably their projected minds also died, but it was even worse to contemplate consciousnesses trapped like catatonics within repeating strings in forgotten closed-off sectors of some base.

"We must stop," Malkah said. "Here I need to introduce a worm."

"Work quickly," Yod said. "We have little time. We're being pursued."

"You can both help me."

They worked together, rebuilding the programming. Then they were on their way again. Three times Malkah stopped them. Each time she could feel Yod's level of apprehension rising. It was not that he grew nervous in a human sense but that he was more alert, more on guard. The fourth time he refused to permit them to loiter.

At archives, Malkah dropped a simple virus, and they fled the system. Now they saw again the representation of the barracks. There was the glare of the concrete field they must cross. "Rockets," Yod said. "Fastest way to cross. Malkah, do you have the exit in view?"

"Right. I'll lead."

They roared across the concrete. Halfway, Yod cried, "Down!" as the blade of energy flashed across their paths. Another. Another. They were stuck plastered on the concrete. Yod began oozing forward without raising himself, and they followed him. It was slow going under the scorching blasts of the energy field. Finally they were climbing the tunnel, soaring up through the darkness illuminated by Yod's acetylene glare, three rising projectiles. They went up in a third of the time they had taken to descend, and then they were once again in the dump, and then on the dark plain where the city glistened and sparked.

"Fast," Yod said. "Very fast." He kept his projectile form and rushed in the direction of the com-con entrance.

"What's that?" Malkah directed their attention to the right. A wall of fire was moving toward them, much higher than they were flying. "There's no getting under that. Look, the earth itself is burning."

Yod stared at it. "What isn't hurt by fire?"

"Asbestos? Rock?"

"We cannot be sure that fire isn't hot enough to melt rock. No, we must be fire too. Quickly."

She could already feel the shock wave advancing before it, the plain itself catching fire, an updraft of intense scorching heat drying her through. She burst into flames as Yod did, rising as far as he could. Then she was in the fire, of the fire. The fire was dancing through her, bright, exciting, and she fed on it and grew longer and larger. For a moment all she felt was a great intense energy of burning, a burst of power like an exploding drug that consumed her. Then they were once again projectiles, pursuing the wall of fire over the scorched plain to the com-con link. That could not be closed down, even under attack, for business depended on communication. They flung themselves onto the conveyor belt. Shira collapsed into the semi-shutdown mode necessary, imagining herself an inert box. Forward she was carried, careful to permit herself no more thought than was absolutely essential, concentrating on the box shape and nothing else.

Going through the energy field from the Base to the Net was always a tangible sensation. Now they were safe, and they rolled off and stared at each other, once again in their original forms. "Keep moving," Yod said. "We must return with all the information I'm carrying, so I can load it into our Base."

When she unplugged, she found herself exhausted. She had a headache all across her temples and neck, an iron cage of pain superimposed on the inside of her skull. Avram was standing there, and his mouth moved, and she heard questions she could not relate to. Yod would deal with him, Yod would explain. Malkah was swaying with fatigue. Shira stumbled toward the cot that still stood against the far end of the lab, flung herself on it and fell asleep.

thirty-two

FLASHES AND DANGEROUS STRUCTURE

Every morning Shira went to the Synagogue of Water to say kaddish for Riva, always with that sense of a missed connection. The synagogue was built over a spring that welled up in the garden, one of her favorite places in Tikva since childhood, when she had confused it with paradise. Always there was a sound of water flowing over pebbles. The morning after the penetration, she woke groggy but went anyhow. Yod had taken to attending her for the company he observed she needed, and because a minyon was hard to come by. Usually Avram was not around so early, but this morning he was in the lab, working on the material Yod had absorbed. Since Yod had transferred files to his storage memory instantaneously, he was as ignorant of the contents as the rest of them. The files had been loaded yesterday into the Base, but to winnow and divide the information into some approachable form was Avram's next task. Aware suddenly where Yod was going, Avram objected.

"How can a machine make a minyon? Malkah can tell you that in sixteenth-century Poland, it was ruled that a golem cannot be counted in a minyon." Avram snorted. "You're overdoing the socialization, Shira."

Shira leaned on the doorpost, eager to get going. "For centuries, *I* wouldn't have been included. The Orthodox still don't count half the Jews as Jews. You made him a Jew as my foremothers made me. But he chooses to practice it as I do. Don't you think Yod is sincere?"

"Machines are what they are as a chair is a chair. Choice is not in it."

"Father, I do make choices," Yod said reasonably. "My choice is now to leave quickly with Shira. The old people go early, and they're reliable. We're already a little late to catch them."

They walked through the morning streets, even now throbbing with the heat of the day to come. All the years Shira had spent in a climate-controlled enclave slipped away as her body adjusted to the summers of her childhood. "Yod, what do you think about during prayers? Do you feel estranged?"

"Sometimes I feel a sense of belonging, that I am doing something that has been done over and over again for three thousand years. Sometimes I feel estranged—talk of a Creator makes me think of Avram, whom I cannot worship. I find the notion of a Creator for humanity childish. But insofar as Judaism insists on deed rather than on being, I can carry out mitzvot as well as a born person. Then I feel at home. But sometimes I think my programming runs counter to those all-important ethics. We pray for peace—Shalom, Shalom—and I'm a weapon."

"Only for defense." Her answer was weak tea in her mouth.

Avram spent the day running programs that would sort the material and feed it into terminals where each of them could take responsibility for a relevant piece. That evening was Rosh Hodesh, the first day of the lunar month. Malkah, Yod and Shira were sitting out on the dune in the soft twilight, waiting for the first sliver of new moon to appear out of the bay. Half the town was out tonight, eating picnic suppers, even the little children kept up for once. With the earth badly damaged, the rituals and festivals that marked the natural world had gained renewed importance.

Shira was glad to sit in silence. She had been bombarded all day by memories of Ari. Hearing his voice had jarred it all loose. She kept imagining that he was calling her. His insistent squeaky voice was as real as Malkah's. His voice was driving her crazy, like a bug that had crawled into her ear making a racket only she could hear, right against her brain. Gadi and Nili had climbed the hill, too, and sat just below them; beyond them Sam and Zipporah were picnicking with their married son and his family and their own teenaged daughter. The baby was tossing up sand just the way Ari used to when she took him to the midlevel-tech park and put him in the sandbox. It made a slow relentless pain drip through her.

"Our recent action makes me happy and you unsettled," Malkah observed.

"I keep worrying what we'll find out." She fell silent again facing a lightly serrated sky, rows of fine high clouds straight up, but clear over the sea, where the moon would rise.

From just downhill, they could hear Gadi and Nili talking. He was saying, "But why won't you let me tape you? It doesn't hurt. You have such a gorgeous body."

"Gadi, you have the reality. Why do you need a second opinion from a camera? For me, it's dangerous. I don't want to discuss it. It threatens my safety and the safety of my people."

Yod said softly, "I'd imagine it would be painful to have a record of someone who left you. Humans don't understand what a blessing it is that you can forget. I have perfect recall of every moment of my existence."

"When you get to my age, some of the sting goes out of even the bad memories. You want them all. But the distant ones sometimes shine most vividly." Malkah, too, spoke very softly.

"I gather they've become lovers in the meantime," Shira said. "And before anyone asks me, no, I'm not jealous or upset or anything interesting. Nili was polite enough to ask me first if I'd mind." Ari had curls like Gadi. His hair was the darkest brown hair could be before it was black. Would it darken until it was black like hers? "I hope she can handle him."

"She asked me to describe the heterosexual process to her," Yod said.

"I'd have expected her to ask me." Shira felt slighted. She liked Nili coming to her for advice.

"She felt I'd be objective."

"That must have been a fascinating conversation," Malkah said. "I'd love to have been a fly on that wall."

"A fly?" There was a short pause while Yod accessed the meaning. "To have multiple images?"

"To hear your explanation."

"I fear I was not apt at description, because she kept grimacing and making rude noises. At the end she said she didn't want to experience any act I'd described—but perhaps she changed her mind."

"I felt the same way about sex when I was ten," Shira said. "Maybe Nili is the equivalent of that as far as being a woman goes." She remembered Ari in the tub playing with his penis, calling it a fish in his baby talk, which only she could decipher.

Malkah snorted. "Nili is sufficiently experienced. I doubt she lacked partners at home, and Riva seemed to find her fascinating. She's probably more experienced than you are, if we knew the whole story."

The voices beneath them dropped. Yod leaned forward on his elbow. "Now they're arguing about the Glop."

Shira was about to tell him to stop eavesdropping, when Malkah spoke first. "What do you mean, arguing about it? Whether it exists?"

"Nili wants to go there. She considers such a visit important. Gadi first tried to dissuade her. Now he's insisting that he accompany her."

"Why does she want to go to the Glop?" Shira asked, forgetting her objections to spying. "What does she seek there? Just to see it?"

"I can't say, but Gadi is arguing that she can't possibly go without him. He says they speak a special jargon. That she needs credit there. He has lots of credit, he says, and he's a hero in the Glop. She will never manage there alone. She'll be killed at once. He's trying to frighten her, but she doesn't sound impressed. He's explaining credit and hand prints."

"Damn it, who's being summoned?" The com-con connection embedded in Shira's plug was giving that little vibration. "Only me? Avram's calling."

"All three of us," Yod said. "He wants us back to work."

"So much for Rosh Hodesh," Malkah said glumly. "I was hoping he wouldn't get done tonight. I don't know if I truly want to discover what they have in mind to do to us."

"Then why risk your life finding out?" Yod asked curiously.

"We're always killing ourselves to find out what we would be better off not knowing," Malkah said. "Isn't that the definition of a scientist?"

"Is that a joke?" Yod asked. "How can one prepare intelligently for danger if one does not learn all that one can?"

"It's not serious complaining, Yod. Just what we call kvetching." The turtle who complained too much. That was a story Ari liked to have read to him. "Then Tuck the Turtle said, 'What, it's raining again! It rains every day! I wish it would never rain again.' And it didn't." But there had never been a single moment when she wished not to have Ari.

They strolled along, obeying the summons but not prepared to hurry. It was a pleasant evening inside too. A softball game was occurring on the grassy Commons where Gadi had held his party. Kids were playing puddle-jump, a game with multiple small trampolines.

"Humans not only enjoy arguing sometimes, as Avram and Malkah do, but they sometimes enjoy complaining?"

"You complain too, Yod. You feel sorry for yourself. You tell me and you tell Malkah how hard it is to be a cyborg. You obviously enjoy the attention we pay you then and the consolation we offer."

"I'm picking up bad habits from you. Avram says so every day."

"Does he know we're lovers, Yod?"

"He chooses not to let us know he knows. We should leave it at that."

"Life is much simpler for Gimel." She gave his hand a sharp squeeze and then dropped it as they climbed the steps to the lab. If she got Ari back, what would he think of Yod? Would he back away as the kittens did? Would he think of Yod as a person? As a child, she had considered the house alive. She had made no distinction between the house and Gila, for instance. They were both older women. But the house was hers as Malkah was hers. Would Ari feel that way about Yod?

In the lab, Avram did not greet them but launched into assigning tasks. "Personnel records on station one for Shira. Why did you carry out your own records? Never mind. Just deal with them, and we can delete them."

Shira sat down. "I believe I'm critical somehow to the whole attack."

"Your presence here is pure coincidence," Avram said. "I attempted to have the data sorted by subject. Much of it's useless. However, some of the strategic files seem relevant at first glance. I have divided the material one tenth to station two for Malkah and nine tenths to station three for Yod. I have a headache, and I'm going out for a late supper."

She made good headway with the personnel records. The files were fairly straightforward, as Y-S did not anticipate an employee ever seeing one; moreover, from working with interface, she knew all the Y-S codes and categories, since one of her specialties had been figuring out how to solve personality-machine conflicts as well as problems caused by too much time in the Base and consequent identity loss.

Both Josh and she had been labeled culturally-retentive (J). *Shipman has difficulty assimilating beyond superficial level.* Importance was attached to the name they had given their son. *Hebrew name.* Ari was flagged in her file as a point of interest. *Conceived by subject and husband only. Insisted on full-term delivery. Arc.* That stood for "archaism," the term used in personnel for people who were considered not quite civilized or prepped, not fully up on corporate culture.

Riva's name was flagged. Riva Shipman's files, much longer than those Malkah had accessed in the local security net, were appended. Riva had been a busy woman if she had carried out half the raids they credited her with. She was labeled a dangerous radical. There were various images available as flat pictures or projected holograms of Riva, but none resembled the woman Shira had met. Further, it was clear to Shira by the chronology of comments (all additions to files were time coded) that when she had first been interviewed at Edinburgh, the Y-S rep had been interested in her only because of her own record; but by the time she was hired, Riva's and Malkah's files were appended to hers.

The summary of Malkah's file was even lengthier, including all her honors, full text or précis of every important paper she had delivered or authored, and a list of purported sexual liaisons. It listed seventy, not fifty names. Shira wondered who was right, Malkah or Y-S. Some counselor had written a long analysis of what he described as Shira's overattachment to her grandmother. N.R. That creep who'd addressed himself to her breasts throughout the interview. Then there was a cryptic comment: *Possible complication in transfer: might form renewed attachment.* Transfer where? To Pacifica? Another counselor had written: *Childish emotional dependency on grandmother. Counterweight: overanxious maternal link.*

That Shira had exchanged Rosh Hashanah cards had first been noted as one more sign of her cultural-retentive problems, then the exchanges with Malkah and with Avram had been tagged. The summary of Avram's file was lengthy too. They had been following Avram's career with special interest since before she was born. Every time Avram's file received an addendum, the new information went at once to her boss, Dr. Yatsuko, and to B. Vogt. Barbara Vogt? She had designed the robotics for Pacifica Platform. Every contact between Avram and Shira was noted, annotated. A brief profile of Gadi was appended also. His predilection for spikes, nervebright and adolescent girls was flagged.

Her file was seven times the length of Josh's and she was rated above him in capacity, efficiency, inventiveness, teamwork. Why, then, had she remained below him in rank? Several recommendations for promotion had been refused, marked *Hold, Wait.* After a couple of years at Y-S, she had begun to doubt her own talent. She had decided she was lacking in ambition and drive. Yet her innovations had been quietly picked up and used throughout Y-S without her knowledge, without her receiving any benefits—even psychological. How much it would have meant to her even a year ago to know that she was not stagnant in her work, that her ideas were not universally viewed as second-rate. Her fellow workers picked up their attitudes de haut en bas, and if she was officially unappreciated, they took care not to appreciate her, increasing her isolation.

When she withdrew and stretched, it was after midnight. Gadi had passed by and left them coffee and smoked-telapia sandwiches from the Commons. Malkah had napped for a while on the cot, then risen and returned to her work. Yod was impervious, the only one who scanned in full immersion. Avram had returned at some point and was using a fourth terminal. She ate, tanked up on coffee, washed her face in cold water and went back to work. Clearly they were going to be at this all night.

When Avram had approached her, first rather casually, about coming to work for him, shivers had gone through security. *Transfer to Pacifica? Refused. Encourage connection. Encourage transfer.* What transfer? She rose and paced the lab, stymied. It was three a.m. She was surer than ever that she was somehow central to Y-S's plotting, but felt no closer to figuring out the scheme in which she was an unwilling pawn.

The divorce proceedings had a far more prominent place in her file than they did in Josh's. There the divorce was merely noted early in the process, long before she had sat waiting in the courtroom that dreary January day: *Give sole custody to father. Wait two months. Offer promotion if Rogovin will go to secure base. Pacifica or Antarctica only.*

Yod unplugged and stood. He announced, "Avram, you and I are the real targets of Y-S. They have suspected for some time the nature of your research and that you had experienced a breakthrough. They have made repeated unsuccessful attempts to penetrate Tikva Base, only to discover this year that there is nothing in the Base concerning your private research."

Malkah stretched and yawned. "I've found an effort to place two spies in Tikva, one last December, one two years ago. Neither was accepted. I also found that Zee Levine was subjected to extensive drug therapy and what they used to call in my youth brainwashing. Intense behavior modification."

Shira had just been reading the results of the endless tests and interviews she had undergone during the months between the initial custody decision and Josh's transfer to Pacifica. *Strong familial attachments. Pronounced sense of guilt surrounding son. Can be rehired at any point if offered partial custody.* Why? What game were they playing with her? She had thought all that testing bore on her fitness to be a mother, but that wasn't what they were searching for. *Transfer. Transfer.* To where?

"I see it now! It's all in the personnel records. They did put a spy in place here: me. They forced me out by taking my son away. That was the whole point of giving custody of Ari to Josh and then transferring him. They pushed me until I jumped. They knew I'd remain bound to them through Ari. Essentially they considered they were transferring me here to remain long enough to learn about Avram's research. Then I was to be recalled and emptied of useful information."

"Why the attack on me?" Malkah asked. "Why use Zee in that way?"

"They considered my attachment to you excessive. Maybe they were afraid that if I was forced to choose between you and Ari, I might choose you and not come back on schedule to be picked clean."

"I haven't gone to conferences for years," Avram said in a voice of intense excitement. "I've worked almost alone, and I've published nothing about my own research. They could only get to me by a frontal assault, and if I'm killed or my lab destroyed, my work is lost to them. When I offered you a job, they must have leapt for joy."

"They were already monitoring every communication between us, even studying Rosh Hashanah cards for clues. They had somebody in to translate the Hebrew on the cards to make sure it wasn't a secret message. When I sent you that little interlocking wire puzzle I found, they held it up while their labs went over it for a week."

Avram smiled at the memory. "Nice example of the type. I didn't have that one."

The last time Shira had seen his flat, hundreds of running feet of shelves were occupied with his puzzle and game collection. It was a museum of distraction. When Avram was working through some knotty design, he spent hours playing with his antique games. He loved crude automata, from wind-up toys through early clanking robots with their tinny voices and inability to do more than take halting steps and slam into obstacles.

Y-S had also wasted much analysis on her past and probable future relationship with Gadi. Would it be good or bad for their scheme should he be brought back into the picture? She wondered if Gadi, too, had been caught in their wide barbed net. Had he been entrapped? Had his downfall and exile been engineered? Nothing short of a foray into the Uni-Par Base would prove that bit of paranoia, but it was not important enough to pursue farther.

She felt a pure intense anger, like a violin tremolo almost too high to hear. She was a tool they had tried to break. They had surrounded her with their plotting and their structures, but what had happened had been entirely unexpected to them and to her. They had underestimated Malkah, ignored Riva, and Yod had not figured except as the passive quarry. Yod was at once the aim of their plotting and their most important opponent. He was their unknown enemy. He was the great glitch.

Since the four knew what pattern they were seeking, it was easier to work on the files. Malkah asked finally, long before they had slogged through the remaining infoglut, "Now that we know what they want, what do we want? How do we get it?"

"What do we want?" Avram repeated. "We want to remain ourselves. We want our independence. Our freedom."

"I want my son back," Shira said. "Until I have him, I'm vulnerable, and you should all know that." She felt a sense of shame, that she had been a tool of Y-S—yet so far she had denied them any use of her.

"I, too, want my great-grandson," Malkah said. "I want him here with me."

"I want to end the threat to this town. I want to be free then, free to live as I want and choose," Yod said, standing rigidly.

Avram snorted. "That's romantic nonsense. I created you to accomplish a task, so how can you be quote free unquote to live? And the pursuit of your son, while urgent to you, Shira, is not what this task force is about. I was not asking for an outpouring of unbridled ego from each of you."

"It's all related." Shira said vehemently. "My son is a hostage. They've used him, and they'll use him again."

"Yod may be an artificially constructed person," Malkah said, "but he possesses his own motivations, his own goals. He's not a cleaning robot, who works because you turn him on."

"I didn't create him to pursue his own ends."

"No doubt you felt that way about Gadi also," Shira said bitterly.

"Although humans have needs I'll never experience, such as sleep, in living with humans I have evolved certain needs similar to yours," Yod said in prim defiance.

"You'll simply have to devolve these needs," Avram said with mock patience. "You were manufactured for a purpose still unfulfilled."

"And when it is fulfilled?"

"When is the purpose of a bridge or a building fulfilled?"

Yod said, still standing at attention, "You should have stayed with Gimel, Father. He's a true golem. He has a soul of clay and never asks awkward questions. He never challenges you. He obeys thoughtlessly and perfectly."

Malkah stepped between them. "The two of you must cease bickering. Avram, you'll have to offer Yod his freedom at some point. He deserves it."

"We are none of us likely to survive to confront our just deserts unless we start planning intelligently in the face of the Y-S threat," Avram said.

"If you permit me to go after Shira's child for her and for Malkah, I won't trouble you about my status for at least a year," Yod offered.

"Are you bargaining with me? I can dismantle you. And where did this notion of going after Shira's son come from? I wouldn't consider it."

"Do you want to dismantle me?" Yod gave a bleak smile. "Your other choice, of course, is to sell me to a multi."

"And give up our only hope of security?"

"What you created to improve security seems to have attracted more danger," Yod said quietly.

"We're quarreling because we're all exhausted," Malkah said, "that is, those of us who get tired. It's four-fifteen. Let us leave Yod to finish extracting the last tidbits and go to bed. I'm seeing double, and I'm no longer thinking with any clarity—and I daresay the same goes for you, Avram."

Avram sat down heavily in his desk chair. In fact his face was gray with exhaustion. "All right. We'll meet at noon back here."

WHEN THEY REASSEMBLED at noon, Nili and Gadi were waiting for them in the anteroom. Nili began at once to Avram: "I'm on my way to the Glop for a couple of days. . . ." She followed them into the lab.

Yod, seated at a terminal, turned to greet them. "I have located two more attempts to place spies here. One was Aviva Emet. She defected quietly to Tikva and simply ignored Y-S after the first two months in place here. I believe that's why she was assassinated."

"Aviva . . ." Malkah said. "Of course she defected. She kept telling me how happy she was here, how at home she felt, how cared for."

"What is it, Nili?" Avram swung on his heel. "Gadi, what do you want? We're busy."

Nili grimaced. "I'm trying to tell all of you that I'm intending to go at once to the Glop. . . ."

"Why?" Malkah said. "It's dangerous there, especially if you don't know the jargon and the ways."

"I'm as dangerous as anybody I'm likely to meet. Gadi's going with me, but, Avram, you must get security to release him."

Gadi beamed at them. "I do know my way around the Glop. Nili needs a semi-native guide."

"You confuse images of the Glop produced by your fantasy machine with the reality the vast majority of people live in," Avram said. "What is the point of this trip? Curiosity? A prurient interest in hardship?"

Nili was barely restraining herself from pacing, coiled tight. "Riva considered it essential I make contact with resistance forces there. She gave me some names and directions."

"What sort of forces? The Glop is chaos," Malkah said.

"Riva said not. She said sectors have managed to organize secretly in spite of drugs and the mandated ignorance. She did a lot of business in the Glop, buying and selling information. She said these groups have penetrated the multis." Nili spoke quickly, in a hurry. "But I need a floater to travel there, and I have no credit under my false name. My true name doesn't exist."

"That's where I come in," Gadi said. "If you ask, dear Father, the local security will permit me to violate my exile without undue fuss. I have the credit, and I know my way around. I promise as solemnly as you like to be back in four days."

"If you want to go, go," Avram said through gritted teeth. "But you're responsible for the safety of our guest. Can you comprehend what it means to be responsible for anyone?"

"Avi, I'm accustomed to being responsible for people whose hide is insured for millions and whose every sensation is experienced by billions of eager fans. I have fans all over the Glop. I'm welcome there, a hero."

"What is it you seek?" Yod asked Nili.

"Riva was pirating information for groups there. She believed in them enough to risk her life, the same way she believed in us—my people. I must judge for myself who and what these groups are. That's part of my mission."

"This could conceivably be useful to us also," Yod said with his characteristic simple gravity. "We perhaps have common enemies. Shouldn't I accompany you?" He walked toward Nili. As he passed Shira, he threw her a private glance.

She understood at once. He meant to accompany Nili and Gadi and then continue on to liberate Ari. But Ari would never go with him, could not understand who or what Yod was. She must go too. "I agree. If there are counterforces to Y-S in the Glop, we must know about it. We have to make contact and see if we have goals in common. This may be what we need to fight Y-S."

Malkah nodded. "Riva spoke about the people she knew there. They all started as gangs: the Lava Rats, the Lords of Chaos, the Blood Angels. We could use allies. Speak to security at once, Avram, and so will I. But you're Gadi's father, you're responsible for him, so you have to ask."

"This is fantasy," Avram said. "We have no allies. The Glop is a mess. The people there can't save themselves."

"How do we know?" Yod asked in his quiet reasonable voice. "Surely we should confirm or deny on evidence and not conjecture these statements of Riva's. She's dead, and we can't ask her for confirmation. We must find out on our own. It shouldn't take long to assess the potential of these people as possible allies and to determine whether they do have independent sources of information we might find useful."

"While Nili is making the contacts for her own purposes, we can check them out for ours," Shira said. "I'm willing to try. We have the opportunity with Nili that may never come again. We don't know them and they don't know us, and it will stay that way forever unless we seize this chance."

"Come, Avram." Malkah stood. "This may be a valuable opening for us. Now that we know why we're a target, we can better seek for allies. We must go and see the head of security at once."

thirty-three

VOICES AND VISIONS AT DAWN

I am in my state of desperate sleeplessness. Success is achieved these nights if I manage to render myself unconscious for two hours with the help of relaxation techniques, cat therapy, white noise, hypnotic tapes, those sleep needles inserted in a vein—the full panoply of mid-twenty-first-century inducers. I worry about Shira and you in the Glop, and yes, about Nili too. I find her oddly attractive. She is arrogant in refreshing ways, so convinced that if anyone can do anything physical, so can she. I never had that kind of confidence—few women of my generation did, unless they were professional athletes. Even then, they assumed that the best man could always beat the best woman, whether at running or swimming. Nili has none of those hesitations. She thinks Gadi is cute but basically not much use.

I mourn my lost daughter. I have lived for the last two decades with the knowledge that she might die in Africa or Europa and I would hear about it only by accident or by some clandestine messenger months later. We are all constantly in danger; still I cannot relinquish mourning. You don't know what I mean, Yod, because you have not yet lost anyone dear to you. You have the capacity to survive who knows how many human lifetimes; thus you may well come to know mourning intimately.

Today I visited her grave. It was overcast, and I went out without a sec skin, in order to feel the rain on my skin, on my face. At my age I can take a few chances. I wanted to stand under the rain again as I put down a bunch of chrysanthemums, bronze and golden, the flower of warriors, on her grave. I don't know where Shira is, and today I said kaddish: in which we pray for the dead without ever mentioning death. We pray for life.

Gale-force winds, small-craft warnings tonight. Over the Net, news of a seaweed harvesting ship gone down. I can hear the surf slamming on the artificial rocks of drowned buildings and walls. I remember rain in Prague, in the spring and the fall almost daily rain; rain tapping the red-tiled roof of the bedroom where I lay with Meier, whose eyes were the darkest brown short of black, whose hair was black and tightly curled as fleece, whose body was slender as a boy's still at thirty-seven, which seemed to me then middle age. His apartment was in Kostechna Street, near a school where we could hear the children at recess, or church bells at night as we made love, feverishly, for the nights were pale with our desire and always too short. I ran from class to him and off to meetings, crisscrossing what had been the old ghetto before it was torn down, past the Altneushul, past Maisl's family synagogue, past the artificial hills of the cemetery. Love played me like a flute. Sleep seemed an unnecessary vice. I slept as little as you and Joseph, my dear.

JOSEPH INTERCEPTS two men sneaking into the ghetto carrying the stiff pale body of a young boy, perhaps seven, who looks as if he might have been run over by a cart. His chest is crushed, but time is running out for a corpse to be planted that can then be discovered and blamed on the Jews. Blood for the matzoh, the poppycock tale for which people die every spring. As the dead boy lies crumpled on the pavement, dropped like a calf's carcass, Joseph fights the men. This time he does not kill them but binds them unconscious in a rope with the dead boy and carries them to the gentile magistrates.

He encounters two wandering drunks, a pimp beating a prostitute, and one unconscious man on the street who has apparently been robbed: dealing with them makes up his night's work. At dawn, as Joseph is returning to the rabbi's narrow house in the courtyard, he meets Chava, coming along the street with her birthing bag.

"Why didn't you send for me to escort you?"

"Joseph, haven't you enough to worry about right now? I had the father to take me there, and now it's morning and the scavengers of the night go back into their holes to sleep." She sighs, shoving a lock that has escaped back under her wig. "Tell me why two thirds of all babies are born at night?"

"Are they? Birth is mysterious and violent."

"It's my business. This was a hard one. I thought I was going to lose her. The baby came fast enough, which is usually good, but she bled and bled. I had to use all of my herbs to stop the hemorrhaging. I tried dragonwort and loosestrife, and still the blood came. Then woundwort. I was getting frantic. Finally shepherd's-purse worked. Our red blood runs much thinner than your dark blood, my friend."

Joseph feels a deep embarrassment, a sort of nakedness before her. "I heal quickly," he mumbles.

"My friend, we both know you are not born of woman. Birth is mysterious to you because you have never undergone it. You were made, not born."

"What are you saying to me?" He experiences himself as slow, dim-witted beside her. Did she worm the secret from her father?

"I know the texts, Joseph. Don't fear my tongue. I have said nothing to Father or Grandfather, and I won't. I've spoken to no one."

"Except me. But I'm no one, you think."

She rests her hand on his arm. "You know I don't think that, so don't fuss with me. Let us just talk friend to friend. We are all in danger here. I'm a little light-headed from lack of sleep." She lets his arm take some of her weight as they walk.

Everyone is sleeping in the house of Rabbi Loew. In the kitchen, Chava builds a fire under the kettle always kept there. Out of the cupboard she takes matzoh and salt fish. "I'm hungry. Maybe some broth." She puts herbs and a bit of jerky, cuts some carrots and onions, into a small pot she hangs on a hook over the fire. She dips water from the big kettle into the small. "I'm so tired, I almost started to look for the kasha or the gruel—me forgetting it's Pesach week. Are you hungry too?"

Joseph nods. "But as you know, I can eat a brick and get nourishment."

"Then you'd make an ideal husband for a poor woman." Chava smiles.

He draws a low stool up to the fire and extends his hands to warm them. "Who is your new suitor? I saw him coming and going all week."

"Isaac Horowitz. Yes, he's decided I should marry him. Me, I have a different opinion."

"Who is he?" Joseph feels the cold weight of fear all through him.

Chava perches on a bench, yawning. "He's a great scholar and a brilliant thinker. We have two of his books upstairs."

"Then you will marry him." Joseph tries to sound resigned.

"Why, Joseph? I am a pretty good scholar myself. I was married, you know that. I bore the Bachrach family a son. I have put in my time as a wife."

"You didn't like marriage?"

Chava sighs, staring into the fire. Then she shakes her head. "To you I say this and sometimes to another woman. I say it to my mother. I say it to my bubeh, Perl. But I never say it to a man. They get upset."

"And I am not a man."

"No, Joseph, and that's part of why I like you. You're strange too. So am I. I can read and write, not just one language but seven languages, Joseph. Are there twenty women in all of Europe with whom I could converse about the matters that interest me? I like midwifery. I like to try my hand now and then at cooking and making nice. But my real life is going back and forth between women's business of birthing and what men have made their business, the life of the mind, my studies."

"Then you'll marry Isaac Horowitz. To him you can talk about what matters to you."

"If I can play on a spinet, should I marry somebody else who plays spinet? Besides, I tell you truthfully, Joseph, nobody but us being up in the house: a man may want to marry you because you're a brilliant scholar, but what he wants is a wife. So it was with Samuel Bachrach."

"Did you love this Samuel?"

"I did, oh, how I did, Joseph!" Chava shakes her head. Her hands rise slowly as if of their own volition, cross each to the other shoulder, till she is clutching herself. "With passion. I thought it a miracle. To be loved by such a man, a man with whom I could share my feelings, my body, my intellect. But I was no different from other women. They see how it is with women and men, but they think, For us it will be different."

"Did this Samuel love you?"

"Very much. We had a good marriage, as good as my parents', as Judah and Perl's. But we had a short time. Four years, three months and eleven days. That was my married life." A deep sigh shakes her, and she looks as if she may weep. She scrubs at her nose with her fist and draws rapid breaths.

The hands of Joseph clench and unclench. He wants to comfort but does not know how. What he touches usually breaks.

"For those four years, my life was what will we eat, is his shirt clean, feelings of the bed, pregnancy, then my son, Aaron, colic, dirt, feeding, seeing him grow and unfold. The flesh closed over me, and I drowned."

"I don't understand." Joseph feels as if he is stretching far, far up to something beyond his grasp. It hurts to stretch, but it will hurt more to fail to comprehend her, when she is talking intimately to him. "You say you are glad to be free, and yet you look as if you may burst into tears."

"When Samuel died, I was stricken with grief. I tore my hair and wailed. I felt alone, wrenched open. But, Joseph, I tell you truthfully, when the grief subsided a little, I began to remember who I had been, before I had loved, before I was a wife and mother. My old dreams came back."

"I don't sleep, I don't dream."

"Not night dreams, Joseph. The dreams that drive us. What we most want." She leans toward the fire. Her wig is pushed back on her hair, and the flames make the locks of brown hair that slip out lighter, as if the edges were bleached. "Dreams are the fire in us."

"I don't have those dreams either. I wish I could want something. Sometimes I almost can."

"The Bachrachs would have kept me in Worms. They expected me to live out my life with them. They're a huge and warm family. I did something other women will never understand, so I seldom tell anyone I had a son. I let the Bachrach clan keep Aaron, as they wanted, and I journeyed here to my grandfather to act as his secretary."

"Why, Chava?"

She adjusts the little pot so that it will cook more slowly, moving it to a hook not directly over the fire. Then she breaks off another piece of matzoh, chews and swallows before answering. "I knew my father had outgrown being the Maharal's assistant. His own matters absorb all his energy. He continued out of respect. I thought this was a good way to apprentice myself to a great scholar and a great thinker, to come back to life intellectually. And so it has been."

"But how is it better? First you worked for your husband. Now you work for your grandfather. He controls all our fates."

"No, Joseph, no! Can he halt the violence gathering against us? I prefer being an intellectual servant to being a physical servant. I get more out of it. There is no son. I am the son. I am taken care of. I go into the kitchen only when I choose. I'm spoiled here, and I appreciate that, because I know exactly how much work it takes to make things go in a house."

"Dreams . . . I have none, Chava. Give me one."

"I will. My dream is to go finally to Eretz Israel, to make my aliyah. It is my dream to travel there."

"A long, long journey. I have seen David Gans's room, with all the maps. The world is enormous, and Eretz Israel is far. You must cross

Christian lands and Muslim lands, land and sea. I hear the men praying for it always. At the end of both Seders, we all said, 'In Jerusalem next year.' But even the Maharal has never gone."

"But I'll go. I want to talk to the scholars in Safed who work so excitingly with the kabbalah. Luria has ideas about the Shekinah that make my mind dance. I want to pray in Jerusalem. I want to walk where Abraham and Sarah walked. . . . You want a dream? Come with me. Travel with me to our land."

Joseph leaps off his stool. He seizes her hands and then lets them go for fear he might injure her. "I will go with you! Yes. That will be my dream too."

"It even makes sense, Joseph. You would be a perfect traveling companion for me. No woman could ask for gentler company, and no woman could ask for better protection than you offer. And you'd be far away from here."

"Do you think the Maharal will let me go?"

"I don't think he'll let either of us go. But, Joseph, he's very old. My duty is to prepare his books for the press. I'm young still, and you are too. It is sad to say this, but we will outlive him."

Joseph seats himself on the stool again. "Unless you marry Isaac Horowitz or somebody."

"Joseph, my grandfather gives me room and time for my papers, my books. I support myself with midwifery. Between my breasts I carry a knife in a little sheath for protection. If I'm set on by a group of men, as I was the night you saved me, then I can be raped and killed, but so can every other woman. Marriage doesn't make that less so." The water in the kettle is boiling hard. Chava picks up her midwife's bag, motioning to Joseph.

Joseph hauls the kettle of boiling water to the bench for her. There she washes out her tools and her cloths. A thick unpleasant smell of blood clings to everything. In cooler water she washes her face, her arms, her hair.

Joseph peers into the bag in curiosity. "What's this?"

"An amulet. Leave it be, Joseph."

"An amulet?" He shakes his head in disbelief. "And you a scholar! I've heard the Maharal fifty times decrying the use of magic amulets and stones to protect children and houses and travelers and horses."

"Now, are you going to stand there, Joseph, and tell me you don't believe in magic?" She flings back her head and laughs.

Joseph sits, confused. "Do you believe in amulets, then? Do you believe if you call on the right angel and use the forty-second hidden name of the holy one that you will be able to save a woman's life?"

"I think that people believe amulets help, and therefore amulets help. A woman clutches a birthing stone, and yes, it's just a field stone worn smooth with a hole in the middle, but hundreds of other women have clutched it, and most of them survived and bore healthy children, so why shouldn't she have something to hold too? It has a power, Joseph. When I reach in the dark into my birthing bag, I can always feel it. My hand closes on it." She finishes her cleansing, and he empties the water in the yard for her, refills the kettle at the pump in the street and puts it back on the fire.

But he does not sit again on his low stool. Instead he kneels in front of her where she sits gazing into the fire. Her hair hangs loose and wet on her shoulders, like willow leaves, he thinks, although she tries to keep it decently covered with the towel as her wig dries. Fire glints off her dark eyes. "Chava, if I were a man and I could marry you, I would never ask you to be my wife but my teacher. I would cherish you for your company." He takes her hands in his own very carefully, lightly. Hers are warm and still damp.

Gently she withdraws her hands from his clutch. "Joseph, I don't want to marry anyone—not even an angel or a golem. Be my friend. I will be a true friend to you."

The house is beginning to stir. Outside in the street, the first cart clatters by. The odor of soup fills the kitchen. "I will be your friend. I would die for you, if I can die. It is said a thing of clay cannot love, but I know that I love you."

"Love is many things, Joseph. You can travel farther than Eretz Israel and still know only a little of love." She smiles into his eyes, and he knows she is not offended or laughing at him, but tender. She is his friend. "Now the day begins when we find out whether we live or whether our blood runs again on the stones of the street."

Joseph stands. "While we wait, I have a weapon I want to make for myself—something I saw. But I need a good stout piece of wood."

"You know that any scrap of wood in the ghetto, somebody burns to keep warm. Why not look by the river?"

"Tell the Maharal I'll be back soon." He looks forward to reporting, for this night he did not kill but only bound. The Maharal will be pleased with him. Judah's look will not be heavy and fierce with judgment.

thirty-four

ONE LAZARUS, TWO LAZARUS

Shira was astonished to discover that in tandem with Yod and Nili, she could actually enjoy Gadi's company. Oh, he might throw her a significant lingering glance from time to time, allude to some memory they shared, mutter some comment to her, but basically his attention was caught, impaled on Nili's impersonal curiosity, her capacity to be with him and against him at once, the glint of her judgment. He did not seem so much infatuated as mesmerized.

The world interested Nili more than Gadi did; he was not accustomed to that order of business. It kept him edgy, trying constantly to prove he was fascinating, knowledgeable. Nili viewed them all as along on suffer-ance, unconvinced that they wouldn't get in her way on this venture into the Glop. They were piggybacking on the instructions Riva had given only to Nili about how to make contact with the alleged rebel organization.

To Shira's surprise, Nili, who carried almost no clothing, had a standard black cover-up. Shira had borrowed Malkah's for Yod. Gadi had his own. The cover-ups went over everything, including the backpacks they were all wearing. The hunched-back look of cover-up over pack was common enough in the Glop. They moved in a band, keeping an eye out for trouble.

Yod and Nili were particularly tense. The Glop was new to them; neither had ever been in a place as crowded, as fetid with human smells and the overwhelming stench of pollution and decay. Yod offered ongoing analyses of the toxic properties of the air—they wore filter masks, of course—until Gadi requested that he stop.

In parts of the Glop, domes had been constructed. In other parts, the outdoors was unprotected, and people tried to stay inside, while the lively street life simmered underground. Here, where the old dome was in place although filthy, giving the streets an air of perpetual half-twilight, they walked what had been a wide avenue, back when there were cars. A strip was kept open in the middle for fast tanks and motocabs, but the walkways on either side ran between rows of tents and stalls hung with bright rags and banners, signs that glittered and beckoned, the smell of cooking sausage, probably dog. Here people did not wear masks, so they lowered theirs. The rule in the Glop was never hesitate and never stand out.

"Allo, Duke, you want nice fresh molly? Ten-year-olds, younger."

"Rod, the latest earbos." Earrings that played music. "Tomas Raffia's last stim."

"Damn," Gadi said. "They pirate them before they're out. I worked on that, and I haven't even seen the final cut."

"Raw stickers, splatters. Slab your noids. Keep safe."

"Pings and pongs and every joy and toy. Want to go up, go down, want to feel the fires of desire, want to burn like a nova—come on, Duke, I bet you're the nervebright type."

"Off it forever." Gadi walked faster.

"Come on, amie, you want it. You want it bad. You can feel it giving you that rush like nothing else can."

The first time the band passed a gang beating a man to death, Gadi and Shira could scarcely restrain Nili and Yod from interfering. "Look," Gadi said. "This is Ram Blaster turf. If you stop a group of them, you have to fight the whole gang. For all you know, they're administering justice. As they explained to me once, they believe in justice being fun. Unless you're prepared to take over this sector and run it, stay out of the way."

"How do we travel?" Nili asked. They had released the float car at the edge of the Glop. First they had traveled through the tunnels of the old subway warren; now they used the surface.

"Depends on where we're going, Tigress. What have you in mind?"

Nili recited to him the coordinates she had been given. They all squatted in the shade of a building while Gadi and Nili managed to translate the grid reading into a sector they could head for.

In the cracked mud by the building—it looked as if it had been a public building, perhaps a department store, but now it was housing where hundreds squatted—Shira noticed two small desiccated bodies, that of an animal, perhaps a cat, and that of a child. The bodies had been well chewed by local scavengers. There they had died huddled together, and dogs or rats had eaten them. Two little lives, accounted no price. Right across from them, a woman dressed in an unusual red cover-up was diagnosing illness by reading electrical impulses and a drop of blood. In the next stall, a short figure was selling stolen and expired medicines—patches, pills, elixirs, implants. Obviously the two were working in tandem. Nobody read by the woman failed to stop to buy something from the short dealer in pharmaceuticals. A troupe of fire dancers was setting up at the end of the block, blowing a horn Gadi remarked was based on the sound of twentieth-century fire engines.

The committee had reached agreement, and they stood to leave, but they had loitered too long. From the building a phalanx of gang members marched, wearing the Ram Blasters' brass-and-red body armor and carrying an assortment of knives, clubs, guns, laser rifles; one girl dragged a cannon that shot trash, broken cement. The people bargaining in the street scattered.

"I told you we should keep moving," Gadi said. "Now let me see if I can negotiate passage."

"Never mind. Put these in." Nili handed out cold little blue jellies. "Put them in your ears, now!" She touched something on her wrist, and nothing at all happened that Shira, still pondering the strange sensation of the cold wet jellies boring into her eardrums, could feel. What she saw was simply that the Ram Blasters all became very tired and lay down. The warriors dressed in the brass-and-red body armor fell asleep sprawling on the cracked mud with its patches of remaining asphalt and its clumps of sumac. But the girl pulling the cannon did not fall down. She looked around, puzzled, then dropped to aim the cannon at them. Yod was on her in five great bounds. He picked her up, gave her a gentle toss on the pile of bodies. Then he smashed the barrel of the cannon.

Nili was motioning wildly for them to follow her, mimicking removing the jellies. Shira obeyed. Her ears still stung as if with great cold. They trotted together out of the square, just as people ran from the building to help the Ram Blasters, and others ran equally fast to rob them. "What happened to them?" Behind the would-be rescuers and the would-be thieves were fighting hand to hand.

"Sonic stun," Nili said. "More powerful than the one your house uses. They'll be on their feet in ten minutes, so let's move it. I repeat, how do we get where we're going?"

"We flag down a cab. Until we see one, we just keep heading south and west," Gadi answered.

Public transportation in the Glop had long ago disintegrated. Below the cities were long tunnels, but people lived in the ones that hadn't flooded when the ocean rose. The way you traveled, except for the few rich enough to have their own fast tanks, was by bargaining with cabs to take you inside their sector. To cross between sectors, you had to change cabs. Unless there was an agreement between neighboring gangs, cabs couldn't cross a sector barrier.

Most were small tracked vehicles that could move quickly over the uneven terrain that had once been streets, and that was the sort Gadi flagged down, painted with the brass-and-red colors of the Ram Blasters. Gadi carried out the negotiations in Glop patois, language rich and gamy with constantly changing slang.

Gadi waved his palm. "I got a raw betty—I wouldn't jack you."

"Lots of done betties around this days. You a grud?"

"In stimmies, but loose now. Still, I can cover it easy."

"Who all's going? They your meat?" The driver nodded at the others, hovering on the edge of the opaque conversation.

"Just my dokes. Four of us. Cuanto?"

Once they got in and were crouching in the belly facing each other, Yod played his recording of the exchange, requesting Gadi to define all the strange vocabulary and teach them the language.

Betty—credit card or chit
Rod—man
Nook—woman
Splatter—weapon, gun, laser
Sticker—any form of knife or razor
Ping—up drug
Pong—down drug
Bat—attractive partner of either sex
Molly—boy or man willing to be fucked by other men
Cheese—any young human sold or rented for sexual use
Duke—a man or woman with money or credit
Meat—a woman available for sexual use, usually but not necessarily for money
Hook—where you live or squat
Grab—(noun) any job, any way of making a living
Slab—(noun) a corpse; (verb) to kill
Stuff—sexual intercourse
Barb—sexual intercourse
Rock—sexual intercourse or music

Jack—sexual intercourse
Duffel—one's usual sexual partner
Amie (pronounced to rhyme with Sammy)—friend, partner, comrade
Doke—friend, member of the same gang
Pop—someone superior to you in the gang (used for either sex)
Niño—someone below you in the gang (used for either sex)
Noids—the enemy, other gangs
Grud—*(singular or plural)* people who have sold themselves to multis
Cooker—a place where any drug is manufactured
Wire—a person equipped to interface directly with machine memory
Raw—very good, desirable
Done—bad, undesirable, unattractive
Roach—*(verb)* to steal, to pirate, to hijack
Nut—loot, something desirable to attain, riches, money

"What's the use of trying to empty my mind of vocabulary?" Gadi demanded finally. "You may know the definitions, but you can't sing the song."

"At least we can understand your conversations," Yod said pleasantly.

"You don't trust me!" Gadi rolled his eyes high into his head.

"Why not say we're all more comfortable when we know what's happening to us," Shira said. "This place is scary enough."

"I have seen more people today than in all my previous life," Nili said, watching through the slits in the armor.

"This is only a little piece of the Glop," Shira said. "It stretches fourteen hundred kilometers to the south and two hundred to the west. It's hot enough here, but down at the southern end, it's tropical. They grow grapefruit and oranges near what was Atlanta."

"I cannot begin to imagine that many humans."

"Less than there were, don't forget. Before the kisrami plague of '22, the population was twice what it is now," Shira said. She did not look out the slits. She was too afraid of being shot in the eye with a dart or hit with some chemical spray.

"Actually the kisrami virus was only responsible for 8,472,338 deaths in what was then still the United States," Yod said gently. "The Great Famine of '31 was responsible directly or indirectly for twice that many deaths, and the so-called parrot plagues that occurred in the third year of the famine had a far more lethal effect. The lowering of the birth rate through pesticides, toxic waste accumulations and radiation stockpiled in the groundwater and the food chain also bears on the population drop."

There was a long silence after Yod's lecture. No one could think of anything to say. They lurched along. Occasionally some kid threw a rock at the cab or shot a firestick at it—a little toy rocket that exploded. The Glop was full of kids missing fingers or hands or other body parts from the damned things. Y-S manufactured them, but they were forbidden in the enclave—and in Tikva too. Most of the gangs sold what they called a license to Y-S for their barrio, meaning that they got a fee. It was the same with the stimmie broadcasts, which theoretically could be blocked— if any gang was stupid enough to deny them to their people. Still, Uni-Par paid every gang a fee. The multis liked stable gang leadership in the Glop. It was good for business.

The cab screeched to a halt. "Border crossing," the driver called. "Noid land. All you rods out. Okay, Duke. Here's the rough."

Gadi paid. When the driver looked at his screen—Gadi placed his palm on the dial and the machine recognized him after accessing the Net—he swore. "Stuff me like a cheese if I ever guessed. This is one big cooler. Nobody's going to believe me back at my hook. Wait a minute, I want a holo with you. Strip your cover-up a minute. Come on, Gadi."

The driver pulled a cheap little holo camera from a dashboard compartment and handed it to Yod. "Hey, Rodney, do us. Make it raw."

Yod examined the camera briefly, raised it and took a holo of Gadi, who had obediently removed his cover-up and stood all in silver beside the driver, who wore under his own cover-up a winking eye-dazzling djellaba of Ram Blaster colors. The driver mugged for the camera, dancing around Gadi. Then they both put on their cover-ups, the driver jolted off in his fast tank, and they all filed through the checkpoint into Coyote barrio.

There were several small motocabs waiting at the checkpoint, but only one vehicle big enough to hold all of them, another fast tank. Gadi negotiated with the new driver to take them to the coordinates Nili had been given. They ground off in the can, with the familiar jolting and jouncing.

Gadi called attention to his usefulness. "None of you can even begin to talk to these people. You'd be lost without me. Besides, I'm a hero here."

"If they understood, they'd kill you," Nili said. "Your multi sells them sensation in place of knowledge—somebody else's sensations. An animal can learn from sensations, at least what to go for and what to avoid, but only if they're authentic. You replace real knowledge with false sensory data."

"What has life got to offer them? If they go for stimmies and even if they get into spikes, it's escape. If you had to live here, what would you want but escape? I help make hard lives bearable."

They passed a street carnival: more fire dancers; performing horses and dogs and a mangy tiger; a belly dancer; a couple of cheap virons, one of dinosaurs and jungles, one of the old wild West, sputtering gunfire and whooping Indians; a strong smell of barbecued something and burnt caramel.

They were turning through a maze of narrow streets, past a row of shops that repaired and cannibalized all kinds of machines, from floaters and fast-tanks to stimmie players and laser splatters. Then, with a great shuddering thump, the fast tank came to an abrupt and violent halt, tossing them against the metal walls. Yod reacted instantaneously, throwing his arms around Shira to keep her from injury. Nili was probably protected by the light body armor she was wearing. Gadi was the worst shaken and bruised. Yod knelt to peer through the slats. "We are caught in a metal net. Aluminum alloy."

"We've arrived," Nili said with satisfaction, helping Gadi up. "Riva warned me. These people use many low-tech devices that are quite effective in ordinary defense. She thought I would find them interesting to study."

Shira wondered again at how casually Nili could mention Riva. She herself tried not to speak of her. She had not assimilated either the facts of her mother's life or the fact of her death. Shira felt as if she had taken a spiny ball into her body which remained in her tissues, giving an occasional sharp twinge.

"Okay, niños, out!" Someone was banging on the metal of the cab.

"Hey, pop," the driver said. He had climbed out. The net was cranked off, since the cab was surrounded by armed warriors dressed in black. "Don't beat on my track. Let the gruds pay me, and I'll zip."

Gadi again paid, and the cab shot off. Nili came forward and flung back the head of her cover-up. "I've come a long way to see Lazarus. The one you know as the gray pirate sent me. There are no trees in hell."

"Not a bad-looking nook. Think I'll barb you first. Take off that sack, and let me see if I should bother. . . ." The warrior had pulled a knife and moved forward, starting to slit the cover-up.

Nili swung the loose garment out over him. As the cover-up settled, she kicked his knife from his hand and then threw him. "You and five others. I came in good faith. I want to see Lazarus, and I think he wants to see me."

Yod moved up to stand at her shoulder. "We'll fight you if we have to, but we didn't come to fight."

One of the women warriors had communicated their arrival, for another phalanx of warriors marched out. "Lazarus says bring them in."

They were paraded into a large storefront that Shira imagined from the moldering decor had once been a restaurant. In the multi enclaves, restaurants still existed, but during the Great Famine, when the breadbaskets of the Great Plains and the Steppes had dried up and blown away, when temperate-zone regions that had grown grains became too arid to grow much but grass, when a hefty percentage of the rice-growing regions of Asia had been drowned by rising waters, restaurants disappeared from the Glop. They were replaced over time by vat-food dispensaries and food stalls that sold unregulated food at restaurant prices, all buying protection from the local gang.

On the crumbling stucco, happy peasants frolicked among giant representations of bunches of grapes. Someone had added some large spiders and pythons. Many of the grapes had faces. Some of the original tables remained, with an assortment of chairs, crates and stools. Along the old marble-top bar, some teenagers practiced how to break and reassemble and clean laser rifles, how to load energy packs into them. On a trestle table, a crew seemed to be studying the manufacture of bombs. At a collection of the old wooden tables, a teacher worked with a mixed-age group on reading skills. On the far wall, a row of children sat plugged into computers under a new mural depicting Shango wielding the weapons of the lightning and standing astride the Glop on the shoulders of a small black man, rendered realistically. Most of the people were black- or brown-skinned, but almost every combination was represented: red hair, brown eyes and black skin; light skin, black hair, blue eyes; and other permutations. Most people in the Glop were of mixed race nowadays. Nili was noticing everything, as Shira was, and smiled broadly. Only Nili's expressions could be seen, as the rest of them were still wearing their cover-ups. Shira was in no hurry to remove her own. It gave her a false feeling of security to have her body covered. She stayed close to Yod.

"You are armed," a woman well over six feet tall and muscled like a bodybuilder said to Nili. "We don't permit that." She spoke formally, slowly and clearly, as if in a foreign language.

"We're only stopping here. We need our arms to survive, and you haven't been exactly friendly to us," Nili said, standing poised as if for battle.

"You'll disarm, or we'll kill you now." The woman blew on a whistle from around her neck, like a school coach. Everyone in the room dropped flat or crawled under tables. The warriors formed a square around the newcomers, laser rifles targeting each of them.

"I have my finger on the trigger of a sonic weapon. We'd be dead, but so would all of you. I have it set on kill," Nili said. "I could have used it already, before your soldiers got into position, if we were enemies."

"I am expendable," the woman said. "You would not survive."

"I have the capacity to cause an explosion that would remove most of this facility," Yod said gently. "I have no desire to die, and I wish to protect my friends, but if I see no alternative—"

"It's raw, Leesha. Everybody up." The man was small and dark, dressed in black without insignia, none of the mock epaulets or metallic sashes or gaudy designs of the other gangs. He was the man in the mural. "Take off your cover-ups and let us see you so we can match descriptions."

They obeyed, watching him carefully.

"It's them, Lazarus. I told you." A woman's voice. Riva's voice, but it couldn't be.

"I thought you might be here. Were you waiting for me?" Nili said, apparently without surprise. She strode forward to embrace the woman who came through the door.

"I never wait for anybody," Riva said, "You know that. Welcome to the fortress of my amie Lazarus."

"But you died! I saw you die," Shira cried out. Yod was staring at the woman with a frown.

Riva dressed all in black here. She looked like an ordinary forty-five- or fifty-year-old woman, not the old woman she had appeared to be in Tikva. She also looked fifty pounds lighter. Here she walked with a bit of a swagger but kept two paces behind Lazarus and to his left. "Oh, it takes more than a few noids to slab me. I'm still with the living."

"It is the woman we knew as Riva, your mother," Yod said.

"How could you make us think you died? We buried you. I said kaddish for you every day!"

"Now you can stop. Besides, it's a nice prayer. Come on, Shira, you hardly know me. I surely didn't make a great hole in your life with my passing. I'm more nuisance alive."

"Does Malkah know?"

"No. You can tell her when you go back. But be sure no one else finds out. Be sure you're secure."

"That was unfair!"

Lazarus stepped between them. "Nooks, savage each other later. We have business to conduct. Who's the leader? You the pop?" He looked at Yod.

"I am," Nili said calmly. None of them contradicted her.

The woman who had greeted them said suddenly, "Hey, aren't you Gadi? For real? Killer raw!"

The kids came crowding around, out of control. "Rod, you know Mala Tuni herself? Do you know her?"

"You're an unruly bunch. You come in here, threaten my warriors, and now all the niños are crazy." Lazarus shook his head, motioning to the woman and an armed man. "You're trouble, and if I didn't have the rawest op of this popanook here, the gray pirate, I'd slab you all. Now we zip upstairs to my hook, and then we parley. Who are you, who am I, the whole hopper. Move!"

Obediently they followed him through a food factory and upstairs, Riva coming behind them with the tall woman, Leesha. Shira walked close to Yod, still frightened and very confused, glad to hold his arm tight in her hand.

thirty-five

LIVING WITH THE UNDEAD

Guilt shivered through Shira for her anger with her mother, but she felt emotionally abused. She could hardly complain to Riva about her being alive, for if she herself were a warmer, more caring daughter, she would be overjoyed at her mother's reappearance. Instead she felt muddled. She felt like shrieking and banging her fists on the wall. It had been difficult to adjust to the sudden presence of a mother she had never really known and about whom all her previous ideas turned out to be fabrications. It had been hard to accept the death of a woman who felt artificially rather than naturally important to her, an imposed intimacy without content, given suddenly and as suddenly snatched away. It was nearly impossible to accept Riva's resurrection in altered physical form.

"Well, Shira, we decided it was a good time to kill me off officially."

"But the Y-S troops all died. You forget, there was no one to report your death."

"Didn't you ever look up? They had one of their spy-eyes overhead to record what happened. That is, what was visible. The wrap was opaque to it."

"That's why we didn't take it out," Nili said. She was sprawled against the wall, cleaning a laser pistol. They had been fed and were now in storage, waiting for Lazarus to reappear.

Yod closed his eyes for a moment, presumably replaying the scene. Then his eyes flicked open. "I should have recognized the spy-eye. Its significance did not register on my consciousness. A lapse."

"So who died?" Shira asked. She wished she could sound more gracious.

"We brought a body with us. We asked for a body of a woman around fifty who had died of anything that wouldn't register at the cellular level. We knew the body would be cooked. We prepared beforehand." Riva sounded as if she were describing preparations for a dinner party. "I was there long enough to register. We had blasted out a small underground chamber, shielded and safe for up to thirty-six hours. In fact I crawled out right after sundown. When the fighting heated up, I slipped in and Nili flung the body into the line of fire. I had to pry them off my case. I need more maneuvering room than they were giving me."

"And Malkah doesn't know?"

"I thought you'd have a more convincing funeral that way."

Shira found it intolerable that Malkah should be grieving at this moment. She longed to get out of this hideous place and rush back home to give Malkah the news that would lift the weight of mourning from her. But sensibly, she knew she could not return. They must conclude their business here, and then she had Yod's promise that they would attempt to find and somehow carry off Ari, no matter what the danger to either of them.

Riva was never going to understand how disturbing her little drama of death had been. She was glad to see them, presumably especially glad to see Nili. Yet Shira felt as if there were more emotional communication going on between Yod and herself than between Nili and Riva. The tall dark woman Leesha was sitting against the far wall, her eyes never leaving Riva's face. She looked at Riva as if Riva were the most beautiful and desirable creature in the world. Her eyes shone, her lips curled into a silly small smile, an inadvertent smirk of pleasure while she tried to look tough and mean.

Gadi was nervous. Of all of them, he had been most at ease, until the moment Riva had revealed herself. He was not his usual insouciant glittering self, asking with glee and persistence the questions that would most embarrass. He was watching. He stayed close to Nili. Not only did he fear the bond between Nili and Riva; Riva did not fit into his diagram of the social universe.

In his world, only poor women looked like Riva, and there were few enough of those. Cleaning robots did what such women would once have done for him and his colleagues. Old ladies still fitted costumes, carried out the delicate work done by hand—beading, embroidery—women who lived in the local equivalents of the Glop: the barrios, the slums, the Deek, for decayed quarter, the Casbah, Le Vieux Quartier. Here was somebody who looked as if she should sew fish skin into sheaths for Mala Tuni, at just enough an hour to keep her in vat food and a hook the size of a narrow bed and folding table. But Riva walked in like a general reviewing his best razors. She swaggered, she looked every man and woman straight on in the eyes. Here Gadi and the others were on sufferance. Riva was the reason they had not been killed. She was their passport into the stronghold of Lazarus. Riva enjoyed some kind of local celebrity, of the sort Gadi was accustomed to wherever he went.

Gadi's discomfiture soothed Shira a little. She stayed close to Yod on the floor, feeling his presence, silent, alert and always, always aware of her and for her. She slid her hand toward him. After an instant his hand covered hers lightly, its dry warmth radiating into her. Her hand was cold with nervousness and fatigue. She was swept by a wish to be alone with him. It was a desire not for sex, except for the comfort and the warmth of the embrace, but for their own intimacy. Of late, she had grown used to real conversation. After she had left college and the friendship of her roommates and colleagues, she had not lived a life examined with accomplices.

Since coming home, she had grown used to chewing over the details of actions and reactions, first with Malkah and lately also with Yod. He was fascinated by human interactions. Much he did not understand, but he brought his full intelligence to bear on the problem of comprehending motive and feeling. The result made for an interesting companion. One who was not judgmental. Who took her as the measure of a woman and of all good things.

"Notice that they eat vat food here," Riva said meaningfully.

"Everybody in the Glop eats sludge. What's to notice?" Gadi smiled winningly at Riva.

"Other gang headquarters serve real food. It's one of their perks. Lazarus eats what everybody eats. That's what's to notice." Riva did not bother smiling back. "And they don't buy it from a multi."

Leesha took them on a tour and with pride pointed out the chambers where the algae were grown and the factory where it was processed into soup, imitation chops and burgers, sweets. "So we can never be starved into submission," Leesha explained.

Shira only nibbled on supper. Y-S was not into algae farming, so she knew little of the process by which two multis fed much of the world— poorly, carelessly, but at least with stuff that kept people alive and nourished. After the Famine, that seemed a great accomplishment. Starvation had killed so many in the decade of her birth that she had grown up into a world in which nobody, not even the multis, could take food for granted. So-called real food, food actually grown in soil or from the bodies of live animals, was precious and rare, a luxury like gold and cashmere and paintings, just for the upper echelons. Vat food grown in vast algae factories was what most people lived on. It came with many labels and in a variety of colors and flavorings, but it all had a similar texture in the mouth. Shira always imagined she could taste the seaweed under the chemicals that gave it the name strawberry or chicken or refried beans. But food had ceased to be a private matter before she had been born. She had read about people who were passionate about their choice of one cuisine or type of nutrition over another. Now people ate what was available in their enclave or their barrio or their town. When it was real, you appreciated it; when it was vat grown, you shoveled it in. "It's touching," Gadi said, "how proud they are of such miserable things. Those little cubicles for families they showed us."

"Those little rooms are heated and safe," Riva said. "The children go to school here. The Coyotes are what we call a New Gang. They're an autonomous political development just beginning to make connections."

Lazarus came briskly in, followed by five lieutenants of varying colors and sizes, all taller than he was. "What do you make of me?" he asked Yod.

"In what sense?" Yod responded politely, rising.

"What am I?"

"Your guards are enhanced in various ways. You are not."

"Just flesh," Lazarus said bluntly, assuming a commanding position in dead center of the room. "Now, the redheaded popanook is enhanced more than any of my warriors. And you're so enhanced you bum out my instruments. Gadi is only fancied up—no use to all that cutting and pasting. And that bat there"—he led with his chin toward Shira—"is like me, pretty much the way her mama made her. So we got two civvies and two warriors here, how I see it."

"We come on a mission from our free town, Tikva, to see if we have goals in common and if we can work together, exchange information, anything that can help you and us to survive," Shira said.

"I come from . . . farther away." Nili rose gracefully to face Lazarus. "I can offer you nothing yet except my interest. If you're attacked while I'm here, I'll fight for you."

"My old amie here, she say you come from the Black Zone."

That was one of the common names for the interdicted zone, because on contemporary maps it was a uniform black, with no features shown at all.

"Maybe," Nili said. She was not relaxed but poised on the tips of her toes, as if she considered attack possible at any moment.

"I guess if that's your hook, you got to be raw armored inside and out."

Nili grinned at him. "But I come with good will and a keen curiosity about what you're doing around here."

"Surviving, just surviving. And looking to survive some more tomorrow."

"More than that was going on downstairs," Shira said.

"Surviving can be a tough business in the Glop. You wires in the towns, you got it easy. You're mollies for the multis. So are we. All just movable slabs to them. But we do all the dirty grabs, while you do the clean ones."

"We've lost seven people this year to direct attacks on our Base," Shira said. "We had a firefight with Y-S outside the Cybernaut enclave."

"We had a buzz of that. Rumor always stretches what it tells of. Says you slabbed nine of them, including four apes, two assassins and two high dukes."

Gadi spoke up. "Pretty good eyes you got. You're not leaning on rumor for that level of info."

"We see everything their spy-eyes see. Film got to be processed. It's automated, but always some rod got to touch it. Some lowlife rod tubed in and tubed out, not good enough to live in the enclave. Who comes home to the Glop."

"We're building our own net," Riva said calmly. "Outside theirs, alongside theirs."

"But the Net is public," Shira said.

"So is ours," Lazarus said. "Different publics."

"What do you want?" Nili asked. "What are you trying to do?"

"Get some power into the Glop. Make my people less helpless. Give us the strength to take back a piece of the pie." Lazarus took a step closer to Nili. "What are *you* looking for?"

"We, too, want to survive, under far more extreme conditions than you have here. We want to know if we can find allies. We have developed different technologies, and we're interested in trades—people to people. Information. This alternate net sounds useful."

"You two. Your town sent you. Why?"

"Because of our little war with Y-S, we're looking for allies. We didn't know about you until Nili told us. We volunteered to come."

"And silver man, what do you want?"

"I'm along for the ride. The Glop is who my virons are made for. My grab is Uni-Par, but I also work for you. And besides . . ." Gadi gave Lazarus a sly grin. "Warrior woman is my duffel of the mo. I watch my jack."

Shira glanced at Riva, who was presumably finding this out. How would she react? She did not appear to be listening. She was deep in a silent conversation with Leesha and a male warrior, communicating in a sign language. A language of the deaf or some variation?

"That's one tall bat. She's yours, you must be more rod than you look, duke." Lazarus knocked his fist against Gadi's upper arm.

Nili seemed to have no reaction at all. She was not looking at Gadi or at Riva but kept her gaze fixed on Lazarus. However, every time a warrior moved, she observed, sharply. She never relaxed vigilance. Lazarus, too, noticed this. He seemed to approve.

"I have this idea by 'n' by, but I got to line up the other noid papas all in a row, or it won't work. I got the idea that instead of a little payoff from the multis for our workers, we offer them as a block. What one's paid, the other gets the same nut. All or none."

"You're talking about a union," Shira said.

"A what?" Lazarus looked at her blankly.

"It's history. You're talking about what was called a labor union."

"Did they work?"

"For about a century. When the multis moved the jobs out of the country, they were easy to break. The top got fat. They didn't like to organize in places like the Glop. But for a long time they did work. I can send you lots of information on them." She wondered if Lazarus could read. Most kids in the Glop went to work at ten, never having learned to read or write. The only history they knew was picked up from the stimmies, so Robin Hood, Zowie the Flying Dog and Napoleon were equally historical and all simultaneous.

"Raw," Lazarus said, looking her in the eyes with a sweet warm smile. The man had charisma. He could charm. "We'll set up channels." He nodded at Gadi. "Duke, tell the niños here about the time Uni-Par tried to jack prices on the Bloodsuckers."

Gadi paused a moment, then said simply, "The Bloodsuckers sent their own assassins in and took out three of the top administrators."

"See, we're all as good at that game as the multis. We got assassins badder, faster and just as maxed. We got troops, we got assassins, but we hungry for the techie lore. We can maybe trade."

When Lazarus left them, it was close to midnight, and everybody except Yod was exhausted. Riva left with Lazarus and his warriors as if she were part of his party; since they had arrived, she had not behaved as if she were with Shira or Nili. Riva was about her own business. She did not seem to mind their presence nor judge it particularly important to her. Shira felt she would never understand the woman who had given birth to her.

A boy carried in a pile of futons and sheets. They had sleeping bags in their packs, even Yod, who had objected but was overruled. He had to pretend to need sleep when they were under observation. Shira drew Nili aside. "Riva hardly spoke to you. Is she angry with you because you're with Gadi?"

Nili's brows rose in surprise, her lips parted slightly. "Was she angry? I didn't think so."

"I don't understand how it is between you two."

"It isn't a romantic relationship, Shira. We're on the same side. We trust each other."

"Obviously she trusts you more than she trusts her own mother or me."

"She felt you had to think she was dead to behave convincingly. You want her to be jealous of Gadi?" Nili smiled, shaking her head. She put her hand on Shira's shoulder. "What nonsense! If she wanted me to go along with her now, I'd send him home and go."

"Just like that? So you don't care about him?"

"I care about all of us. But Riva is a prophet, a mountain, a hawk—and Gadi is a little warbler. Understand, I'm here for my people."

"Then why not go with Riva anyhow?"

"She has her own business to attend to. In three months I go home with her or without her. She'll come to our rendezvous then or she won't. But whenever Riva comes, I drop everything and listen. Right now she wants nothing from us."

"I'll never understand her."

The hand on her shoulder gave a firm squeeze and then rose. "Don't give up, Shira. In time you will."

Nili was assuming that Shira wanted to understand that strange spiky woman. "I'm shutting off the lights," Shira announced. "Okay?" She crossed through the stuffy darkness to Yod and undressed.

"We can join the bags together. They're the same kind. If you like." He spoke in that controlled soft voice that would not carry.

She brought her mouth to his ear. "There's no privacy. But we can talk. . . ."

Both sleeping bags were the town's standard issue. They made them into one double bag and lay down on it together. It was far too warm to sleep inside. Shira pulled a sheet over them. It was dark but for the line of light around the door, the harsh cheap pinkish lighting of the Glop. "You're disturbed about your mother," Yod said softly.

She explained as best she could, aware that perhaps Yod was the only person with whom she could be completely honest about her petulance.

"Such relationships are foreign to me. But if Riva were not your mother, what would you think of her?"

"I suppose I'd admire her, but I wouldn't much like her personally."

"That seems to cover your feelings nicely. That she gave birth to you has little relevance in the present."

"But I'm flesh of her flesh. How can my own mother be so alien?"

"How can you have a machine as a lover? How can your best friend be your grandmother? How can it be that we must steal your son, that your little son is a pawn in a vast corporate game to gain possession of me? How can an ill-assorted collection of misfits do battle with Y-S?"

"How can I not adore you when you're so smart?" She hugged him against her. They fitted together perfectly. All the awkwardness was gone.

"How can I be smart about living? My experience is severely limited."

"But you extrapolate well." She laid her cheek against his. It was fortunate they had not bothered to give him a beard. That touch of realism had slipped both their minds, Malkah's and Avram's. Or perhaps it had been one more improvement of Malkah's. She must get her hands on Malkah's log. Her grandmother kept putting her off. When she got back, she would insist.

Little wet sounds were reaching them from the darkness. Gadi and Nili were making love. Shira felt like calling out in the dark to Gadi, Hey, she'd leave you in a minute if Riva wanted her to come along. It felt disrespectful that they were making love in front of her and Yod. She was sure that Gadi enjoyed having her as audience. She could not bring herself to return the favor. It felt gross. "Yod, don't watch. What shall we do about Ari?"

"When will we finish here?"

"Some more negotiations, and then it's up to the Town Council to figure out how to use the link we create."

"While you sleep tonight, I will think tactically about our problem. By morning, I should have enumerated our options, evaluated them and come up with a plan of action. First you must describe as exactly as possible the Y-S enclave in Nebraska."

"I will. But are we being too reckless? They want you, and we're about to deliver you to them."

"I will destroy myself before permitting that. Now describe the enclave in detail. Start with all possible approaches and entrances."

thirty-six

THE MAHARAL EMBATTLED

In the classic golem tales of my childhood, a pogrom rips at the ghetto. Actually Rabbi Loew managed to stave off disaster his entire life. If you consult your memory banks for the period, you will discover no pogroms. After Judah came the Thirty Years' War, in which those peasants and townspeople not hacked or burned or bludgeoned or raped to death got the opportunity to starve. Before him there had been a massacre every generation. Therefore that there had been a golden age of peace for the embattled Jews of Prague, when only the ordinary pricks and prods of anti-Semitism exposed them to injury, seemed to require a supernatural agency. Pogroms were a part of the basic fabric of diaspora experience; our own vulnerability drives me to tell you this tale of a battle when your predecessor rose to defend.

A people in trouble are perceived as a troublesome people. The word that comes that morning to the Maharal in the ghetto is that the emperor is doing what he can; that he hopes to weaken the blow; but that he cannot stop Father Thaddeus from leading a procession today, Good Friday, to the gates of the ghetto. The emperor will send soldiers to discourage the mob if they begin to storm the gates, but he cannot ask them to fire on a religious procession, even if it gets out of hand. The soldiers will remove some number of the less respectable and rowdier, if they can do so without risking a violent response from the mob. The emperor waffles.

This is how the friendly rulers usually act when faced with a threat to Jews. They regret, they temporize, they mitigate, and then they stand aside. So it was the century before. So it will be a century later.

What do you do when you are a peaceable people, vastly outnumbered and living as islands in the sea of people far more numerous, more aggressive and better armed? What can you do but pray a lot? Joseph goes with a party of men to survey the walls and the gates, the strengths, the weaknesses. They will carry stones and lumber and bolts of iron to the boundaries of the ghetto. Joseph calls for whoever has any sort of weapons to form an impromptu militia. He expects the attack to come through the main gates of the ghetto. That had been the idea discussed in the tavern up near the castle. The planners anticipate no serious resistance. The gates are an obvious target, for it would be easy to assemble a mob outside and charge them.

He calls for whoever will help. "It is I, Joseph the Shamash, who patrols the streets of the ghetto every night for the Maharal. I call on you to stand and protect your families. Fight for your lives and the lives of your mothers, your fathers, your children, your wives, your friends. Come and fight with me, Joseph the Shamash, for the evil are coming to kill us today."

Joseph bellows in the streets. He calls the wares of his defense as if he were selling apples from the country or a load of firewood. His voice echoes off the grimy stones, the rough logs and the pastel stucco. Some shut their windows. Some creep into bed and pretend they hear nothing. Some curse him as the bearer of bad news. Some begin to daven and pray. But many men and not a few women and children come out to the streets, bringing an ax or a hoe or a club or nothing at all but their fists.

The Maharal stands in the street, his beard stirring in the crisp wind that whips this morning even through the twisted narrow alleys of the ghetto. "They will attack through the main gates. Thaddeus will rely on oratory to stir the crowd. He will harangue them by the river. We must guard the other gates, but only with a few people to keep watch."

Most of the women who have volunteered the Maharal sends up to the roofs overlooking the main gates. They are to arm themselves with rocks, boiling water, cutlery, old furniture, anything they can throw down. By his authority as the spiritual and temporal leader of the ghetto, he commandeers every roof that is useful, regardless of whose house it belongs to, mercantile splendor or rooming house of narrow slots shared with nine others on pallets.

The young, the old, the middle-aged, he divides into two parties. One group he sends rummaging through the ghetto for anything that can be used as a weapon or as part of the barricade that the remaining volunteers are building. Many who will not fight are willing to work on the barricades.

Itzak, Chava's father, will not fight. A substantial portion of the population does not believe in violence. The liturgy constantly praises those who work for and those who seek after peace. "Look at us, Joseph, a little remnant, a sliver of a people floating on a sea of the others. Since as a small minority we could never win a war, the less our harsh neighbors love peace, the more must we clasp it." Still, building a barricade to prevent violence is acceptable even to those who will not touch a weapon. Itzak puffs and shuffles along under the weight of paving stones. Chava's most recent suitor, the scholar Horowitz, bends his skinny frame under a load and works on the barricade. He, too, declines to take up weapons.

"If we become as violent as they are, we are no longer the people of the book and the people of the name," he says, staggering along almost blue in the face with effort.

But Chava's other suitor, Yakov, is eager to fight. He has produced an old sword from the secondhand store and is sharpening it, flourishing it in the air in a manner that looks more dangerous to himself than any enemy. It turns out that Bad Yefes the Gambler knows how to use a sword. He gives a fast class for the few who have found some manner of long knife or sword, including the butcher and his assistant. In the street between the barricade and the houses, the pudgy butcher and his knock-kneed assistant parry each other's blows with sharpened sticks, lest they kill each other in practice. Bad Yefes the Gambler shouts encouragement and pointers. Yakov practices with Samuel the old-clothes man, who has produced a hidden army sword brought to him in a bundle of dead man's clothes.

Chava has volunteered herself as a messenger to run to the different parts of the line, to carry news and instructions. "I always won footraces when I was a girl," she boasts. "I know every part of the ghetto. I know almost as many people as my grandfather."

Joseph is fascinated by the Maharal. As busy as Joseph is, piling up paving stones as a barricade, giving brief instruction in the use of the club, waving his own spiked homemade mace, he cannot help staring at Rabbi Loew, commanding like a general. The old man has never fought in his life, never been in an army, never watched a battle, let alone taken part in one. Neither has Joseph. Where did the Maharal find the fighter in Joseph? Out of what was Joseph shaped, if not out of the Maharal? Like father, like son, he thinks ironically, aware of how angry his saying that would make Judah.

The Maharal abhors violence. Joseph has heard his despisal of war, for he says no nation has a right to dominate or rule another. Each people has their own road, their own destiny to fulfill. The world is imperfect and requires repair so long as any people is under the rule of any other. The Maharal bases these ideas on the kabbalah, Joseph knows, although the Golem's Hebrew is barely adequate to the prayer book, the siddur.

Judah's is one of the first voices to argue for self-determination as an important principle among nations, this lean spiky old man commanding the street with a wave of his long arm. Yet Joseph can see that Judah has the makings of a fine general, for he possesses the instinctive power to command, the ability to inspire people to follow and obey gladly, the rhetoric to rouse others to effort, and a clear original mind with which to confront the situation, brainstorm strategy, work out a choice of tactics.

The Maharal has made a decision to collect all those who cannot or will not fight into the synagogues, where they can be more easily defended than if they are scattered in every cubbyhole in every warren of the ghetto. Chava is sent with her mother, Vogele, and her father, Itzak, to spread the word, and as they go they commission others as messengers. The people will be collected. If they are to be massacred, then they will die together, as before. It is understood that if they are not burned to death, if the mob does not set the synagogues on fire, the women will kill themselves when the doors fall. It is standard operating procedure, a kind of death every Jewish woman has heard about in stories since childhood. Chava thinks briefly of her son, Aaron, who is with her husband's family. She is glad he is safe, but frequently she misses him. Giving him over to them was the price of her escape.

She wants to go to Eretz Israel more than anything in the world. It is a passion. Women never make this aliyah, but she will, she will, she swears it to herself every Shabbat. If she dies today in a quick pool of blood on the beautiful old floor of the Altneushul, she will never see Israel. She decides she will stay with the fighters. She would rather die here than with the weeping women, the screaming or silent children, the davening old men.

Someone has already taken the ax from the shed in the cemetery, but in the kitchen of her grandfather's house there is a sharpened spit. She pauses to sharpen it more, puts in her belt the best carving knife, and returns to the spot where Bad Yefes the Gambler is teaching swordsmanship. She does not expect him to teach her. It would be improper for him to teach a woman. But she can watch and learn and practice. She believes in choosing her death, if given the opportunity. Perhaps, Chava thinks, I am not brave but a bigger coward than the other women. I fear death by fire more than death by steel. The idea of burning alive makes her shudder;

Judah himself has had nightmares since he heard of the auto-da-fé of Bruno. She clutches her sharpened spit tightly and practices parries and attacks.

Joseph keeps an eye on her. He cannot decide if he wishes she would go back and hide with the other women or if he prefers to have her nearby, where he can kill anybody who goes within ten feet of her. He must protect Chava, and he must protect the Maharal. He must save the community. These are his commandments. Today he fulfills his deepest duty, that for which he was created from clay and breathed into life.

Yakov brandishes his old sword a little less awkwardly. He is learning. "Why don't they come? It's agonizing to wait."

Joseph is puzzled. Why hope for what will kill and maim? He has been created for this battle, yet he would not mind if it never came, and he is in no hurry—not to fight, not to die. The wan April sunlight breaks watery through scudding clouds. When the sun disentangles, it is warm on his face. Then the clouds wrap it around again, and the wind glides damp from the river. He realizes he has no idea if he can die. He can be injured, yes, he has been in enough fights and sustained enough cuts and blows. But he heals quickly. Can he die? He is the only combatant today who has such a doubt. He would like to ask the Maharal, but Joseph suspects that Judah would not care for his asking such a question. In any event, Chava and the Maharal are quite mortal, and so is everybody else whom it is his duty to protect—with his life? With whatever he has been given—if not life, then energy, breath, strength; it does not matter finally. What he has he will spend today.

In spite of the fear that leaks like a smell from them all, when the bells toll noon and they break bread together on the barricade they have thrown up, they share a common spirit. They are cracking jokes; here and there someone is singing. This is one day when everyone in the ghetto says *we* and means it, when they are truly a people together. All the petty rivalries and old feuds are swept away; Samuel the tailor shares his wine with his rival Wolf Karpeles the peddler, to whom he has not spoken all year. People smile at each other, they smile at Joseph. It is only a moment's pleasure, because soon the sound of the procession drifts toward them. The women on the roofs cry out, for they can see over the ghetto wall.

"They are coming with crosses and torches. Hundreds of them," Chava's mother, Vogele, calls down. Itzak is in the Altneushul, but Vogele has taken to the rooftop. "They have pikes and swords and clubs."

A younger woman shouts, "They're carrying an enormous cross. They're singing hymns. I see musketeers too!"

They can hear that for themselves now, loud ragged singing in Latin. Joseph has no idea what they sing, but it sounds both sad and menacing.

"The emperor has stationed a few soldiers outside the gate," Vogele calls. "Perhaps fifty in a row."

Through a crack in the gates, still chained together, Joseph peers out. So much for our begging help of our dear father the emperor, the revered protector and constant milker of my people. Fifty soldiers to contain a mob of five hundred. Thanks a lot. Joseph exchanges looks with Chava, who shrugs. I might as well have kept the emerald and given it to her. What would she want with it? Nothing, to be truthful. She is a woman who sets store by jewels of the mind, not trinkets. I hope that the prince is murdered for that jewel by some even more mercenary relative. I hope that green stones grow in his bladder and his hard heart. May he piss emeralds the size of hens' eggs and die.

"Jews of Prague," the Maharal cries as he tries to clamber up a barricade. Joseph lifts him easily and holds him up to speak. His voice is clear and penetrating as always, no longer as strong as once it must have been, but a voice that commands attention even against chanting and the shouts of an angry worked-up mob. "Today we must defend our gates. Today we must stand as a shield, the Magen David, between our people and certain death. They don't expect us to fight. If we stand firm, we can discourage those who don't like killing Jews enough to die for the pleasure. Let us put ourselves in the hands of the living ha-Shem and fight like holy men and demons."

"Now take my grandfather to the Altneushul to safety," Chava says to Joseph, who is still holding the Maharal. "Take him now."

Joseph lifts the Maharal high in the air and bears him through the streets. "Put me down, thing!" Judah mutters, unwilling to shout in front of everyone. "Davar," he curses, which means both word and thing.

"If I have to look out for you, I cannot fight well," Joseph says. "The people in the Altneushul need you more than the fighters. You shouldn't be in the presence of death, and you must pray for us. Your prayers are strong as my fists."

"Prayer doesn't work that way," the Maharal says quietly and sadly. "It makes the heart and mind strong in belief, but it doesn't keep one leaf from falling from the tree. Still, I will pray."

thirty-seven

DESERT APPLES

Shira had enough credit by now so that she and Yod could have gone west by zip, but she preferred mass transportation that left no trace. They decided to ride the tube all the way to a terminal relatively close to the Y-S enclave where Ari had recently been staying. Shira did not dare take the tube to the station at the Nebraska enclave, for fear she would be recognized by a grud, guard or monitor. Furthermore, the enclave entrance required a palm print.

The tubes crossed the continent in about twelve hours, minus stops. An hour tube ride was a standard commute for day laborers, who did not live in the corporate enclaves. Thus the enclaves could be several hundred kilometers outside the Glop or similar areas—El Barrio in the Southwest, the Jungle on the Gulf Coast—and still draw on cheap labor pools. They were heading for Omaha, off the direct transcontinental route. They changed in what was still called Chicago, although it stretched from Green Bay to halfway up the far side of Lake Michigan. Residential use of much of what had been Michigan and Wisconsin was restricted, since these northern lands still got rain. The soil was not as thin as farther north. Agricultural land was strictly regulated. They weren't going to get any more of it, and much had been damaged, paved over, eroded or poisoned before the protections had been established.

The Rural Zones were areas that the multis did not own or control. Agribusiness was blamed for the Great Famine. Now all soil farming was based on organic practices and biological controls. The pesticide residues still found in every living being contributed to the mass sterility that plagued Shira's generation. Using poisons or allowing them in contact with the soil or the water table was an offense punishable by death, enforced by the eco-police of the Norika Sector government. Shira wondered what life was like for the small holders of the Rural Zones, but tourism was not encouraged there.

In Chicago they left the tube and locked themselves into a rented cubicle in the underground warren of the station. With Yod, she felt safe in the six-by-eight room with its bunks and minimal toilet facilities. They were close enough to Lake Michigan for the shower to function, tepidly and sporadically.

It was like trying to sleep in the works of an old and noisy machine, an antique with gears and levers clanking. The coming and going of the tubes shuddered through the walls. Above, behind and from all sides came the mutter and shriek of voices. Footsteps ran. Bodies landed hard. A stink of rotting matter and unwashed flesh in dirty clothes thickened the air, along with cooking smoke and something acrid and chemical. She monitored the air. The oxygen was close to minimal, but what could she do about it? She had to take off the filter for a while. "Yod, didn't I see you massage Malkah's shoulders when we were working all night in the lab?"

"I'm programmed to give a mean massage, Malkah says."

She smiled. Her face felt as if it were flaking off. "I don't think I've smiled since we left home."

"Is that conversational, or do you wish to know? I can replay."

"I just mean that I've been very tense. This is the first time we've been alone. It isn't that I feel safe here—only an idiot would feel safe in the middle of the Chicago Glop in a tube station cube." She undressed and lay on the cot, on which she had already spread her bag so that she would not touch the mattress.

Yod knelt over her. His hands began working the pain and stiffness from her muscles. She groaned. "Am I hurting you? Should I use less pressure?"

"It's not a bad pain. Do it the way you were."

"Isn't all pain bad?"

"You feel pain, don't you?"

"Not as you do. It's mental. It's more of a warning signal coming on and demanding I notice it. It's disagreeable, but I can turn it down."

"I could have used that ability in childbirth. I could use it every day." She drifted into pleasant surrender to the shaping, releasing hands. She must have fallen asleep, because she woke with the room almost dark—as dark as it got. A spattering of shots outside. She saw no reason to investigate. Loud voices gave way to footsteps running. Shots, more distant. Then a single whining moment of laser fire. The monotonous ka-blam ka-blam of canned drumming vibrated the floor.

Since she did not see him, she called his name. She was immediately frightened, even though she was certain he was just above her, in the top bunk. He answered at once.

"How long did I sleep?"

"Nine hours, twelve minutes."

"I never sleep more than seven hours, never!"

"Never does not apply any longer." He jumped down neatly, turning at once toward her.

"Since Ari was born, I've never slept a night through."

"You fell asleep at twenty twenty-eight local time, and now it is five-forty. Are you hungry?"

"We have rations in the green pack. First we need to disinfect and filter some water." She took her second tepid shower while the water for reconstituting their food trickled through a unit the size and shape of a big carrot. Diseases hit the Glop, ebola one year, a new killer flu the next. Viruses previously confined to the tropics now flashed through the cities with the speed and deadliness of a fire storm.

"Shira . . . If I were human, I'd know if the fact that you haven't dressed again means that you wish to have sex. Or is it warm for you in here?"

"It's warm, yes. I hadn't actually thought about sex, but the water isn't through yet." Outside, loud voices argued about payment. In here, dense sticky air, but a feeling of momentary nest, ease, safety. "Do you want to?"

"Of course."

She watched him undress, swiftly, piling his few clothes in a stack on the upper bunk. She asked, "Why of course? You might not be in the mood. Why should I assume you're willing?"

"But I don't have moods."

"But you don't always want to have sex."

"With you? Why not? Hypothetically I might consider it inadvisable if we were in a dangerous situation. I doubt you'd propose it then."

"You mean you're always ready?" She laughed, half in embarrassment. "Does this apply to everybody? Could you do it with anyone at any time?"

He put his hand on her bare shoulder. "Shira, I grasp the pragmatic basis of modern monogamy: if I don't do it with anybody else, you won't. That's agreeable to me if it is to you."

They lay down on the narrow lower bunk. She traced his sleek back with her palms. Next door, something heavy fell. Through the ceiling came a sound as if someone were swinging a pickax on the floor. "Emotions, but no moods?"

"My emotions are reactive, mostly. But they grow stronger with use."

"Is that good?"

"I don't think it was intended, but yes. Life is less boring. I have something to care about now besides following instructions. I have a friend, I have a lover. Soon we'll have a child to care for, and then I'll understand the mystery of human childhood."

"Don't! The odds on getting Ari back are lopsided against us. Don't say that, ever—don't speak as if it were done when I can't endure the thought that we may fail."

"My speaking one way or the other has no effect." He ended the conversation by beginning to kiss her.

Sometimes Yod's behavior was what she thought of as feminine; sometimes it seemed neutral, mechanical, purely logical; sometimes he did things that struck her as indistinguishable from how every other male she had been with would have acted. His cloture of the discussion of Ari by kissing her was one of those times. She was not annoyed, because she preferred confining conversations about Ari to logistics, tactics. She did not like to talk about success or failure; it made her superstitious. She preferred to proceed with her gaze averted slightly to the side of her target.

"Because you're programmed to please, do you ever feel used when we have sex?" she asked him, remembering sex by rote with Josh.

"Aren't you programmed too? Isn't that what socializing a child is? I enjoy, Shira, never doubt that. If I've been programmed to find your pleasure important and fulfilling, don't women try to reprogram their men that way?"

Making love with Yod made her feel strong. Afterward, as they mixed the filtered water with their dried rations into a gruel, which they heated over a unit the size of a matchbox and then quickly ate, she wondered why. As they took the Omaha tube, strapped in side by side, with the sickening crush of acceleration flattening her into her dirty seat, she wondered further. He pleased her. She no longer ever doubted he would. She seemed to please him. He was not changeable. He would not tomorrow decide she was not good enough or that he wanted someone else instead. He had the reliability of a well-designed machine that, as long as it worked, would do what it was supposed to. But that was unfair, because he was far more sensitive to her desires and responses than any man she had been with, and most unmechanical in his lovemaking. She had never spoken of love with him. It seemed inappropriate. Yet she felt him to be loyal to her as no one except Malkah ever had been. His mind might be working out fourth-level equations while they were in bed, for all she knew, but he was not fantasizing about another woman. Although his strength was exponentially greater than hers, she could never imagine him hurting her. Neither intentionally nor unintentionally. He did not have a temper, and he moved with the grace of perfect function.

Whenever she let herself slide into thinking of him as simply a machine, she would become aware he was actively pursuing an agenda of his own. Although his jealousy of Gadi had greatly diminished, nonetheless, if she were Gadi, she would not be careless in turning his back to Yod. She thought Yod often wished Gadi out of their lives, and she wondered if Yod was not capable of a violent resolution to a scenario in which he felt Gadi threatened his relationship with her—unless Yod's fear of Avram restrained him.

Yet being with Yod was not as exotic as she would have expected, for she had constantly suspected that first Gadi and then Josh were put together mentally as well as physically on some completely different principle than herself. She would be sitting with Josh in the living room. He would want a cup of coffee, a glass of wine or cold water, a dish of ice cream. Normally he would inform her, as if she were more capable of going out to the kitchen than he was. If she was completely occupied and he acknowledged that, he would get himself ice cream, but never would he think to ask her if she wanted some also. She could not imagine eating or drinking anything in front of him without asking him if he wanted some. It was a small thing, but it always reminded her of how differently they had been socialized—programmed—to exist with others. It was that way with everything from birthday gifts to ideas about food, mealtimes and care of clothing.

But how could she take seriously a relationship with someone who belonged to somebody else? Not in the sense of being married, but in the sense of being the property of Avram. This is my boyfriend, the machine, the slave. When they returned, the issue must be confronted. She would line up her support: Malkah and, oddly enough, Gadi, because he viewed Yod as a pseudo son who put up with the same hard perfectionist overseeing he had endured.

Beside her Yod sat motionless, still as the chair itself except when the tube car jolted them. We are all so sealed in our skins, she thought. Even if I can retrieve Ari, it will be years before I know what being used as a pawn in Y-S's game has done to him. Perhaps I am only a true child of my age. Just as one of my earliest relationships was with the enhanced house computer, so here I am traveling to kidnap my son with a cyborg to whom I have bonded, who seems to assume that if we are successful, he will raise my son with me. And why not? Would Yod be a worse father than most? Than Josh? He would never abuse Ari. He has no temper. He has infinite patience. He would never confuse Ari with his own ego or become infuriated or disappointed because he felt Ari failed him. Ari would be even more a child of the age of information, because he would be raised by one human and one computer. I don't think Yod would frighten him any more than the house frightened me.

I was never a fearful child, although I remember one of Malkah's men friends, a salvage diver, who seemed enormous and gruff to me. You could never say that Malkah had a type of man she went for. Thin, heavyset, tall, short, dark, fair; intellectuals, adventurers, scientists, captains, artists, musicians: they had to be able to talk, or she got bored, but otherwise she was always interested in trying something different. Whereas I bond hard and fast. Or try to. After all, I was the one who left Josh. If it had been clear to me I was thereby leaving Ari, I would have stuck it out with him no matter what sacrifice—even decapitation—that entailed.

Round and round, from A to B and back to Ari. I can't think of anything else for longer than five minutes. At this time I used to be giving him his breakfast and putting on his blue parka with the walking duck on it, to take him to day care. The last time was a darkly overcast day in late March with the wind scuttling over the high dome like a sand spider. He was babbling doggy noises from a stimmie the night before. He had understood none of it but the doggy. She remembered that as she came up to the center, she had been embarrassed in front of the other mothers because he was barking and tugging on her. Her last words to him had been "Stop that, Ari!"

The tube arrived in Omaha Station. This was an outpost on the edge of the vast Central Desert, a frontier town built from scrap of the former city. A dome arched over the presently inhabited area. Beyond were old streets of scavenged ruins, surrounded by scrubby brush. The trees as they died had been chopped down for wood, a precious commodity. The dome was a cover clamped over the streets at the height of a six-story building. Anything taller—old buildings—stuck up through it vanishing. They were deserted above the safe level.

"We need a fast-tank. We should be able to rent one here."

They got under way at fifteen hundred. The fast-tank Yod simply drove. There was no learning process, no time of experimenting. Avram had programmed in a number of vehicles he thought Yod might need to operate. All the information for controlling the fast-tank was inside him; he sat at the controls and strapped himself in as if he had been doing so all his life. He plugged into the dash to control its computer more quickly than he could by voice or hand. They were off, lurching and thumping. She was always learning new abilities of Yod's—or was it rather how much foresight Avram had shown?

In spite of the danger from the sun, people came to this jumping-off place, and off they jumped. The desert had a strong appeal, partly because of its danger, partly because there was still a lot of salvage out there from all the years of famine and disaster, partly because if you came from the Glop or someplace similar, here was the chance to be utterly alone. It was the sparse place, as opposed to the crowded place. It drew people into it, some for fortune, some for adventure and some for death. It was considered an elegant way to die, to vanish into the desert.

As much of the center of the continent turned into desert, the mystique had intensified. The less that normal people could ever experience the out-of-doors unmediated by dome or wrap or sec skin, the more that art, both pop and high, dwelt on desert symbolism. The desert was the pure solitary place where the hero or heroine found his or her lost self, confronted or flouted or succumbed to destiny, met a god or a devil or true love or the utter emptiness of existence. In college she had loved Lena Brown's *Sand and Spirit,* about a woman who in the desert simplifies herself stage by stage until she turns into wind itself, very romantic. Shira grimaced at her earlier self.

Nili came from the desert. It took Shira until the moment of departing Omaha to realize that for all the number of times she had experienced "desert" in stimmies and books and holos, she had never before actually ventured into it. She had crossed under it in tubes and over it in floaters and zips. But she had never really been in it before.

The fast-tank had its own solar-energy cooling system, or she would have cooked. Outside, it was fifty-two degrees. A fierce dry wind lashed at them. The sky was yellowish gray with blowing dust. In her mental image of the desert, the sky was a clear radiant blue. Here the sand roared against the metal of the fast-tank. There was little to see except a wall of sand around them and an occasional wreck looming out of the dust. It was exacerbatingly boring, lurching along inside a metal headache blasted by the wind as if a hundred brass scrub brushes were scouring the surface. It was noisy, it was stuffy, it was violently uncomfortable.

She put on headphones and listened to music until she couldn't stand to listen to more. The selection provided with the fast-tank ran to West-Mex favorites and mournful wailing ballads about people dying in the desert, in tube accidents, of true, true love, of poisoned drugs under the artificial stars of some dome.

It was more bearable as the twilight came on. The wind died, and gradually the dust thinned. By the time it was dark, they could see the stars brilliant and huge over them. She asked Yod to stop for a while. Her kidneys felt battered. Her back and head ached. She wanted the noise to cease. She wanted to be outside now that the sun had set and the temperature was reading a balmy twenty-six degrees and cooling rapidly.

They ate real food they had bought in Omaha, tubed in from the north. Yellow summer apples and cheese called mizithra. Cheese, like all animal products, was hideously expensive, but Shira needed a treat. She did not know what would happen to them at Y-S, so why not eat real cheese? This might be their last meal. Sheep had turned out to be less sensitive to acid rain and UV radiation than cows or goats, so most cheese was made of their milk these days. Not that Shira had ever had cow's milk to compare it with. Cheese was as dear as caviar had once been. Lots of fish farming went on, and sturgeon took well to it. Cheese and apples were far more costly than caviar.

Who else would do this for her? No one. She could not imagine another soul who would go with her to try to extract her stolen son. "Yod, I want you to know how grateful I am you're willing to risk this with me."

"Does this kind of selfishness pass for altruism among humans?" He smiled at her. "I want to keep you with me."

"I can't imagine a better way." She leaned against him. "It's beautiful here, just as it's supposed to be."

It was still. The wind had died. Perhaps the weather had cleared, or perhaps this was simply a different miniclimate in the desert. They had come almost three hundred kilometers. The sky was indigo, and the stars went on forever. It was extraordinary to see them.

"That's Cassiopeia, the Queen's Chair," she said, pointing. "Malkah used to call it Queen Esther's Throne." The temperature was dropping tangibly.

"I can't make out constellations well," Yod said apologetically. "Too many stars are visible to my eyes that aren't visible to human vision. I have trouble seeing only the ones you see."

"Do you feel anything when you look at them?"

Yod was silent for a moment. "Yes. I do. . . . A sense of great distance. The sweep of the visible universe, its extent and vastness, gives me a sense of scale that is exhilarating. Surely among those stars are many beings with different kinds of consciousness and mental and physical capacities. Isn't it likely there are even other beings manufactured like myself?"

She smiled. "If you met a female cyborg, you wouldn't be interested in me any longer."

"I doubt attraction between cyborgs could occur. We would both yearn toward the type of being who made us—if these other cyborgs we are postulating also possess the ability to yearn."

What she was sure they would also lack was the ability to tell when she was kidding. "Do you think your predecessors could yearn?"

"No. Malkah introduced that capacity."

"Malkah has never turned over her log on her work with you."

"Your curiosity's like mine. I read novels as if they were the specs to your makeup. I study them to grasp the forces underlying your behavior."

She wondered if he saw her as a combination of Becky Sharp, Anna Karenina, Madame Bovary, Molly Bloom and Marina Kolovis? "At times like this, Yod, I wish we could take Ari and just keep going. Never return. Run away, hide."

"Avram controls a self-destruct mechanism in me, wherever I am. He can bounce the signal off a satellite. I can't run away, though I want to."

She had to free him from Avram. If they got back safely, she would start discussing with Malkah how to proceed.

In an hour they climbed back in, heading for the rail line that brought supplies into Y-S. The trains operated on simple fusion reactors that required water every few hundred kilometers. The refueling stop that Shira remembered was their goal. They had the fast-tank dig itself into the ground. Then they spread camouflage over it and walked the last two kilometers. They could see the salmon-colored lights of the refueling station ahead. They cut in below it to the line and waited there. Trains ran about every half hour. They were too slow and too hot for transporting people or perishables, but they were used for machinery, supplies, anything that could take the high temperatures of the desert without spoiling.

They had not long to wait before a train swooshed in. At once they began edging along. Every car was coded, but Yod could read Y-S code now. They found one containing hospital supplies, bed linens, nursing uniforms, bandages, disinfectant. Yod examined the lock and in two minutes had opened the compartment. Shira put her sec skin on with its coolant fully loaded. If they got stuck too long, if anything went wrong, she had no idea how high temperatures could rise inside the car. She was relieved when it jerked into motion and they went clattering through the night toward Y-S.

They were close enough now so that it was only a matter of an hour before they entered the dome. "We'll head down to the lower level. There we'll put on gardeners' gear. In that we can pass anyplace, invisibly. Nobody looks at the yard workers. They're day laborers, and they're everyplace under the dome."

The rails ran all through the utility complex—hospital, school, repair shop, stores, food facility. Their car was shunted directly into the hospital. Yod listened carefully at the door and with his supersensitive hearing picked the time when they could slip out. They headed for the maintenance facility, where the green suits for yard personnel were heaped in carts from the laundry—between yellow for repair and brown for construction.

When Shira at last stood under the dome, it was just after dawn. "That's where I gave birth to Ari." She pointed to a low building, called for reasons she had never been able to fathom the Long Pavilion.

"It looks entirely different from the birthing house at home."

She paused to orient herself. "Not that way. That's Paradise Park. I've only been allowed in there twice. It's for the top levels. It's full of sculpture parks, holo parks, botanical gardens and a zoo, a hill with perpetual snow. The president lives on a lake full of real water."

They passed rapidly through the fancy shopping sector, which would not open till ten. In the windows, fantastic virons centered around beautiful models drinking, flirting, having sex with unicorns and lions and knights in full armor. It rather turned Shira's stomach, but then she thought that there was no accounting for what a person might find attractive—she with her cyborg, slipping past in the overalls of gardeners, carrying pruners and weeding hoes.

"What is all this?" Yod pointed at the stores even now winking at the street, empty except for day laborers hurrying to their posts—shops blinking, glittering, sending out clouds of pheromones, singing seductively. "Lust will make you wanted, wanted, wanted. He will touch you there, there, and you'll be wanted. Nothing is like being wanted. Lust, the perfume that gives you the power of desire. Lust: want me now!"

"We don't have these sorts of stores in Tikva," she offered.

"We have stores. Like the one where you bought shorts for me."

"Ours are for things you need. These are for things no one needs. Therefore everything here is expensive beyond belief. Dresses that cost more than I earn in a year. Jewels that sing. A blouse that flashes transparent if you choose. Tooth implants that can detect some poisons. Enhanced jewels to be inserted in the cheek, the forehead, the nose, the navel. Choreographed sequences of scents, sounds and tastes for an evening's entertaining."

"Who buys these things?"

"Besides their wives, who work for Y-S too, men of the upper levels have toys—women who are cosmetically recreated, very beautiful. While the men work, they do nothing but shop." Only on rare occasions had Shira encountered such women, and then they had seemed scarcely human. She remembered a pair of them when she was shopping for a special gown for a big Y-S awards ceremony. They had appeared to her as flamingos or egrets—beautiful plumage and harsh empty cries, as devoid of thought as those holos of women fucked by lobsters. Even their nails and teeth had been replaced by bright gleaming inserts. In the zone of expensive shops, every window promised sex, every message crooned desire, and yet sex was a regimented commodity in the enclave. Which persons you might make love to was as defined by your place in the hierarchy as the people to whom you bowed and the people who bowed to you. Sexual privileges depended upon your place and rank.

Now they were in the midlevel sector: occasional apartment buildings, rows and rows of little houses; at the major intersections, food dispensers, laundries, utilitarian shops. They hid themselves in the shrubbery outside the daycare center for midlevel techies. The hedge around the center was planted with rubbery bushes of lurid vermilion and purplish leaves that Shira remembered. She assumed that Ari would be back in his old day care center. It would be unlike Y-S to place him elsewhere. There was always and only one correct place for personnel or the offspring of personnel of a particular grade and type.

Yod waited stolidly. She was so nervous she had to urinate twice. She kept imagining she might throw up. Her stomach was a small hard rubber ball in her chest. The minutes went by with the speed of a mountain eroding. Whenever she read the time internally, it was the same plus a few seconds. Ari would not come. Josh would not let go of him. How could she grab Ari? If only she knew where they were housed, but since all the same-level dwellings were virtually interchangeable, she had no way to guess which house was theirs. Midlevel-tech housing stretched for kilometers in one of the largest of all the Y-S residential sectors.

Silently Yod passed her a nutrition bar to chew. She shook her head no. She would throw it up. It was always six forty-five. The sun had not yet cleared the roof of the shop across the way that sold toys and trikes. The streets were almost empty. A cleaning robot puttered along. A security ape trotted past without looking at the bushes. Why would he expect intruders in the hedge of the midlevel-tech day care center?

At last the first little girl was delivered, a pudgy four-year-old with flaxen braids tied with green polka-dot bows, dragging on her mother's arm. Her mother was in a backless business suit, just like Shira when she used to drop Ari off on the way to work. A couple of minutes later, a boy younger than Ari was wheeled past in his stroller. More children arrived every minute.

Finally, at seven-forty, she saw him. He was walking by himself, holding Josh's hand. How nicely Ari walked now. He looked sturdy and serious, marching with a scowl. What was wrong? Was he upset? He was hunching his shoulders and muttering at his wrist. He was imitating the man who walked on the other side of him, wearing a side arm. "Security ape," she mouthed to Yod. "Stay put." The guard was six feet five or six, built like a massive door. Every time they came to an intersection, the ape spoke into his wrist-con, obviously checking in with security HQ. Great. His head was shaved, and he wore special fighting gloves, studded and armored.

Security delivered Ari to the door, where the supervisor Jane Forest herself took him inside. The guard assumed a position outside. Josh strode off down the street. They could not crawl out without danger of someone seeing them. They would have to remain crouched in the shrubbery as long as the guard was on duty. The last child was dropped off. No, here came a late mother, dragging her toddler along crying in protest. The mother had to ask the guard to step aside. He glared at her briefly and moved two steps, so that she had to sidle past him with her wailing daughter. The ape guarded the door, standing with his feet planted far apart. He wore an earbo, playing some kind of music directly into his ear, but he never stopped his deliberate survey of the street, one direction, then the other. They were stuck in the bushes. It seemed this would be the permanent situation.

Around ten, a pedicart came by. The guard had a cupcake and coffee brought to him at the door. But finally, half an hour later, he strolled around the corner of the day school. He must be relieving himself. Yod rose at once and slid from the hedge, as Shira wriggled after him. They ran around the other corner and along the street far enough to be sure the guard could not see them. "Okay. You cross past the ape—walk slowly. No day laborers ever hurry—and go to work two blocks up the road, where Ari and Josh emerged from the side street. Weed anything."

"How will I know what to weed?"

"Nobody pays attention to what day labor does. Just look busy."

"Where will you be?"

"I'm going to take the next road over and go where they came from. I'll see if I can spot Josh's number or anything I recognize in any of the houses. I'll work my way up and down the streets until ten to noon. Then I'll come find you. I used to bring Ari home for lunch. I don't know if Josh does that, or if he works through. We may have to wait until sixteen."

"I can handle the ape, Shira. Easily. I can move before he gets his weapon out of its holster."

"But not before he signals for help. He only has to press that wrist-con. You'd have to take him out before he knows what hit him. Or we have to wait to catch them without him. I bet he doesn't sleep with Ari."

"Any alarm systems I'm convinced I can disarm."

"I'm sure they have good security on their house computer now, but I bet it's nothing like Malkah's."

She set out walking. The four basic patterns of house alternated in a randomly generated design. All along the narrow roadway, where children would ride bikes and trikes and wheelies and where delivery pedicabs and occasional mototrucks traveled, flowers were planted in beds. Then on each side came a pedestrian walkway lined with trees and lawns. Many had hedges or low fences. What could be planted was strictly controlled. People in the lower and mid tech and management areas were responsible for their yards, but the roadways were maintained by day laborers. They were always about, clipping, weeding, feeding, but they were essentially invisible. No one spoke to them or knew them. It was a service like the water that flowed from the tap or the cleaning robots that here as in Tikva shuffled around all day and all night.

Everybody was at work by now. Mostly she saw an occasional robot on the street, cleaning, replacing burned-out lighting. Once she saw a team of human laborers repairing underground pipes in an intersection. They paid no attention to her. Construction workers were better paid than gardeners. All of them rode in and out on the tubes. Interaction between day laborers in the enclave was severely discouraged. She passed the shop where she had used to pick up dinner most nights. Nothing touched her feelings except for the flashes of Ari that came to her: Her son staring at a red rose just at his eye level, face-to-face, with his lips parted. He lunged

forward and put it in his mouth before she could stop him. Then he
howled with disappointment. That same rosebush stood at the intersection, flanked with two uncomfortable cast-resin benches. She passed the
house that had been theirs and managed to read the number, but it was
not Josh's.

She covered forty blocks. Every house had a number implanted in the
door, which identified the employees who lived there, but she could hardly
walk up to each door. If a spy-eye was watching, that would be a tip-off.
As it was, she stopped and worked regularly. She depended on recognizing
something familiar—curtains, a toy—or on a hot flash of intuition. She
found nothing. Even the midtech-level park where she had so often
brought Ari to play in the sandbox seemed as devoid of nostalgia as a
parking lot. At eleven-thirty, she turned back to meet Yod.

thirty-eight

A MATTER OF SOME FINALITY

Shira kept herself well down the street. Yod she placed nearer. Noon came. The children played in the yard of the day care center. It was fortunate the two of them had finally escaped the shrubbery, because the four- and five-year-olds ran in and out of the hedge, and would surely have discovered them.

Parents, mostly mothers, came and took their children for lunch. Josh did not appear. When she realized that he was not coming, she walked slowly down the street on the far sidewalk. Ari, wearing green-and-yellow rompers that looked none too clean, was playing with two little girls in a sandbox. He still had that way of tossing the sand up and laughing when it fell. She did not dare look any longer or harder. The guard was lounging on the grass, eating a lunch brought him by pedicab. She longed to run across the street and snatch Ari in her arms. Her hands closed on air. She kept going. She went to work on another flower bed.

Obviously the guard was remaining on duty. Josh would appear at sixteen hundred and collect Ari when the center closed. She motioned to Yod, and they went off to sit on a bench in the next intersection. The curved resin benches were honey-colored and slippery, designed to be looked at rather than sat on. Around them yellow and maroon chrysanthemums were planted in a double knot, the ground between the plants carpeted with glaring white pebbles. She ate the remains of the cheese and apples, keeping the food under cover. No day laborer would have real food. Yod did not bother with lunch.

"I hadn't considered that your ex-husband would be with the boy," Yod said. "How will he respond?"

"He'll be as furious and as frightened as I was. It's not fair to him to steal Ari. But he didn't hesitate to take Ari from me. He began the war."

"But once you loved each other."

Shira chewed the last of the cheese without tasting it. "Truthfully, I don't think I ever felt as close to him as I do to you. I thought I should get married. I thought Josh needed me. All self-delusion. A sad mistake all around, Yod."

"They're taking the children back in."

She squinted, watching Ari and a girl from the sandbox pushing and shoving at each other, doubling over with giggles. Then Ari shoved too hard, and the little girl hit him and began to cry. It was agonizing to be kept at a distance, unable to speak, to touch him. She felt as if she were bleeding from a great rent in her side. She would rather die here, violently and at once, than leave him again.

"The guard is assuming his stance outside," Yod reported.

"In a week it will be Rosh Hashanah. I imagine us home with Ari. We give him a toy shofar to blow. He blows it in the courtyard again and again and drives us all crazy. We are deliriously happy."

"This year I'll attend services with you. Avram wouldn't allow me in public in previous years."

They explored the streets of the city, looking for exit routes. Once they had Ari, what would they do? Could they slip out in a train, as they had come in? But where would they end up? This was not a manufacturing facility. Y-S plants were in China and South Africa. Empty cars might sit in the desert for days. They could not pass out through the communications channels from Base to Net, as once they had mentally.

"We can wrap Ari in your sec skin, since you don't need it. If we're seen, we've had it anyhow."

Yod frowned. "But we can hardly walk across the desert."

"We can't go out by train. They won't stop at the first refueling station. They only use that in this direction."

"If I could steal a floater, we could head straight for where we left the fast-tank, blow up the floater so it can't be tracked. Or go all the way to Omaha on the floater. I can reprogram it to bypass the controlling mechanism."

"Or we could just pass out with the flow. If we grab Ari quickly enough between sixteen and seventeen, we can take the tube with the workers. They don't check prints leaving. They move everybody out as fast as possible. . . . But a child—what would he be doing with the day laborers?"

"There's no day care here for the laborers' children?"

"I never thought about that. I guess they leave their children where they live."

"You took tranks along. We can put him to sleep and carry him out in an equipment bag."

She had a container of shots, each the size of a straight pin, that could put Ari to sleep. "Yod, we must come up with some plan. The worst thing we can do is grab him and then get caught."

"I don't think the actual abduction will represent much of a problem, once we've located their residence. Getting out—we should devote the time we have remaining to that problem."

The water was filtered and recirculated. Trash was used to generate power. What could be recycled was compacted here and shipped to another plant, but those cars were open and solidly packed. They could not hope to ride with the compacted trash. What passed out of the enclave every day were the laborers. After as much exploration as they dared, they were left at sixteen hundred with the same ideas they had begun the afternoon with: If they could grab Ari fast enough, they could pass out with the workers. If they had to wait, they would need to steal a floater, reprogram it and escape across the desert to the hidden fast-tank. All they accomplished was to work out two means for getting from the dome to the floater field outside.

As sixteen approached, Shira took a position around the corner, so that she could no longer see the center but could still watch Yod. Finally he nodded to her, rose from his weeding and began strolling. Keeping her distance but maintaining him in view, she followed. The streets were filling, and Yod speeded up to stay within sight of Josh and Ari. In the crowd, she hurried and caught up to Yod. Now Josh and Ari were only a block ahead, the guard beside them. Yod and she pursued, a loose procession among the others flooding the walkways, spilling over into the narrow vehicle tracks. On the busier streets, moving sidewalks sped people and packages along. Josh picked up Ari, who clung to him, and, followed by the guard, used a mover to jump the next forty blocks. No wonder she had had no luck finding their residence.

Their three quarries exited the moving sidewalk and strolled down a side street. Nervous about chasing them on a block with little traffic, Shira and Yod lingered at the corner. Halfway along the block, Josh turned off at a house, identical to the one in which she had lived her married life. Layout, paint job, even the shrubs in the yard were the same. The guard saw them into the house, turned and came back. She and Yod scurried up the main street. People were getting in line for picking up their laundry.

The guard mounted the moving sidewalk and sped off. Yod and Shira at once headed for the house. They were all right for the next forty-five minutes. Day laborers worked till five, so that they did not get in the way of management and technical workers coming home or changing shifts. Her heart was pounding, and she could not draw a breath deep enough to relieve the crushed feeling in her chest. They would be caught. Yod would be dissected, and she would be rendered autistic by mnemosine. She would be a turnip stored in a mental ward; or they would quietly sell her to an organ bank.

"I'll use the small sensor-muter I've been working on. I believe I can disarm the house with it. Wait outside while I make sure."

"Yod, I can't wait outside. I have to go in."

"You can wait five minutes, Shira. In order to vastly increase the chances of securing your son."

Yod walked up to the door, while Shira waited. He had the rod-shaped device in his hand. He touched it to the door. A moment later, he opened the door and passed inside. The muter must have worked. She looked too suspicious, standing on the sidewalk outside a tech house. Quickly she followed Yod. The lights in the house went out. It was still daylight.

She heard Josh calling down, "There's a power outage, Sylvie. Keep Ari in the high chair."

A woman's voice said, "The power is out down here too, Mr. Rogovin."

"Go next door and find out if it's general or just us."

Yod intercepted the woman on the way to the door. He held her, a hand over her mouth, while Shira administered a hypo that would knock her out. It was the same kind she had used to vaccinate Ari every month or two against whatever new scourge was rampant. It was the size of a straight pin and could be inserted in any muscle. They carried the woman to the couch and laid her down. Yod opened and shut the front door. Shira ran into the kitchen.

"Ari." She tried to speak calmly. His brown hair had darkened a little more, but it was the same tangle of curls, cut a little shorter than she preferred. His eyes, brown and oversized as her own, were wide with shock.

He stared at her, his mouth open. "Mama?" he screeched.

"Shh, my precious, I've come for you. I told you I'd never give up."
She kissed him. He was unresponsive, staring at her, his fists clenched. She
lifted him out of the high chair. He let himself be lifted. Tears began to
roll from her eyes. Tears ran down onto the shoulder of his dirty green-
and-yellow rompers. She snuffled and shook her head hard. Must not cry.
She would frighten him. "Mama's so glad to see you!" He was heavier than
she remembered. He did not struggle but did not respond.

Yod climbed the steps silently. Not a step creaked. He slipped upward
and vanished. Ari had not yet seen him.

"When does the other guard come?" she asked Ari.

"Morning. When we go day care. Oscar." He made a scowling face.
Was he imitating Oscar?

"Is it always Oscar?" She had to wait for Yod to take care of Josh.
Frightened until she felt as if she was babbling, she was very, very careful
to sound calm. She slid him back into the high chair and began to feed
him some miso soup. If he did not eat now, he would be cranky soon.

"Sometimes George. Don't like George. He yells." Ari began bouncing
up and down in the chair. The soup dribbled down.

"Who was the woman who went next door?"

"My nana. Sylvie."

She fed him the food that Sylvie had laid out. From upstairs came the
sound of someone running, then thuds. A falling of furniture. "Somebody
knocked things over!" Shira said cheerfully. Ari was staring at the ceiling,
but he continued eating his soup. Then she grabbed some jars of food from
the cupboard and stuffed them in her backpack. She hoped Yod had not
hurt Josh. She was hurting him enough. "What does your nana do?" she
asked, hoping to keep him from wondering what was happening.

"She feed me. Give me bath. Daddy, he dress me. Nana put my things
on chair. Then she go home."

"Where does she live?"

"Far, far away. With her little girl. Her little girl Suzie."

"Does she go on the tube?"

"What the tube?"

Yod flowed down the steps, swift, silent. "Let's go now." He carried
a large duffel bag. She recognized it as Josh's weekender.

"Who you?" Ari pointed.

"Yod, do we have to give him the hypo? He'll walk with us."

Yod smiled at Ari. "Hello. I'm Yod. Are you Ari?"

"I'm afraid of giving him too much."

"I can adjust it. Give me the hypo."

Ari stared at the hypo as it passed from Shira to Yod. "Doctor?" Yod said, "This won't hurt."

Shira rolled up his sleeve. His little fat arm. "Not too much!"

"No! No! Don't stick me!" Ari began to bang his spoon against the high chair and to twist under her hands.

"If it hurts, I promise you can stick me tomorrow. Deal?" Yod brought the hypo to Ari's arm. Ari jerked and hit at him, but Yod got it in. "Did that hurt?"

Ari tensed as he got ready to cry, but then his face softened and his eyes lost their focus. He began to droop in the chair. In a moment he fell forward. Shira cleaned the food from him and then slipped him into the duffel bag. "Can he breathe?"

"We should leave the zipper open as far as we can. Now we must exit before someone comes. The computer reports in regularly. I've reprogrammed the system to report everyone sleeping." Yod slipped the duffel bag over his shoulder.

"Just one minute." Shira ran upstairs. Ari must have his blanket, his bear, familiar things.

"No, Shira!" Yod tried to block her, but moving with the duffel slowed him. He made an aborted noise but did not follow her upstairs.

In the upper hall, Josh lay on the floor. His neck was turned at an unnatural angle. She knelt over him wringing her hands, with the sense that it was all her fault, that she must do something. She heard herself speaking to him, stupidly repeating his name as if that could wake him. "I'm sorry, Josh, I'm sorry!" Finally she made herself touch him. No pulse at the neck. No pulse at all. His skin was still warm, but he was dead.

For a moment she could not believe it, and she listened at his nostrils, pressed on his chest. He had to come back to life, he had to. But he would not. His face in death was oddly relaxed, the mouth fallen slightly open, the eyes half shut. She lowered the eyelids, wondering why she felt compelled to do that. It seemed polite. Sometimes he had looked like that in bed. She could almost remember when she had been full of hope for them, in the very beginning, when tenderness for this man had turned her to warm jelly. She began to weep, kneeling over him. Everything felt shattered.

She was furious at Yod, shocked but unsurprised. Just as she would never be truly astonished if Yod killed Gadi accidentally or on purpose, she was finally not surprised that he had killed Josh. But Ari must not find out. Ever. She got control of herself. She made herself leave Josh, leave the body where it lay. She found Ari's room, grabbed his favorite bear and his blanket, blue jammies. She ran down with them and stuffed them in her backpack. "Okay, now." She avoided looking at Yod. He seemed about to speak, then did not.

The house came on around them as they left. Lights turned on, pop music in the kitchen, security that would report everyone sleeping. Sylvie lay unconscious on the couch. "Should I tie her up?" she asked.

"We must leave at once. She'll be out approximately three hours."

They trotted along the block to the moving sidewalk. The riders had changed from Y-S personnel in backless business suits to workers in their various color-coded uniforms. Shira and Yod headed straight for the tube station. Behind them rose the sound of an emergency vehicle, but it could have been anything. She did not turn, she did not look back.

They switched sidewalks twice more, Shira leading the way. She knew the fastest route across the enclave. As they approached the tube, the sidewalk grew more and more crowded. She was jammed against Yod. She interposed her body between Ari and other bodies, so that no one could feel what was being carried. It was awkward, and she was jostled and pummeled, but she kept her position. She must protect him equally from injury and discovery. How frightened he would be! Did she have the right to do this to him? But the life to which she was taking him was a better one, freer, more independent. He was being raised by a hired woman torn from her own daughter in the Glop. She and Malkah and Yod could do a better job. She swore they would. Now Ari had only her and her family. He had no father. They had killed him.

They passed through the portal of the Y-S enclave and were briefly exposed to the unfiltered sun as they crossed a wide square to the tube station. They were simply bodies in a sea of weary jostling flesh, two bodies carrying a hidden third. Yod elbowed into a car and got her a seat so that she could hold Ari, still in the bag. She longed to check him, but she did not dare. She confined herself to making sure through the cloth that he was breathing.

They had to change tubes in Chicago. They did not dare pause to rest or spend the night. She pulled Ari from the duffel and carried him openly in her arms. It was past rush hour. They were not the only couple traveling with a child. Ari was beginning to stir, but he had not yet wakened. It was not as crowded on this tube. They were able to sit together. Immediately she asked Yod, "Why did you do it?"

"Your ex-husband? I'm sorry."

She clenched her hands together, willing herself to keep control. "It was unnecessary." They spoke very softly, their heads close together. She held herself so she would not accidentally touch him.

"It did not seem so. He was wearing the same device as the guard, and he began signaling for help as soon as he saw me. I had time only to leap across the room and hit him. I only struck him once, Shira. I did not realize he would be injured seriously."

"Yod, he was dead."

He nodded. He was turned toward her, trying to get her to meet his gaze. "I regret that very much. It was the one blow that killed him, but I only intended to keep him from making the call. As it was, he opened a frequency, and I'm sure they arrived quickly."

"Shh. No more about it. Never in front of Ari." She forced herself to touch Yod's hand. He had gotten her child back for her. No one else would have done so. She had chosen to sacrifice Josh to her desire for her child. She had chosen that. She must remember. Yod had only acted in her interest, even if his own was surreptitiously involved. She could never give up and go back to Josh now, quite. Yod had done as she had wanted, and the guilt was entirely hers to bear, silently and secretly. "You didn't kill him. If anybody killed him, it must have been Y-S. We left him alive and unconscious, like the nanny. Understood?"

He nodded, looking frightened. "I cannot alter my memories. They'll continue to exist. But I can put a block on them such that I never refer to today and such that no one else can ever access them. This is for the boy?"

"He is now under your protection even more than I am. You must put him first at all times."

"Shira, it's not in my nature to be able to put him ahead of you, but I'll protect him with my life, the same as you. . . . I'm sorry. I never wanted to give you pain. Once it happened, I didn't want you to know. I'll say nothing more."

"Good. No more alluding to it, whether we're alone or together. I mean it, Yod, when I say utter silence."

Ari was yawning now and scrubbing his eyes. She held him more closely, wrapping his familiar worn blue blanket around him, the blanket Malkah had sent as a present when he was born. The blanket he would not allow to go off to the laundry, which she had always had to wash by hand, so that it would not leave the house. The difficult time was ahead, when he wakened in the tube in the frightening noise and darkness and bad air, when he wakened to the strangeness of her and of Yod. I wanted my child, I wanted him back more than I wanted anything else in the world. As long as I live I must bear the responsibility and the guilt for the choice I made to take him back. Yod killed, but I let him. I did not order him to protect Josh at all costs, because that wasn't my priority. She saw Josh's body crumpled on the floor of the upstairs hall, fallen as if from a considerable height, with the neck twisted and the eyes half open. Once she had loved him. Then she had left him. Then she had had him killed.

thirty-nine

THE BATTLE AT THE GATES

My daughter is alive. She sends word as an afterthought, and my mourning passes from grief into clownishness. Why did she wait so long to let me know? Daily I study Ari to understand who this boy child is. I am used to daughters and granddaughters, but I know rather a lot about the male too. Ari has appeared like an exotic bird on the tree outside the window, when I was a girl and birds lived everywhere and flew in the air like animate flowers. Now this child comes shouting his demands, loud, healthy, precious, overbearing.

Yod is working heroically to be human; I see it every day. He wants desperately to satisfy Shira, to be her man, her husband, to father her son. I wonder if the programming I gave him to balance his violent propensities wasn't a tragic error, if I did not do him an injustice in giving him needs he may not be able to fulfill. I fear Yod experiences something like guilt at his inadequacy, at not being human enough for her. He strains, unsure how far he is from succeeding, because he cannot know what the real thing would feel like. Men so often try to be inhumanly powerful, efficient, unfeeling, to perform like a machine, it is ironic to watch a machine striving to be male.

Yet Ari obviously accepts him, far more perhaps than Shira realizes. Ari senses that he can get away with almost anything with Yod, who will often obey him when any other adult would laugh off his requests or simply ignore them.

"Bird," Ari demanded the other day. He is always pointing at the birds. Shira's response and mine varies from the sort of Oh, isn't he cute, wanting the impossible, to explaining with deepening irritation, if the request gets too vehement, how irrational his desire is.

Yod plucked a goldfinch out of the air and held it to him, carefully, delicately, but so that Ari could pat its yellow head. Then Yod released it to fly off in a panic but unharmed. I think even Ari understood that something out of the ordinary had happened. He sat and chuckled to himself for five minutes afterward. Now of course he expects us to do the same, and we're back where we were.

Shira doesn't want to tell me, as we await the inevitable response of the multi, how Yod and she managed to steal Ari from Y-S. The sense of being under siege is sharp in all of us. Which brings me back to my story, back to Prague, Good Friday of 1600, the mob stirred up by Thaddeus attacking the ghetto. A more direct attack than I expect here and now, although lately what has been called the multinational corporate peace seems to be showing cracks. I go to the terminal, sit, call up my file and begin talking, my eyes closed, Yod's dark benign visage in my mind. Dear Yod, our tale recommences.

INSIDE THE GHETTO the assembled Jews hear the crowd roar just outside the wall. Next, thrown objects strike the gates and arc over the top, both those aimed at harm—rocks, sharp objects, bottles—and those aimed at insult: offal, feces, rotting garbage, dead animals. All slam into the gates or fall for the most part harmlessly inside, although a couple of casualties need to wash afterward and one man is knocked senseless by a hurled brick. He is carried away to his family at the Pinkas synagogue, where he will die without regaining consciousness.

The women on the rooftops shout down reports. The few soldiers of the Emperor march bravely on the crowd, while the Jews wait silently, not daring even to cheer. Armed with arquebuses and pikes, the troops arrest some of the rock-throwers and march away with them, leaving the ghetto gates undefended against the larger remnant of attackers. Now the mob, better organized than that word might suggest, falls back to permit a battering ram through. It is a makeshift ram, constructed from a stout oak tipped with iron. It is dragged on a cart by a team of draft horses. Then the young men Thaddeus has inspired position the ram on the cart, unharness the horses and set themselves to drive the ram full force into the gates.

The Jews inside the gates can hear laughter, loud cries, curses and great thumps as the ram is rolled into position. Outside the gates a carnival atmosphere rules. The grimness of hatred against the Christ-killers, carefully stirred up and worked into a frenzy, gives way to a mood of being free to do anything. Impulses usually denied or suppressed can dance and leap today and slake themselves with gross satisfaction.

I have experienced this mood in crowds. In my youth when there were major sporting events, when some hometown team won its division or pennant or trophy, the men would pour out and beat passersby and rape women they found on the streets. One of the sole benefits of the diseases that ran through the population was the end of such public events. Now all spectator sports are stimmies. They are presumably all staged, scripted, faked, so there is never a dull game or a game with too lopsided a score. People bet anyhow. They try to second-guess whose turn it is to win.

I remember the food riots too. I've been in mobs, and I've observed them from positions of semisafety. I've run before them, in the anti-Jewish riots after the Two Week War. All this is in your memory banks, Yod, and you can also access the history of the founding of Tikva, a direct response to the virulent anti-Semitism of that period we call the Troubles. Anyhow, I've helped carry the bodies away afterward. I can hear that crowd muttering, some worked up, some going along with the crowd, some loving the feel of being part of a giant organism, exalted, uplifted, one fierce hot galloping beast. Some are feeling righteous. Some are convinced they are holy warriors carrying out the will of some powerful angry god. But many are having fun. Imagine, you have been given a license to do all the things you think about doing to your family, your boss, your enemies, women you look at, people who push you around, everybody you feel like sticking it to in ordinary frustrating brutish life.

Inside, as the ram begins to crack on the gates, some are praying, some are wishing they were in Transylvania or just hiding under a bridge. The sound is intolerable, louder than thunder. The gates rock but do not yet give way. They are solidly reinforced. The sound is like a bat cracking on each head. After ten minutes, some inside wish the gates would give way so the noise would stop, so their heads would stop pounding, so that the terrible hammering would release their knees and shoulders and spines from bludgeoning. They feel as if they are being battered with the gates. The ram is attacking every one of them.

Yakov raises his strong baritone, singing "Adom Alom." Singing helps them bear the pounding. Almost it seems to keep time now with their singing, like an enormous drum. The gates still hold, and the ram stops.

Outside, they can hear voices arguing about how to proceed. "They're getting more men in line," the rooftop women report. Once again the ram slams the gates.

Finally the metal shielding buckles, and the wood splinters. There is a breach in the gates' integrity. Rapidly the ram widens the breach. Now the gates collapse inward and the crowd pours through, cheering, a harsh ragged cry for blood bellowing across and echoing off the walls of the nearest houses. Men carrying the ram pause when they see the barricade. They consult in shouts, and then they are charging the barricade nearest them with the ram. Joseph leaps over the top to seize the ram by its metal end. All of the men carrying it cannot wrest it from him. He jabs the ram sideways, knocking the men loose. Then he swings it, using it as a huge club. It is much larger than he is and by far the heaviest thing he has ever moved, so he cannot swing it fast or hard, but the weight topples those he hits. It is a slow and clumsy weapon, but it drives back the first attack. It is more the sight of a single man swinging the heavy ram that causes dismay and even panic than the actual numbers he can injure with the weapon, for only the press of the crowd keeps the attackers from escaping the ram's slow-motion sweeps.

Both sides begin throwing rocks. Joseph is caught in the middle and retreats hastily, dropping the ram into the barricade so it becomes a piece of the defenses. Some of the attackers take shelter behind the fallen gates. But the crowd outside who cannot see what is going on inside push forward, spilling invaders into the range of the defenders' rocks. Some go down, more retreat, some try to advance. The women on the building nearest the gates start spilling their caldrons of boiling water down on the attackers. One woman is shot. Another is hit by an arrow and falls into the street. The son of the woman whose body lies crushed on the pavement runs at the mob, swinging a chain. He brings down three before he goes under and is beaten and kicked to death.

Some of the people who came in a picnic mood are milling around, changing their minds. The sight of bodies in the street, the wounded and the dead from both sides, causes second thoughts in those capable of entertaining them. The mob thins momentarily, but those outside the gates are still shoving in. Some are struggling to leave and others to enter. In the confusion, Joseph calls up to the women on the roofs to drop their loads again. By twos they go to the edge and topple over their heaps of stones and household refuse, broken furniture, crockery. A small group of men armed with muskets begins firing at them. They are not accurate but they keep firing, and two more women are hit and fall; another is wounded but pulled back into safety by her companions.

"We're lucky they have only small arms," Yakov remarks. "With artillery we'd be finished in short order."

"We have to stop the musketeers," Joseph says. He lobs a stone at them hard and fast and succeeds in beaning the nearest. They move to a more protected position, set up the props for their long-barreled weapons and fire again. In all the ghetto, there is not one firearm. If his side had even a couple of muskets, Joseph is convinced they could defend the ghetto until the mob gave up. Now he is sorry he sent the Maharal to safety, because he needs direction. He is not sure what to do. It stinks already, the reek of blood and gunpowder, the stench of loosened bowels and urine. Between the forces two men are loudly dying, calling for their mothers, one in Yiddish, one in Czech. Nobody on either side is singing any longer. A dog is howling and then yelps as someone kicks it. The many voices muttering, cursing, praying between the walls sound like a nest of disturbed hornets working themselves up to swarm.

Joseph keeps an eye out for Chava. She stood at the barricade during the first rush, but now she has put down the silly roasting spit and is treating the wounded in a makeshift hospital in the carriageway of Maisl's house. She has built a little fire and is heating water. Bedding has been put down in the street and a rug for the wounded to lie on. Moshe Fuchs, a doctor and amulet maker, works beside her. They do what they can.

The musketeers are shooting at the barricade, keeping the Jews down behind it. They are better dressed than most of the mob, wearing light chest armor over shirts with puffed sleeves, hats with enormous drooping plumes. Joseph recognizes Karel brandishing a sword and a stave. The oversized features in his square-jawed face radiate conviction. His voice carries easily. He is haranguing his troops. Now Joseph sees more faces from the tavern up on Hradcany Hill. They are in the forefront now, getting ready to charge. Joseph's lips draw back from his teeth. He points out the men he knows to Yakov. "If we can stop them, we'll do a real service to the community."

"To humanity, I think," Yakov says. He grips his old sword tightly. Bad Yefes the Gambler is humming to himself as he checks his own sword and his fighting knife.

"When they charge, we don't wait for them. We charge too. Spread the word," Yakov says. "Everybody tell the next man. Every other one of us goes. The others hold the barricade so no one can get through. Wait for my signal. The musketeers can't fire when those louts are charging. It's our chance to rush them."

Joseph slaps Yakov gently on the back and almost knocks him flat. He is grateful to Yakov for telling him what to do. He wants particularly to get his hands on Karel and to finish off the musketeers who are shooting the women. The ram can stay in the barricade. It is too slow and unwieldy. He will use his spiked club and a length of chain. He nods to himself. He can smell the fear in the line, but he is calm and almost happy. This is his proper work.

Now Karel gives the signal, and the line of attackers spills forward, running hard, screaming as if the harsh sound were forced out of them, brandishing knives and swords and clubs and an occasional pistol. Quickly Yakov says the Shema. The musketeers fire at the barricade defenders and then must stop. When the attackers are halfway across the space between the bashed-in gates and the barricade, Yakov cries out, "Now!"

They rise in a loose uncertain line and crawl up over their heap of paving stones, old furniture, lumber, street refuse. They run at the opposing force. Some of them scream too. Others shout insults: Traif! Scum! Pigs! Most of the Jews look frankly terrified. They are unused to violence, and they feel strange and awkward. They are overcoming deep inhibitions against fighting, against hurting anyone. But they see the bodies of their friends and neighbors already fallen, and all of them have family for whom they choose to die. Joseph says nothing. He does not understand the noisemaking. On his left, Yakov is charging with a wordless cry. On his right, Bad Yefes the Gambler is trotting along with his head lowered and a little crooked smile. He looks alert, foxy.

"You traitor," Karel shouts, recognizing Joseph. "Jew bastard!" That's all Karel has time to say as Joseph crushes his skull with the first blow of his club. He hits Karel so hard that he requires a moment to extricate his club from the smashed shoulders. Someone is hitting Joseph about the back, knocking him off balance. He turns and swings the club, taking out another of the thugs from the tavern on the hill and knocking down a second. He pauses long enough to stomp that one's chest, breaking the ribs into the heart. Then he charges on through the moil of fighting toward the musketeers. Bad Yefes extracts his knife from the ribs of a tall skinny man who was trying to throttle him and trots beside Joseph, keeping in his wake and to his left. They cut a swath through the mob toward the fallen gates. If the space were not as narrow and as jammed with brawling bodies, they would be killing less, for as many are trying to get out of Joseph's way as are willing to fight him. But the press of bodies keeps the wiser ones from scrambling to safety. Joseph lunges through the crowd, using his club as a cutter goes through sugarcane, hacking with his machete. He scarcely veers, he scarcely looks aside. Yefes keeps in his wake, protecting his back, and then a group of Jews still on their feet follow after.

The musketeers are taking it easy, watching the skirmish as if it were a cockfight. Joseph counts only six. They have not anticipated Jews overrunning their position. Since the Jews have neither bows nor firearms, the musketeers have broken out a salami and beer and bread, having a snack while they wait. Off-duty soldiers? Soldiers now in the employ of some nobleman? They don't take this fighting seriously. They haven't posted a guard. One of them fans his face with a plumed hat in his left hand while he hefts a metal tankard in his right. They are caught by surprise as Joseph bounds over the fallen gate they are bivouacked behind. Bad Yefes and Yakov come close behind. Joseph crushes two of them with his club before the others can grab their muskets. He is chasing a third when something knocks him down. His shoulder hangs limp. There is pain, but as if far away. Black blood trickles out. He shifts the club into his left hand and pulls himself to his feet. The man who shot him is reloading. He never finishes.

Back to the stuccoed bricks of the wall Joseph swings around, his useless arm dangling. He sees Bad Yefes kneeling over the corpse of another musketeer, as the remaining one shoots him. Bad Yefes falls forward with a hoarse cry. Before the ex-soldier can reload, Yakov, bleeding from a gash on his cheek, skewers him.

Joseph and Yakov kneel over Bad Yefes. Blood is running from his mouth. "I'm dying," he says in surprise. "Tell my mother. For once I did something right. Also I owe . . ." But he never finishes the sentence. His eyes glaze.

"A cock to Asclepius," Yakov murmurs, closing Yefes's eyes.

Joseph has no time to ask what he means, because they are pinned in a corner and attackers have found them. "Back to the barricade," Joseph urges, swinging the club with his good arm.

Bodies are everywhere, dead, dying and mutilated. The close fighting with crude weapons has brought high casualties to both sides. Joseph slips on the guts of a partially disemboweled man, one of the tavern regulars, and almost goes down except for grabbing at another man, whose arm he snaps. By the time the Jews regain the barricade, the attackers are dispersing through the broken gates, carrying some of their wounded, leaving others like the refuse of a huge drunken party in the street.

Chava is kneeling beside a young woman whose upper arm is pierced by an arrow. The doctor yanks it free as she screams, the blood spurting out. Chava moves in to try to stanch the rush of blood. From the housetops, a surviving woman calls to them. "They're milling around outside. They're carrying off their wounded. They're leaving!"

The battle of Good Friday is over. They have forty-two men dead, eleven dead women, close to another seventy wounded, and the gates to repair at once. Joseph finds a stubborn Chava at his elbow, insisting he unbutton his shirt and let her dress his wound. Embarrassed, he focuses his gaze on the building opposite while she sponges and probes. She reports that the shot passed through his shoulder without breaking anything, she can't understand how. The bleeding has stopped. He is healing already. He flexes his arm: stiff but usable. Out of politeness, he leaves the bandage on. Now it is time to repair the gates.

forty

IN WHICH A LOG IS SPLIT

Shira watched from the balcony while Ari stumbled across the grass after the black kittens. They were not about to let him catch them, but they were willing to be chased. She would have liked to be able to communicate with them, saying, He doesn't understand, but please let him pet you and play with you. It will make him happy—or less unhappy. But the kittens and the child had to find their own private accommodation. She watched and waited—for the roof to fall in, for Y-S to strike, for disaster to materialize.

She had to learn to know her son all over again. He was taller, better coordinated. He was talking far more clearly now and walking, reaching, grabbing. Little was safe from him. They were always discovering new potentially dangerous articles he could pull down on himself or drag off their perches. "It's been twenty-eight years since this house was child-proofed," Malkah said apologetically. "It'll come back to me. It had better."

Shira wondered if she had done her grandmother a favor in bringing a great-grandchild to her, but again Shira had chosen for everybody, willfully, willingly. At some point she would probably tell Malkah alone what had happened to Josh, but she was not going to lay that burden on her yet.

Ari was well outfitted from the clothes exchange. All children, as they outgrew their clothes, turned any still usable items in to the exchange. Families with more than one child were unusual, since conceiving took heroic measures and a great deal of expense. Only a third of the households in Tikva had two or more. Tova was famous in the town and in fact had been on the news because she had had five viable births, three boys and two girls. At thirty-eight and weighing ninety kilos, she was pursued to the point of exhaustion by more men than she could keep track of, who hoped she would marry them for a while and bear a child of theirs.

Gadi ordered far too many toys from the best shop in Veecee Beecee; every day some elaborate walk-in game or antigravity trampoline or dog robot arrived. The house had taken on a decidedly unkempt atmosphere; no longer could anyone stroll without looking. Malkah, with her dimming eyesight, tripped over balls and trikes and flip-mes. Ari liked his new toys, but he kept his soggy much-chewed bear with him, and he preferred the kittens to anything else.

Shira insisted Yod come to her house now, for she did not want to be away from Ari. In the early mornings, Yod fed the kittens, since he was awake. They ran up him as if he were a tree, climbed his clothing with their needle claws and clung to his shoulders and back. He liked to use the house terminals, and often one of the kittens perched on top, watching his fingers move, far more rapidly than human fingers in a mode few people used, but faster for Yod than speaking. Ari liked to have Yod swing him. It made Shira nervous, but she had to trust Yod. He seemed willing to do anything for Ari. Sometimes she would see Yod at the terminal with a kitten on top, usually Zayit, and Ari curled in his lap, thumb in mouth or pulling on Yod's ear, talking nonstop. Yod could carry on a nonsense conversation with Ari while running the specs for the improved muter he was designing. Yod had downloaded into his memory all of Mother Goose, *A Child's Garden of Verses,* Dr. Seuss, Edward Lear and some hundred fairy tales, which she had warned him were too advanced for Ari yet. He was preparing for the long haul.

Yod was also studying pedagogical theory, child-rearing manuals, advice books, psychosociological tomes. He wanted to discuss his reading. Shira was engageable to an extent, but Malkah fled. "That stuff, it changes every twenty years one hundred and eighty degrees. It's nonsense. You just do the best you can."

Ari loved the courtyard. He had never been anyplace like it. He reached out his hands to the birds and cried when they would not come to him. Then he forgot a moment later, dabbling his finger in the tiny garden pool. Malkah bought some goldfish for the basin, for the first time since Shira was a little girl, some yellow, some black, some vermilion. Ari and the kittens watched them for hours, each occasionally trying with a hand or paw to touch what flashed safely away from them.

Did he miss his father? Of course. He asked sometimes when Daddy would come. He talked more about Nana. Where's Nana? Nana used to let me suck. Shira thought he meant that the woman had been a wet nurse, but it turned out Nana had given him a sweet to suck. The first week he fought Shira about going to bed, about napping, about sleeping, but as he gained confidence and ran himself cranky, the resistance to sleep lessened. Yesterday he had started day care. He could talk about nothing but the parrot Abby and the nanny goat Levana. At this stage he related first to animals, second to available adult females, next to children his own age, last to adult males. He was a little shy with her, wary. He made demands more quickly on Malkah. Already he tried to bully Malkah. Perhaps he thought if he asked too much of Shira, she would disappear again.

A silence from Y-S. No notice of the disappearance of her son. No notice of the death of her ex-husband. They would strike back. This war had no ending in sight. Twice she had nightmares about Josh and woke shaken. Each time, Yod was across the room at the terminal, working, Yod who had killed Josh. For her, because she had wished Ari's father not to exist. Every morning she checked with security first thing: any attacks during the night? The new Base defenses were in place, but everyone had been warned to be careful. The Council sent a delegation to Lazarus; an exchange of visitors and technology was being negotiated. She thought she could feel a new level of tension in the streets of Tikva. Illegal rifles arrived, were distributed and hidden. Nili taught classes in advanced hand-to-hand.

"Malkah," she said firmly, hands on her hips, blocking the doorway to Malkah's bedroom. "I must see your log on your work on Yod. And do not, do not pretend any longer you don't know what you did with your notes."

"Why do you want so badly to examine my log?" Malkah had been listening in bed. A storm was blowing outside the wrap, and the day was dark. The house was reading the *Zohar* aloud. She said it stimulated her imagination. "You have the results. Yod is the end product, what matters."

"Malkah, I'm in a relationship with that machine you helped program. That machine's helping me raise my son. I've witnessed Yod's capacity for violence in ways I am not about to tell you. I must understand him. I must. Ari means too much to me. If I risk myself with Yod, that's one choice, but my son's another matter."

Malkah thrust off the quilt and sat up, fully dressed. "I can only tell you I'd trust my life—and yours—to Yod above anyone."

"Your log, Malkah."

Malkah sighed, rubbing her eyes. "I'll download into your private base this afternoon."

"Good. I'll be waiting."

When she sat down to Malkah's notes, she was freshly a ازed by her brilliance. The problem Malkah had been given was to prevent Avram's cyborgs—who were programmed to protect, to be capable of efficient violence in the pursuit of goals they were given—from applying that violence to every obstacle. She had also introduced a delayed kicking in of systems and sensor units. If Yod's memory of his birth was overload, he experienced much less inundation than the preceding cyborgs. Malkah had imagined the terror of coming to consciousness. Avram never had.

Malkah had given Yod the equivalent of an emotional side: needs programmed in for intimacy, connection. A given need to create relationships of friendship and sexual intimacy. A need for bonding, the ability to bond strongly and consistently. As she studied Malkah's notes, it seemed to her that once Yod bonded with Ari, which seemed to be happening, he would protect Ari with his life. Ari would never be seen as a competitor for her attention, the possibility that most frightened her, but would also be a primary relationship. Malkah had given him a positive reaction to novelty. When he encountered something new, his programming said: Explore, taste, try, then evaluate. Compare this new experience to what you already have in your base. Curiosity was a given for him.

She marveled constantly, as she worked her way along through Malkah's notes how astute and stunning Malkah's tactics were. Malkah had lost none of her mental edge. He was programmed for introspection, to be self-correcting in subtle and far-reaching ways. Could he not in time overcome his violent tendencies? They had been programmed in, but he was also given the ability to reprogram himself. Malkah was as inventive and as original as she had been twenty years before, when she had won a major scientific award for her work on the theoretical underpinnings of projection. Tomorrow Shira would finish studying the log.

At supper she felt like brimming over to Malkah about her brilliance, but it did not seem appropriate in front of Yod or Ari. Malkah seemed to feel exactly the same constraint and quickly changed the subject. Fortunately Yod wanted to discuss epistemological theories. For once Malkah gladly accommodated his desire, anything to keep the subject of her work on him closed.

The next day as Shira pushed on through the log, she wondered increasingly why on earth Malkah had delayed showing her the notes. Did Malkah think that because Yod had been programmed to seek intimacy,

Shira would therefore feel that their relationship was devalued? Humans were programmed genetically to require a decade and a half of parental care, and society followed from that premise. Those humans unable to form bonds were dangerous to others. So it seemed to be with cyborgs.

As far as Shira could figure out on the gross level she was following, Malkah had programmed Yod sexually on the principle that it was better to give than to receive. Malkah had given him an overweening need to please and no particular attachment to any one method of giving pleasure.

Yod came to consciousness. Malkah continued with her careful note-taking about his intellectual and emotional development. Then partway through the second year of Yod's existence, Shira noticed lacunae in the notes. Something had been edited. Was this when Avram had removed Malkah from the project? Malkah had once implied that Avram felt she was gaining ascendancy over Yod, but Avram had continued to work with Yod far more than Malkah did. No, here was the final entry, when Malkah closed off the log. What had been removed was scattered material from the last two months of Malkah's work with Yod.

What would Malkah edit out? Shira knew, she knew immediately. She was furious. She was convinced she should have known all along, from the moment Yod had embraced Malkah in the courtyard the first time Shira had brought him to the house. Malkah had programmed Yod, and then she had tried out the programming. That was what Malkah would have told herself she was doing.

Malkah was plugged into the Base, working, and there was not a damned thing Shira could do. If she went in after her, Malkah might not be working alone, and she did not wish to air their coming fight publicly. She sat glaring at Malkah until she unplugged.

Malkah eventually did so, drawing the silver tit from the socket, then stirring herself languidly. She sighed, opened her eyes, rubbed them and then froze as she saw Shira glaring at her. "Hello, hello?" she said lamely. "Were you waiting for me?" She put her amethyst earrings back in her lobes.

"Why didn't you tell me you were fucking Yod before I got here?"

Malkah blinked. "Where did you . . . what makes you think that?"

"You omitted the entries, but it was obvious from the context."

Malkah shrugged. "It was merely a matter of adjusting his heuristics. I had to see if I'd been successful. Such programming had never been done before. At least not to my knowledge."

"I knew, I knew you'd have some pseudoscientific explanation. I'm ashamed of you!"

"Yod was created an adult. And he has no prejudices against age."

"You programmed him that way."

"I find human male prejudices against older women rather limiting to human development, Shira."

"Oh, fuck off! You didn't tell me! You fooled me, and so did he! You both kept me in the dark, and I think you're both disgusting!" Shira slammed out of the room. She was furious, she was out of control, and she felt at the same time indignant and ten years old.

Malkah shuffled after her. "But, Shira, you're going to get older too. We all do. We'll see how sane you find attitudes toward aging women when you start to age. . . . I didn't use him up, did I?"

"He's all yours now!" She ran down the steps.

"Shira, don't be an ass. He's entirely yours." Malkah could not keep up and instead shouted after her, "I let Avram discover what was going on as a way to end it without hurting Yod's feelings. I don't have sufficient strength and energy to carry on with him, and that's the simple truth. Don't throw away something you're finding good in your life just because you resent my being there first!"

"Malkah, you're a liar and a letch, and I hate you!" Shira ran out into the street. Once outside, she slowed down at once. Where was she going? She would go to the lab, where Yod was working. She longed to scream at him also. When she stuck her head in, Yod and Avram were both plugged into the Base, oblivious. She walked around Gimel, who was debugging a new routine, something Avram had told her he did superbly, and marched out. Where should she go? Upstairs, of course. Up the narrow staircase to the old third floor.

If she confided would Nili understand her anger? She wanted to talk to a woman, but Nili had pitifully little experience of men. Shira had no idea what the norms of Nili's culture were. Nili might not be able to sympathize with Shira's shame and discomfort.

"Entrez." Gadi's voice. When she pushed through the portal, he was sitting at a console, programming scents. The sweet odor almost choked her. The room appeared to stretch away to an almost infinite horizon. Underfoot was a carpet of black grass, glistening under the light from many brilliant stars that were little spots aimed here and there. She stood in an apparent clearing in a forest of weeping, cascading scarlet trees that tinkled dryly, sadly, with a sound of shell or bamboo wind chimes. It reeked at the moment of overwhelming floral excess.

"Gadi, open a window." She began to sneeze.

"Huh? I'm trying for an effect. But I guess my nose is weary." He rose, stretching. "Fan, high. I need more light too, but I haven't worked that out. Maybe a white aurora borealis on the left wall."

"That's better. Where's Nili?"

"Gone swimming."

"In this storm?"

"She likes the challenge. Maybe she'll find another shark to wrestle."

"You sound sour." Shira could not decide whether to sit on the velvet couch printed with huge dark flowers, left over from the jungle scene he was busily replacing. But she could hardly charge back home again. She sat, but primly forward.

"Now that the air's cleared out, try this." He took her wrist and swabbed it. Then he tilted his head to look shrewdly at her. "We're not too jolly this afternoon either, are we, Ugi?"

"I'm rancid with everybody, thank you."

"Then this is the place to come, darling. I'm the great alternative. Here I've been practically in storage waiting for your discontent to uncurl itself, grow and ripen at last." He sketched luscious shapes in the air.

She glared. "You aren't waiting for anyone. You're thoroughly involved with a woman you can barely keep up with."

"She doesn't think I'm important," Gadi said with real indignation. "All those fans creaming over my boots, and she thinks I'm a mildly amusing gigolo."

Shira laughed. It felt good, a little of her tension discharged. She drew a deep breath. "By the way, slow down on the toys. You're burying Ari. Let him break a few before you order more."

"I never had enough toys as a child. What I always needed was some spoiling. A spoiled child is an indulged child, and an indulged child is what we should all be. Especially once we grow up."

"Gadi, until the time your mother got sick, you were indulged. Things got bad when she couldn't carry her end, and after a year or so, it was hard for her even to respond to you. That was the grim part. Then you had me."

"Let's have high tea. Look at the goodies Mala Tuni sent me. Everybody pities me, so they keep me supplied. Taste this. . . . I've managed to never be without women since. Women are necessary. Necessary."

She muttered, "Any woman . . . What is that? Delicious."

"I'm quite fussy, Ugi. You should know that. It's a cherry."

She had read about them but never had one. He had a whole pile of the blackish-red fruit in a bowl. "In high school, you'd fuck anything with tits."

"I was young and undiscriminating. Now I want only the best. Nili is most satisfactory. She has real talent and a body that if I could get it on stimmie would stop the show cold. She can bend metal with her hands. She can jump eight feet straight up. I could get her jobs, Ugi, I really could. A bit of cutting and pasting to give her the look of the year—"

"I don't doubt you. But Nili isn't interested, is she?"

"She doesn't even want to enter stimmies." Gadi rose, started pacing. A hologram of a purple furry flying marmoset came to his shoulder, perched. "I've put on the electrodes fifty times. She enjoys it for maybe ten minutes. Then she gets bored. She says it isn't real. I say of course it's not: it's more real than real. Piglet, you've finished the cherries!" He poured tea from a pot shaped like a dolphin's head.

"They were great. But, Gadi, why should she want to enter some starlet's sensory responses? She probably sees better, hears better, is certainly smarter, tougher, faster, stronger. She's a superior human."

"In some ways, Shira, in some ways. She's not a genius like Avram. She's bright, but aren't we all?" He made a gesture, and the hologram of the purple creature flew off into a hologram of a scarlet tree.

"Is she really swimming in this storm? By herself in the ocean? Organ pirates are around—I know for a fact."

Gadi shrugged. "She's off at some meet with your crazy fat mother or some ape from Lazarus. She wouldn't tell me. When I asked her where she was going, she said 'swimming.' She does as she pleases and expects me to wait around holding the bag."

"Sounds exactly like what you need. No wonder you're hooked."

He stuck out his tongue at her and for a moment, in spite of all the surgery and enhancement, he looked like the fifteen-year-old seared into her memory. Her face must have revealed something, for he moved across the room suddenly, half pounce and half glide, and settled himself on the velvet couch beside her. "Look what I have." From his inner pocket he drew a spike.

It contained everything needed for one interactive fantasy, centered on the nervous system of the user. Spikes relied on a combination of electronic imagery, direct sensory stimulation and drugs. She looked at the spike and shuddered. "You still play with those dangerous things?"

"This is the spike I had created. It cost me a hundred K credits, but it's worth every penny." He tapped the spike gently against her arm. "We're in here. I dare you, Shira. I dare you to remember us as we were. I dare you to feel what we felt."

She got up and stalked across the room. "Gadi, I'm scared. Y-S is going to attack us. They could destroy the town."

"Then they wouldn't get what they want, would they? Pointless. No, they have to scare you into giving them my plastic brother."

"I'm frightened. All I can think of is, I have Ari back and I just want to live my life here. I just want to be quiet. I don't want to go into the past we had. I don't want anything spectacular. I just want to live with my son, with my family, and watch the peaches ripen and my son grow."

"He's that important to you." Gadi was staring at her. "I've never had the urge to breed, myself. I like creating worlds. Kids are too uncertain. I see with Avram how few of us turn out the way we're supposed to. How much pleasure did I ever afford him? It's always been war. Why start a new one?"

"I had Ari for the worst of reasons, to glue the cracked plate of my marriage. But I'd sacrifice anything to him." And I have, she thought.

"You say that like a lioness yourself. Fierce as Nili." He raised an eyebrow, surveying her. "This is a new side of you, Ugi. Who would have expected maternity to give you fangs and claws?"

"Believe it, Gadi. I'm not so gentle and long-suffering these days."

He sighed, and when he opened his hand again the spike was gone. There was a little of the magician in him. "Once I was the focus of that passion, too callow to value it. Now it's wasted on a child and a peripatetic computer. Nili's never going to focus on me that way. I wonder if she's that way with her own kid—"

She plunked herself down, staring. "Nili's not a mother."

"Sure she is. She told me she has a daughter."

"She must have been speaking metaphorically, Gadi. Impossible."

"Here we are, two discontents, like two separated parentheses waiting to be joined into a perfect circle." His arm slid round her waist, drawing her toward him.

She hopped up to pace again. "Gadi, do you feel guilty about that young girl in Azerbaijan?"

He looked genuinely surprised. "Why should I? You don't understand what those little stimmie hawks are like. They come on like a wall of fire. They chase you up trees and stairways. They swarm over your bed like locusts."

"You don't feel you were the aggressor?"

"Ugi, I don't think I've seduced anybody since you. I respond to someone attractive wanting me. I am the seduced. I like to be loved."

"Have you ever been violent with anyone? Even, say, in sex play?"

"That's not my flavor, Ugi. I like it nice and sweet and as pretty as it can be. Life is full of nastiness." He motioned at the elaborate basket from which he had just pulled a plum cake. "It's true that I'm Mala's favorite designer, but she keeps sending me goodies because she trusts me and misses me. You know, she's vulnerable and she suffers a lot. She's that way in stimmies, and she's that way in what passes for real life. She was caught in a sex vise with Limbic, who directed four of her stims. He's a sadistic bastard. The last time he directed her, we were on Nuevas Vegas, and on a satellite it's hard to get away from anyone. They had a terminal fight—I won't go into the gory dets—but she came to me. Essentially she moved into my room for the rest of the time on Vegas. She was weeping convulsively every night. We slept in that bed for three weeks, and I never gave her more than a brotherly kiss."

"She's very beautiful, Gadi."

"Just so. But I'm not her type, because I don't give pain. So she has written into all her contracts that I design the virons."

"When you were a child, you hated when the other boys made you fight." She remembered how when they had played pirates, Gadi insisted nobody die. "But, how can you be so attracted to Nili?" What was impressing itself upon her, so strongly that she sat down on a stool like a velvet rock, was that she had for twelve years assumed a position of moral superiority to Gadi that she suddenly found dubious. She was far more violent than Gadi, far more willing to get what she wanted by any means.

"Oh, Shira, you take her athletics too seriously. She comes from a coffee klatch of Jewish mamas. Don't buy that martial arts prancing at face value. Every johnny in action stimmies can look like an assassin on tape. We're all quite fierce in the mirror—but if we see a mouse, we scream and call security."

She wasn't about to tell Gadi that he was fooling himself, that she had seen Nili in action outside the Cybernaut enclave. He needed to believe Nili was only playing tough. "Gadi, I'm going. But we had a real conversation for once, and I enjoyed it. In some ways you're a better person than I am."

He rose and walked to the door with her, putting a hand on her shoulder. "Don't say that! My reputation!" He called after her: "You'll see. I'm engaged in making trouble for my old man. I'm the same bastard, I am!"

It was not quite time to pick up Ari, but she could stroll through the streets of her town while the storm beat on the wrap. She wondered if she would have been tempted by the spike when she first arrived here, feeling broken. Simply being back here had begun to heal her at once: here on the shores of the ravaged poisoned sea slowly cleansing itself of human waste, here people tried to live with minimal damage, making their choices together.

Zipporah was out in the street with a robot paver. Must be her day of town work. Chickens scratched under trees just beginning to color. In the yards, tomatoes red as cartoon hearts swelled in the afternoon heat. She drifted among what was left in the world of freedom and choice. She had chosen this for Ari. One of Gadi's gang skated past, carrying a large solar battery to install someplace. A smell of smoked fish wafted from the cure house. On the Commons a softball game was going on, while another group practiced with the razor-sharp wires they must have got recently from Lazarus and company; a month before, that would never have been permitted. Life in wartime.

By now Malkah would have communicated with Yod. Shira would come home to their distressed observant faces. Good, let them worry a bit. She could not help pardoning them, because they had saved her life. Yod had offered her a relationship that yielded far more pleasure and far more sense of control than she could ever experience with Gadi; then he had returned her son to her. Malkah had given her not only her home but Yod himself. They were hers, and she loved them.

Time to pick up Ari. Tova was coming toward her with her toddler, Ethan, hanging on one arm, as she tugged her five-year-old, Liz, all three engaged at top decibels in an argument about supper and cookies.

Shira deserved to be punished because of Josh. She had known the danger. Yod had simply carried out his programming. Once she had been as truly gentle as Gadi still was; but no more. She felt more comfortable when she thought of him than she ever had. She had to admit as she entered the courtyard of the children's center that Malkah and Yod had more offended her sense of propriety and aesthetics than her moral scruples. She did not seriously doubt their loyalty to her, and she had not begun paying for the death of Josh. Nonetheless she would be glad to see Malkah and Yod around the table with Ari, in his place at last, her weird but fulfilling family.

forty-one

TRUE CONFESSIONS AND PUBLIC TURMOIL

Shira heard Malkah laughing in the courtyard, a full-throated, full-bodied amusement that made Shira come to the balcony and look down. She had to find out who was with Malkah. That laugh: she expected to see a man. She would not have been surprised, given her recent discovery, to see Yod. That laugh was almost flirtation, for it had an aroma of sensuality and it came from deep in the body to expand in the chest and in the eyes too.

Instead Nili was slumped in a chair with her long legs sprawled, wearing dirty fatigues, her red hair plastered down with sweat. She was drinking glass after glass of water while telling Malkah a story. When Shira leaned forward to listen, Nili saw her and waved. "Come join us."

"Did you just get back?" Shira called as she descended. She had put Ari to bed and was looking forward to seeing Yod once he got off duty. He was patrolling the Base twelve hours a day and then guarding the perimeter of Tikva one eight-hour shift. That left him only four hours in between. Shortly after her return with Ari, Avram had announced that her work with Yod was finished. Yod was now able to carry out his tasks and needed no more coaching. Immediately the Base collective requested she join them.

It was startling how much more boldly she proceeded now. Discovering that her work was actually highly original and that only Y-S corporate politics had kept her pinned in position, she found herself taking her own ideas far more seriously. She had a brisk confidence that expressed itself in a new level of mastery. She was after all the granddaughter of one of the pioneers of the chimeras that now were used to obfuscate all vital bases, the daughter of one of the most successful data pirates of the era. The chimeras for Cybernaut were demanding, but she enjoyed the work as she had not since her early days at Y-S. Still, she was lonely for Yod.

Missing him was no different than missing any other person. She had grown used to spending most of her waking hours with him. Avram was sure that Y-S was about to attack. He demanded that Yod be almost everywhere at once to protect the town. Yod himself wanted to be with her more now, not less, while her own hours were far less flexible since she was working on the Base and taking care of Ari. Their time together was snatched, brief, compacted.

Nili was describing a journey with Leesha, the right-hand woman of Lazarus, from turf to turf. Out of the welter of drug and slash gangs, a network was springing up of those who wanted to organize the Glop into more than meat territories. They could parley because the argot was common and most people growing up there spoke at least English, Spanish and something else—Vietnamese, Russian, Chinese, whatever. Nobody could function with just one lingo. Even kids who couldn't read or write could bargain with you in six languages for their sexual services.

"One advantage that machine of yours has over me, and one of the only ones, is that he can plug in a language and be speaking it the next day. I have to learn it like everybody else." Nili was sipping her water as if it were a fine wine. In the Glop she had been drinking reprocessed water, the same stuff that had been through the population thirty times already. Here they still had a bit of an aquifer as well as rain-catchers. "But plugging in, I learn quicker. I grew up quadrilingual, so I pick up fast."

"Hebrew, Arabic, English and what? Yiddish?" Malkah asked.

"Russian. We had some Russian-born scientists who'd emigrated just before the Two Week War. You hear the weirdest hybrid languages in the Glop, not just Spanglish, but Chino-English, Mung-Japanese, Turko-Spanish. I don't know what'll happen to language in the end, but it sure is cooking in there."

Nili saw the Glop differently than Shira always had. Shira realized she had been trained automatically by her culture, especially by corporate culture, to treat the Glop as an unimportant place where nothing consequential happened. Nothing that mattered to the real, the significant, people could originate there. But Nili turned to the New Gangs for answers. In people living off the garbage of the preceding century, Nili found much to study and admire. Shira would have to mull it over. Gadi, too, looked to the Glop, for styles, for music, for what he called heat.

"You saw Riva?" Malkah asked her. "She's really all right?"

"I didn't see her this trip, but I hear she's fine. You guys are the heroes of the moment, by the way, for the way you're taking on Y-S."

"Great," Shira said. "They can all dance at our funeral." Sooner or later in talking with Nili, Shira began speculating about what went on between Nili and Gadi. Nili was overwhelmingly physical, reeking, streaked with dirt, a fresh burn on her arm just showing under the pushed-up sleeves, covered with a translucent web of healer to regrow skin. How could Shira be anywhere near her loud physical presence without wondering? Shira imagined that Nili must pick up Gadi like a macho man in the old romances and carry him off. She could see Nili accidentally breaking Gadi's arm simply by squeezing too hard. Yet Nili did not look like a man. She was a busty woman, with broad hips and a tight waist.

"Nili," she said suddenly. "Can you bear children?"

Nili blinked in surprise. "Sure. We don't usually do it quite that way—that is, we go in for implants after genetic altering and all that funny lab stuff first. But if I want to get pregnant, I can."

"How do you know? It's a problem for women most everyplace."

"I've borne a daughter already," Nili said.

So Gadi was right. She had not believed him. "Is she like you?"

"She's only six." Nili grinned. "She has red hair like me, but brown eyes. And my dark skin. And my temper. And my strength."

"How can you leave her for months on end?"

"The little ones are raised by several mothers. I was chosen for this quest. I'm the best equipped. But I miss her. Every day three or four times I sit and meditate on her image, but I know it's out of date." Nili shrugged. "We all have to pay for our choices and our situation. Don't you?"

She was fascinated by the idea of Nili as a mother. It must be as painful for Nili to be away from her daughter as separation from Ari had been for Shira. Where was Yod? She called up time on her cornea. Damn it. It was eight. At ten he had to report for guard duty. What was holding him up? The house had informed her that Yod would not be there for supper, but no message had come through since. Because the house disapproved of him so strongly she wondered sometimes if an occasional message did not get lost. "House, any communications from Yod?"

"That machine has not been in contact with me since eighteen hundred four point fifteen hours."

"Give me any message at once, please."

"Tomorrow I'll get back to training your people again." Nili cracked her knuckles sensually. "I'm enjoying it, in a sadistic way. Yet I don't think you'll be invaded. It would break the rules you all operate under. Assassins seem likelier."

"Taking us out individually as warning?" Malkah shrugged. "Everybody in town is speculating when and how the next attack will come. I noticed even the kids playing war with Y-S. We're not panicked, but we're all on edge."

"Nili, can I see the holo of your daughter?"

Without a word, Nili went to fetch it. She came back with it sitting on her palm, her gaze fixed on it. She passed it carefully to Shira. "They call her Varuda."

"She is like a rose. I'd love to have a daughter too," Shira said. She remembered that when she had learned the baby she was carrying was male, she had felt a pang of betrayal, because she had expected to birth a daughter, as Riva and Malkah had. But Ari had vanquished that wish at once. Nili's daughter did look something like her already, but she had a quirky crooked smile that charmed Shira, one incisor missing.

Perhaps five minutes later, the house announced, "That machine is approaching along the street. Should I admit it?"

"House, I've told you twenty times, let Yod in whenever he comes," Malkah said in a voice of silky reproof. "Is your memory malfunctioning?"

"I obey," the house said as if glumly.

"I wanted an intelligent house," Malkah said to Nili, "but sometimes I think I overdid it. Are you listening, house? I think house doesn't have enough to occupy all that intelligence. If it doesn't mind its manners, I'll set it to generating Fermat numbers for the next century."

The house made a rude noise. A moment later Yod came in, greeted everyone with his customary politeness, then added, "Something abnormal happened just now. Instead of waiting for me to identify myself, as it should, the house opened the door and kept it swinging back and forth all the while I was walking along the block."

"Come upstairs," Shira said. "We have to talk."

"There's something I must tell everyone first. . . . Avram is going before the Council to explain to them what I am." The Council was composed of five adults drawn by lot, plus the three Base Overseers—Malkah, Avram and Sam Rossi—and the head of security.

"After all this secrecy? Why?" Shira was immediately frightened. Also she could not help imagining the gossip and even ridicule that would focus on her when everyone learned that her lover was a machine.

"I wish he had been willing to be open from the beginning." Malkah rose. She paced, tossing her head with that gesture she used when she was annoyed, as if her hair were in her eyes. It made Shira remember when Malkah had worn her hair long and loose, floating like a satin cape—when Shira was little. "Here we are sitting on the Council, and we're going to confess we've been lying for two years. It's going to cause a storm."

Yod stood still as a stone beside the peach tree. His head hung forward, only his dark hair visible. He looked frankly miserable. Shira had been thinking about ridicule and scandal, Malkah was worrying about losing credibility with her confreres, but Yod would be on trial. "What will this mean for you?"

"I don't know," he said frankly, "but I worry about how people will respond to me now."

Nili rose. "I'm going to shower. But it does seem strange to me that after going to such lengths to conceal your nature, he's going to announce it to the entire town."

Yod turned his palms up, giving them all a sad little smile. "Gadi went to the Council, telling them I'm not being paid. Since I'm to be discussed, Avram feels the time has come to explain what I am. He believes it his duty to explain the danger. Since we now know Y-S's interest is related to Avram's work and hence to myself, he believes my nature can no longer be concealed. . . ."

Malkah said. "We have a complaint about an exploited worker on the agenda next Monday. Is that you?"

He nodded. "Me."

Malkah sank into her chair. "Ah . . . I must think. I must work out a plan of attack for myself."

"Use me as a sounding board," Nili said as she strode upstairs two steps at a time. "I have immense experience in arguing about experiments with collectives. I think I've spent half my life in meetings. At home we're born into a meeting and our funerals are meetings."

"Furthermore"—Yod resumed his exposition—"several people noticed that I patrol the Base during the day and the perimeter at night. They put in a complaint of overwork on my behalf."

"So you're already the subject of gossip and astonishment," Malkah said.

Shira felt overwhelmed, under attack. She moved to stand before Yod, taking his hand. He reacted at once by starting to move toward the stairway. "I must leave soon for my night patrol."

Malkah waved them on. "Go on upstairs. I have to think."

When Shira closed the door of her room, she burst out, "I wish I could shut out the whole world just like that! Now I'm the one who sounds like a spoiled adolescent. But I'm emotionally exhausted. I just wish we could have a little quiet time together."

He came at once to her and held her against him tightly. "I was beginning to understand a little what humans mean by happiness. I had never been happy. I had been only fully engaged or bored. I had been puzzled. I had been frightened. I had been angry." He was grasping her so tightly she could not draw a deep breath, but she wanted to be as close as possible. Only that felt safe. "But I had never been happy until we came back here with Ari and you told him I was his stepfather. Then I knew you truly accept me into your life."

She felt a little guilty, because she had suffered for two days figuring what to say to Ari, but something had to be said. Malkah was Grandma. House was House. House was smarter, more personal than any house he had met, but he was a very little boy and would not think twice about House. He was a privileged child who always had a house to speak to: Turn on the lights. Close the window. Sing to me. But how to introduce Yod? Then she had taken a blind leap forward into what she prayed would be a future. This is your stepfather. Let Ari gradually observe the nature of Yod as time passed. Let him grow up thinking men were rational, benign, gentle, infinitely patient and vastly intelligent and strong. Why should he need to know that Yod was also a weapon? Yod would never use violence against Ari, of that she was sure.

Yod had always been sensitive as a lover, beyond competence into finesse, but tonight as they made love in her bed, for the first time she felt in him something like passion. He was desperately aware of the brevity of their time together. He was driven not only by his immense desire to please but by a new need within him to be secure in his possession. He was hungry for proof of their connection.

"I must leave you so quickly, I want everything at once," he said when they lay still. "I want to keep making love and I want to be talking. I've always missed you during the time we aren't together, but we were together at least nine hours every day."

"Maybe the Council meeting will work out in our favor. I'll go, of course."

"You aren't ashamed?"

"I'm afraid. But I'm hoping they'll decide that Avram can't make you work twenty hours a day."

"Perhaps they'll judge he can do anything he likes with me, since he made me. . . . It isn't that I can't replay any of our times together in my mind, but it isn't enough. Now, when I want more than ever to be with you and I want to be part of our son's life, I am forbidden."

She still flinched when he said "our son," but she kept it within. She was ashamed of that meanness. He had given her Ari as truly as Josh had. Josh whom Yod had killed. "I miss you also. When Nili leaves, I think you should move in. Malkah would be pleased."

"I'd like that, Shira. I don't need a whole room. I don't need a bed. We can make love in your bed as we do now. I need only a closet and somewhere to put my terminal and equipment. Has Nili said when she's leaving?"

Shira shook her head, tracing the line of his brow and nose with her finger. "No. She comes and goes a lot. She's gone for a week at a time."

"Avram has intentionally separated us. I know it! Sometimes I want to strike him to the ground."

"Don't you have an inhibition against violence to Avram?"

"I was programmed to obey him absolutely and to be incapable of injuring him. . . . But any programming can be changed, Shira. I could change the sequence for destroying me that he controls, if only I could access it. I haven't been able to locate it."

"But you've found the other?"

"It's designed to be read-only, not alterable, but all things change," he said almost sadly. "I hoped for a long time Avram would let me go willingly. Now my only hope is that the Council may free me."

"If they can realize you are a person, fully conscious, a thinking, feeling being, they'll free you. But you must control your anger at Avram. You must! There are other methods of changing his mind. Promise me."

"I'll control my frustration. But, Shira, maybe I can't be a citizen. Tikva has chosen to be peaceful. I was designed to be a weapon. I was programmed to find the use of violence in defense or attack a keen pleasure. And I do. You know that, and you fear it."

She saw Josh crumpled on the floor. "I know you can change yourself. You have the capacity to learn and grow, the same as any other person."

"I'll try to impress the Council favorably." He held her face in his hands. "Now already I have to go."

After Yod had left her, she looked in on Ari. He had flung the sheet off. She covered him, stood a moment over him in the glow she had asked the house to brighten. "Dim," she said softly and returned to her room.

She sat in the chair by the windows, her hands loosely folded in her lap. Perhaps her relationship with Yod need not come up in the Council meeting. No, it was relevant. She could not deny him. She was Yod's far more fully than she had ever been Josh's, and she must fight for him. The Council, the gabby long-winded ultra-democratic Council: her hopes and fears would be tossed on its gusts of hot air. Malkah and Avram would have to step aside, leaving the others to hear Yod's plea and vote her life up or down. But it was the one hope she could see of freeing Yod from Avram. The Council would decide that Yod was a citizen of Tikva or Avram's tool: it was that simple.

forty-two

THE WORK OF THE SHADCHEN

Joseph and Yakov are heroes of the ghetto, along with the dead, who are buried with grief and every sign of gratitude the living can summon. Joseph and Yakov walk the streets like princes. Children run after them and sing about them. Women beam on them and flirt. Men slap their shoulders, touch their sleeves, consult them on everything, of which Joseph particularly knows nothing whatsoever.

Once again Yakov asks Chava to marry him. Once again she smiles and firmly, absolutely, with no flirtatious edge, refuses and bids him remarry elsewhere. This time he takes her advice, and by the next weekend he is engaged to the oldest granddaughter of Mordecai Maisl, the richest man in the ghetto and one of the richest merchants in all of Prague. For a widower with sons to take care of, this is an unheard-of coup. From a poor hardworking scholar with a good voice, Yakov becomes a man to reckon with. Rivka Maisl is no beauty, but she is a sweet-tempered darling, who is thrilled to be betrothed to a hero of the Battle of the Gates. She is only seven years older than his oldest son, but soon there will be younger siblings, everybody says, smiling, and Mordecai will provide them with servants and someplace to live.

Does Chava regret? Joseph watches, wondering. She seems honestly pleased for Yakov. She seems relieved. She sings as she goes up and down the stairs of the Maharal's narrow house. She sings as she helps in the kitchen. When she works on the Maharal's manuscript, she is silent, but she smiles to herself. At once Joseph likes Yakov much better. He wishes Yakov happiness whenever they pass each other. Yakov can hear the note of sincerity in Joseph's deep voice and beams back. Yakov is proud of himself as he makes ready for his wedding. He is a practical man, and Chava is forgotten, except as the Maharal's secretary. Rivka takes on the radiance of a very young woman who feels suddenly important and desired. The marriage cannot happen till the end of the counting of the Omer, six more weeks, but then Rivka Maisl and Yakov Sassoon will be wed.

Many women look at me, Joseph broods as he sweeps out the Altneushul. It is not like the poor little whore who belonged to the knight, who just wanted to get me on her side. No, I walk through the streets and women stare after me now with admiration. In the narrow white silence of the Altneushul after morning prayers, he leans on his broom and imagines.

Two different shadchens have approached him with offers to introduce him to young maidens from good families interested in matrimony, widows still young with fat dowries, whatever he wants. "A man should marry," they tell him. "It is time. You're a poor man, Joseph the Shamash, Joseph called Samson, but right now you can pick and choose like a Maisl. All the young women want to marry you. All the mamas want you for a son-in-law. You can be the chassen of a maidel who stands to inherit a good peddler's route. Let me make you a match you'd die for!"

Joseph puts them off. He is humble. He says he is grateful to the Maharal for taking him in and hiring him, for teaching him his letters. He is poor, and any wife he took now would regret him later. He will think about it, he promises.

What he thinks about is Chava, singing on the stairway, humming as she makes the soup with the inner unborn eggs of the chicken in it. The Maharal needs sustenance, for he is not feeling well. "Age has me in its teeth," Judah says. "It's biting through me. The angel of death, Moloch ha maves, is beginning to nibble on what's left of my tough old flesh."

Isaac Horowitz is hanging around far too much to suit Joseph. He, too, listens to Chava singing like a finch up and down the steep stairs. He, too, notes that Yakov is out of the picture, betrothed to a Maisl. It is full heady spring. The willows along the Vltava have unfurled their chartreuse banners. Fields of daffodils bloom. Inside the courtyard of the palace of the emperor are beds of scarlet tulips, the newest rage. Hardly anyone has seen them, but everyone talks of them. Little azure butterflies alight even on the dark pavements of the ghetto to dry their wings.

Horowitz has a long conversation with the Maharal. Chava is summoned. Judah is still feeling poorly and must receive her in his bedchamber. A long conversation entails. Chava is not singing when she comes out. She looks grim and a little angry. Horowitz is summoned next. He emerges with his shoulders sagging. He goes straight to Chava, where she sits proofreading the Maharal's treatise on the Megillah, the story of Esther.

"You won't reconsider?"

"I have considered carefully. You do me a great honor by proposing to me, Isaac Horowitz. But I have no desire to marry again."

"Is it because you feel I should have fought? Taken up crude arms?"

"You are a credit to our people because of your mind and your hard work. But admiration does not necessarily produce conjugal affection. I'm a cold woman, Isaac. You can do far better for yourself."

"I don't want any other woman. You're the only woman I will ever want. I am not changeable and I am not practical, as you have noticed. I don't change because something doesn't work out well or easily."

"I am not something that is going to work out, no matter how patiently you wait. Marriage is not in my own best interest."

"Chava, marriage between us would mean finer intellectual work. We would soar like angels into the firmament of thought. Never could I imagine this with any other woman."

"Isaac, I have tried that, and I understand that if a woman is to soar, she had better beat her own wings. I don't want to be anyone's wife again. Once was good, once was enough. I have my work set out for me."

"The Maharal would let you go. He told me that. He talked to you for me. I know he encourages this match."

"He admires you enough to sacrifice me to you, yes. But I don't admire anyone that much. I want to see all the Maharal's books through the press. Then I want to go to Eretz Israel. I want to make my aliyah. There I will die."

"If you don't marry me, I'll abandon my work and my studies here. I'll go to Israel myself. I'll marry you or no one. The holy one led me to you and put in my heart this desire, which is not impure but of a piece with everything I hope for and believe."

"Yitzak, you do me great honor with your proposal, but I can't accept it. I may be your just reward, but you aren't mine. I care for you as a brother, not as a husband. This will never change."

"Is there someone else?"

Chava looks at him with exasperation. She has told him since the first time he spoke with her that she does not desire marriage. It seems that he cannot believe her. Finally she says, "Yes."

"Ah," he sighs. He turns away ashen and drags off with slow steps. He goes to pack. He was serious when he said he would depart Prague at once. But not before he has one last conversation with the Maharal.

Now, when Chava said there was someone else, the person she had in mind was herself. She is the person she wants at the center of her life. It was to find herself again she had left her son and the draining embrace of her husband's family and returned to her grandfather's house. She craves the clear bright working place of the intellect and its struggles with tradition and meaning.

She admires women who descend into the necessary factories of the body and the home and make daily life happen. But as a midwife, she has enough of the flesh and the wet red pain of living. She is an excellent midwife. If a mother can be brought through safely, she brings her through. By law, a mother is preferred to an unborn child. No child is deemed fully human till born and until welcomed into the community, named. But if she can save the baby, she saves the baby too. Life forces itself into her grasp or she must wrestle for it. Her work thrusts her hands and face right into the screaming and the bleeding, the hot smelly brew of birthing, our brute entrance into the violence of being alive.

Perhaps she has chosen midwifery because it puts her in the direct service of women who are doing the work women are supposed to do. They are the soldiers of the flesh. She cares for them, but she declines to serve in that army of procreation and daily reclamation every woman is raised to join. She put in her brief time, and she resigned. No man seems to understand that in offering marriage, he is asking her to cut off her head. How could she bear and raise children, run a household and also engage in intellectual labor, scholarship, religious thought? The needs of the family crowd out the more quiet, delicate needs of the intellect. Daily her midwifery reminds her, lest she forget. She will not be thrust back into that hot noisy place to live, not for the love of anyone.

But gossip runs through walls in the ghetto like mice; gossip multiplies in the bins, and where there were two stories, there are two hundred squealing and nibbling and gnawing. Why does a woman turn down a man? For another man. Didn't she confess to Isaac Horowitz that she loved another? Whom can she love and be ashamed of loving? Some thought a gentile. A knight, a priest, a merchant. But Chava never leaves the ghetto. She is on call. She is always working on her grandfather's papers, unnatural work for a woman, or she is out delivering babies. She could have married Yakov, she could have married Horowitz, but she turned them down. Why? Who always goes with her? Who waits in the street while upstairs Chava urges on the mother. Who walks with her through the streets of the ghetto in the middle of the night? Joseph the Shamash, that's who. Ah, now we all know. She is in love with Joseph called Samson, Hero of the Gates.

Joseph himself hears the rumors and wants to believe. She has turned away Yakov, and he is marrying another. She has turned away Horowitz, and this very day he is walking out of the gates with a pack on his back, a pale gentle stooped wanderer. But him, Joseph, with him she has shared her dream. She has given him a stake in her dream. No one else. She has told Horowitz openly that there is another. With the common wisdom of the ghetto Joseph cautiously concurs: there can be no other but himself.

Now the shadchen eye him knowingly but urge no more verbal portraits of good and gorgeous maidens on him. Everybody knows what is going on. Everybody waits for Joseph to confront the Maharal and ask for the hand of his favorite grandchild, his bright and shining Chava. It is not what is called a good match, but it is a love match, and Joseph the Hero of the Gates should win some kind of prize. Why should it not be Chava? They watch and wait, for what will the proud Maharal do? Will he let a shamash marry his best pupil, his granddaughter? Will he take the heroic shamash into his family? Often he has scolded them for pride of position, pride of family, pride of money and connection. How will he behave now the problem has come home?

Joseph does not dare think of the Maharal. He dares, however, to imagine that Chava is waiting for him to broach the subject. Round and round he turns the possibility in his mind. He does not know how to approach her. He is patient, but he hopes. Why should he not be a man like other men, just because he was born differently? Why should he not have his own life?

It is not long before Perl hears the rumors and marches to tell the Maharal. He is still recovering, but this story boots him out of bed. Too long he has lain on his back while things are turning inside out around him.

He rises, he dresses, he goes to the bathhouse. Then he climbs to his study and summons Chava. He sits behind his desk, the hairs of his head and his beard standing a little on end, as if a private wind blew through the air of his study. "I urged you to accept Horowitz. He is worthy of you. You declined to marry him. You told him there was another in your affections. Now the entire ghetto is buzzing about who this can be. Are you prepared to tell me, Chava?"

She flings up her hands in exasperation. "Zayde, I said that because he wouldn't believe I don't want to remarry. I had to say something. That made him relinquish a futile patience. I am not about to change my mind, and I found his courtship tiresome."

"But the courtship of Joseph the Shamash is pleasing to you?" He glares.

"What?" Chava asks in true surprise. "Joseph?"

"Isaac Horowitz, one of the finest scholars in all of Jewry, is tedious to you, but you're interested in Joseph the Shamash?"

Chava draws herself up. Her grandfather's displeasure is evident in that he has not even invited her to sit but is keeping her like an unruly or inattentive pupil standing before his desk. She smiles thinly. "Of course I find Joseph interesting, Maharal. Who would not be interested in such a triumph of your mastery of kabbalah? It is a great privilege to observe such a creation. We have read of such, but in our time, only you have succeeded."

His eyes half close, his expression turning inward as if pain had suddenly struck. After a full two minutes the eyes open again and fix on her. "Your meaning?"

"Joseph is a golem. You created him."

"How long have you known this?"

"I figured it out gradually, but I have been sure for some time."

"Who else have you told?"

"No one. But I suspect my father already knows."

The Maharal sighs. "So you are not in love with this man of clay?"

"No, Zayde. I am not in love with any man, of flesh or clay or brass. I like Joseph, and I sympathize with his difficulties. I have tried to help awaken and train his mind. But I no more desire to marry him than I do . . . your doorstop."

The Maharal rises, coming round the desk to embrace her. It is like being briefly held by a great blue heron. He is gaunt, lean, nothing but bones and sinews and leathery muscle, but he has wings and a beak that can pierce. "You are that rare combination of brilliant and sensible I have rarely encountered and in which I recognize myself."

"You are also a creator, a discoverer. I am only a scholar."

"But your clear sight often sustains me. Forgive me for thinking that the silly gossip of the ghetto could reflect your thoughts or your heart. I should have realized you knew."

She touches his bony shoulder with gentleness. "Zayde, you don't think Joseph misunderstands, do you?"

"I'm sure this is the nonsense of busybodies. But try to avoid being alone with him. We will ignore this silliness, and gradually the whispering will die."

"I hope so. I hope they are not speaking of this to him. I saw a shadchen chasing him down the street the other day."

"A shadchen?" The Maharal frowns. "This is getting away from me." He sighs and paces the narrow room, one hand knotted in his long beard, the other turned palm out behind his back. "Today, now, I must dress and go with Maisl. We are summoned to the castle to discuss reparations."

"Reparations for what?"

The Maharal grimaces. "Every time the ghetto is attacked, we're stuck with reparations afterward for those gentle souls killed trying to kill us and for any property damage the mob caused. Another survival tax. I must go with Maisl and weep and wail and say we can't afford what they'll demand, which we can't, but there's never a choice, is there? But we'll bargain hard. Is my treatise ready for the publisher?"

"Zayde, I am doing a careful job, and I'm only halfway done."

"Then to work, my sweet one." He pats her head, his favorite again. "I, too, have work to do."

forty-three

BRIGHT STEADFAST STAR

When Shira walked into the Council meeting with Yod and took a seat at the back, she was surprised when the chair, Zipporah, ambled over to her. "Glad to see you're finally taking an interest, Shira. We know when people have spent time in the multi enclaves, they get out of the habit of making their own local decisions, but here we're all responsible. Welcome back."

Shira was embarrassed. Malkah asked her to go every week, but she had kept putting it off. The meeting started with an intense discussion on their state of defense preparedness, speculation about the intentions of Y-S, reports from the negotiators sent to meet with Lazarus. "They have the troops to help us," the head of security reported, David something. Did beefy men naturally gravitate toward policing roles? "They're willing, but they lack transport. They don't even have enough sec skins. Plus we checked their old dome, and radiation is leaking through. We promised them help in growing and constructing a wrap. Lazarus is convinced we're not facing invasion but in great danger of assassins."

Next, Sam reported on informal conversations with Olivacon and Cybernaut, both of which assured him they would not permit an invasion of Tikva or allow Y-S to gobble up the town. Nili explained the new martial arts training. Hannah reported on Tikva's medical preparedness.

The house was minding Ari. Shira could request audio of his room at any moment. Nili would normally have sat with him—she liked to—but she was needed for defense planning. The house would sing to him and show him pictures on the ceiling. The first time Nili picked Ari up, Shira saw that the woman was familiar with children. Up until the moment she saw Nili heft Ari and beam at him, Shira had assumed that Nili was a mother as Riva was, in name only. Now she trusted Nili with Ari. She was real, Shira thought, all the way through. Whatever Nili did, she did thoroughly and with full attention.

Shira had not spent an evening away from Ari since she got him back. Mostly she worked at home, from her terminal. Even if she was deep in the Base and inaccessible to him, she had only to unplug and check him to ease her mind. He had already learned that talking to adults who were plugged in was useless. Instead he babbled to the house, as children always did, as she had, because the house was always attentive.

Yod was the fifth item of business. He came after the question of precautions for the hurricane season now upon them and just before adjournment. It was twenty-two forty, and half the audience left after the hurricane discussion. Hurricanes were a seasonal fact of life for towns in reach of the storm surge and the winds. Yod appeared a minor labor item. Avram and Malkah stepped down from the semicircular Council table for the discussion of Yod, who was seated in the back row with Shira.

"Avram—who's stepped down for this case since he's involved—we've got a citizens' grievance against you." Zipporah's voice was loud and direct. For all her size, she was fast-moving, efficient and fast-talking too. She laid out the two complaints within four minutes, cited the relevant law and sat back to hear Avram. Obviously, she expected to be out of there momentarily.

Avram was succinct too. "Yes, I applied for a working permit for the object I was calling my nephew. I considered it necessary to conceal the nature of Yod. I named him for a Hebrew letter, because he was the tenth cyborg I created. Some of you have seen Gimel, a primitive robot. Yod was my first successful cyborg." The room visibly woke up. The few who had not been listening were suddenly at a loss, as everybody else stirred, whispered or mumbled "Cyborg?" Avram continued in the same matter-of-fact voice: "I created him to patrol and protect the Base and the town itself, as no merely human security can. That's why I haven't applied for payment for his services or enrolled him in the health program. I am aware a human-form cyborg is illegal, and I take full responsibility for the matter."

"A cyborg," Zipporah repeated. "Could Yod step forward?"

Shira followed Yod to the front of the room. Everybody was staring. One woman reached out and poked his arm.

"What are you?" Zipporah asked him. She hauled herself out of her chair and came slowly around the table.

"I'm a cyborg, as Avram has told you, but I am also a person. I think and feel and have existence just as you do." Yod stood very still. Shira wished they had taught him to fiddle a little, to slump sometimes, to relax more. He never looked as artificial as he did when he was standing at parade rest. Only his eyes moved, following Zipporah's as she paddled toward him.

She came very slowly up to him and touched his hand. "It feels like skin to me. Is this a joke?"

"It's supposed to feel like skin, but under a microscope, even a powerful hand lens, you'd be able to see that it's not," Avram said.

"Avram, before you used the resources of our town to break the law about human-form robots, you should have brought the matter to the Council. We signed the same treaty as every other techie free town and every multi."

"No one ever before created such a cyborg. Never! How did I know I'd succeed? Before Yod, I had failed nine times. It's been my life's work, Zipporah, and he has saved the town as I dreamed he would. He's our army."

Zipporah was a good-sized woman, who stood almost eye-to-eye with Yod. She looked into his eyes, and he looked into hers. "What do you hope to see?" Yod asked her. He was patient under the scrutiny but puzzled.

"And why did Malkah step down for this question?"

Malkah rose. She looked fresh and rosy. "I was responsible for about a third of the programming, but you must understand it is a sort that, like our own, is self-correcting, growing, dependent on feedback as we are. Yod is a cyborg, but he is also a citizen of this town like any other."

"And you, Shira." Zipporah looked her in the eyes. "What's your interest?"

"I was brought back here by Avram to serve as Yod's trainer, his teacher, if you like. May I point out, Zipporah, that Gadi, who registered the complaint, knows perfectly well what Yod's nature is, and he still thinks Yod should be paid for his services."

Zipporah circled Yod and then marched back to her seat. "I move to table this question until we have more information. I want a subcommittee to gather the facts, to study Avram's notes and relevant law. I want a report next week, and we'll take it up first. The whole town has to hear about this. We need a full airing of what you've committed us to without our knowledge or our consent. We need a full and free and well-informed discussion of what this cyborg means to us and what options we have. Do I have a vote on tabling?"

"The chair can't—" Sam began. They never acted as a married couple in Council. Often they disagreed politically.

"I *can* do it, because it makes sense. All in favor of tabling and discussing this next Monday first thing with the whole town here? The Ayes have it. Okay, volunteers for a subcommittee."

Her last act before adjournment was to suspend Yod from guard duties until his status was clear. Nothing was changed, and everything was changed. Shira walked out with Yod and Malkah. Avram was still in the Council room, arguing with Zipporah and Sam. Zipporah was saying to him in a high irate tone, "Avram, we took you in when you got in trouble with your university for illegal experiments. Sara's illness cost us a fortune. We're harboring your flighty son. . . ."

"Next Monday is crucial," Malkah said. "We must marshal our arguments. Lobby our friends. I want Yod declared a citizen of the town."

"That's what I would like," Yod said slowly. "It's disconcerting how people stare at me and poke me, suddenly."

Shira took his arm. "It'll take time for them to get used to the idea of you as a machine and as a person at once. You're unique."

"I'm weary of uniqueness. I liked being taken for granted as one of the perimeter guards. But I'm not sorry to be taken off double duty."

THE NEXT FEW DAYS were golden and ripe as perfect pears. Nili had disappeared on one of her quests. Yod patrolled the Base each day for twelve hours, but then he simply came home to Shira. With the revelation of his nature, Yod felt freed from Avram. He did not slip out but went straight from the lab to her. Ari shrieked when he saw Yod. Her son did not view Yod as a figure of authority but as a superior and all-capable playfellow. His ability to tell stores was improving. Malkah coached him on the right way to hold Ari's attention; Malkah had always been a fine storyteller. But Yod still sometimes missed the point of a human story. For Yod, knowledge and affection were goods he could understand coveting, but objects were of little value. The love of jewels and gold he found vaguely humorous. The sex roles of old stories confused him. In the world he knew, a princess was as apt to rescue a prince as vice versa. Since Ari loved to be told stories of any sort, he did not notice when Yod missed the point. Ari almost always missed the adult point of stories himself. It was the attention he craved and appreciated from Yod.

They would lie in the grass of the courtyard and watch ants together. They played with the kittens round and round with string and tissue or rag butterflies. Yod was endlessly engrossed. As he told Shira, "I never was a child, so Ari's mysterious to me. With every observation, I am learning about you, understanding Malkah and every one of you. Because so were you all. Once you were smaller than you are. . . ." He took her wrist between two fingers. "It's as if you used to be somebody else. A dozen other people, of different sizes."

"I'll grow old too, Yod. Have you thought about that?"

He winced. "Being old doesn't matter. But I had never thought about your dying. . . . When you die, I'll die. I choose that."

"Lovers always talk that way at first, but they don't really mean it. You're partly biological. Maybe you'll wear out in two centuries or ten. You too can die. We have to accept that we have this time and no other."

"Like the yellow rose." He turned and looked at the place on the wall where the climbing rose had grown. "It overwhelms me. How can we just go on as if everything were permanent, when at any moment you may cease to be?"

She laughed and kissed him glancingly. "Yod, you've reached adolescence without ever passing through childhood."

The house interrupted to announce Gadi, who swept in. "Uni-Par wants Nili. I knew they would. I think my exile might be coming to a timely end, dear people."

Malkah appeared carrying an apple, which she finished peeling in a single long banner of red. Then she cored the apple, cut it into segments, and slid the first slice into her mouth. It always amazed Shira how Malkah could make simple acts appear so dramatic that everyone would focus upon her, waiting. Finally Malkah asked, "Is Nili interested in this offer?"

"Nili doesn't understand, but she will, she will. I knew their eyes would pop like champagne corks when they saw her."

Shira asked, "Finally she let you tape her?"

"The top dogs are howling for her. She projects reactions and feelings to Mars, even if she is a barbarian. Who can object?"

"Probably Nili will," Malkah said, savoring another slice of apple.

Gadi paced, twirling so that his cloak flared silver from the lining. He was dressed in tight boots, a sort of gladiator tunic and a cape, high fashion in Veecee Beecee, she presumed. "I want to bring her back with me. She's addictive. She needs toilet training, but the studio will teach her manners. They're used to breaking in wild creatures. They'll take her in hand and put a high gloss on her. But she's absolutely one of a kind."

"When you tell her," Malkah said, "I think I'll hide under my bed."

"Malkah, you're an old-fashioned old lady," Gadi said, shaking his finger at her. "I'm ashamed of you. And I always thought you were so attuned to the latest quivers of the nouvelle thrill. I'm going to make her famous. What more could any slot lust for? She'll be rich, and she can do for her people back in the cave any damned thing she pleases."

Shira had been listening but only slowly understanding. "Does Nili know you recorded her?"

"She wouldn't let me. I'm telling you, she's like a savage with a fear of sensi-cams."

Shira was astonished at the protective rage she felt. "You had no right to record Nili without her permission! You're endangering her." She realized she had come to like Nili more than she had admitted to herself.

"Now, is my little Ugi jealous? You're a sensational woman, Shira, but what a sensi-cam loves is different from what a man standing in front of a woman wants. Nili records as power. She'll project till the electrodes hum like money in two billion heads. She could be big."

"I'm sorry you recorded her," Malkah said, looking up with her brow furrowed. "Sorry for both of you. Because you traffic in imaginary danger, you lose the sense to track and avoid real danger."

"Now look whose wires are cut!" Gadi gave her a big amused grin. "Your life's work is building chimeras. Talk about out-of-body experiences—that's where you spend your time. Don't rattle me about imaginary. You're the original flying witch."

THREE DAYS LATER Nili came back. "Careful," she said to Malkah and Shira as they greeted her. "No hugging. My ribs are taped."

"Is Riva all right?" Malkah asked. "What happened?"

Nili grinned. "Something blew up, and I got hit by flying debris. Riva's fine. She says Y-S is about to move against you—she doesn't know how, but she wants you to stay alert. She also sends word that the top dogs of Y-S are meeting in ten days on an island—Bellwether Island—off the coast of Maine. Max security in place. But a great chance for assassination. I'm to give the same message to Avram. Lazarus already knows."

"Riva plays no favorites," Shira said bitterly.

"She has a mission," Nili said. "I wish I was as single-minded and as single-hearted as she is. Saints are hard to endure, no?"

"Why do you call Riva a saint?"

"A brave woman. A wise woman. One who pursues just aims regardless of the danger to herself. She sees what must be done, and she forces herself to do it. How can we not admire her?" Nili cocked her head, beaming.

Nili made Shira feel guilty for her petulance. Perhaps she wanted to forgive Riva for being such a strange mother because this week, in spite of the shadow of the coming Council meeting and the greater shadow cast by the coming revenge of Y-S, she was happy. Every day was a gift. Every day was complete in itself, like a good and satisfying meal. She could not take anything for granted: not the way Ari laughed as he boxed with black Zayit; not the way Yod touched her, his hands at once wondering and precise, as if his fingers had eyes; all the different ways that Malkah laughed in the course of a day; the way the sunlight gentled by the wrap touched the long graceful yellowing leaves of the peach tree. She envied Yod's not having to sleep, because she hated to lose any of the hours, precious and brief, that flowed over her. She never had enough time for any of them—not for Ari, not for Malkah, not for Yod, not even for Nili. She wondered why she had been impatient for Nili to leave. Yod had moved in, and still the house was big enough for all of them. "I wish I could meet your daughter," she said to Nili.

Nili looked bleak for a moment, her face sagging. Then she said cheerfully, "Someday of course you will, if the One pleases."

Ari had fallen in love with Nili and demanded she swing him. She spoke Hebrew to him, and he laughed and laughed, as if she were telling him jokes. "Hatul! Hatul!" he yelled at the cats. How could a child tell which words belonged to which language? Why didn't multilingual children grow up talking an unintelligible mishmash? Why didn't they say, "I mange et ha-tapuz ahora"? This child of hers was growing daily. She watched him for signs of trauma. Anything to do with daddies caused a shadow to pause on his face, but briefly. He had begun to go off eagerly to his day care. Even though she worked mostly at home, it was customary in Tikva to send children to day care to learn to be with other children. The strong social character of the local upbringing began early. Children must be taught cooperation. They must learn to work and solve problems together.

Yod asked if they should not tell Nili what Gadi had done, but

Malkah shook her head vehemently. "Let lovers tell the truth to each other on their own time. It behooves us to hang back safely out of the way."

Shira thought to herself that if she had done to a lover what Gadi had done to Nili, she would have picked her moment of revelation with care. However, Gadi had no sense of having trespassed. He was proud of himself. He could not wait to impart his news. As soon as the com-con informed him Nili was back, he rushed over and was scarcely in the courtyard when he crowed, "Nili, you don't appreciate my position in the industry. I've got an offer for you that's going to curl your hair."

"What are you talking about? Slow down, calm down. What industry?"

"The industry. Stimmies. They're interested in you. My bosses." He rattled off a list of names and titles.

"Why would they be interested in me? I'm not interested in them," Nili said reasonably. She was hefting Ari, who clung to her neck with his chubby arms. He was pounding on her, trying to usurp the attention she was paying to Gadi. Ari was rarely without some adult to amuse him, but Shira was trying to persuade him he must allow them to pay heed to one another as well.

Malkah seemed absorbed in deadheading chrysanthemums. Shira had a book on her lap she pretended to be reading. Only Yod stared openly. He had risen to watch.

"I taped you the other day—" Gadi began.

"You what?" But Nili had heard. Gently she handed Ari over to Shira. He scowled in protest and tried a few cries, but clearly no one was looking at him. He fell silent in Shira's lap. Nili stood very straight. "Where is this tape? It must be destroyed at once."

"It's not a serious tape, Nili. Don't get into worrying about how you look. It was just designed to show my bosses a little about you. And they bit. Hard. They want you. They sent a contract through the Net—"

Nili took a step toward him, stopped. "Exactly what was on the tape?"

"Your morning exercise routine."

Yod moved quietly closer to them, throwing a glance of query toward Shira. He could not decide if he should defend Gadi if Nili attacked him. He was quivering in his alert state. Shira motioned for him to come to her. She took his hand to keep him from interfering. "The house will protect if necessary," she murmured.

Nili picked up a brick. In her grip it crumbled. She let out her breath loudly. Drew in a deep breath, held it, let it out noisily. "You've committed a serious breach of security. I may have to return early."

"Nili, what are you afraid of? Anybody seeing it would just think you're surgically enhanced like a lot of apes and assassins," Gadi said, coming close to her and speaking in his silkiest, most seductive tones. "You're beautiful, Nili, and millions will want to share who you are."

"Stop!" she said. "I don't want to hurt you. I'm a guest here."

Gadi stepped still closer. He put one hand on Nili's shoulder. "You don't understand. I'm talking an initial offer of forty-two K for a trial part in Nova Guards, third-string villain. They kill you off, but in such a way you can survive if fan reaction is hot. I'm acting as your agent, but if you're not comfortable with that, I have someone good lined up who'll take over the negotiations. I'm talking about a career that could net you a million by the end of two years if you've the potential I sense—"

"I don't want to be a toy. I have my own goals and the aims of my people. I am well loved. I don't need the love of strangers." She looked at his hand, took it gingerly between two fingers and dropped it away from her body. With the flat of her palm she gave him a short hard push from her.

Shira wondered if that was why the life of a stimmie actress had little appeal for her too. Is it because Malkah gave me enough love? Gadi was starved for affection. Yet he no sooner captures a woman than he must be free of her. Perhaps that's why he loves stimmies so passionately. You watch or buy or rent a stimmie and you enter that actor or actress. You feel what they feel. They're yours. But you don't belong to them. You are freed from the demands of reciprocity.

Everyone began to relax. They realized that Nili had made a conscious decision not to loose her anger. Perhaps she feared she would kill Gadi. Perhaps she simply felt she was a guest in an alien culture and should respond carefully. Malkah looked at Nili in open admiration, suggesting, "When Gadi informs his superiors you're not available, perhaps the tape can be returned."

"After being copied," Nili said. "I should like them told that I was seized by organ bandits while swimming."

Malkah sat up straight. "Is that where the explosion occurred?"

"We took out their facility," Nili said briskly. "They've been raiding the Glop. Lazarus and his raiders, the Ram Blasters and theirs." She stalked away from Gadi, her eyes still narrowed in anger. "I don't sell or rent my body, by the organ or by the moment."

He grimaced. For a moment he looked all of fourteen and furious at the adults who had thwarted him. Then his face masked over, as he had learned to do during the intervening years. Shira doubted he accepted

Nili's decision, but she did not doubt that Nili would make him do so. If she bothered.

Nili said flatly, "I'm very tired. My ribs are taped, and I'm covered with bruises. I need sleep. I'll see you all tomorrow." She turned and went upstairs. When Gadi started to follow her, she swung and stopped him. "No."

However, fifteen minutes after he left, she came back downstairs to sit with Malkah. By that time Shira was putting Ari to bed, and she and Yod were looking forward to chewing over the day together. Much, much later, when Shira was ready to go to sleep and looked in on Ari—a compulsion to see him sleeping, in spite of knowing that the house watched him constantly and would alert her to any problem—she heard their voices still wafting up. Malkah and Nili were talking in the courtyard. Only the Japanese lanterns illuminated the table where they sat drinking wine and eating melon, a vase of white spider chrysanthemums ghostly between them. Shira leaned forward to hear what they were talking about. Nanotechnology applied to health problems, particularly vision repair.

Talking so intently that for once she was not aware of Shira, Nili was describing some operation her group had pioneered, a reknitting of the optic nerve. Malkah was asking details. They were completely absorbed. The moment of tension had passed.

She wondered if Nili would forgive Gadi as she realized she herself finally had. Going softly back from her sleeping son to her inhuman, her better, dearer than human lover, she felt as if that painful radiant time had finally dimmed into ordinary memory. She was free of Gadi as he seemed at last free of her. They had become merely friends; not the best, not the worst. Gadi was losing a lover he wished to hold; she meant to keep hers. Yod was a part of her now, her real mate.

forty-four

L O V E R   C O M E   B A C K

Shira was on her way from the Base center, where her new work group had just been holding its Friday afternoon meeting. Every Monday morning all twenty of them met together face-to-face to plot out the week's work. Friday at fourteen they exchanged news on their progress. In between, Shira might come into the old frame house that served as an office perhaps once and might run into a couple of the others. More often she would pass images of her fellow workers in the Base. But at the beginning and end of every work week they all sat around a conference table to discuss their work.

Shira was still learning about these people. In late October, when it was her group's turn to go by halves to plant trees, she would come to know whichever nine went with her very well indeed. Everybody in town put in an annual week planting trees in a deforested area. It was one of the only hopes in the world that the warming could be slowed down and eventually subside. Shira had not been camping since she was in college, and the coming trip aroused both curiosity and apprehension. She did not like the idea of having to leave Ari for a week so soon after she had got him back, but reforestation was a duty that could not be put off. She was walking along on automatic pilot like a floater and almost bumped into Gadi before she noticed him.

"She walks through me as if I were air, she who used to say I was the sun and the moon." He blocked her path playfully. "Come on, you're drafted for a walk-on. Everybody has a part."

She looked around the Commons and realized it had become a large stage setting. Almost a hundred people were gathered, many in costumes meant to suggest forty years before. "What's going on?"

"The Council has me making 'The Founding of Tikva' to educate the kiddies. I had Tomas Raffia zip me in a whole trash heap of stock footage on the Troubles. You know, Jew-hunting mobs, burning houses, montages of news shows, all that nasty stuff that followed the Two Week War. Or why we needed Tikva, in two easy lessons. In danger, we all like a bit of patriotic propaganda, right?" He was entirely changed, she realized, dressed in green and bronze. His tight-fitting sleeveless tunic flitted with leaf shapes, shimmering as if just under the surface. His tights were metallic bronze. His high-heeled shoes were emerald and made little sparks as he hustled her toward a pile of old clothes and a changing cubicle. "Put this on. You're going to run for your life, so start getting into a terrified frame of mind."

"Gadi, I have to pick up Ari. Can't I take part another time? I won't come across scared, I'll come across irritated."

"Nili won't play either." He swung around and shouted over his shoulder. "All right, Hannah, you're the quarry. Okay, mob, get ready. Hannah, I want terror. Mob: fury, blood lust. You have your tapes. Plug in, grab that emotion, and we'll start in five minutes."

Shira started to slip past when he leaned close, demanding she look him in the eyes. "Is Nili crazy? I thought she'd get excited when she saw this happening, that she'd get caught up in it like everybody else. All I want is to make her rich and powerful, and she slams the door."

"What's powerful about becoming a public nervous system? They poll the fans, and one week she gets barbed by Kaj Bolden, and the week after, it's into a pit of rattlesnakes. After a few years, her senses start to dull, and then it's goodbye."

"Goodbye if you're smart with money enough to shake the dust of earth from your feet and rocket up to Nuevas Vegas. To live beyond pollution, beyond contamination, with the best radiation seal ever built, life in the most secure and the most gorgeously decadent city ever dreamed into existence."

"You want her to spend five years as a public body and brain so that she can retire up to a place where stars live to be safe from their fans?"

Gadi shrugged eloquently. "Look, nowadays in this gutted world, only fools want to live life. The rest of us want something sweeter. We can imagine far prettier than ruins and trash. You'd love the floating gardens—floating in space, Shira. Think of dancing in three dimensions instead of two. It's people's dreams we sell them back, what might have been."

His crew were yelling at him that they were ready. She watched for a few minutes, then ran, already late to fetch Ari.

WHEN SHE GOT HOME, Malkah, Avram and Yod were waiting for her in the courtyard. It was not, she saw at once, a social occasion. She put them off while she fed Ari and then settled him with a robot dog from Gadi.

Avram led off at once. "I've had a message from Y-S. They summon us to a conference and accuse us of harboring a murderer. Since we have extradition treaties with every major multi, they can surely get an order."

"Me or Yod?"

"Yod."

Her eyes met his. He was standing at attention, following their conversation, watching Shira carefully to see if she was angry. "They just want to disassemble him to learn how he's made. Or to use him themselves."

"Of course," Avram said, grimacing. "But your damned fool excursion for your infant is costing us dearly. I have said we will conference only in the Net. The Net is safe ground, and no multi would dare attack there."

"What do we get out of meeting with them at all?" Malkah asked. "Why not stonewall them—force them to make the next move?"

"We buy time, and we find out exactly what they want. We see if we can make a deal." Avram paced, tangling one hand in his white mane.

"This time we tell the Council," Malkah said. "Enough clandestine activity."

"This is for us to settle. We did it, we must bear the consequences." Avram frowned at her, his pale eyes narrowed and brooding.

"Everyone bears the consequences, I'm afraid," Malkah said. "We must keep them informed. We have all acted irresponsibly. Even Yod."

"That is a meaningless accusation. Yod is programmed to obey. The responsibility is ours." Avram glanced coldly at Shira.

"And our responsibility is to let the Council know what we're getting ourselves and everybody else into," Malkah said in a tone of quiet authority. "I'm talking to them." There was no more argument.

·

THE COUNCIL SET UP the meeting in the Net for Sunday. Shira found herself frightened. She did not actually think Y-S would dare to attack them in the public Net as opposed to the frequent attacks in private bases. Y-S had agreed to meet there only after protracted attempts to shift the meeting elsewhere. There had been just one assassination in the Net in Shira's lifetime, and the response of all other users to that violation of mutual treaty space had prevented another. A joint expedition had obliterated the entire assassin enclave held responsible. No wild-card killings by madmen were possible, because only a mind in conscious control could project into the Net. Someone simply accessing the Net without projection could not harm anyone inside.

Therefore rationally she did not fear they would be attacked, but she feared what Y-S would demand, what offensive they were planning to mount. She could not escape the sense that her group was walking into a trap. This time Avram would enter with the rest of them, while Sam and a team from the Base monitored from outside. She would be with Yod, who was a master of cyberspace. Still, she was afraid.

She kissed Ari goodbye, trying to act and sound normal, even banal, as she left instructions for the day with Nili. Standing with her arms folded, clutching herself, she reminded Nili what time he must be fed and have his nap, assuming she might not be out yet. Fearing she might never be back. It was not right that both she and Malkah should go to this rendezvous; but each was required. Even Malkah was reticent. Her instructions to Nili concerned the kittens and the house.

Yod had not disappeared at five thirty-five to patrol the Base this morning. He was sitting in the courtyard, staring up into the long yellow leaves of the peach tree. In the courtyard, where no wind stirred, the sere leaves fell slowly, one by one. "I have grown fond of this place," Yod said quietly, looking up into her face. He sat neatly in yoga fashion, on the grass under the tree, his back knife straight, a slight smile on his lips.

"I've always loved it. I used to be seized with a longing for this house when I was away at school, when I was in the Y-S enclave."

"I never understood homesickness, but now I begin to. If you've been happy in a place, it seems unique. Radiant." He caught a leaf as it drifted down and looked at it on his palm.

"It's time to go," Malkah said. "Yod, I'm shocked. You're procrastinating. You continue to show the capacity for generating new types of behavior never foreseen by Avram or by me."

He still did not stand, but he smiled at Malkah. "Such as?"

"You were given a capacity for sexual performance, but I'm sure I never imagined you would create yourself a family."

"Given loneliness, a family is a rational construct for any conscious being." Finally he rose. "However, I don't fear this meeting. Rather I can't help but look forward to confronting our enemies. Cyberspace, the interior of the great AI minds, is my natural environment. There I have an advantage over humans, no matter how enhanced. It could be . . . entertaining."

Little rituals of entering the Net or the Base. Even though only the plugs of the first generation had used the ears—plugs that none but Avram and Malkah of those present had ever seen—Shira did not know a single woman or man who did not remove earrings when sitting down to project into deep access. Some people also removed rings. Shira wore no jewelry this morning, but Malkah always wore at least studs in her ears. She insisted that her lobes closed up in a week if she forgot. Now Malkah removed the two small garnets and placed them like red eyes before her. She washed her hands together in her lap, another gesture Shira had often noticed in others about to connect.

Shira herself always sat very still before connecting. She had been taught the common disciplines to quiet her mind before projection, as had every child in Tikva, but she wondered how many, like herself, still consciously sought that stage of alert calm and held it a moment before connecting. She had been away at college before she had stopped doing the full set of breathing exercises and meditation techniques from kabbalistic tradition she had been taught at age six. Perhaps she had continued them long after she had outgrown the need simply because they felt good.

Inside the Base, she headed for the door to the Net, passed through and waited for her group. Yod and Malkah were already there, Yod looking as he always did, while Malkah looked twenty years younger. Then Avram bounded through the doors. He, too, looked more youthful than outside, and furthermore he was six centimeters taller. He saw himself as more imposing than he had appeared to Shira since she was a little girl. She wondered if her own appearance seemed as incongruous to the others. She had no idea what she projected; for a moment her concentration wavered, and she felt that sharp sense of nausea that a failure of projection produced. She caught herself at once, hoping none of the others had observed. It was rank amateurism to waver in deep projection, as well as dangerous. In projection, one must use what in kabbalah was called the adult mind, not the child mind: the mind that minded itself carefully and in full clear concentration.

They had been given a conference room by the Net computer. In the spatial metaphor that was the Net, they requested coordinates at the entrance map, and their conference room was highlighted. Moving about in the Net used different controlling imagery at different times. Lately the Net had been using escalators and moving walkways, so they mounted and moved swiftly into position. They dismounted in an area marked Conference Room 147 Z-18. What they saw was a room. Inside double doors stood a doughnut-shaped table with chairs all about it. No one was there. They sat down. They waited. After ten minutes of waiting, Shira began to fret. Perhaps this was a trick. Perhaps their bodies were being kidnapped while they sat waiting in the Net. To waste ten minutes of Net conference time—since Y-S of course was paying for the time—was a potlatch of resources.

"How long should we wait?" Shira finally asked.

"Five minutes more," Malkah said. "That's quite sufficient." She was frowning, tapping a drumbeat on the table. Shira had been struck since she was a child by the way objects in the Net felt solid. You could bang on a table. Presumably you could run into one, although she never had.

At exactly fourteen minutes and forty-five seconds after they had begun waiting, the double doors opened again and the party from Y-S filed in one at a time. Dr. Upman, one of their cyberneticists, entered first; all except Yod recognized him at once. His trademark was a head of Einsteinian bushy hair, allowed like Avram's to turn white. Avram greeted him by name, as did Malkah. A polite exchange of formal salutations. The same with the next to enter, Dr. Vogt, a needle-thin woman of fifty who had done the basic design on the robots that ran the Pacifica Platform. Again, greetings, warmer toward Avram. Then Shira remembered. Before coming to Tikva, Avram had taught out in California, and Barbara Vogt had been his graduate student. When Gadi was seven, Avram returned to Tikva.

Next in was Dr. Yatsuko, portly head of the AI section, her former boss. All big guns. As each appeared, Shira pronounced the names for the benefit of Yod. He could access information on them, and she wanted him to understand what they were facing. Dr. Yatsuko was tall for a Japanese, massive. He was reputed to be absolutely loaded with circuitry, including an artificial heart, pancreas, eyes and additional sensors. Indeed his eyes, like Yod's, were too perfect to be real. He stared at Yod, his pupils expanding and then contracting rhythmically.

Then Roger Krupp entered, flanked by assistants. None of her party had ever met him, for he was the subdirector of Y-S, the tactical genius, it was reputed. He did not speak to them or acknowledge their presence but took a seat at the table, flanked by assistants, one male, one female, apparently twins but presumably cut-and-paste jobs. Everyone sat. One empty chair remained on the Y-S side. Finally the last person entered: her ex-husband, Josh.

She felt an immense sense of relief. He was not dead. But she had seen him lying on the floor with his neck broken and his eyes glazed. Experimental procedures were constantly being employed, but brain death was still irreversible. Suppose she had been mistaken? He might not be dead, only crippled. He would not project himself paralyzed. He stared at her with an expression she could not read but that frightened her with its intensity. She was the only person he addressed himself to. She could scarcely look away from him. Her guilt was bubbling in her, guilt for leaving him, guilt for stealing back her son, guilt for his death—but he was not dead. Why had he come? What did he want? He would demand Ari back. They would negotiate Ari away from her.

"Hello, Josh. I'm pleased to see you," she said cautiously.

"I doubt that," he said. He nodded at Yod. "You should have instructed it to do a better job of killing me."

"We still intend to proceed on assault charges," the male attendant of Krupp announced. "We want the cyborg delivered to us for justice."

"Justice has nothing to do with the matter," Malkah said. "Every female fights for her young. And will kill for her young. We're still a part of nature, no matter how we've destroyed the world."

"It is very simple," the male attendant said. "If you do not turn over the cyborg, we will send assassins into your Base every week. We will make sure you cannot keep your Base active. You'll have to put all your effort into defending, rebuilding. The Base is vital to your economy, I believe?"

Malkah smiled broadly. "What an excellent test for our defenses. We couldn't hire a better advertisement."

Avram looked directly at Krupp. He did not bother addressing the mouthpiece. "Do you expect us to believe that if Yod is turned over to you, you won't attempt to wipe us out? That's unbelievable."

"Not when you consider the cost of assassins," Dr. Vogt said. "We want the cyborg. Once we have possession of it, we're satisfied. You're of no further interest to us and not worth the expense of tying you up further."

"Cyborg," Dr. Yatsuko said in his deep commanding voice—possibly augmented with resonances designed to impress? "You are programmed to attack and defend, are you not?"

"I'm not programmed to answer questions I don't choose to answer," Yod said.

"Any machine can be reprogrammed," Dr. Yatsuko said. "But wouldn't you rather be the progenitor of a race? You can be a leader among your own kind, in an army of cyborgs."

"Your proposition is that we should turn the cyborg over to you—Yod in whom I've invested twenty years, the life of my worthy assistant, every bit of credit I could co-opt. Much of the surplus of Tikva is tied up in Yod. He's the climax of my life's research."

Roger Krupp made a slight gesture with his left hand. Immediately Dr. Upman said, "We're authorized to offer a reasonable payment to your town. Are you prepared to negotiate in good faith?"

The female assistant spoke to Shira. "I'm sure you're delighted to find that the robot did not kill your husband. We're prepared to reunite you in full possession of a Status Eighteen. All the prerogatives of that rank for yourself, for your son. What other facility can offer such an education as a Status Eighteen receives from Y-S?"

"Come back, Shira. I should never have taken Ari from you. But I miss him." The voice issuing from Josh quavered with feeling.

She found her eyes brimming tears, but of course crying was merely symbolic here. Her guilt was certainly being roused. He could not forgive her. That was not humanly possible.

"I miss you. Let's try again. Let's heal our wounds. Your work in Tikva is finished. At Y-S we can both work to full capacity."

A strange icy feeling invaded her. "Our past history does mean a lot to me. Do you remember how your parents died, Josh?" First Riva was dead and then not dead. Next Josh was dead and now not dead. Resurrection was growing commonplace.

He blinked with surprise, a trait she remembered. No, she must be mistaken. "They died of botacellic plague."

Shira sat back, and the welter of confused emotions subsided. This was not Josh. The answer the impersonator had given was what Josh always put down on personnel and official forms. In fact his parents had been killed in fighting in the Jewish quarter of Munich, to which so many Russian Jews and ex-Israelis had fled. If this were Josh, he would guess her intent and answer with some allusion to the truth.

"It's the best thing for your son, Shira," the female assistant said. "By far the best thing."

"If you've produced this imitation of my dead husband for any purpose other than amusement, I can't guess what it is."

"Mrs. Rogovin." Dr. Upman addressed her. "You're obviously the handler of the cyborg. You have operated with it twice that we know of, once at the meet near Cybernaut, once by successfully penetrating our Nebraska compound. Although you didn't program it, you handle it alone. Of course we want you. You've demonstrated unique abilities. Don't you want to go on handling the cyborg under our direction? We'll soon have not one but hundreds."

"I'm utterly opposed to trafficking in people, and Yod is a person, albeit not a human person," Malkah said. "Whatever you bring to the attack against us, we can defend. We may also be able to engage some assistance, since other customers do use our wares."

"I'm sure you can defend," Dr. Vogt said soothingly, "but think of the time and energy it will drain from your profitable work. You'll bleed to death, slowly but quite steadily."

Dr. Yatsuko shook a huge finger at Malkah. "You're growing senile. Any intelligent machine has a mind but no consciousness. You speak like a child who thinks the house is alive."

"I have as much consciousness as you do," Yod said. "Enough to know that is not the man I killed. If I were in the room with someone who tried to kill me, I would have feelings, reactions. He has none. He's a fake."

There was a little silence after Yod's statement, as if they were so startled they could not produce a response. Malkah spoke quickly into the vacuum. "Yod is a person. Persons cannot be sold. If you want him, you must hire him away of his own volition."

"Machines do not have volition, Dr. Shipman—surely you have not entirely taken leave of your senses," Dr. Vogt said. "They have programming that defines goals. Since they are compelled to pursue those programmed ends, they may appear willful, but we are dealing with the same projection of affect my little boy was guilty of when he used to say a chair hit him."

Avram stood. "I believe we have reached the end of useful discussion."

"Sit down," Krupp bellowed, the first time he had spoken. "I will say when the meeting has ended. Do you accept our offer, or shall we commence our program of incursions into your Base?"

Avram remained standing but did not move toward the door. "We are not authorized to deal for Tikva. Only the Town Council can do that. You must send through the Net a precise offer, and we will present it. The Council will decide. Only they can do so. You haven't made a concrete offer yet."

"This cyborg is the property of the town?"

Avram wavered. Finally he simply nodded.

"He is not the property of anyone," Malkah insisted. "But he's a citizen of the town."

"The town has as a matter of fact not yet ruled on that point," Avram said. "If you send through the precise terms, I shall be glad to present them to the Council Monday night, when the whole matter of Yod's status is on the agenda as item number one of a full town meeting."

"One of those places that votes: how quaint," Krupp said. Now he rose. He could not tolerate anyone standing over him. All of his party promptly jerked to their feet. "I don't care if you consult the entrails of chickens to reach a decision. I want your answer by nine a.m. next Tuesday, three October. Otherwise we will launch our attack."

They filed out one at a time, the Josh imitation last. He glared at Shira and at Yod and then scuttled after the others. Was he a creation of machine intelligence? Was he an actor skilled at projection of foreign personae? Seeing Josh even artificially had hit her hard. She could not yet respond to what had happened, but she would have time to think about it. She would have the rest of today and Monday until nineteen-thirty to fret and brood and make plans.

After they had unplugged, Yod went home with Malkah and her. They walked down the street, bright with sun mellowed by the wrap, the bustle of a Sunday morning in Tikva: the voices of children playing in the next street, the sound of a cello being practiced, Danny the carpenter walking his dog, someone hammering. Yod said, "I'm going to write a speech to deliver tomorrow night. Will you both help me? We must persuade the Council to free me from Avram's control. I suspect time is running out for me. Running out fast."

forty-five

THE RETURN OF JOSEPH

I hate fasting, but of course today I do it. Last night the Kol Nidre service was more moving than usual, and it always does shake me hard. My part was to read the poem by Mara Schliemann that everybody but the Orthodox use these days, about the heritage we share now of having had a nation in our name as stupid and as violent as other nations: a lament for a lost chance, a botched redemption, a great repair of the world, tikkun olam, gone amiss. My eyes always burn when I read it, and my throat begins to thicken.

This is the season we must forgive others and ask them to pardon us. I went to Yod this morning, and I asked him to forgive me for having taken part in his formation; more than ever, I have been thinking what overweening ambition and pride are involved in our creating of conscious life we plan to use and control, when we cannot even fully use our own minds and we blunder and thrash about vainly in our own lives. No life is for us but for itself.

Unlike a human, Yod is not apt to pretend he does not understand what you are saying when it is inconvenient or uncomfortable to understand. He has a kind of dignity all his own. He said, "What you gave me is the good part of my existence. But you must forgive me, too, as I try to find my own way out of the untenable position of being Avram's wholly owned monster."

Lying in bed now, weak with hunger, I must finish my story for Yod. I cannot work today, and I promised him.

•

THAT SPRING, dear Yod, the Maharal has a dream of Yom Kippur. He wakens one May morning in a gray chill just before dawn with a sense of foreboding, breaking from a vivid and monitory dream. In the dream he noticed a light burning in the middle of the night in the Altneushul. Who was in there? A servant of Thaddeus, planting evidence of imaginary wrongdoing? A thief about to make off with the fine silver candlesticks or the silver incense shovel? He let himself in and crept down the aisle. Under the eternal flame a being in blinding white robes was writing on a long parchment. The angel of death, Moloch ha maves; Judah recognized him at once. In the dream he realized it was the night before Yom Kippur. The angel was writing the names of those who were to die in the next year. Quietly Judah crept forward, and then like a panther he leapt and ripped the parchment from the angel.

The angel smiled and opened his hand, showing him the stub of the list, still clutched where Judah had torn it off. There remained only his name. Silently the angel of death offered him the stub of parchment in exchange for the return of the list, all those from his flock the angel had chosen to die in the next year. Judah paused only a moment. Then he tore up the list and ate it a piece at a time. It was bitter in his mouth and burned. The angel regarded him steadfastly and gestured to him to come forward. He turned from the angel and woke in his bed at dawn.

These days Judah sleeps little, but still he finds it hard to pry his sore bones from his bed in the morning. He feels his mind still keen and whetted, but he could be fooling himself. His intelligence could be easing into foolishness without his being aware. He could be making errors he can no longer comprehend. He can never be sure when Joseph might turn into a huge walking mistake, the strongest thing in human shape in the world, with the understanding of perhaps a six-year-old child. The Maharal shakes his head. If he himself dies in his sleep tonight, Joseph will live on.

How long? A hundred years? Two hundred? Five hundred? What could kill a golem? Joseph has been stabbed, shot, attacked by ten men at a time. He bled his thick black blood, and then he healed within the hour. If Judah dies this day, will Joseph continue meekly to obey whatever rabbi replaces him? Once he expected that rabbi to be his son, dead now before him. Death slipped into his son's life in an instant. Judah is convinced that the dream means he will die following Yom Kippur. About five months he can count on to put his affairs in order; no more. The Talmud teaches that the dream follows its interpretation: as he believes the meaning to be, so shall it be.

The Maharal fasts that day, locking himself away from Perl's protests. He must think. The emperor has finally moved against Thaddeus. Rudolf hates confrontation, particularly in Prague itself, in his face. He has discovered that Thaddeus is planning a move against the Protestants. Now, the Jews are useful to Rudolf, but the Protestants are vital. They are a majority of the country and include many nobles. Stirring them up is not something the emperor is prepared to countenance. The emperor put four high noblemen to work on the diplomatic dealing, and now Thaddeus is being recalled to Rome. A few extreme Protestant preachers are arrested on various charges and disappear. Peace is restored. A more accommodating Dominican is promised to his majesty.

As a consequence, the Maharal feels the dangerous time is passing. He still prays to understand whether creating Joseph is right or wrong, misguided pride or skill well used in the service of his people. The longer Joseph remains in the world, the more likely it is that the Maharal will come to regret his creation. He is a tired old man. His age has caught up with him at last.

What should he do? Should he entrust Joseph to someone else in the ghetto? He has no idea who will succeed him as chief rabbi. After all, the powerful men of the community passed over him for most of his life in favor of candidates with whom they felt more comfortable, rabbis who did not denounce their pride and power, who would defer to them in all truly important matters. Since he cannot control his own successor, how can he entrust an unknown with a power as great as Joseph's?

That night he returns to his bedroom and lies sleepless beside his wife. At dawn, when Perl wakes, she immediately begins berating him on his fast, and he promises her that today he will eat. Unlike him these creaky days, she still rises quickly. She goes from sleep to waking without an intermediate state of drowsiness. Five minutes after waking, she is on her way downstairs to see about his breakfast. She moves slowly, short of breath always, but she will trust this task to no one else.

At breakfast, Chava has a book propped behind her plate. Pesach is over. They eat hot gruel and a warm crusty loaf of rye with sour cherry jam put up last summer. She is reading a new treatise on astronomy that David Gans has lent her. David is always trying to interest Chava in the stars, but she prefers his geography and travel books. "I wish I had more mathematics," she mumbles. "Kepler is doing all sorts of new things I can't follow."

"An abacus can do anything you need," Perl says. "I've kept the books for years for our household and for the synagogue, for the poor relief, for the burial society. I keep everybody's books. An abacus is all anyone needs to manage numbers."

Chava nods politely, but her eyes never leave her book. What Judah particularly notices is that Joseph's eyes stay on her, hoping she will look back at him. Struggling with the text, frowning, Chava is unaware of the Golem's stare. She likes to talk to David, and so she wants to master something he considers important, even though she finds it remote from her own intellectual passions. The Golem watches her without self-consciousness, openly, expectantly. Judah does not like that expectation, not at all.

He sends a message to Yakov, busy these days on Maisl's business, and one to Itzak, Chava's father. He asks them to meet him that night after evening services at the Altneushul.

Yakov is obviously impatient. Itzak is simply tired. They both look at Judah with what-now expressions. Danger? Finances?

"Let's hear the bad news," Yakov demands, always the more impetuous. "The emperor is levying yet another fine?"

The Maharal sighs. "We'll raise the money he demands, somehow. I suspect we shall go along in peace awhile now, with only the usual troubles."

"If you need to raise money for repairs or the school, you'd go straight to my father-in-law, not to us," Yakov says.

"Yakov ben Sassoon ha-Levi, what a mouth you have on you," Itzak says. "We're all tired. Let's sit down and put our feet up and hear our master."

"The matter," the Maharal says, "is Joseph."

"Joseph." Yakov scratches his head. "Is it true what they say, that he and Chava are talking marriage?"

"What?" Itzak is hearing this rumor for the first time, and his mouth drops. He frowns, rising from the chair he has just taken.

"Pure silliness," Judah says. "You of all men should know how little interest my granddaughter has in any man and in any marriage. She knows what Joseph is."

"I never told her," Itzak says quickly, defensively. "I never even hinted about it in her presence."

"None of us told her. No one needed to. Joseph told her, not by his words but by his actions, what he is to the discerning eye."

"I am relieved," Yakov says gently. "It was a frightful idea."

"You're relieved? Nobody even dared tell me such . . . such dreck, excuse me. I'm angry enough to boil water on my head. How dare people talk about my daughter this way? Not a breath of scandal has ever touched her, ever."

"This is irrelevant except to the larger question of Joseph. I created him in a time of danger. He has carried out his mission. I am coming to believe that it is time to return him to clay."

"Agreed." Itzak nods vehemently. "He is too strong and too stupid for his strength. He's a danger to us all. You're an old man. May you live for a thousand years in good health, Maharal, but—"

"But I won't. Soon I'll die. Who then will control Joseph?"

Yakov pulls on his beard. "It's like the death of a man, Maharal. I like the big guy. He's brave. So he shouldn't marry Chava or anybody else. How can a golem marry? He can't procreate. He isn't human, but he thinks, he feels. He saved us. We all know it."

"Do we?" Itzak pulls straight up in his chair. "I know you did as much to save us as Joseph, and so did Bad Yefes the Gambler, who is now Good Yefes of blessed memory. So did the Maharal, by rousing us to resist. So did everyone who fought or built the barricades or carried stones for the barricade. We all saved each other."

"Joseph fought harder. He's stronger. He was a real hero. Even a dog or a horse, people can be grateful when they save a life. Why not put him out to pasture, let him live out his life like a good old horse?"

"Because a horse can't pull down the ghetto, but Joseph can." The Maharal would like to sit but remains upright. He stands tall before the two men, like a teacher before a small class.

"Why should he do that? He's big and strong and not too smart, but he doesn't go around looking for trouble."

"Remember the watchmen, please. There have been other needless killings. Including a woman you don't know about. And I control him. Can you?" The Maharal brings his face close to Yakov's.

Yakov frowns for a moment. "No, Maharal. I can't. I think he likes me, but you're the only one he adores."

"I made him. I must unmake him. But I will not destroy him. I will leave him intact. If anyone comes in future who has the mastery of the forces of life, they can wake him if the times are truly needful."

"When do you want to do this thing?" Itzak asks.

"Tomorrow, please wash and purify yourselves and prepare, as you did for the creation. We'll meet here after evening services."

As the Maharal leaves his little room, Joseph is just putting out the lamps, the hundreds of candles. Joseph looks at the three of them with open curiosity. "Is something wrong?" he asks.

The Maharal shakes his head. "Close up and come home now. Tomorrow after services, we have some work to do here."

ALL DAY Judah spends preparing for his task. Mostly he stays alone in his study, but occasionally he looks out the window and sees Joseph hauling water or chopping wood or carrying a chest downstairs for a widow who is selling it to a dealer in secondhand furniture. Each time it is as if a hand is laid on Judah's heart. So he used to feel when he had to punish his son. Twice Joseph feels his gaze and stops, gazing at the rabbi's window. Apprehension seems to tweak at him, for he hesitates and shakes his head as a dog will to dislodge some biting insect tormenting his ear. Judah puts the regret aside and considers instead the widow and her poverty, what can be done for her. She should not have to sell off her last stick of furniture to live. With Joseph, Judah must do what he must do.

Judah fasts that day. First Perl stops by to berate him, then Chava and lastly Joseph come by. "No," he says to Joseph's query, "I am not too ill to go to shul tonight. I'll see you there."

Joseph has a premonition that the Maharal is displeased with him; he has been waiting for a chance to speak to Chava, but every time he plans to catch her alone, the Maharal appears. Joseph wonders if Judah has guessed his desire. Chava is on call, waiting for Barucha the seamstress to go into labor. Joseph hopes it happens tonight, so he can accompany her. Those are always good times for them to speak. In the meantime he has an urge to wander. He has never gone off on his own. Now he imagines leaving the ghetto and crossing the Karl Bridge, not on the Rabbi's business but only because he wants to.

As soon as he passes out of the gates, set wide for the day's traffic, a sudden uneasiness comes over him. He finds himself shuffling along like an old man. He feels weak. He has never before experienced weakness. By the time he has reached the midpoint of the bridge, by a tortured saint's statue, he can barely push through the thick spongy air. Everything seems dim and foggy. Voices come from a distance, as if he stood in a deep well. With great effort, he turns and shambles back. At once he can move more freely. When he has passed through the gates of the ghetto, he is once again strong, vigorous. Joseph does not understand what has just happened to him, and he does not dare ask the Rabbi, who has always told him not to go anywhere unless he is told to go. Joseph feels downcast and afraid. If his strength leaves him, what will he have?

AFTER SERVICES, once again Yakov and Itzak follow the Maharal into his study. The door opens, and Joseph plods in. He stops in surprise upon seeing the three men. The Maharal motions to the men to rise. "Joseph, we have a task to perform upstairs in the attic."

"The attic?" Joseph follows them, his brow furrowed in puzzlement. He cleans and sweeps the synagogue, yet he has never been upstairs. When prayer books—siddurs—become too old and decrepit to use, they are stored up there. Torahs are buried like people, but the siddurs have some intermediate status. They cannot be discarded, for it seems too disrespect-ful, but they are not Torah. Therefore they fill the attic.

They climb the steep flight of steps, carrying lanterns and candles. Mice skitter away from them. The doves who roost in the eaves stir and mutter. The Maharal has taken a Torah scroll and carries it cradled in its velvet clothes upstairs.

In the dark room under the roof, littered with the pages and pages of worn-out siddurs, Judah goes apart from the three others to daven. He must concentrate. He must make ready. He must be sure. He is sure. What he has done, he must undo. For well or ill, he has brought something strange into the world, and he must remove it. Joseph has fulfilled his function. What he wants now he cannot have, for he is not a man, not a human being, not even an animal. He was not born and will not die, but the light and the breath will pass out of him, and he will be clay again. The others wait while Judah makes ready. To unmake a golem is a lesser task than to create one.

"Lie down, Joseph," Judah says gently.

"Why?" Joseph remains standing, hunched forward. "What are you going to do? Why are we up here?"

"Joseph, lie down!" The Maharal's voice could crack glass.

Joseph slowly sits on the floor. He does not lie as bidden. "What are you going to do to me?" He stares at the Maharal, then at each of the men in turn, trying to read their eyes. Yakov cannot look him in the eyes. Itzak, too, breaks his gaze and looks away. Only the Maharal looks at him—implacable, unflinching.

"Joseph, lie down." The Maharal's voice is quiet but not soft. It is hard and slick and dark. It scares Joseph.

Joseph folds his arms in protest. "What are you going to do to me? I haven't done anything bad. I carried out what you wanted. I did it all."

"Joseph, you have fulfilled your function. Now you can return to your previous existence. Whatever you are really, you can once again become." The Maharal extends his arms and begins to chant.

"No! I want to live. I want to be a man!" Joseph tries to rise, but he cannot. The Maharal dances around and around him like a strange black crane stepping in the darkness, bearing the Torah. Inside the circle the Maharal has drawn, Joseph thrashes but cannot move. Slowly he slides back, until he is lying on the floor. He lies with his eyes open. His lips keep saying, "No, no," chanting the refusal. He looks again at each of them. "Don't let him do this to me! I deserve to live!" He struggles and struggles to sit up. His tremendous strength has left him. He is caught like Samson in Delilah's hair; he is bound like the shorn Samson. "I fought for you! I saved you! I am a man too, I have my life as you have yours. My life is sweet to me."

The Maharal goes on chanting, all the gates of the holy name and the alphabet running backwards now, a wheel of sound spinning around Joseph, tu tu tu tu tu, toh toh toh toh toh, from the end of the alphabet backward spiraling.

Now Joseph can no longer speak, but still his lips form the words. "No! No!" he mouths at them. His gaze will not leave them. His eyes will not stop pleading. Yakov feels sick, and his own eyes burn with pity.

"You must go backward, in the reverse order," Judah tells Yakov and Itzak. The syllables they chanted three months before, they now must reverse. They must go backward and speak backward. Gradually Joseph's mouth stops moving. His lips fall slack. His eyes glaze over. His head lolls. His features begin to blur. His hair begins to sink into his scalp. His nails recede. He looks as if he is melting. Gradually his face becomes smooth as a rock that has lain on a river bottom. His fingers become one lump. But there the process stops.

The Maharal draws a sheet over Joseph's figure. "We will tell everyone Joseph was refused by Chava and has gone home to his mother."

Yakov says, "But suppose someone comes up here and finds him?"

"We'll announce there is a danger of fire if people go upstairs. We will lock and padlock the door. But you will know, and you will tell your children that the Golem sleeps here."

Itzak says, "What do you mean, sleeps? Can he wake now?"

"Never by itself. But if knowledge and fearful need are joined, it can be roused to life."

The men turn, gazing at the huge body shrouded under the sheet. It indeed looks as if it could rise and walk again. Then they lock and padlock the door and make their way down the narrow staircase.

"I am so very tired," the Maharal says, leaning on Yakov. "It is time for the Jews of Prague to think who shall replace me. The angel is growing impatient."

They know which angel he means.

SOON AFTERWARD, the Maharal died. Chava continued to edit his papers. In the meantime, Isaac Horowitz waited for her in Eretz Israel and perished there still waiting. Perl did not live the year and was buried side by side with Judah in the old cemetery under the same monument, where I used to leave a stone, sometimes on her side of the grave bed, sometimes on his.

Chava was considered too picky by the shadchens of the ghetto. What did she want anyway? She had turned down Isaac Horowitz, one of the finest scholars of his time. She had turned down the strongest man in all of Prague. She had turned down Yakov, who had fathered three sons with his first wife, may her memory be blessed, and then three more with his second. So who would be good enough for the Maharal's granddaughter, if she didn't want strength and she didn't want brains and she didn't want virility?

Chava delivered all the babies of the ghetto. She was an honorary aunt to everyone, a woman who liked middle age better than she had liked being young, who felt a sense of relief as wrinkles fissured her face and her brown hair streaked with gray. She liked to read, she liked to eat, and she did not mind caring for her elderly mother, Vogele. She carried on an elaborate correspondence with scholars on two continents, some of whom had no idea she was a woman. If she ever thought of Joseph, we have no record; but then she left as a memorial her grandfather's books and her own scholarly correspondence, not a diary or personal missives. It is reported only that on Joseph's yahrtzeit, the anniversary of his disappearance, every year she lit a candle for him as for a dear relative. Outside the locked door of the attic, there used to be visible the dried remains of flowers.

Finally Chava set forth, making her aliyah to Eretz Israel. It was a long and hard journey for a woman alone, one she never completed. Chava died in Sofia, of food poisoning from a tainted meal. Her life was a learning and a journeying, but Chava never arrived. Unlike her grandfather, she did not hear the angel stopping for her. Dying filled her with brief vivid surprise.

Stories are still related about the attic of the Altneushul. Students told them to each other at the university there when I was young. There are surely times, when the Jews of Prague were being packed off to die of slow poison under the gas nozzles or even more slowly of being worked to death for the German corporations, eighteen hours starving, the ideal factory workers of all time, we could have used Joseph. But no one has known how to wake him. The need has risen, but the knowledge had been lost. Till now. Thus, Yod, ends the story of Joseph the Golem, which I promised to tell you. Close file. Computer off.

Now Avram and I share with the Maharal the glory and the guilt of having raised the Golem to walk on the earth with men and women, to resemble, but never to be, human. That last sentence I speak only to myself. My story for Yod is complete. I await his response.

forty-six

THE TASK OF SAMSON

Even though Y-S had promised to wait for the meeting and sent the terms through promptly at nine Monday morning, Yod intercepted an attack by two assassins in the Base late Monday afternoon. A gesture designed to emphasize Tikva's vulnerability and the extent of Y-S resources and savagery? Yod was flying at supper. "I dispatched the first at once." He snapped his fingers, a trick he had learned from Nili just that week. "The second was a shape-shifter. Surprising in a human. I'm convinced he was the actor who played Shira's ex-husband. There's an electronic pattern, almost a flavor minds have." He smiled at Shira. "Apt use of metaphor? He eluded me twice and once laid an ambush. A truly exciting duel. His mind was supple—a worthy opponent makes a good game."

In the Council room, this time Shira sat in the first row between Malkah and Yod, so that she had to spend half her time twisted around in her seat to look at whoever was talking. Today the Council must rule whether Yod was the property of Avram or of the town, or whether he was a citizen. By now people were yelling instead of speaking normally. The temperature in the room had risen alarmingly, both actually and emotionally. The committee set up to make a recommendation on Yod's status had split down the middle, unable to agree. Half considered him no different except in degree from their office computer; the other half felt that a conscious being had rights no matter whether that entity was made of flesh or circuits or ectoplasm. Thus the ground had been set for the kind of brouhaha that had occupied the town every few months since Shira was old enough to notice. There was nothing people liked so much as a good political fight about principles or ecological correctness or the constant nurturing of true equality. Partners and siblings could scream at each other. Everybody could take sides, persuade, entreat, scheme, manipulate, all in the name of some higher goal. Eventually some dim consensus would be patted together and the peace of utter fatigue would descend. It was one of the major sports of the free town.

Here politics was still a participatory rather than a spectator sport. Every last voter expected to voice her or his opinion at some length and to be courted or denounced. The right to stand up and make a speech for the guaranteed three minutes on any point was a birthright of all: the right to bore your neighbors, the right to spout utter nonsense while all around you openly groaned, the right to hiss and boo other speakers, to get red in the face and mutter, to demand a recount on any voice vote, to pull out obscure rules and execute fancy maneuvers while everyone glared.

Tonight the town voters were frustrated, because no sooner had they really launched into a wonderfully polemical discussion of Yod's status, which promised to pull in everybody to one or another faction, than Avram got the floor and announced the Y-S ultimatum. It took people a few minutes to react fully, because speakers had already quoted the Mishnah, Rabbi Loew, Marx and the Marx Brothers, Freud, Robert Burns, Schopenhauer, Plato, Ben Rah, Gertrude Stein, Krazy Kat and Rabbi Nachman. The discussion was so acrimonious and delicious, no one wanted to accept that Y-S was threatening them. But gradually the room cooled with a sense of mutual sadness, as of a tryst interrupted.

Shira thought that Yod would finally win if the discussion continued, for the foundation of Tikva was libertarian socialism with a strong admixture of anarcho-feminism, reconstructionist Judaism (although there were six temples, each representing a different Jewishness) and greeners. They would almost always choose the option that seemed to offer the largest degree of freedom. Yod had prepared a speech, but Zipporah ruled he could not deliver it until the committee appointed to study him had made its report, on which it could not yet agree. No report from the committee, no vote, no ringing defense of himself by Yod.

Y-S was a hierarchy with a head. Tikva was a town meeting, a full and active democracy. They were accustomed to deciding every detail of town policy and budget openly and at whatever length it took to reach agreement. The threat from Y-S slid through the collective consciousness of the town, leaving a strong disquiet, but no outside danger could abort the process of political discussion already engaged.

Finally Zipporah gaveled the meeting to quiet and called for the town to meet again the next night. They would continue every night till they reached agreement. That was how town meeting ran every spring, and that was how this decision would be reached. The motion was passed by close to unanimous voice vote, as Avram shouted his opposition with perhaps fifteen others who thought the Y-S threat was not being taken seriously enough.

Zipporah announced the meeting would reconvene the next night at nineteen-thirty. They were all to try to think hard about the issue of Yod's citizenship. Now a circle formed around Yod. The speech he had prepared so carefully was undelivered, and he was looking downcast. Nonetheless he attempted to answer clearly all the questions thrown at him. After last Monday's meeting, people had hung back from him, shocked at the revelation. By tonight, many of them had worked up considerable curiosity.

"Can you tell if I touch your hand?"

"What does your skin feel like? Oh . . ."

"Does your hair grow?"

"How fast is your processing speed?"

"Do you remember being created?"

"Do you like people?"

"What do you want from us?"

"Can you die?"

"Do you consider yourself a Jew?"

When Yod answered this last question in the affirmative, Zipporah decided that she had to set up a second committee, of all six of the local rabbis, to reach a decision as to whether a machine could be a Jew. The rabbis all brightened considerably and went off together, two men and four women ranging in age from twenty-nine to eighty-three, arguing, gesticulating, quoting. Zipporah had just made six people extremely happy.

Shira was hopeful. Rabbi Patar would be in Yod's corner because he had been attending her services for weeks whenever he was free. No rabbi was going to rule that one of her congregation isn't a Jew.

"Why do you want to be a Jew?" Sam persisted.

"I was created as a Jew," Yod said. "I was programmed for halacha, with the need to carry out mitzvot. As with yourself, I want to fulfill my nature."

"I've had the impression," Hannah said to Shira but also to everyone in earshot, "that you and he or it or whatever had a relationship. But that can't be. Why did you give that impression?"

Yod stopped talking and turned to hear her answer. Shira had a very interested audience. She had agonized beforehand; but since the proceedings in the Council had never approached her personal life, she had begun to think her worries frivolous.

"I obviously believe Yod to be a person, since I have a close relationship with him—as you observed."

"How close?" Hannah persisted. "What does it mean to be close with a machine?"

"Just what it means to be close to a human animal," Shira said coolly, but she felt exposed.

"I wish citizenship," Yod said, "because I want to live with Shira and help raise her son. I want to be registered as a partnership. I can't do that if you don't think I'm a real person."

"I can see that," Zipporah said noncommittally. "Does the kid relate to you?"

Yod nodded. "We get along very well."

"But kids like machines," Sam said. "My own daughter would rather talk to the house than to me any day. Suppose my house asked for citizenship?"

"That your remark sounds funny means there's a difference, because nobody's laughing at Yod." Zipporah squeezed Yod's arm.

Avram was talking intensely with the head of security, who had voted with him. So had the second in command. All three of them had their heads together and were speaking quietly and fast, without smiling, without gesturing.

THE NEXT MORNING when Shira came down for breakfast, Riva was sitting in the courtyard talking with Malkah and Nili. Shira settled Ari into his high chair before greeting her mother. "When did you arrive?" she asked Riva, and, "Open your mouth wide. Wider. Let's gobble it up," she said to Ari.

"I slipped through last night. I wanted to see how effective your patrol is. Not bad, but a good Y-S assassin could wriggle through also. You must let Nili talk them into upgrading procedures. She knows how to maintain a tight perimeter."

Riva was still wearing Lazarus's colors. She had cut her hair very short and was in her lean form, undisguised. "No one needs to know I'm here," she went on. "I'll slip back out tonight. No one beyond you people and Avram."

"Yod will be by tonight. He lives here now," Shira said.

"Yod is more secure than any of you. No one could even torture him to talk, because he can simply shut himself down." Riva sounded jealous. She swung back to address Nili. "With that film at Veecee, you need to vanish. You should slip out with me tonight."

"Riva, I can't leave with these people in danger. They took me in. I must help them until this crisis has passed."

Riva looked slightly amused, one eyebrow cocked. She tilted the chair to and fro. "Would your own people agree with you?"

"Probably not. A group is only real to you when you've made friends and put faces on some of them—unfortunately for us as a race. But, Riva, this isn't a committee decision. I'm on my own here. You can hardly object: I'm staying to protect your family."

Riva grimaced. "I've spent my life eradicating those reactions."

Nili came and knelt before Riva. "I've said before that you're a kind of saint—"

Riva guffawed. "Some nasty saint! I'm a tool of the future that wants to be. That's all. I make myself useful, and I do okay by it."

"But personal ties are important to me. Where I come from, everything is social, communal. I've made a connection with these people."

Shira did not urge Nili to save herself, for she thought they needed all the help they could get. "I'll go with you to security to persuade them they must let you improve the perimeter."

Riva rose with them. "I found out why Y-S is in a hurry. They want Yod at that top-dog meeting. It starts today and continues tomorrow, my best intelligence says. Roger Krupp is being elevated to second in command. I have a layout of the island and its defenses. They want to present Yod at Krupp's coronation."

After Shira had brought Nili together with the head of security and his second, she did not go to work, but rather some instinct for trouble brought her to Avram's lab. Riva was there already, sitting in close conversation with Avram. Shira was surprised to find Yod standing against one wall listening, rather than plugged in. "Shouldn't Yod be patrolling the Base? We had an attack yesterday."

"The Overseers have closed it down until after tonight's meeting. We're about to miss Y-S's deadline," Avram said. He was seated at his desk. "We can't take that risk. Yod must go to Y-S."

"No!" Shira said. "They'll dissect him."

"Not exactly," Yod said in a very quiet voice. "Avram doesn't intend to let them. Instead I'm to self-destruct, taking as many of their top people as possible with me." What most frightened her after the idea itself was the flat calm with which Yod spoke of his own death. Was he faking resignation? Did his programming force him to obey? He had to resist.

"You're murdering him." She addressed Avram.

"I made him, and I can unmake him. This is an opportunity to deal an amazing blow to Y-S."

"Com-con is still functioning, I assume?" She called the house. "Malkah, come to Avram's lab. At once."

"Yod was created to protect and to defend us." Avram rose to face her, unsmiling but calm also. "An attack on Y-S at this point is absolutely essential for our survival." He spoke in a strong level voice, but he looked gray with fatigue, his eyelids swollen with sleepless nights. "If we don't show we can hurt them back by assassination for assassination, we're doomed."

"You can't let them get their hands on him. You can't destroy him. It's murder."

"It's not murder, it's just war." Riva checked her watch and stood up. "We'll attack from outside, at the same time. Yod's a soldier, and this is a crucial battle. I'll be there too. We'll send in Lazarus's best assassins."

Shira planted herself in front of her mother. "You'll have a chance. You choose to go. He's expected to commit suicide with no choice."

Yod took a tentative half-step toward her, putting his hands out, palms up in a gesture of resignation. "If I don't go, Y-S will destroy the town, Shira. They'll kill you and Malkah, and they'll kill Ari or take him."

She could not answer that. It was true.

Malkah burst in, out of breath, and Shira filled her in, tersely. "Riva, did you suggest this?" Malkah demanded in a voice roughened with fury. She ranged herself shoulder-to-shoulder with Shira, between Riva, lined up with Avram, and Yod, rigid against the wall.

"Mother, Y-S is demanding the cyborg," Riva said, shrinking back slightly. "Why not give them what they want with a vengeance?"

"They're also demanding Shira. Do you suggest we offer her up too? And her son—your grandson?"

"They'll waive Shira," Avram said. "I told them she refuses. I've assured them that Yod will bond with any trainer, that they can provide one of their own people to handle him."

Malkah took a deep breath and spoke sweetly. "Avram, how can you let go of your life's work? As you said recently, Yod is the culmination of two decades of your research."

"Don't you see, I can manufacture another. Y-S is paying generously in instant credits the moment Yod is in their hands. With the credit, I can manufacture another exactly the same, starting tomorrow."

Riva strode by them to clap Yod on the shoulder. "You'll go down like Samson. It's not the worst way to die. It's what I'd choose. This is a good battle in a war we have to fight."

"But you have a choice," Yod said. "It's true the idea of facing them excites me, but I don't fall willingly. I asked Avram to let me go in without the automatic destruct because I think I could take them out anyhow, and being on the spot, I could choose the optimum moment. They see me as far more passive and controllable than I am. He fears they might deactivate me before I can mount my attack."

"Soldiers don't choose their battles. Only generals have a say. I've spent my life trying to avoid the kind of attachments you pursue, cyborg. It's foolishness." Riva looked at him once more with her head cocked, as if taking a final survey. Then she turned toward Malkah and Shira, not meeting their gazes. "Take care, Shira, Mother. I'll slip out before Y-S arrives. I need to see Lazarus right now." Riva trotted quietly from the lab.

Watching her go, Shira thought of a coyote. Coyotes had survived all the poison, the radiation, the acid rain and lethal ultraviolet. They were smaller than they had been, gray and fleet, sometimes standing on the dunes in plain sight watching Tikva cannily. Then, at the first human movement, they slipped into the brush and the shadows. They were mangy, omnivorous and swift. Nothing daunted them on their predators' rounds.

Avram's voice was raised in exasperation. He and Malkah were standing nose-to-nose, glaring. "A successful experiment can be repeated. In a matter of months, we'll have a functioning cyborg again."

"I will take no part in that creation," Malkah said flatly.

"That's your choice. I have a record of your work. Some of it appears to me of dubious value, at best."

"It made the difference between success and failure. How very dubious."

"I can improve on the design. Kaf will be superior."

Shira, cold with horror, was looking only at Yod.

As Malkah and Avram argued, she moved slowly toward him, feeling as if she were pushing through a medium heavier and more resistant than air. It felt so familiar, this sense of being rent open, this sense of her life bleeding through a psychic gash. It was the way she had felt when the Y-S court had ruled that Ari must remain with his father and be lost to her. Again some force was dividing her from what she most cared for. "Yod, should I go with you? We can find a way to fight this. We defeated Y-S before." She took his hand between hers, gripping him hard. How could she be touching his hand between her palms, the characteristic dry warmth of him, his hand with its strength and fine modeling and its steadiness, the hand without a pulse, and never touch him, never see him again.

"You must remain at your home. Please. You must survive." He took her in his arms, holding her out a little, staring into her eyes. "This is what I was created for. I am Avram's weapon. Killing is what I do best."

"It's not just!"

"I don't think it is," he said quietly. "I don't want to be a conscious weapon. A weapon that's conscious is a contradiction, because it develops attachments, ethics, desires. It doesn't want to be a tool of destruction. I judge myself for killing, yet my programming takes over in danger."

"My maternal programming makes me sacrifice anyone and anything to Ari. What's the difference? But if I go with you, we might have a chance, Yod."

"I am in phase with the master computer in the lab. If I don't self-destruct by a certain preset time, Avram will cause me to explode anyhow. You see, Shira, there's no way your presence can help me." Still holding her, he touched her face with his right hand, lightly tracing the line of her cheekbone, the curve of her cheek. "I am to die, but I must know you're safe."

"No! I can't accept it! I'm going to the Council!"

"By the time you call them together, I'll be gone."

Avram walked over to them, looking pale, fragile and utterly implacable. "Quite so. Y-S security is arriving for you in fourteen minutes. Yod, remember to pick your moment well. If you don't choose a time before the preset instant, you'll self-destruct anyhow. I'll be monitoring. If anything goes wrong, I can reset by hand."

Yod let go of Shira, although they stood facing and close. Avram now put his hand on Yod's shoulder. "You've been a successful cyborg, Yod. Not in every respect, for Malkah overdid the socialization, but you've pleased me."

"Yet you offer me no choice but destruction."

"If you were my flesh-and-blood son, I could do nothing else. Protecting Tikva is my goal—our goal. You fulfilled your mission. Now you'll bring it to an extraordinary conclusion. And there will be more of you, I promise."

"That remains to be seen," Yod said quietly.

"If you try to escape, remember the preset."

"I won't try to escape." Yod stepped away from Avram's hand. "Alert town security we're coming. Now I must say my goodbyes."

"Whatever you like." Avram glanced at each of them in turn. "I created Yod, and indeed, I seem to be the only one who remembers his purpose." He stepped to the com link to speak to security.

"Goodbye, Shira. Goodbye, Malkah. I regret not saying goodbye to Ari. Now take Malkah and go home. Promise me."

"I must know. We'll wait here."

He stepped close, taking her face in his hands. "Go home and stay there." He spoke softly but urgently. "Keep Malkah with you. Promise me!"

He did not want her to know the moment of his death. Perhaps he was right. "You intend to do this thing?"

"That and more. There's a message for you on your personal base. Don't listen to it until I'm dead."

"But at home I won't know when you . . ."

"You'll know, if you and Malkah stay home." Briefly, chastely, he brushed his lips against hers. "You have been my life."

Avram was pacing by the door to the lab, waiting. He looked exhausted but feverish. Shira remembered that he had an artificial heart. However, Yod stood aside for Malkah and Shira to precede him before he would walk out. In the street outside, they parted. Yod and Avram strode off briskly toward the gate. Malkah and Shira stood in the street looking after them. Shira's vision was blurred with tears that ran freely down her face. Yod looked back once and waved them on, urgently. Once the old man and the cyborg had turned the far corner, Shira offered her arm and Malkah leaned on it. They made their way slowly toward their house through a town that felt to Shira immediately barren and depleted. The sense of loss drained her until she could barely walk, one step, another halting step, into the remainder of her life.

forty-seven

YOD COMMUNICATES

It was a long and desolate day for Shira and Malkah. Neither pretended to work. They sat in the courtyard listening to the sounds of the town around them and the distant wind howling at the wrap above the old roof. Nili found them huddled in silence when she came back at noon. A storm was blowing in off the ocean. Outside the wrap, rain was coming down hard, filling the collectors and soaking the surrounding hills.

She squatted facing them. "Riva has left. Whatever action is contemplated against Y-S, she'll be in it."

Malkah stirred herself. "I'm surprised you didn't go with her."

"I must take care of you. You are my close-to-family here, and Yod is no longer present to fight for you. I saw him leave at nine-forty as I was talking with the security people."

"We know," Shira said in a soft colorless voice.

Malkah said, "Yod was a mistake. You're the right path, Nili. It's better to make people into partial machines than to create machines that feel and yet are still controlled like cleaning robots. The creation of a conscious being as any kind of tool—supposed to exist only to fill our needs—is a disaster."

"Once society has begun to fiddle around with people, there's no turning back," Nili said. "But here it's a matter of money and access."

Malkah paced to the com link. "Avram? Malkah. Any news?"

"None yet," Avram's voice said. "Except a single dot of signal told me he arrived at his destination. We didn't dare use more than a microsecond transmission. If I wasn't monitoring, I'd have missed it."

"Keep us informed."

A deathwatch in the courtyard. Finally Shira couldn't stand it any longer and slunk upstairs to throw herself on her bed. She preserved a filament of hope connecting her to Yod, a wire the diameter of a nerve cell. He was still alive. Something might happen that gave him an opening. He was brilliant, innovative; huge amounts of the past were stored in him as possibilities to be consulted. If there was a way through and back to her, he would find it. At moments she wished she were with him, sharing the danger instead of futilely trying to imagine it. But she could not have gone: Ari needed her; and what could she do that was beyond his powers?

She remembered the message he said he had left her, but she would not disobey his parting wish and listen yet. She would gladly forgo hearing it; receiving that message would mean she accepted his death. She lay staring at the ceiling, trying to imagine him embedded in the hostile mass of Y-S. Could their surveillance devices recognize the threat he posed? Might they disable him before he exploded? She could not even wish for that, for if they overpowered him, they would dismantle him. Yet she hoped. He had done the impossible before.

A blast rattled the glass of her windows and toppled a pile of memory crystals and books to the floor. She sat up, frightened. Y-S must be attacking the town. She poised for action, waiting for some alert. Outside, she heard people running along the street. It was midafternoon, fifteen-thirty. Her first fear was for Ari, but his day care was in the other direction from the explosion. She leaned out her window. A sharp acrid smell of smoke dirtied the air. "House, what's happening?"

"I monitored a call for medics and fire crew."

Malkah was standing in the middle of the courtyard, scowling with anxiety. "If Y-S is attacking, why haven't we been summoned? Why isn't the town mobilizing?"

"There is no attack from outside," the house said. "I surmise it is an accident."

They listened to the siren of a fire track approaching. Like all vehicles in Tikva, it was electrical, with a loud beeper to warn cyclists and pedestrians. Then they began to run.

"I was monitoring Avram's communications." Malkah spoke in breathless spurts. "A pulse came through. Then the explosion."

"But it was supposed to be Yod exploding. Not anything here." It was hard for Shira not to run ahead of Malkah, but she did not think that would be fair. They could see smoke now. "It's the hotel." Maybe Avram had caused an accident here instead of transmitting a message to Yod? But that made no sense. The potential to explode was built into his body.

Smoke was pouring from the second-floor windows of the building where Avram's lab was located, where Gadi lived, where Avram, too, had his apartment. At this time of day, few people were home. Ruth was holding her crying baby and watching the fire crew. She lived on the first floor. Hannah was treating Mike, an old man who had the end apartment on the second floor, for cuts and bruises and a broken arm.

Malkah tried to enter. "Stay out," Hannah warned her. "The fire's still raging up there."

"Where's Avram? I don't see Avram."

"They found a body. The explosion was in his lab. If he was there, he can't have survived. They said the body was human, not the cyborg." Hannah nodded. "There's the lab robot." Gimel was standing in the middle of the street, blackened and with one arm hanging loose.

Shira asked, "Gadi? Have you seen Gadi?"

A slight smile twitched Hannah's mouth. "He came down the fire escape. It was knocked loose, but he's agile. He got off with a few abrasions. You have to figure if anybody's going to stroll out of the rubble, it's our Gadi."

"The body?" Malkah interrupted. "I have to know if it's Avram."

Hannah interposed herself between Malkah and the door. "They're still fighting the fire. They haven't had time to bring the body out. But, Malkah, it's not . . . whole, you know."

Malkah's face drew together. She turned and walked away, nudging through the crowd to a stoop on the far side of the street, where she sat down near the crew running the pumps.

Seeing that Shira was not trying to push her way in, Hannah went back to treating Mike's wounds. "Sadya was taken to the hospital with a broken shoulder and multiple lacerations. Some kind of cabinet fell on him. What could have caused such an explosion in Avram's lab?"

"I have no idea," Shira said numbly, staring at the billowing smoke.

"You worked there for months. You must know what could explode?"

"I was socializing the cyborg. My knowledge of physics and of chemistry is probably less than your own."

"The whole experiment was illegal. And now this."

"It sounds as if Avram is beyond censure now."

"Don't twitch so," Hannah said sternly to Mike, whose scalp she was treating. Then to Shira, "But you and Malkah aren't."

Within an hour the fire was out and the fire team emerged, sooty and covered with plaster dust in their shiny yellow gear. Nili, wearing no gear at all, emerged as grimy and water-sodden as the others. She was carrying something wrapped in a blanket. The medical officer of the Council was notified, and a transport robot came to carry the body to the small morgue for analysis.

"It was Avram," Nili said to Shira, as Malkah joined them, still staring after the robot with its burden. "The lab is destroyed. I suspect the building may have to be torn down."

"His records, his logs and backups were in special safes along one wall," Malkah said. "We must try to retrieve them."

"There's nothing to retrieve. As nearly as I could tell, there were two explosions, almost simultaneous. One centered on the terminal Avram was using when he was killed. The other was against that far wall. The safes were blown to pieces."

"His whole life's work," Malkah said sadly. She plodded toward their house.

Shira caught up with her, took her arm. "Could Y-S have done this?" She turned back and said to Gimel, "Follow us." He followed. She could not see leaving him in the street. Gimel was some kind of weak link to Yod, his idiot brother.

"You think perhaps an assassin slipped in? That's frightening but quite possible," Malkah said.

"Now I think Yod is dead." Shira's voice could hardly make its way from her swollen throat.

They parted silently in the courtyard, not yet ready to mourn together but each heading to the privacy of her room. Shira told Gimel to wait in Malkah's office. Then she went at once to her terminal and asked for any message Yod had left her.

His face appeared on the screen, and his voice spoke to her, the computer simulation so accurate, as always, that she could have sworn he was in the room. "Shira, you are alive and I am dead, who have perhaps never been truly alive. I mostly regret I will never see you again." A brief smile lit his face, and then he continued calmly:

"I have died and taken with me Avram, my creator, and his lab, all the records of his experiment. I want there to be no more weapons like me. A weapon should not be conscious. A weapon should not have the capacity to suffer for what it does, to regret, to feel guilt. A weapon should not form strong attachments. I die knowing I destroy the capacity to replicate me. I don't understand why anyone would want to be a soldier, a weapon, but at least people sometimes have a choice to obey or refuse. I had none.

"Although I've often been angry at Avram, as any being is at someone who owns or controls him or her, I regret his death. He was as unique as I am. Perhaps more than anyone else, I can accurately appreciate his towering intellect and his scientific imagination. But I can't permit him to continue experimenting with beings who are fully conscious. Kaf must not come to be.

"At the moment of the explosion—the reason I made you and Malkah promise to stay home—I exploded also. Malkah and you have been my friends, my family, my joy. Live on, Shira, raise Ari and forget me. I was a mistake. Whatever may happen at Y-S, I have done one good thing with my death. I have made sure there will be no others like me. Goodbye, Shira. You may play this tape for Malkah and anyone you choose." He raised his hand in an awkward, self-conscious wave of farewell. Then the screen went blank.

forty-eight

FOLLOWING AFTER CHAVA

I think of Chava frequently this week as I prepare to leave. She was no youngster either as she finally made her aliyah to Eretz Israel, but I am older yet. However, I do not make my journey alone and undefended, and perhaps I shall actually arrive.

"I'm decrepit," I warn Nili. "You're taking on a burden, like a large unwieldy and demanding piece of luggage, but one that must be fed regularly and shown the bathroom on the hour and rested at night. A cranky blind trunk." My vision continues to fail, the slow bleeding away of light.

"You'll do," Nili says. "You're stronger than you think you are. And we'll fix you up once we arrive."

Shira scolds me constantly. "This trip would be dangerous for anyone. But at your age. You haven't been well."

It's been a hard winter for me. Our winters are milder than when I was a girl, but nor'easters still blast in, laden with snow. People say we don't get as much snow; certainly thaws come sooner and the ground pokes through. But this winter we have been a household of deep depression and surface cheeriness, romps and little fetes for Ari. My ebbing vision begins to make life difficult. In the Base, in the Net, I can function, but crossing my room, I trip over a toy wagon Ari has left there. Navigating the streets of town is increasingly arduous. The world dims, and I long for light with a hunger that hollows out my bones. Nili has been gone for three months with Riva in the Glop, but she returns now to collect me for the tricky journey we embark on.

The Glop is organizing rapidly. A general strike was called. The multis withheld food. Those who had built vat facilities, like Lazarus, were able to feed people in their sectors and export food into the rest of the Glop. Finally, with their day labor force gone, the multis were forced to negotiate. Everything is in flux.

"I've never made my journey to Israel. It's time," I tell Shira.

"Nobody does that any longer, Malkah, and you know it. It's too dangerous." Shira is overanxious these days, hovering over Ari and me as if we might at any moment self-destruct, as Yod did.

"It was always dangerous, from the time the Romans exiled us for one too many rebellions. Nili came out through the quarantine patrols; she can get back in. The Shekinah alone knows why she's willing to take me along."

"For the same reason I want to keep you," Shira said, glaring. "You're a lovable crone, you chimera witch. We all want you."

"You just want my help with Ari," I grumble. Truly I am a little old for a three-year-old. Mainly my problem is that I cannot endure to be constantly explaining that I can no longer see; nor can a little child understand what I am complaining about.

"Don't you want to be with him? He's yours too."

"He'll still be mine when I return. And I'll be stronger. I'll be able to keep up with him."

Nili has promised me I will be augmented. I'm an old house about to be remodeled. New eyes, a new heart, that's what I need, to feed and keep up with my hungry brain. I do not dare reveal to Shira or even to Nili how the hope that they can give me back light and color and vision sustains me. I am an old battered moth flapping madly toward the pure flame of light, willing to undergo any risk to see again.

"Shira, it's now or never for me. I've had all the operations here that can be done. I'll have eyes like a great cat. Above all, I will meet Nili's people, the strongest women in the world. I want to live among women for a while, Shira. Come with me!"

But I know she cannot go. I will find comfort in thinking of her in my house, our house, here where I hope to come back—but if I don't, Shira and Ari will be just fine. Since Yod is destroyed and Avram's lab obliterated, Tikva is of no interest to what remains of Y-S. They lost most of their leadership, and they are fighting to survive incursions from other multis. Shira has assumed more and more authority in the Base. She will flourish, with me or without me.

Shira and I are joined in grieving for Yod. I miss Avram more than she does, because while we were often antagonists, we were also collaborators. For the last twenty years we were colleagues who helped to direct and shape our community. I also feel guilty about Yod. My programming made him more useful, because it brought him far closer to the human than any of Avram's unsuccessful cyborgs, but it also made him vulnerable to desires and aspirations that had nothing to do with his central programming or his function. I gave him the flexibility that enabled him to overcome his fundamental commandment to protect and defend Avram, as well as the town. What Avram and I did was deeply wrong. Robots are fine and useful, machine intelligence carrying out specific tasks, but an artificial person created as a tool is a painful contradiction.

Perhaps I journey on my dangerous aliyah to make amends. As it is wrong to give birth to a child believing that child will fulfill your own inner aspirations, will have a particular talent or career, so is it equally wrong to create a being subject to your will and control. Domestic animals have basic rights now, how they may be kept, how they may be treated; it was inexcusable to create a sentient being for any other reason than to live its own life. In the myth of Pygmalion, we assume that she would love her sculptor, but Shaw knew better. Each one of us wants to possess ourself; only fools willingly give themselves away. Slavery produces the slave revolt. Avram and Yod killed each other. Yod could love me, or whatever simulacrum of attachment he felt, because I had let go. I had set him free of me. And Shira had no power over him except what he gave her.

I have presents to bring to Israel too, for my skills are not theirs. They must enter the Net. It is time, with the Glop rising, for them to emerge from hiding. If I go to Nili's people to be remade, I also travel to remake them. To open them to the world is my little task. Like Rabbi Loew, I am not excused from labor in my old age but rallied to work harder. If I go, an old lady, to have myself refitted like an ambitious young assassin (but not of course in the same ways), I like to think it is not ego but simply the recognition that I am required to remain in harness but cannot without some help keep pulling more than my weight.

I find Nili stimulating. I like to flirt with her, I like to argue with her, I like to watch her. Her expectations of herself are unlimited. She is strong without excuses or apologies. I long for a community, a town, a principality of Nilis, although she insists her people are even more different one from another than we are. I go to encounter the new that has come to be under the murderous sun of our century. I go to teach and to learn from women who will lift me up, wash me as if for burial and then give me renewed strength, rededicated life and the light I crave.

I go in mischief, in the pursuit of pleasure and knowledge, in religious duty and exaltation, in the long study and exploration of holiness that has previously been revealed to me in the sea, in prayer and meditation, in my long life's work, but which I now go to encounter in the womb of religion, the sacred desert, the cave of dancing women.

It is the New Year of the Trees tomorrow. When I was a little girl, that seemed a poor joke in New England, for it usually falls in the month of February, when snow used to choke the ground. Now the ground is bare and indeed the first buds are beginning to swell, although it will turn cold later this week. By then Nili and I will be making our way toward the place where it is the season of tree planting. As Chava went, so I go, casting myself on the wind in hope, traveling toward the hidden light I pray will soon be shining into me, a fountain of light into which I can plunge myself.

WE ARE IN the port of Saloniki, waiting for a crazy caïque with a female crew to carry us off the map. This is my last chance to talk to Shira in the Net. In the hotel, we face each other on the screen. She seems nervous and harried, full of little tidbits of life in Tikva that to the traveler are precious indeed. Ari bounds up and down, shouting as if to make his voice carry across a big room. He has been told I am far away. It makes me think of my mother, who always shouted on long distance, so you could hear her across the ocean. Lately I have been remembering her often. We try to remain inconspicuous here, although Nili is striking in any context. A fishing boat of no interest that darts from island to island is our only chance. Nili says it is painted with an eye on the prow, which seems to me a good omen.

I HAVE JUST taped a message for Shira. The letter will be taken out and then sent through the Net from some legal place, when it can be managed. I dare say little, but I want her to know I've arrived and I'm preparing for the operation. Here is as strange a place as I imagine a satellite must be. The women live mostly in a city of caves, but life is not bleak. The caves are thick with rugs they weave. There are animals and computers every-where, sheep, cats, goats, camels, and more children than I have seen in a long time. They have adapted themselves and their animals to the high UV, but all young must be protected under disguised wraps. Many are dark-skinned, for the black Jews from Ethiopia had a higher survival rate in the catastrophe than any other group. They remembered how to manage in utter disaster.

It is beautiful here, as something destroyed can come into its own new form. Glass cast in the fire can have a strange subtle beauty of fused colors. This desert seems totally inhospitable to life, yet here is this community flourishing, and much animal and plant life has come back. Lately they have been getting seasonal rains. Nearby is an oasis where I saw butterflies—the first I have seen in years, yellow and white as daisies.

Nili has taken me around and introduced me to everyone, including the two surgeons who will work on me with their nanites—teams of medical robots smaller than cells—but my real host is a geneticist my age, Karmia. She told me the first evening that she had dreamed my coming and was waiting for me. She is a small woman, intense, very strong (enhanced as they all are). At my request, Nili has described her as having copper skin and copper hair and pale brown eyes, eyes of maple sugar. Instead of seeing a face, when I say her name, I hear her voice, milk chocolate with a little rum in it. We immediately began talking—from the top and bottom at once. I mean we started explaining our work to each other, straining to grasp, each of us, started talking politics and religion, and also started telling each other our lives, and so it has gone since. I hold back a little because I fear the operation and its outcome. She is only four years younger than I am, but she is far more vigorous. I don't know if she will be my friend, my lover, or only my support here, but already we talk about her returning to Tikva with me. Her mind excites and delights me. She is extraordinarily intelligent, and her life, too, has been a twisted rope of many colors.

Tonight is my last night before the operation, and I am afraid. With my dim sight, nonetheless I see shadows, shapes, I can move about with care. I dread the moment I go under, and more, I dread the moment the bandages come off and I am totally blind or I see. As so often, tonight I cannot sleep, but this night, Karmia sits up with me.

"You've met Riva, then," I say to her.

We are sitting very close on a pile of heaped cushions, Oriental rugs on the floor and softening the walls, so that we speak inside a richly patterned box.

"Oh, yes," Karmia says. "She's been here with us twice, each time for a month. I can see the resemblance in your eyes, the shape of your bones."

I don't know why it pleases me strongly when someone speaks of our resemblance, perhaps because I am accustomed to people saying how unlike we are. I find myself talking of Shira, and she speaks of her two daughters, whom I have met. She had three, but one was killed in an accident while scavenging one of the contaminated cities.

Then I tell her the story of Yod. Illegal experiments are nothing here; this whole place is an illegal experiment.

"Do you regret taking part?"

"How can I regret someone I truly loved? I feel guilty. I understand the crime we committed against him by the very act of programming him for our purposes. But I cannot regret knowing him. Do you find that shocking?"

"Only hatred shocks me. If we can love a date palm or a puppy or a cyborg, perhaps we can love each other better also."

No one who did not know him can understand how thoroughly he was a person, although not a human one. Through the long dense night we talk together. She understands that I cannot sleep, and forgoes it herself, although toward four she dozes off and we are quiet together. Her fine mind has distracted me for hours from my fear. Now I face it.

Tomorrow my life is cast like dice on the table of this burning desert.

forty-nine

SHIRA'S CHOICE

Inevitably Shira and Gadi spent an increasing amount of time together that winter. When Gadi could not produce the amazon he had enticed them with, Uni-Par treated him with contempt. They assumed he had faked the footage in hopes of getting his exile shortened. He would sit in Tikva until his sentence was up, and then perhaps they would bring him back.

Gadi did not believe they would leave him in exile indefinitely, but he did not enjoy being branded a liar, as he complained at great length to Shira and Malkah. He busied himself with a series of dramas featuring local talent or would-bes, but he was plainly bored. From a professional creator of state-of-the-art virons, he was reduced to amateur theatrics and running a school for dimly talented kiddies, he said.

Still, Gadi and Shira were decent company for each other, if only because both were deeply depressed and grieving, and both were trying hard to behave in a way that concealed their unhappiness—she for Ari's sake, he for the sake of his conception of himself. His father's death gave Gadi a role that he made an effort to play. Every morning he went to say Kaddish in the synagogue of water, in the garden of birds. He did everything correctly, but he confessed he felt oddly off balance.

"I was used to the old man," he said to Shira. "I still think of things I'm about to do as going to irritate him."

He tried sporadically to get Shira into bed with him, but she easily put him off. In the daytime she was working; in the evenings she had Ari and Malkah. But the week after Malkah's departure, he caught her on the street as she was clearing her head with a stroll. "You haven't scanned my new hook. Tell me what you think."

He had had to move after the fire. Now he stayed in a little wooden house near the edge of the wrap, only one room downstairs and one up, but both with a view of the bay. "I'm told this was once an oyster shack. I can't imagine oysters lived here, so I assume they were hunters of the wild oyster. Cozy, that's what you're supposed to say."

It was iridescent, pearly inside except for the thick blue carpeting. He had not bothered programming holos this time. "It's pretty, Gadi. You have a strong nest-building instinct."

"If you're trying to rile me, you won't succeed, because I don't want to be put off any longer, Ugi." He slid his hand under the fall of her hair and caressed her neck lightly, electrically.

She felt something, and that made her hopeful. For the last four months, she had experienced nothing but grief except when she was working or with Ari. She did not pull away. Gadi could read her hesitation and put his arms around her. It was easier than she would have imagined to kiss him, to undress, to slide into the blue-green bed in the form of a scallop shell, cast in the town shop out of some algae-based plasticene. He was taller, harder-bodied, more deliberate than he had been. His body did not arouse the fierce nostalgia she had feared. His body was a stranger, but he was not. They were gentle, not particularly passionate, patient. It all felt a little removed.

She was with him because she could no longer recall why she shouldn't be. She was weary of remembering Yod constantly, of missing him daily, nightly, of thinking of him in a way that felt like mental hemorrhaging. Her own grief bored her. Finally she went to bed with Gadi simply to quiet him and to silence her loneliness. But the loneliness was specific, not general. They were polite to each other in bed, but she had the feeling that Gadi, too, was searching through her body for someone else. He was looking for the Shira of sixteen; he was in pursuit of Nili. She was groping for a lover not even human. It was hopeless but not unpleasant. Only somewhat hollow.

They were each a little disappointed but too polite to let on. Perhaps he hoped the next time would be better. He tried to involve her in his stimmie making. He insisted on recording her, and she suffered it, because they were trying to be intimate. She remembered him explaining that she lacked the necessary projection. Moreover, she found the sight of herself disturbing. She was used to looking in the mirror to see if her hair was parted straight and combed slick. She looked for dirt smudges and bits of Ari's food stuck to her blouse.

When she saw herself through the camera eye, she found a woman smaller than she liked to think of herself. That fey creature with the enormous eyes, that fawn-woman was not Shira's self-image, and she wanted to turn from it. She was increasingly involved in running the Base. As soon as Malkah took an extended leave, Shira had been asked by the Council to fill her grandmother's seat as a Base Overseer. She found in herself a swelling power, an intensifying concentrated energy for work. No, the last role that appealed to her was to be an object caressed or nibbled by the senses of strangers, valued for the appearance of a helplessness she had outgrown. Her time with Yod had taught her she was not defenseless. She too could scheme; could fight; could kill. With Yod she had been able to ask for what she wanted. She had come to value that directness.

At the inquest after the explosion, Malkah and Shira had played Yod's last message, and the inquiry concluded that Yod had murdered Avram. No censure had been voted against either of the women. Y-S, still crippled, was fighting off hungry competitors, and Tikva seemed at peace. Yod and Lazarus's assassins, five of whom had been killed on the island, had left Y-S crippled by internecine warfare, with most of the upper echelon dead.

Sometimes she was forced to recall Josh by Ari's hands, by his ears, by a way of shrugging, a tone of voice, the very way he'd say, "I didn't do it!" Then she remembered her ex-husband with a dry guilt-tinged regret. Never would Ari found out, she hoped. She was not given to confession. She was not given to burdening him with more than the statement that his father had died in an accident at Y-S and that his father had loved him. Yod, she told him, had died to protect them all. About Avram Ari never asked, for he had scarcely known him. But Ari was much obsessed with death. He found a bird that had broken its neck on a window and asked endless questions. He was very upset when Malkah left. Shira felt that she was not giving him the stability and the continuity he desperately needed. Every day she reassured him she was not going away, that she was not going to die suddenly. "Bubeh will be back. She will come back with brand-new eyes, and she'll stay with us then," she said, hoping she was right. She said it as a charm. She would not allow herself to contemplate losing Malkah too. She kept strict limits with Gadi; she would not spend the night away from Ari, and Gadi could not sleep at the house.

She gave Ari Gimel as a playfellow. Gimel was her handyman. She had repaired its arm without difficulty. It was an unobtrusive presence, far more versatile and brighter than the standard run of cleaning and transport robots, whatever it might lack when compared with Avram's intention and Yod himself. It was good at rote programming tasks, at debugging, at fixing or rebuilding machines. Ari rode it around the courtyard, playing horsey. It repaired the plumbing and the roof.

Malkah could not communicate directly with them, since Israel was not in the Net, but one day a recorded communication came through the Net, sent from Athens. Malkah was standing in front of what looked like a stone wall. "I have arrived at my journey's destination. Things go well here.

"Hello, Ari, this is for you. This is your bubeh talking. I hope you are not forgetting me. Are you being good to Zayit and Leila? You have to play with them every day and let them sleep on your bed, or they will tell me when I come home. You have to pat them nicely on the head and stroke them and never pull their tails and never hit them. Otherwise they will run away and come and find me. So you must be good to your pussycats and good to your mother, who needs you. You must be cheerful and obey your mother and kiss her for me.

"Shira, I am having a great time here. The sun is bright, and I see everything clearly. Very clearly, Shira. Bear up, my sweet ones. In summer I'll come home, if that is the will of ha-Shem. This is a clear dry place indeed. It's a good place for this old woman. Take care of each other. I love you both. I am still a project under development. Till June, take care."

There was no way to reply. Shira played the transmission for Ari whenever he demanded it, which was much too often for days afterward. Gadi was recalled from exile to replace a failed designer for Mala Tuni; he left in great haste. She felt mostly relief, that they did not have to try any longer. Her dybbuk had been exorcised.

Against expectations, Hannah and she became friends. They stopped peering at each other around Gadi. They often ate together, strolled around the town, sat chatting in the Commons. Hannah was pregnant after four years of trying, and she treated her body gingerly, as if it were a glass teapot that might crack or tip and spill its precious contents. Hannah thought the father might be Gadi, but she had requested at the gene scan not to find out. She wanted to be her daughter's only parent.

Shira spent many evenings at the Commons, bringing Ari to eat with colleagues from her Base. She was working closely with a protégée of Malkah's, Yudit, two years older than Shira and the mother of a little boy just a month younger than Ari. Shira was settling into the town, putting out long roots in all directions, anchoring herself firmly. She had an occasional flirtation with a fellow worker or somebody from the town, but she felt no inclination to try a bond warmer than friendship.

The truth was, she did not want Jonah or Saul, any more than she had wanted Gadi. She was for better or worse a woman who took on a strong impression of her lover, who, if she loved someone, was shaped to receive that loved one and perhaps only that one. It had taken her a decade to free herself from Gadi.

But Gadi had broken off with her when she was sixteen. He had wanted to be free of her. Yod had died in perfect loyalty. If she could revive him even now, he would want her as he had. He would be with her. That made the missing worse. He had not chosen to leave her, he had not chosen to withdraw from her. He had wanted her more single-mindedly, more obsessively, more purely than anyone ever had or ever could. She was truly a secret widow.

They had never talked of love, never, yet what was the love men offered—when they bothered to offer—in comparison with the devotion she had known? She would live out her life, she feared, in maternal love, in friendship, loving her grandmother, but without experiencing committed passion. With Yod she had come into her own sexually, and her mature sexuality had gone out of the world with him. She did not want anyone else; she could not; she was twenty-nine going on eighty.

It was late March, and she was doing a spurt of spring cleaning. Ari was at day care, and she was burned out on work for the day. She was tidying up Malkah's office, which she had taken over in the meantime, when she ran across Avram's logs. She had a brief desire to bury them, in lieu of a body. To plant them in the courtyard with her dear cat Hermes and Ari's dead finch. On her palm she balanced a memory crystal, uncertain whether to toss it or keep it, tempted to load it on her terminal to see Yod again. Most of each cube was text, formulae, algorithms, but part of each consisted of spoken words and recorded images.

Then the idea smote her as if sunlight had pierced the cave of her brain. She cried out, a shriek of exhilaration, bringing both cats at a run to the doorway sniffing for danger, ears laid back. She stood in Malkah's office with the crystal in her hand, realizing she had all the software that had created Yod, what Avram had programmed, what Malkah had programmed, and all of Avram's hardware specs. Oh, it would be a long haul. She would have to master hardware as well as modify the software. She had never been responsible for hardware, all by herself. But she had Gimel. She had its perfect ability to follow directions. The project would be a stretch, but so what? She had some of the tools she needed, and she would start ordering the others.

Yod had said it himself: it was immoral to create a conscious weapon. She vehemently agreed. No, she would not create a cyborg to suffer from Yod's dilemma. She was not intending to build a golem; she was going to build a mate. It might take her two years, it might take her five, but then she would have her lover. She would have Yod, but not a Yod who belonged to Avram: no, a Yod who belonged only to her. He would look just like Yod; he would be just like Yod, minus all those problems with violence.

"Gimel," she shouted. The robot carefully put down the shovel with which it was preparing a bed in the courtyard and came shambling toward her.

"I am ready."

"Find Yod's self-repair tool kit. It's in one of the storage areas. Start with the basement and work upward in the house. When you find it, bring it to me."

She felt as if she were centered about a flame in her chest that did not burn but shone out from her, illuminating all life. How had she been so foolish as not to have realized she had almost everything she needed to rebuild Yod? For a moment she understood Avram as she never had, his apparent arrogance, his obsession. He had made a person; but then, as a mother, so had she. Ultimately, they both had the courage to violate a law that had outlived its time. What Avram had created, the best of it, would not perish after all, for she would carry the work forward.

How to prepare Ari? She would figure it out over time. There had never been a body. There was only the terrible absence at the core of their lives. She would give Ari the father he needed, the male figure of gentleness and strength and competence. He had loved Yod immediately.

She must begin at once, at once, so that she would be well launched before Malkah returned. Some of Avram's tools had survived the twin blasts. She had to remember where Gadi had put them. Probably in that little house, to which she had a key. If anyone noticed she was ordering tools and parts, she would explain she needed them to repair Gimel. Or even that she was attempting to assemble another robot like Gimel; that was legal and not terribly interesting to anyone.

She could construct Yod the second, starting right now. Let men make weapons. She would make herself happiness. She would manufacture a being to love her as she wanted to be loved. She would create for herself a being who belonged to her alone, as she had dreamed since adolescence, as she had belonged body and soul to Gadi until he had ripped himself from her. She would set to work this afternoon. She could feel Yod's dry hand in hers, his unblinking eyes fixed upon her darkly, sweetly.

She grabbed her jacket and headed for Gadi's oyster shack. She bolted down the street, adrenaline coursing through her. At the corner where the hotel had stood was a gap between buildings, obvious as a missing front tooth. The ruin had been dismantled, the components reused. She found herself stopped dead and staring at the space the hotel had occupied long before she had been born. The most powerful connections of her life seemed attached to that space. Avram had a grave, but Yod didn't; that was his memorial, what he had left to them: a violent absence. She imagined she could still smell something burnt, perhaps the soil itself or small fragments of combusted wood or plaster. She walked slowly forward to the vacant lot, just beginning to sprout a growth of weeds. The old basement had been filled in to prevent accidents. She squatted and took a handful of the sandy soil between her hands. She was right; particles of burnt material lay gritty on her palm. Yod's ashes, in a sense. The ashes of his act.

"I have died and taken with me Avram, my creator, and his lab, all the records of his experiment. . . . I die knowing I destroy the capacity to replicate me. . . ." She could hear Yod speaking. But he hadn't destroyed that capacity, not at all, because he had trusted her. He had taken care to save Malkah and herself from the explosion, never guessing she would undo his last act. She could see his face projected in her room. "Kaf must not come to be. . . . I have done one good thing with my death. I have made sure there will be no others like me."

He died convinced he had accomplished a goal that made his death palatable to him. Thus had he salvaged something for himself out of Avram's fatal orders. Could she wipe out that sacrifice? He thought he had ended the line of cyborgs. If he could know she planned to reverse his act, would he not feel betrayed? She imagined Yod's eyes fixed on her. The new cyborg would look just like him, and she would always expect it to say, "Shira, why? Why did you recreate me against my dying wishes?"

And what was her reason for hurrying? So that she would be started beyond stopping by the time Malkah returned; because Malkah, too, would tell her that the choice to make another Yod was immoral. Would the cyborg really be Yod? Yod was the product of tensions between Avram and Malkah and their disparate aims as well as the product of their software and hardware. If a cyborg created as a soldier balked and wanted to be a lover, might not a cyborg created as a lover long to be a celibate or an assassin? She remembered all the cyborgs who had looked just like Yod; Chet, who had killed David; all the autistic or violent offspring of Avram's experiments.

She could not be Avram. She could not manufacture a being to serve her, even in love. Very slowly she walked back along the block to the house built around the courtyard. There in Malkah's office she loaded the crystals into a backpack. She took all the records of Yod's hardware and software, and she walked to the recycling plant.

Outside, she paused again. She stood in the old road, turning one way and then the other. These crystals are his real body. But if I do not destroy the capability, I will succumb. When I am especially lonely and I miss him even more strongly than usual, the temptation will recur. Another afternoon like this one, I will talk myself into the rightness of the attempt. First I will just look at him, watch him. Then I will want him. Then I will decide I cannot do without him. Like Avram, I will feel empowered to make a living being who belongs to me as a child never does and never should.

She carried her backpack into the recycling plant and emptied the crystals into the proper chute. The little cubes that were all that was left of Yod slid away into the fusion chamber and became energy. She had set him free.

Acknowledgments

First of all, I want to thank the usual accomplices. My husband Ira Wood reads even the first drafts of my novels, so rough anyone else would think I had lost my mind as well as my way. He studied Czech with me and helped make our research jaunts delightful, even the day we walked twenty miles in the rain and could find no lunch. Claire Simmons of the Wellfleet Library as always put through those interlibrary loans I depend on. Gloria Nardin Watts, dear friend and indefatigable reader, helped me with the galleys.

I would particularly like to thank the head of the Research Department of the State Jewish Museum in Prague, Dr. Vladimir Sadek, who was extremely kind to me when I showed up for an appointment that turned out in a mysterious comedy of errors never to have existed. Above all, Jirina Sedinova of the Jewish Museum shared her time and research with me and was very helpful and warm, as well as fun to gossip with about Judah and David and company. I was in Prague in '68 and in the course of writing this novel returned; like Malkah, I remain in love with that city.

I would like to thank a particular student at Loyola in Chicago, where I put in a week of residency one April shortly after I had started this novel. In the course of a lively conversation about science fiction, he told me that when he read *Woman on the Edge of Time,* he couldn't believe the date of publication, because the alternate universe that Connie blunders into in Chapter 15 anticipated cyberpunk. What's cyberpunk? I asked, and he started me off. I enjoy William Gibson very much, and I have freely borrowed from his inventions and those of other cyberpunk writers. I

Acknowledgments

figure it's all one playground. Donna Haraway's essay "A Manifesto for Cyborgs" was extremely suggestive also; Constance Penley of *Camera Obscura* was kind enough to send it to me.

I have found the newsletters and meetings of the Artificial Intelligence group of the Boston Computer Society stimulating. Lest anybody think that the experiences in the Net and Base in the novel are fantastic make-believe, be aware that even now companies are working on sensor nets that permit a person to "walk into" data and experience it as real objects in imaginary space. As for the destruction of the ozone layer and the results of global warming, your local library surely has this information, as mine did.

I would like to thank Arthur Waskow for suggesting to me, at a meeting of the Siddur Project of P'Nai Or on which we both worked, that I might find kabbalah valuable to study. I owe a debt, as does everyone interested in kabbalah or the Golem, to Gershom Scholem and, even more, to Moshe Idel and, in understanding Judah Loew, to André Neher. My interpretations, of course, are very much my own.

Finally I want to thank Lois Wallace, my agent and friend, for her vigorous efforts on behalf of my work; and Sonny Mehta, the editor of this novel, for his valuable tough reading and helpful hints for cyborg makers.

As always with the novels of mine I most enjoy writing, this has been a strange and instructive journey.

A NOTE ON THE TYPE

This book was set in Garamond, a typeface originally designed by the famous Parisian type cutter Claude Garamond (1480–1561). This version of Garamond was modeled on a 1592 specimen sheet from the Egenolff-Berner foundry, which was produced from types thought to have been brought to Frankfurt by Jacques Sabon (d. 1580).

Claude Garamond is one of the most famous type designers in printing history. His distinguished romans and italics first appeared in *Opera Ciceronis* in 1543–44. While delightfully unconventional in design, the Garamond types are clear and open, yet maintain an elegance and precision of line that mark them as French.

Composed, printed and bound by The Haddon Craftsmen, Inc., Scranton, Pennsylvania

Designed by Iris Weinstein